An epic saga of love and war, *Shadow of the Swords* tells the story of the Crusades— from the Muslim perspective.

Saladin, a Muslim sultan, finds himself pitted against King Richard the Lionheart as Islam and Christianity clash against each other, launching a conflict that still echoes today.

In the midst of a brutal and unforgiving war, Saladin finds forbidden love in the arms of Miriam, a beautiful Jewish girl with a tragic past. But when King Richard captures Miriam, the two most powerful men on Earth must face each other in a personal battle that will determine the future of the woman they both love—and of all civilization.

Richly imagined, deftly plotted, and highly entertaining, *Shadow of the Swords* is a remarkable story that will stay with readers long after the final page has been turned.

Also by Kamran Pasha

Mother of the Believers

SHADOW OF THE SWORDS

An Epic Novel of the Crusades

KAMRAN PASHA

WASHINGTON SQUARE PRESS
New York London Toronto Sydney

Washington Square Press
A Division of Simon & Schuster, Inc.
1230 Avenue of the Americas
New York, NY 10020

First Washington Square Press trade paperback edition June 2010

WASHINGTON SQUARE PRESS and colophon are registered trademarks of Simon & Schuster, Inc.

For information about special discounts for bulk purchases, please contact Simon & Schuster Special Sales at 1-866-506-1949 or business@simonandschuster.com.

The Simon & Schuster Speakers Bureau can bring authors to your live event. For more information or to book an event contact the Simon & Schuster Speakers Bureau at 1-866-248-3049 or visit our website at www.simonspeakers.com.

Manufactured in the United States of America

10 9 8 7 6 5 4 3 2 1

Library of Congress Cataloging-in-Publication Data is available.

ISBN 978-1-4165-7995-3
ISBN 978-1-4165-8070-6 (ebook)

Dedicated to my father,
who taught me that love is mightier than the sword

SHADOW
OF THE
SWORDS

Prologue

Sinai Desert—AD 1174

The Cross burned red against the soldier's white tunic.

Red had always been her favorite color, the little girl thought. The color of roses. Of the sun as it set over the shores of the sea near her home. The color of her mother's hair.

Her mother.

The girl felt the steel talons of memory tearing at her heart. She had seen her mother's hair for the last time that morning, before it had been tucked away inside the modest head scarf that all good Jewish women wore in Cairo. She was too young herself to hide away her own dark locks, as the scarf would become obligatory only after her cycles began. In that, the Jews and Muslims of Egypt were of a common opinion. Although her breasts had begun to bud earlier that spring, the dark flow of menstrual blood had not yet arrived to welcome her into the fold of womanhood. She had always been impatient and had begun to pray to God that the blood would at last be released and her life would begin anew.

And today God had heard her, and granted her prayer in a way she could never have expected or wanted. For the blood that had flowed this morning was not her own, but of those whom she loved. And her life had truly begun anew in the chaos of screams and death.

They were supposed to have been safe. The coastline of Sinai was guarded by the Sultan's men. The handsome new Sultan who had swept into Cairo and overthrown its ailing king, ending the Shiite dynasty of the Fatimids and restoring Egypt to the fold of Sunni Islam. She should have been too young to understand these complex matters of state, but her father had always insisted that Jewish children should be well versed in the politics of the day. For it was the curse of her people that the changing winds of nations inevitably brought with them storms of tragedy and exile.

There had been many who had feared that the new Sultan would persecute the Jews for supporting the heretic kings who had ruled Egypt in defiance of the Caliph of Baghdad. But he had proven to be a wise man, and had reached out in friendship to the People of the Book. The Jews had found in the Sultan a patron and a protector, and her own uncle had been welcomed into the court as the ruler's personal physician.

How she wished her uncle had been with them today. Perhaps he could have saved them from the warriors of Christ who had descended on their caravan like locusts. Stanched the flow of blood from amputated limbs. Applied his special salves on the burns inflicted by flaming arrows. Maybe if he had been with them, the others would have lived.

But in her heart, the girl knew that it would have made no difference. Her uncle would have been slaughtered with the rest. And perhaps he would have been forced to endure the horror of watching his sister— her mother—be violated by the very monster that stalked her now.

The monster whose face was streaked in blood as bright as the Cross he bore upon his breast. In that, the girl could find some solace, some cruel satisfaction, for the blood belonged to the killer and not his victims. And it was she who had drawn it out. A tiny act of revenge, forever scarring the young man's once handsome features. Whenever he looked in the mirror, he would remember the cost of the horror he had inflicted on her family.

The warrior was coming closer to her hiding place, his broadsword held aloft, black with gore and entrails from the massacre he had unleashed. The girl pushed herself farther into the shadowy crevices of the cave. She could feel something crawling on her back. A spider, or perhaps a scorpion. For a moment she hoped it was the latter, and that its lethal sting would take her before the bloodied knight could finish what he had begun. Her loins still burned from his brutal attack, and she could smell the sickly odor of his seed drying on her thighs.

The soldier's bright eyes scanned the desert plain, like a wolf searching for a wounded lamb. Her footprints should have given her away. But the area was littered with camel tracks from another caravan that had passed the day before, and her markings were lost in the confusion of upturned earth. The red hills were rugged and lined with boulders large enough to hide a girl of her size. It would take hours to search through all the crags and crevices of this forsaken land.

He should have turned back and rejoined his men, who even now were dividing up the booty from the successful raid. The caravan had been headed to Damascus laden with bountiful items for trade—gold and ivory from Abyssinia, beautiful woolen shawls woven by the Berber nomads to the west—and the haul had made these murderers rich men. If her hunter had been wise, he would have forgotten a wayward little girl and focused his attention on securing his share of the wealth.

But she could see in his eyes no sign of wisdom. No sign of humanity. Just a darkness that terrified her more than the cruel sheen of his blade. It was a hatred so visceral, so pure in its ugliness, that he no longer looked like a man, but a demon that had escaped from deep within the bowels of Gehenna.

And the demon was almost upon her. She could hear him breathing, the air sounding like the hiss of a snake as it escaped his lungs. And for a second she imagined that she could even discern the terrible drum of his heart, thundering in its call for revenge.

His eyes fell upon the dark opening to the cave, the crevice covered in shadows from the heavy curtain of rocks all around. And she saw a smile cross his face, his teeth glistening in the harsh desert light.

And so the end had come. And yet somehow she felt no fear. In fact, she felt nothing at all. Her heart was empty of all emotion, and she could not even remember what it felt like to laugh or cry. All of that had been taken away from her in the horror of the attack, in watching her loved ones torn to shreds by men who saw themselves as the warriors of God. The same God that her own people believed had chosen them for a great destiny.

All the terrible stories her father had told her of her people's past had finally become real to her that day. The stories she had dismissed as tragic fables of the ancients were all true. In fact, they were the only truth for a people who had been singled out by a God that demanded a price for His love that was too great.

In that moment, as the bloodstained warrior moved closer to her tiny refuge, she hated God for choosing her people. For placing upon the Jews the curse of being special, a burden that brought with it nothing but sorrow and loss. It was because of her people that this foreigner with his pale skin and strange language even knew of the God of Abraham, and yet that knowledge had not made him a better man. Indeed, it had inflamed in him a righteous anger that brought only suffering into this world. Her people had taught mankind about God, and in return men only became devils in that God's name.

She wanted to curse God, to renounce Him even as he had renounced His own people, had expelled them from their homeland and left them to wander the world as the most hated of clans. And she would have done so, had she not seen it.

The necklace.

A simple stone of jade held in a silver clasp lined with sparkling beads. It had belonged to her mother, had been torn from her defiled body by this monster only an hour before. And he was wearing it around his neck like a savage trophy. At that instant, she wanted to leap out from the shadows and tear the necklace from around his throat. It would mean her death, but at least she would die holding this precious little trinket that her mother had loved so much.

The fire in her heart burned into a savage rage, and the girl curled her fingers into claws, ready to strike. She would put out this murderer's eyes with her tiny fingers, rip open his neck with her teeth like a lioness bringing down its prey. He was not a human being, and neither was she anymore. The savagery that the girl had witnessed today had ended any illusions about that. Despite the Torah's call for men to be better than the angels, the truth was all men were animals and would never be anything more. The God of her people had failed them, and now she would show Him what He had wrought.

She bent forward, her knees pressed to her chest, poised to spring as the soldier came closer to the cave. She had to move now, to leap out like a cheetah, to use the advantage of surprise to bring down her prey.

But as she prepared to move, she saw a small flash of light, like a star glittering on the man's chest. It was the necklace, the jade stone reflecting the sun in its desert fury. And then her eyes fell on the symbols carved on the jade. Four Hebrew letters—*Yod, He, Waw, He.*

The Tetragrammaton. The sacred name of God.

The holy word, which could not be pronounced or spoken aloud, shimmered like an emerald against the warrior's white tunic. As she stared at those mysterious letters, the girl felt something strange happen to her. The fury that was within her subsided. And in its place, she felt a remarkable upwelling of peace and serenity. Gazing at the name of a God she no longer believed in, the girl found herself remembering all the gentle nights she had looked up at her mother as she sang them both softly to sleep. When the girl saw that necklace, that sacred stone, she suddenly felt safe again, as she had always felt resting in her mother's arms.

She leaned back, the tension in her body disappearing. The man could come inside, could take her body and her life, and ultimately it would make no difference. Her people would go on, and her name would be added as another sad yet beautiful note in her nation's song.

Strangely, considering her uncharitable feelings about the Deity, an old prayer entered her heart. She felt the words of the Shema coming to her lips, and she mouthed them silently.

Hear O Israel, the Lord our God, the Lord is One.

The wind rose and sand swirled outside, a curtain of dust rising between her and her enemy. A sandstorm was upon them, blotting out the light of the sun.

She closed her eyes, allowed herself to fall into the shadows, to let the dark embrace her. She did not know what world she would awaken to, or if indeed there was any world beyond this one that had reached its end. But she did not care.

In silence, there was peace.

— — —

THE GIRL STIRRED AND saw that the darkness that had covered the cave now blanketed the whole world. She could see nothing, and yet she knew that there was a vastness all around her that stretched toward infinity. Was this the realm of death?

And then she heard the sound of a jackal's howl and the rustle of wind on the sand and she knew that she was still in the world of men.

Crawling on her knees until she emerged from the cave that had been her sanctuary, she stepped out onto the desert plain. Night had fallen and the heavens were lit by more stars than she had ever imagined. It was as if the sky were a sheet of white diamonds, burning with cold fire.

She shivered and hugged herself tight. The temperature had fallen rapidly and she found it hard to believe that only a few hours before the desert had blazed with such angry heat. The girl looked around and saw that she was alone, with only towering sand dunes and a sea of rocks to keep her company.

There was no sign of the man who had raped her and killed her mother.

At that thought, she felt the knives of memory shoot through her heart again. The girl's knees gave way and she fell to the ground, vomit erupting from her throat, the ugly taste of bile overwhelming her senses.

She lay still on the desert ground for some time. She wanted to cry, but she could not. It was as if the girl she had been the day before, full of life and feeling, was lost forever. Try as she could, her heart would not stir. Would not let the excruciating pain that was tearing her apart emerge and find release.

And so she locked it away, closed that door forever.

The girl rose and stood straight, her head raised in dignity, her face as cold and unflinching as the ancient statues of Isis that still stood in Egypt. She looked around her again, and saw in the distance the flickering of lights. Somewhere at the edge of the horizon there was a campfire. In all probability, it would not be the soldiers of the Cross, who would not risk sleeping in the Sinai and falling victim to the Sultan's patrols. Bedouins most likely, goat herders living out in the open, very much unchanged from the days when Moses had wandered through this desert as an exile. Which was what she was now as well. An exile.

The Jewish girl knew that she had to find help. Without food or water, the desert would claim her in a few days. The Bedouins were her only hope.

She turned to move toward the distant light, and then stopped, her eyes falling on something at her feet that glittered under the starlight. She bent down and saw that it was a piece of limestone that shone like the moon.

The girl held up the rock, felt its soft powder caress her fingers.

She looked to her right and saw the red-flecked boulder that had served as the roof of her tiny shelter. And then she walked over and scraped the stone, writing on it with her makeshift pen, spelling out letters in Arabic. Her own ancient language was no longer used by her people outside of the rituals of prayer. And she felt no desire to pray anymore.

The girl did not know if she would survive. In all likelihood, the wilderness would consume her before she saw another human being. And so she wanted to leave this behind, this one final record that she had existed, that she mattered.

God may have forgotten her and her people, but she vowed that at least here in this tiny corner of a broken world, the stones would remember her name.

Miriam.

1 The Horns of Hattin—AD 1187

*I*t is said that God favors irony. Perhaps that is why His city, named for peace, has known only war and death."

The rabbi's father had said that to him once, when he was a restless youth and a virgin. He had changed much in the untold years that had passed since then. His desire for adventure had been supplanted by a desperate longing for serenity. His wedding night was a distant but still tender memory. The old man had learned that much of what he had believed in the morning of his life was incomplete at best. False, at worst. Yet these words had proven true, time and again. The God of irony was an accurate description of the ineffable, unpredictable Being from whom the cosmos derived its essence. Perhaps it was not fair to call God an outright trickster, but He undoubtedly had a sense of humor.

Like his people, the old man was a wanderer. He had sought the Divine Countenance in the shadowed gardens of Cordova. His weary feet had traced the Queen of Sheba's paths through the African desert. His gray eyes had filled with tears before the Pyramids, which were ancient even when Moses played in their shadow. Yet he knew from his journeys that all paths returned here, to the navel of the world. To the Holy Land. To Jerusalem.

Jerusalem had been the prize of many conquerors, few who had been friends to the Jews. His people were banished and scattered to the winds, yet they never forgot the city of David. It beckoned them in their souls, their dreams.

Then the sons of Ishmael arose from the desert to claim their share in the legacy of Abraham. And, for a time, there was peace and the sons of Isaac began to return home.

So it was, until the Franks arrived on the horizon. Poor, illiterate, filled with hate. They sought to regain Jerusalem in the name of their

Christ. The rabbi had read the sayings of this Jesus of Nazareth and had not found in them anything to explain the horror of what they did.

The Franks slaughtered the old and the weak. The women. The little ones. They killed the Muslims as infidels, and then they killed the other Christians as heretics. They gathered all the Jews who remained and locked them in the main synagogue. Then they set it on fire.

In the end, the lamentations ceased, for there were none left to lament.

Frankish historians would later boast that blood ran down the streets of Jerusalem up to the ankles of their armored soldiers. But the slaughter of tens of thousands in the Holy City was the least of their crimes. In the once pristine town of Ma'arra, emerald with vineyards and fields and olives, an evil beyond evil rose from the very bowels of Hell. The rabbi had vomited after he read the full account of Albert of Aix, the Frankish chronicler who witnessed and glorified the greatest victory of Satan over the hearts of men. For in Ma'arra, the Crusaders not only massacred the population. They cannibalized their victims. Men and women cooked in clay pots. Their children impaled on wooden spits and grilled alive.

The rabbi had once thought that these stories were the typical exaggerations of warmongers and madmen, much like the bloody tales of Joshua's conquest of Palestine in the Holy Book. Ballads of fury meant to debase the humanity of the opponent, not actual accounts of historical events. But he had come to learn that the Franks were a literal bunch, not given to poetry or figures of speech.

Like his people, the rabbi was known by many names. To the Arabs and his brothers among the Sephardim, he answered to Sheikh Musa ibn Maymun, chief rabbi of Cairo and personal physician of the Sultan. The pale-faced Ashkenazim knew him only from his detailed and eloquent writings on matters of law and theology, which had spread through the glorious Spanish highlands into the darkness that was known as Europe. They called him Rebbe Moshe Ben Maimon in the tongue of their forefathers. The most enthusiastic of his followers revered him as "The Rambam," although he did not consider himself worthy of any special devotion.

And the Frankish barbarians, at least the few who could read and write, referred to him as Maimonides. They also called him Christ-killer and a few other choice epithets that were reserved for his people as a whole, but he tried not to take that too personally. They were ignorant primitives, after all.

Maimonides walked slowly toward the pavilion of the Sultan, rustling his hand through his shaggy beard, as he often did when he was lost deep in thought. His body was not tired, but a force greater than fatigue burdened his soul. The oppressive, crushing weight of history. He did not know if he would live beyond the day and he wanted to treasure every breath as if it were his last. But the stench of torches and dung, both human and animal, poisoned the air. Maimonides would have laughed, had his sense of humor survived the horror of war.

The rabbi's mind asked a thousand questions of his Lord. O God of irony, do You find pleasure in even the subtlest twists of fortune? That a peace-loving scholar should meet his doom caught in the bloody swath of a Crusader's blade—is that not enough to tickle You? Is it truly necessary that his final memories should be forever marred by the reek of disease and defecation, the scent of the battlefield?

But his God, as usual, did not reply.

Maimonides turned to watch the preparations for battle. Turbaned Arab soldiers, working alongside fair-skinned Kurdish horsemen and statuesque Nubian warriors, milled like ants through the battle camp. Their bonds of communal purpose were intensified by an urgent energy that seemed to crackle through the air. The sensation was so real that Maimonides felt the hair on the back of his hands rising. Such was the power of destiny. These men knew that they were standing at the doorway of history. Regardless of whether they lived or died, their actions would be forever inscribed in the ledger of time. Their deeds would be weighed on the judgment scales of a thousand generations yet to come.

The old man continued on his way, navigating through a maze of mules and Arabian steeds, as well as the occasional goat that managed to escape the butcher's pen. He passed a line of camels, some carrying razor-tipped arrows from Damascus to resupply the army, while others brought precious water from Lake Tiberias to the north. His escorts on the long journey from Cairo had said that the *jihad* would be won or lost on water. The Sultan had formulated a strategy that relied on cutting off the Franks from their water supplies just long enough to weaken them before the onslaught of the main forces.

The heavily armored warriors unloading the camels ignored the aging physician. They were filled with the fire of youth and paid little thought to those walking down the final paths of life. They were under the spell of the God of irony, of course, as Maimonides knew that he would probably outlive most of these boastful and confident lads. He wondered how many of them would be buried tomorrow under the twin hills known as the Horns of Hattin. He wondered whether there would be anyone left to bury them.

Maimonides reached the Sultan's pavilion and nodded to the two Egyptians who stood before its entrance brandishing massive scimitars. The guards, twin brothers with equally cruel eyes and stony jaws, stepped aside. They did not particularly like the Jew, but he held the confidence of the Sultan. Maimonides knew that only a handful of men had access to the ruler's presence, and fewer still could call him a friend. It had taken the rabbi years of loyal service to earn the Sultan's trust, a journey that had begun when he had been summoned to the Citadel in Cairo to cure its newly installed conqueror of a painful fever. Maimonides often pondered the strange twists and turns of destiny that had transformed him from a modest physician to an influential adviser of a king.

The rabbi entered the tent. He marveled again at its simplicity. There was little to distinguish the pavilion from the humble dwellings of the Egyptian foot soldiers. No grand trophies or ornaments of gold. No plush carpets imported from Isfahan to cover the dry Hattin earth. Just a cabin made of striped green linen with the eagle flag of the Sultan flapping from a makeshift pole at the entrance. The Sultan eschewed the normal displays of power. Maimonides knew that this was one of the many reasons he held the undivided loyalty of his men. He was one of them in life and, perhaps by tonight, in death.

Inside the royal tent, the rabbi found his master poring over maps of the surrounding countryside. The Sultan was a brilliant military tactician whose secret lay in his attention to detail. A general must know every twist of terrain, every hill, every gulley of the battlefield better than he knows the contours of his wife's body, the Sultan had said once. In war, there was no room for error. One mistake could set back the advance of an army, could thwart the destiny of an entire civilization, as the Arab blunder at Tours 450 years before had halted the Islamic expansion into Europe. The Sultan lived in the unforgiving glare of history and could not afford the luxury of even the slightest mistake.

Maimonides stood at attention before the Sultan, careful not to interrupt his concentration. His master ran his hand across the worn parchment one last time before glancing up at his adviser. His tanned brow had been creased in thought, his face a mask of iron focus, but his dark eyes now lit up with genuine warmth.

Sultan Salah al-Din ibn Ayyub, known to the Franks as Saladin, was a man like no other. Like King David, Saladin inspired in his followers a sense that they were in the presence of something larger than life, as if a spark of the Divine had flashed from heaven and lit a fire that consumed the hearts of men. Saladin was more than a leader. He was a catalyst. Like Alexander and Caesar before him, Saladin had come to turn the world upside down with the singular force of his will.

The Sultan stepped forward and embraced the rabbi, kissing his cheeks. Maimonides was struck again by how young he appeared. No, not young. Ageless. His beard was midnight black, without a hint of gray, but his brown eyes were ancient pools that shone with an ineffable sadness. The years of war with the Franks had made Saladin a walking enigma. His body seemed to grow younger with time, but his eyes much older. It was as if each victory against the Crusader menace reinvigorated his external form yet drained his soul.

"Peace be upon you, old friend! When did you arrive?" The Sultan led the rabbi to a silk cushion and bade him sit. Saladin's robes, dun-colored like his beloved desert, rippled with the natural grace of his movements. The Sultan walked like a tiger, every step conveying an aura of spontaneous ease, but brimming with the barely suppressed tension of a predator.

"The weapons caravan from Cairo just pulled in, *sayyidi*," the rabbi said. "We were delayed due to a Frankish ambush." Maimonides gratefully accepted a silver chalice filled with chilled water from the Caucasus.

Saladin's face darkened.

"Were you hurt?" he asked, his eyes narrowing with concern and a hint of quiet anger.

"I am fine, praise God," Maimonides replied. "It was a small band that has been raiding the Sinai since winter. Your men dispatched them easily."

Saladin nodded.

"I will get the details from the captain-at-arms later," he said. "My heart is glad that you are here. We will need the skilled hand of a physician when the battle is over." The Sultan stood up and returned to the map. Maimonides set aside the chalice and followed him. Saladin pointed to the parchment, which was marked with mysterious symbols. The Sultan never remembered, of course, that military plans were as unintelligible as hieroglyphics to the rabbi, but Maimonides played along, feigning comprehension as his master's voice rose with excitement.

"The Frankish army has gathered en masse at Hattin," he said. "Our spies claim that the entire Jerusalem legion has joined the coastal forces in a bid to crush our army."

Maimonides frowned.

"I am not a military tactician, *sayyidi,* but that does not strike me as a wise move on their part," the rabbi said. "Jerusalem is the true goal of the *jihad,* as the Franks assuredly know. Should our forces break through their ranks, the city will be open for the taking. They must be very confident."

Saladin laughed, his eyes suddenly youthful with mirth.

"They are not confident, only brash," he said. "I have no doubt that this suicidal tactic was devised by the great Reginald himself."

Maimonides stiffened at the name of the Frankish noble who had terrorized the Holy Land for years. Reginald of Kerak was a true barbarian whose bloody exploits embarrassed even the most ruthless Franks. The rabbi's sister Rachel and her family had the misfortune of being caught by Reginald's men thirteen years before in a raid on a trading caravan near Ascalon in the Sinai. Only Rachel's young daughter Miriam escaped alive and hid in the desert before she was found by a kindly Bedouin who helped her return to Cairo.

Miriam had never spoken of what happened during the ambush, or how she managed to survive. It was enough for a heartbroken Maimonides to know that Rachel and her husband, Yehuda, had perished in the brutal attack. Maimonides had never truly known hate until he saw Miriam after the raid. Her sparkling green eyes dead, her laughter quenched. The war ceased to be a matter of distant gossip in that moment. Driving the Franks into the sea became the goal of his life, not just the empty slogan of the average patriot, safely lounging on a feathered couch while others fought on his behalf. Maimonides wondered how many men in Saladin's army were here for similar reasons. To avenge a personal atrocity committed by the Crusaders. To avenge themselves against Reginald of Kerak.

Saladin noticed the crack in his friend's composure and he touched his shoulder sympathetically.

"I promised Allah that I will show the Franks mercy if He grants us victory today," he said. "But I made no such promise on Reginald's behalf."

"As a man of God, I cannot preach revenge," Maimonides said, a tiny hint of regret in his voice.

"Leave revenge to the warriors," Saladin said. "I would like to think that there are at least a few men unsullied by blood in this world."

The Sultan was interrupted by the arrival of his brother, al-Adil. Larger in size than Saladin, with a wild shock of almost crimson hair and pitch-black eyes, he was brave and forceful like his kin, but did not share the Sultan's knack for diplomacy. Al-Adil entered Saladin's chamber and eyed Maimonides suspiciously. The rabbi was always a little uncomfortable around the flame-haired giant. He did not know why Saladin's brother disliked him so much. At times he thought it was because he was a Jew. But the sons of Ayyub had been raised to follow the best of their prophet's tradition and respect the People of the Book. Al-Adil had always treated other Jews with courtesy, but for whatever reason, he chose not to extend it to the chief rabbi himself.

Saladin turned to his brother.

"What news?"

Al-Adil hesitated, glancing at Maimonides as if considering whether the old man should be made privy to councils of war, before continuing.

"The Knights Templar are gathering into formation at the Frankish camp. Our archers are preparing for the charge."

Saladin nodded.

"Then the trumpet of Allah has called us to destiny."

He gestured to Maimonides to follow him as he stepped outside the tent, his scowling brother in tow.

A hush fell on the camp as the Sultan emerged. His arrival signaled the beginning of the end. For nearly ninety years, the Muslim armies had been trapped in a losing battle against the Frankish invaders. They had suffered grievous losses and humiliations, none greater than the occupation of Jerusalem and the desecration of the Al-Aqsa mosque. Their tribal pettiness and fratricidal wars had made the dream of victory over the barbarians seem like a desert mirage—seductively inviting, always appearing to be within grasp, but fleeting and illusory at its core. Until today.

Saladin had achieved the impossible. He had united the warring kingdoms of Egypt and Syria after a century of chaos. The Crusaders were finally hemmed in, trapped by the sea and their own shortsighted infighting. And now the unified Muslim armies stood with a dagger poised at the heart of the Frankish kingdom. The Battle of Hattin would determine the future of the Holy Land and the destiny of the Arab people. The soldiers knew that victory today meant triumph over the forces of barbarism and ignorance that threatened to plunge the civilized world back into the illiterate darkness that still covered Europe. If Saladin were defeated today, it would leave Damascus and Cairo open to the Crusader invasion, and the caliphate would vanish into the sewers of history.

That was why he was here, supervising the final battle himself. Saladin trusted his commanders, military geniuses such as the Egyptian general Keukburi and the Sultan's courageous nephew Taqi al-Din. But the outcome of this conflict, for good or ill, would rest solely upon Saladin's shoulders in the annals of history. So when word had come that the Franks, desperate for water to replenish their dwindling supplies, were on the move toward the wells of Hattin, Saladin had left behind the safety of his encampment at Kafr Sabt, halfway between Tiberias and the Crusader stronghold at Saffuriyah, to take personal charge over the impending battle.

Saladin gazed with pride at his men as he approached the forward line of defense. The archers on horseback, dressed in silk tunics over cuirasses, were poised like Greek statues of Artemis, ready for the hunt. The regiment stood proudly behind red and jasmine standards. Banners bearing roses and birds fluttered in the wind around them

The Sultan pulled out a small viewing lens and gazed across the fields of Hattin. He squinted and peered through the glass toward the Crusader encampment below. Saladin's strategy had successfully divided the Frankish army, which had been organized into three columns. Raymond of Tripoli led the forward regiment, which was currently busy defending itself from Taqi al-Din's ambush on the road to Tiberias. Saladin had had many dealings with Raymond over the years and had come to respect him. Unlike most of his compatriots, the nobleman was a man of honor who had sought a lasting peace between their peoples. But Raymond had been thwarted at all turns by hate-filled fanatics like Reginald and was now compelled through a sense of duty to participate in this destructive war. Saladin had once told Maimonides that he would regret it deeply should he be forced to slay Raymond on the battlefield. But there was no doubt in the rabbi's mind that the Sultan would do what needed to be done.

The middle contingent of the Crusader army, which confronted them below, was led by Reginald himself, the brutish thug whom Saladin had vowed to kill with his own hands. Maimonides knew that Reginald had personally led the attack that had resulted in his sister's death. As a doctor, he abhorred the taking of any human life. But the rabbi had long before concluded that Reginald had left behind the hallowed status of a human being with his unbridled savagery.

The rear contingent of the Crusader army was led by Balian of Ibelin and contained the heaviest concentration of the fanatical Knights Templar and Hospitallers. Maimonides knew these men would fight to the death and would never surrender, and he uttered a silent prayer of thanks that the knights had been substantially weakened as a result of lack of water and the never-ending skirmishes that Saladin's men inflicted on the Frankish army. The fools were so busy swatting the minor attacks the Muslims were provoking from the rear that they could provide little support to Reginald's central column. Those forces now found themselves alone, facing the full mass of the Muslim army at Hattin. The divided Crusader regiments had unwittingly walked into Saladin's trap.

Maimonides watched his master as he scanned the distant Crusader camp. The Sultan's eyebrows rose as he focused on a crimson pavilion at the center of the base. A blue standard bearing an embroidered golden cross flew arrogantly in the wind.

"So it has come to this at last. King Guy himself graces us with his presence," he said, with a trace of wonder.

Maimonides turned to the Sultan, startled. This was unexpected. "I'm surprised that cur would find the courage to step outside the gates of Jerusalem."

Al-Adil unsheathed his scimitar and held it high, a towering symbol of power and defiance.

"I shall take great pleasure in separating Guy's head from his shoulders," he said. "Unless you would prefer the honor yourself, brother."

Saladin smiled, accustomed to al-Adil's outbursts.

"It is not fitting for kings to tear each other apart like rabid dogs," the Sultan said.

Al-Adil snorted. His was a world of blood and iron that had little place for idealism.

"They will not show you such mercy should their knights come upon you in battle," he said.

"That is why we are better than them, my brother," Saladin reminded him. "Our compassion is our greatest weapon. With it we slay the resistance in a man's heart and quell his hate. When you defeat the rancor, you have replaced an enemy with an ally."

Al-Adil turned away, shaking his head, but Maimonides smiled. Saladin was a man unlike any the rabbi had met in his life. A Muslim who bowed his head to Mecca, he nonetheless embodied the highest teachings of the Talmud. If such men led every nation, perhaps the Messiah would hasten.

The rabbi peered across the desolate field to the Crusader camp in the distance. Regardless of the course that the battle took, he knew that the end was nigh. He said a silent prayer for the men who would lose their lives in the next few hours. Maimonides forced himself to include a prayer for those among the Frankish enemy destined to die as well, but his heart was not in it.

2

Reginald of Kerak felt his blood boil. He glanced at the line of armored men on powerful steeds, lances raised, ready for the order to advance. The Knights Templar, and their brothers the Hospitallers, were the most disciplined fighters Christendom had ever produced, ready to sacrifice their lives without hesitation to defeat the enemies of God. His bile rose when he thought of how their strategic advantage was being wasted with each passing hour that the opposing forces stared each other down on the plains of Hattin. King Guy, a weak imbecile, had mishandled the entire operation, the most critical error being his decision to forgo extra supplies of water carts. Guy had expected that their men would reach Lake Tiberias well before they faced Saladin's armies, but the infidels had unexpectedly blocked the route. Running out of provisions, his men had begun to despair, especially when they saw Muslim troops mockingly spilling pails of water on the parched sands beyond them. The sight of the precious, life-giving liquid wasted by their laughing enemies had proven a powerful psychological weapon, causing morale to plummet further.

Reginald knew that another day under the merciless Palestine sun would weaken their forces to the point where retreat was the only option left. He had done the best he could—many of his men were supplied with colored surcoats to limit the heat absorption of their armor, a trick he had picked up from the Muslims over the years. But Reginald did not have enough to supply the substantial portion of the army that consisted of recent arrivals from Europe. Unlike the native Christians, these soldiers had been completely unprepared for the weather and the terrain, and they were falling victim to dehydration.

Reginald stormed into the royal pavilion, brushing aside the guards poised at the entrance to the inner chamber. What he saw brought his rage to a level that he had not known was possible outside the flames of Hell itself.

King Guy sat at an elegantly crafted ivory table with a rat-faced aide, playing chess.

Breathing heavily, Reginald moved forward until he was towering over the frail regent. The king did not look up from the game to acknowledge the knight, but his nervous aide stared at him as if he were the Reaper himself come to collect an overdue soul. Guy lifted a bony hand and moved his rook to take the aide's bishop.

"My lord, the Templars await your command," Reginald said, his words reverent, but his tone far from respectful. "Your Majesty should not hesitate at this, our greatest hour."

Guy paused, finally raising his head and eyeing the haughty nobleman. His dark hair was thin and his pocked scalp clearly visible. Even in the midst of his rage, Reginald felt a moment of cruel merriment at the ludicrous sight of the regent's overly bushy eyebrows rising in response to the knight's challenge. Reginald had little doubt that the king's lice infestation had found its way into the coarse labyrinth of fur that shadowed his eyes. How many times had he imagined the exquisite tortures he would inflict on this pretender when he deposed him?

"There is wisdom in caution, Reginald," King Guy said after a long moment, his voice deep and sonorous. "I wish you had learned that by now. Perhaps we would not be here today."

Reginald could no longer contain his fury. He had been forced to uphold the pretense that Guy was more than a ceremonial figurehead for far too long. The fool had been presented with the throne in Jerusalem as a compromise to keep the feuding nobles from one another's throats after King Baldwin succumbed to leprosy. Reginald knew that he and his brothers in the Knights Templar were the heart of the kingdom of Jerusalem. While petty politicians like Guy played their little court intrigues, his soldiers were at the forefront of the war, risking their lives, and sometimes their sanity, to beat back the infidel hordes. While Guy bathed in rosewater, Reginald bore the scars of the holy war on his face, and even deeper ones in his soul.

"Spoken like the coward you are," Reginald said to his nominal master.

Guy's aide blanched. Reginald had given up all courtly pretenses, and the cold hate of his spirit laced his words with menace. The king, for his part, appeared unperturbed. He rose to face his nominal liege, and for a fleeting instant, his regal bearing hinted at the man he could have been.

"Tread lightly, Reginald," he said. "I am still the King of Jerusalem. For what little that may be worth now."

Reginald laughed.

"Fear not, Your Majesty, today I will unburden your shoulders of the weight of the land," he said. "Once I have slain the infidel Saladin, I shall mount your head next to his."

In one swift, contemptuous move, Reginald knocked the chess pieces all over the sparkling board with the back of his hand. Guy's mousy aide cowered and appeared ready to wet his pants. But the king met the nobleman's iron gaze with his own. Reginald thought he saw something in the regent's eyes that enraged him far beyond any taunt the monarch could have hurled at his errant knight. He saw pity.

"If your boasts ever held any truth, our dominion would extend to Mecca today," King Guy said.

Reginald's face turned red with anger and embarrassment. Guy referred, of course, to Reginald's most infamous exploit, his raid on the Muslim holy cities. He had defiled the Sanctuary Mosque in Mecca that contained the Kaaba, the cube-shaped temple that the unbelievers faced in their daily prayers. Reginald and his men then set their sights on Medina, where their false prophet was buried. His plan had been audacious, even by Crusader standards—to dig up Muhammad's bones and put them on display as proof of the infidels' failed religion. The pagans would see that their prophet was nothing but a dusty corpse, while the glory of the resurrected Christ reigned transcendent and eternal.

Reginald's foray into Mecca had the advantage of surprise and sheer bravado. The Sanctuary Mosque was weakly defended, its wardens complacent in their expectations of Allah's protection. His men swooped down on the unarmed pilgrims, all dressed in pauper's robes of white linen, as they circumambulated the Kaaba in their vile pagan ritual. He quickly dispatched the unbelievers to the damnation he was sure awaited them, then proceeded to set fire to the mosque after his horse defecated in the main courtyard. He then turned his attention north.

By the time his men reached Medina, however, Saladin's forces had arrived, seeking furious vengeance for the desecration of their sacred sites. Reginald had been surprised by the ferocity of the infidels' counterattack. His charge on the gates of Medina had been met with a maelstrom of arrows and spears that blocked out the sun. Dozens of his men were captured and paraded around Medina before they were publicly decapitated. Reginald had just barely made it out of that scorpions' nest and was forced to retreat with a few stunned survivors. They had clearly underestimated the passion that these pagan ruins held for the unbelievers. But despite his setback at Medina, he had ridden home to Jerusalem with laughter in his heart. He had proven to the world the hollow core of the Muslim myth—the invincibility of Islam's sacred shrine was as much a fairy tale as the story of their false prophet's Night Journey to Heaven. No angels had flown from the sky to save the Kaaba. It was just another empty, pointless brick building. He had cut the last tendons that held together the infidels' shaky morale. Or so he had thought.

When Reginald returned, he was met with a cold reception, even among his most formidable allies in the court. He had walked through the grim stone corridors of the Templar castle in Jerusalem feeling every eye on him, and not in admiration for his initiative and courage. Reginald would soon discover the reason for his comrades' antipathy. Having prided himself on his reputation as a man with no moral limit, he had finally crossed a line that would prove a turning point in the conflict. Reginald's raid had sent a shock wave through the entire

Muslim world. He had pierced the very heart of Islam, and his actions had given rise to a unifying battle cry among the divided heathens. His enemy Saladin became more than just another ambitious soldier to his people. He was now the sword of Allah that would drive the blaspheming Franks into the sea and avenge the violation of the holy sites.

Reginald had watched with growing alarm as Saladin rode the wave of anti-Crusader hatred and successfully unified the warring kingdoms of Egypt and Syria, a seemingly impossible political task. The Franks had played the two rival nations against each other for almost a hundred years and ensured the survival of the kingdom of Jerusalem in the process. Now the soldiers of Christ found themselves surrounded on all sides by enemies who saw their presence as a daily reminder of the violation of Mecca. Reginald knew in his heart that he had made a strategic error, but his pride would never permit him to admit so much aloud.

"Go, Reginald," Guy said. "See if you can regain your honor. My head will still be here when you return." The king turned away in dismissal, picked up the fallen gold pieces of his chess set, and returned them to the wood and ivory board.

Reginald's hand briefly flitted to his scabbard. He fought back the urge to run the man through. The blood of this fraud was not a worthy polish for his blade. He turned from the king and his quaking aide and thundered out of the pavilion.

Outside, the knight looked up at the unforgiving sun. He stared straight into its blinding rays, an act of pride and defiance against the forces of nature that were conspiring against them in this final battle. The priests had told him as a child that this world belonged to the devil, and over the years Reginald had come to believe it. The world indeed belonged to Satan, its elements in constant battle against the servants of God in this forsaken land that someone once proclaimed holy. The wind and the sun were often worse enemies, far more ruthless and hardhearted than the dark-skinned mongrels who denied the divinity of Christ. As his wavy, straw-colored hair flew in the parched desert breeze, he knew that the forces of nature were definitely in the devil's favor today. In Saladin's favor.

But Reginald's heart rose when he saw the horses. Armored stallions reared in the stables of Byzantium, trained with single-minded purpose—to carry the warriors of God into the midst of the Saracen hordes. Like their masters, the Knights Templar, these mighty beasts knew no fear. Standing proud, the horses bore the soldiers of Christ who waited in strict formation for their leader.

How he loved these men! In a world where madness reigned, they alone stood for order and discipline. Reginald knew the knights would follow his charge without question, even into the bowels of Hell. If such a place existed. After years of being enmeshed in war and death, Reginald no longer believed in any Hell beyond the world created by men.

Reginald climbed his own ivory steed while a page bearing his dagger-tipped lance ran to him. He put his helmet on and lifted the visor before turning to face his men.

"The king and the priests of Holy Sepulchre have blessed the battle with divine favor," he said. "Today, we shall stab at the heart of the Beast, and the kingdom of Satan shall fall!"

Reginald raised his lance for proper dramatic effect, but the gesture was unnecessary. The white-robed Templars and black-mantled Hospitallers cheered with genuine enthusiasm. They had trained all their lives for this moment. In their minds, they were the brave defenders of the Holy Land from the Muslim plague. They knew that they were engaged in the final battle of the heavenly war. Saladin was the Antichrist, who had managed at long last to surround Jerusalem with his demonic hordes. And they were its chosen defenders, guaranteed Paradise regardless of whether they lived or died.

None of these young men feared death on the battlefield, but many hoped to live long enough to see Christ Himself descending from the heavens at the moment of victory. Reginald doubted that any such miracle was in the making, but he saw no advantage in deflating the knights' hopes.

He turned his horse and pointed his lance straight at the Muslim camp across the plain. His herald obeyed the signal and blew a mighty blast on his horn. The trumpet's blare cut across the battlefield like a flash of sunlight breaking through storm clouds. With a throaty cry, Reginald of Kerak, Lord of Chatillon, master of the Knights Templar, charged across the dusty plain. The thunder of hooves echoed through the hills like the clarion call of destiny.

The Battle of Hattin had begun.

rrows swarmed across the plain like bloodthirsty wasps. The Crusader knights were caught in a vortex of death as the cloudless afternoon sky turned into a rain of flying daggers. Their heavy steel armor, which often proved a curse because of its lack of maneuverability, served its primary purpose now—shielding the horsemen from the storm of razor missiles that flew at them like an onrushing flood. Their horses were not as well protected, however, and many valiant steeds toppled over in mid-charge, pinning their riders underneath. Those fallen knights who did not immediately break their necks quickly joined their deceased comrades as Reginald's cavalry rode over them without hesitation. Not that any of the dead men would have protested. The Templar Knights had been conditioned to understand that their individual lives were nothing compared to the success of the sacred cause.

Saladin watched the knights charge forward against his archers' barrage through his viewing lens and shook his head.

"They are courageous. It is a tragedy that men of such valor should serve the barbarians," he said.

Maimonides strained his eyes but could not make out the details of the battle unfolding a thousand feet away. It didn't matter. His hearing sufficed. The pitched screams of dying men echoed across the plain, a cacophony of misery that the physician was all too familiar with. The vibrations of their final, agonized cries would penetrate his soul, as they always did, to be replayed again and again in his nightmares.

Saladin glanced over at his grim-faced courtier and smiled. He slid the lens shut and turned away.

"I take no joy in watching the dogs of war go about their business," the Sultan said.

"Neither do I, *sayyidi*," the old doctor responded. "My healers will have much work to do when this is over."

"Then you are more hopeful than I am. I fear that the Angel of Death may claim many more men than your medicines will save this day."

Across the plain, Reginald and a group of knights crashed through the belt of archers and rode straight into a phalanx of Syrian guards that had been lying inside a trench, covered in ruddy cloaks that effectively blended them into the parched terrain. The Arab infantrymen jumped up in unison, attempting to skewer the Crusader cavalry with jagged spears. Several of the knights' horses fell, but their riders managed to jump free. The battle quickly turned into a melee of hand-to-hand combat. Sword met scimitar in a flash of savage might.

Maimonides knew that this was exactly what Saladin wanted. The Sultan needed to get the Crusaders close enough to his own troops that they were forced to abandon their lethal crossbows, whose bolts easily penetrated the Muslims' lamellar armor. At this range, the knights had to rely on their hand weapons. The broadswords of the Franks were heavy instruments of death that served their purpose well, but the curved Muslim scimitars, forged with almost unbreakable Damascus steel, were more than a match in such combat.

As he watched the Frankish knights riding up the hills toward the camp, Saladin raised his hand, signaling his men to unleash their surprise. Soldiers in crimson tunics bearing torches and bronze kettles of oil ran to the front lines, setting fire to every bush and tree that stood between the Crusaders and the heart of the Muslim army. Smoke and flame billowed toward the charging knights, causing many of their horses to rear in fear. Archers shot the confused beasts, who threw their riders to the earth as they let out heart-wrenching screams of agony. Maimonides covered his ears to try to block the horrific sound. But he could not escape the thunder of death all around him.

—◆— ◆— ◆—

MANY OF THE CRUSADER knights were blinded or choked by the smoke, but a core group led by Reginald himself tore through the waves of attacking Saracens. The Lord of the Templars charged like an enraged bull into the heart of the Muslim defense ranks. His lance smashed into the breastplate of a Kurdish warrior before the unlucky man could raise his shield. Reginald felt the spear pierce his enemy's heart with a satisfying thud. The lance ripped right through the Kurd's back, covered in gore and quivering tissue. The skewered man attempted to scream, but a wave of blood rushed into his throat and erupted out of his mouth and nostrils. He managed a faint gurgle, and then collapsed into death's welcoming embrace.

Reginald tried to pull out the lance from his victim's torso, but it was embedded too deep in the dead man's rib cage. Cursing, the knight let go of the pike and grabbed hold of his broadsword. As he raised his blade, he caught a sudden movement from the corner of his eye. Reginald managed to raise his shield in time, absorbing the full brunt of a javelin that had been aimed at his throat. The spear shattered against the reinforced steel, sending shock waves of pain up his left arm. Reginald cried out in agony as he felt a bone crack in his forearm. Every nerve in his body screamed, pleading with him to drop the heavy shield before his fractured arm broke in two. But he couldn't, unless he wished to make himself an open target for every archer in the enemy camp.

Gritting his teeth, Reginald lifted the shield, forcing himself to ignore the lightning bolts of pain that shot through every sinew in his battered arm. Fueled by rage and bloodlust, he viciously spurred on his horse. The stallion trampled to death a fallen rider and kept moving. He didn't know if the unfortunate fellow was ally or foe, nor did he care. Reginald could see Saladin's tent city looming before him through the cloud of smoke. He was determined to break through the shield formation—fifteen men deep—at the outskirts of the enemy camp. If he died today, Reginald intended to do so fighting in the heart of the infidel army.

A bearded Nubian charged toward Reginald, his scimitar covered in grime and the bodily fluids of dead Christians. The black warrior's helmet had been knocked off and the left half of his face had been torn to shreds, an eyeball dangling precariously from the ruin of its socket. By all rights, the man should have been dead, but some unholy fire burned in his remaining eye. Reginald had seen that look before—the flame of fanaticism that was kindled in the hearts of the infidels as they happily raced toward extinction and the promise of seventy virgins in Paradise. If this man was so eager to return to Allah, then Reginald would oblige him. Reginald swung his broadsword with full might as the African bore down upon him. Had the man possessed both his eyes, he probably could have parried the blow with ease. But his diminished perspective gave Reginald the advantage. His sword struck his enemy's thick neck, severing the cords that had kept the Nubian's head on his shoulders. As the decapitated infidel fell from his steed, Reginald caught a glimpse of his head flying through the air. It landed on the blood-soaked earth of Hattin, and burst like a watermelon as a dying stallion dropped its hooves on what remained of the man's forehead.

Reginald resumed his charge, all of his attention focused on the enemy base that was almost within his reach. But even as he rode forward, cutting a path through bone and steel, an image flashed through his mind's eye. As the head of his nameless foe fell, the African's ruined face was frozen in a smile, the remaining eye staring off into infinity as he returned to meet his Lord. Reginald shuddered as the Nubian's beatific smile mocked him from across the valley of death.

+ + +

As THE SURVIVING FRANKS waged war within the very outskirts of the Muslim camp, Saladin moved toward his steed. Maimonides knew that the Sultan could never quell the warrior blood in his veins, and it was time for the general to enter into the trenches of war with his soldiers.

Saladin mounted al-Qudsiyyah, his most prized Hejazi stallion. Black as midnight, al-Qudsiyyah was like a beast from ancient fable, springing forth from the south wind to conquer the world. Al-Adil mounted his own stallion, a gray charger with a temper as foul as its master's. The sight of the two heroes prepared to ride out and face the barbarian menace sent a wave of quiet awe through the Muslim soldiers. Even in the midst of the raging battle, a strange serenity seemed to flow from the two men into the hearts of their followers. Saladin lifted his emerald-encrusted scimitar and pointed toward the Frank encampment.

"The moment has come, my brothers," he said. "As we face the tides of this last battle, remember the words of our Holy Prophet: 'O men! Do not seek an encounter with the enemy. Pray to God for security. But when you must fight, exercise patience. And know that Paradise is under the shadow of the swords!'"

His words stirred the soldiers, who raised their scimitars in unison, blocking out the blazing sun in an act of pious defiance. Maimonides saw Saladin smile softly as he gazed across the gathered throngs, shaded by their own weapons. Men who were willing to sacrifice this paltry life in a valley of tears for an eternity in the Garden. And then the rabbi understood for the first time how deeply the Sultan loved these men. They held a place in his heart that no woman could take, no child born of his blood could lay claim to. They were mirrors of his soul, and he was proud to fight and, perhaps, die among them.

And then he spoke the words that Maimonides knew could be his last. An oath the Sultan had waited all his life to make.

"May the sun above be my witness. Either I shall return as the lord of Jerusalem this day, or the vultures will feast on my dishonored corpse. *Allahu Akbar!*"

His cry of "God is Great" echoed through the camp. Saladin and al-Adil rode forward, followed by a wave of the army's finest warriors to confront the last of the Franks. Maimonides knew that he was witnessing the end of a chapter in history. For better or worse, the world would never be the same after this day.

Saladin rode straight into the thick of the Crusader onslaught. He was like a living eye at the heart of a hurricane. The Sultan's blade flashed almost faster than human sight could follow, cutting through every obstacle that stood in its path, sending a dozen Franks to meet their Maker. His fearless charge rallied the Muslim soldiers, who set upon the Franks with renewed vigor. The overwhelmed Crusader knights were unprepared for the fury of Saladin's advance and several began to fall back under the attack.

Even as Reginald reached the edges of the Muslim camp, he saw his men starting to retreat and rode forward, propelled by all-consuming fury. He cut through the Arab defenses with unrelenting force until he broke through to the center of the raging storm. And there, at long last, Reginald of Kerak came face-to-face with Saladin.

Perhaps the soldiers on both sides only imagined what happened next, carried away by the emotion of the moment, many would recall that a strange hush seemed to fall on the battlefield. Yes, the din of war and the cries of the dying surely must have continued unabated, but it seemed to the warriors that a force greater than any of them had blanketed the camp, muffling the ongoing devastation if only for a brief moment. It was as if, in that instant, history held its breath.

Saladin and Reginald locked eyes and rode toward each other without any words. None were needed or warranted. Each man had existed solely for one purpose—to slay the other—for so long that any greater goal of the war was forgotten in that instant. Saladin's scimitar, forged with the finest Damascus steel, met Reginald's broadsword. Sparks flew, as if the blades themselves were charged with the hate that filled these adversaries. Blow after blow, their weapons danced. The battle around them raged on, yet for these two leaders, the world was invisible. They were fighting alone on the vast, empty battlefield of their souls, each man focused only on his opponent.

And then Saladin struck Reginald hard on his sword arm, cutting through steel and mesh, slicing deep into the bone. The knight screamed in pain and dropped his weapon. The Sultan wasted no time. He swung at Reginald's head. His nemesis reacted instinctively, moving his neck and letting his helmet absorb a blow that would otherwise have decapitated him on the spot. Reginald was thrown from his horse and collapsed in the mud, unconscious.

＊ ＊ ＊

KING GUY OF JERUSALEM watched the battle unfolding in the distance. He saw the flag signals from the heralds at the forefront of the fighting. The code was new and hastily devised, as the Muslims had recently uncovered the secret of their former system through a captured spy. He thought he could make out the message that was being urgently flashed to his generals on the field. The flags rose and fell, each color and number of twirls sending a complex system of information to those who needed to make decisions in the heat of battle. If he was reading the blue and green standards correctly, Reginald had been captured. A flash of purple followed by orange. The forward assault was in disarray. Red. Black. Red again. The Hospitallers were scattered across the field, unable to form a defensive perimeter to protect the Templar Knights. The king knew what that meant. His men were separated and vastly outnumbered. They would all be dead in a few minutes. Gray. Purple. Black. Raymond was trapped at Tiberias, Balian to the rear. The divided columns of the Frankish army could not come to his aid.

Even as he pondered this terrible turn of fortune, King Guy witnessed a sight that cut deep into his heart. A terrible commotion erupted only a hundred feet away, at the top of the hill known as the Horn of Hattin. There the Archbishop of Acre, wrapped in full armor under his clerical robes, stood with the most sacred relic of Christendom, the wooden plank that was believed to be a piece of the True Cross upon which Christ himself had perished. At the onset of the battle, Guy had grimly noted that the Horn was believed to be the famed Mount where Christ had preached his great Sermon. How ironic it seemed to him that the archbishop was goading men on to war from the very spot where the Lord had called on Christians to turn the other cheek in the face of aggression. And now, covered in gore and the bodies of the dead and dying, the Horn stood silent witness to the consequences of his people's failure to heed the Word. Even as they held the Cross aloft in their hands, they had failed to carry it in their hearts.

The archbishop had stood through the battle on the hillock, surrounded by fanatically loyal Templars, his raised hand holding the sacred relic in view of all the believing warriors. The men had hoped that the sight of the True Cross would inspire and rally the badly dehydrated and demoralized troops. But a swift-moving regiment of Muslim cavalry now rode about the hill, surrounding the valiant defenders and cutting them off from the rest of the Christian army.

Guy watched with helpless horror as the Muslim archers shot their way through the last line of defense. As the brave Templars fell under the never-ending onslaught of missiles, one of the infidel horsemen rode through an opening in the circle of protectors, heading straight for the terrified archbishop. With a piercing scream of victory that seemed to echo through the valley, the turbaned warrior thrust his scimitar with such force that his sword shattered against the archbishop's breastplate. There was an explosion of light and sound as the blade splintered into a thousand lethal needles that seared through the cleric's armor. The old man fell backward in a spray of blood and torn flesh. The Muslim knight reached forward and pried the sacred wood of the True Cross from the dying archbishop's grasp and held it aloft for all to see.

The Cross had fallen into the hands of the unbelievers. The war was over. His people had been defeated.

Guy let the finality sink in as he stood outside under the blazing sun, silent. For what was there left to say? This day had been long in the coming. The Franks had been profoundly shortsighted in their war against the unbelievers. Ninety years ago, his forefathers broke through the gates of Jerusalem and initiated a massacre the likes of which had not been seen in the city since the destruction of the Jewish Temple by Titus and his centurions. Even the corrupt and despotic Pope had distanced himself from the cannibalism and other heart-wrenching atrocities the so-called Warriors of God had visited on the innocent residents of Palestine. His countrymen had controlled the land by terror and ignored all laws of God and man. The Franks thought that they could hold sway over the Holy Land through the unholiest of means. They had lied to themselves that their sins against the Muslims and the Jews would be forgiven through the sacred blood of Christ.

As a young man, pride flowing through his veins, Guy had believed that he and his people were invincible because they were on the side of God. But the years of war and cruelty had quelled that fire. He could not say for sure which old woman's cries for mercy, which child's terror at the cruel flash of a Frankish blade, had finally turned his heart. There were so many, their pitiable screams tormenting his restless nights. Guy knew that the vivid nightmares that consumed him were sent by God as a taste of the Hell that he and the other nobles had earned. He was painfully aware that his men had long since stopped serving Christ and now worshipped only their own glory. This war was the ultimate blasphemy. Their perversion of Christ's love could not go unpunished by God, and Guy accepted that the time for payment of their debt had come.

Reginald's knights were crushed, that was clear. The Muslim army had gone from shield formation to an offensive barrage. He saw their turbaned infantry swarming across the plain like the unleashed battalions of Gog and Magog. The Templars who remained to protect the camp would be unable to hold back this wave of enraged soldiers that descended on their pavilions like a sandstorm. He returned to his tent, ignoring the rush of cowardly nobles who nearly fell over themselves in their desperate effort to flee. Guy smiled grimly. Where did these men think they were going? There was no escape from God's judgment. The Pharaoh and his chariots had learned that lesson bitterly at the Red Sea. But, of course, most of the Franks were illiterate and had never read the Bible that they claimed to be fighting for.

→　→　→

THE MUSLIM ARMY'S ADVANCE was quick and lethal. The surviving Knights Templar bravely stood their ground at the outskirts of the Crusader camp, absorbing a torrent of arrows and javelins, until they were inevitably cut down by Saladin's men. The Sultan led the charge, his eyes focused on the king's pavilion, its crimson trappings fluttering like a virgin's heart in the hot desert wind. He rode up to the tent and jumped off his horse. The Muslim soldiers, engaged in fierce hand-to-hand combat with the surviving Franks, created a corridor of body armor through which their noble leader could cross safely. Two Frankish guards, the last of the royal protectors, moved to intercept him, but he quickly dispatched them, plunging his sword into the hearts of his opponents with calculated ease.

Saladin entered the deserted pavilion alone. His men knew that they could play no role in a confrontation between thrones. The Sultan strode through the cloth corridors unchallenged. Once a beehive of activity, filled with plotting courtiers and boasting generals, the command center was now an empty tomb. Desolate, forlorn, covered with the oppressive silence that follows the end of every epoch in human history. The Sultan knew that silence well. It was the same shroud that hung over every palace into which he had entered as conqueror, from Damascus to the Fatimid caliphate in Cairo. Saladin was the walking void that silenced the final gasps of a dying civilization and replaced it with the newborn cries of the next era.

The Sultan entered the king's inner sanctum, covered in rich purple silk curtains, and was met with the scent of myrrh and rosewater, a striking contrast to the stench of blood and sweat that blanketed the world outside. Across the room, Guy sat alone at his chess set, pondering the pieces. Saladin did not interrupt him. The king looked up at long last and gazed at his archenemy. Then he stood up with the last vestiges of royal pride.

"I am King Guy, Lord of Jerusalem and liege of the Vicar of Christ," the king said, in the flawless Arabic of a man who had spent years living among Muslims.

Saladin bowed low. Then he spoke to his counterpart in French, a language that he too had become conversant with over a lifetime of struggle that had finally come to an end. His voice was booming yet melodious, pregnant with the power of destiny.

"I am Salah al-Din ibn Ayyub, Sultan of Egypt and Syria, viceroy of the Caliph of Baghdad. I regret that kings must meet under such circumstances."

Guy stared at his victorious nemesis, and then smiled. He reached down and turned over his golden king on the chessboard. "Checkmate."

4

Maimonides felt like he was in a dream. He looked around the Sultan's private chamber in wonder. The most powerful and feared men in the region all stood together in one room. Enemies who had spent years trying to kill each other now spoke as if they were old acquaintances. Saladin sat on his royal cushion, a lush velvet of crimson hue, one of the few amenities he allowed himself on the battlefield, with a stern al-Adil at his side. King Guy stood a few feet away from him, next to a scowling Reginald, the knight's face bandaged from the Sultan's blow, the dressing already deeply stained from the wound. Two towering Nubian guards, their heads shaved and tattooed with bloodred swirls of some pagan tribe, were poised next to Reginald, in case the prisoner made any untoward advances, but he stood rigid. His face was passive, ironclad, but his eyes burned. Saladin met his glance, but said nothing. He reached casually for a golden chalice and offered King Guy a sip of water flavored with rose sherbet.

"Fear not, my lord. You are my guest and will be protected by the honor of the House of Ayyub." Guy smiled feebly and took the drink. The old king sipped it and passed it over to Reginald. The calm expression on Saladin's face turned to hot fury.

"I did not extend my protection to this swine!" Saladin's outrage slashed out like a dagger. Guy froze, but Reginald seemed unconcerned. A haughty smile played on the knight's lips.

Saladin locked eyes briefly with the nobleman, and then returned his attention to the old regent.

"It is time, Your Majesty, to discuss the terms of your surrender. Once we have subdued the coast, my men will march on Jerusalem."

Guy nodded, accepting the inevitable.

"What guarantees will my people have?" he asked, realizing full well that he was in little position to negotiate.

"Your churches will be protected. Your innocents will be spared. We will not do unto you what your people did to us. I swear to you in the name of Allah," the Sultan said.

Reginald chuckled softly to himself. He obviously did not believe that oaths sworn to "false gods" held much weight. Guy glanced over at the bearded Maimonides.

"What of the Jews? The Church cannot allow them to return. They bear the blood of Christ on their hands." Guy repeated the age-old charge as a leader of the Christian faith, but his voice held little conviction.

The rabbi's eyes flashed hot. He felt the sullied honor of three hundred generations of his people fill his heart and he spoke before he could stop himself.

"You cowards have hidden behind that lie for a thousand years!"

Saladin raised his hand and shot Maimonides a stern look. Guy was under his protection and the doctor had insulted his guest. Maimonides calmed himself, realizing that speaking without permission during such an august occasion—worse, bringing embarrassment to the Sultan—could prove to be a fatal mistake. The rabbi mused over the irony that, like Moses, he might live long enough to see the Promised Land, but not long enough to enter it. Maimonides met Saladin's eyes, but instead of anger, he saw patience and compassion. The rabbi nodded and stepped back apologetically. The Sultan turned to King Guy.

"I regret to advise you that I cannot comply with your request," he said. "The Jews are People of the Book and are protected by our religion. The Holy Prophet, peace be upon him, forbade us to oppress them."

Guy accepted the response gracefully, his heart clearly gratified that his enemy could act with the mercy that his own people had long forgotten. But the comment obviously struck a nerve with Reginald, who turned on Guy with unrestrained fury.

"You will rot in the bowels of the Beast for your deal with this devil!" he said.

Saladin stood up. He walked toward the proud Reginald, a courtly smile spreading across the Sultan's face that nonetheless failed to mask the deep hate welling in his eyes.

"I must thank you, Lord Reginald," he said. "Without you, this victory would not have been possible. Your crimes united the believers after a century of division."

"I have committed no crime," Reginald responded, his chest expanding pompously.

There was a moment of silence so deep that Maimonides thought he could hear the palm leaves falling in distant Cairo.

"The massacre of the caravans? The rape of entire villages?" Saladin's voice quavered. He was obviously incredulous at the man's lack of decency right up to the very end.

"Casualties of war," Reginald said dismissively, his eyes never leaving those of the Sultan.

"Perhaps, under your twisted code of combat," Saladin said, his voice pure steel. "But, when you attacked Mecca and Medina, I knew you were indeed mad. My lord, what exactly did you hope to gain by laying siege to the holy cities, save an everlasting *jihad*?"

Reginald's face contorted at the mention of his greatest debacle, the foolhardy adventure that had changed the course of history, culminating in his present humiliation before his sworn enemy.

"Nothing of value, really," he said, his anger finally overwhelming any caution required by his situation. "I was planning to dig up the grave of your false prophet and put his bones up for display. Even thought of charging a few dinars for admission."

Maimonides would later wonder whether it was just his imagination, but the light in the room seemed to change, as if the sun had been momentarily eclipsed. Reginald had crossed the final line with the Sultan, and the cosmos seemed to tremble in anticipation.

Saladin unsheathed his scimitar. In one swift movement, he sliced through Reginald's neck, sending the noble's head flying across the room. The knight's decapitated body stood still for one moment, as if trying to process whether this had really happened, and then collapsed in a rapidly spreading pool of blood.

Guy was rooted to the spot, staring at the nobleman's remains in horror. But Saladin turned to him and smiled apologetically, as if he were a host embarrassed by a minor faux pas at a banquet. Still holding his dripping blade, Saladin stepped forward and put a collegial arm around the terrified king.

"Perhaps we should continue our discussion over dinner."

5

Maimonides stared at the ancient stone walls of Jerusalem with wonder, tears welling. He sat astride a gray horse in the procession of honor as Saladin marched into the Holy City. Forty of the Sultan's top generals and advisers were gathered on a train of steeds and camels to witness Saladin's historic entry into Jerusalem. It was quite a mosaic, representing the great and the good from all corners of the caliphate. Kurdish soldiers in polished armor and saffron-robed nobles from Egypt mixed with the bejeweled courtiers from Syria and the blue-veiled Moors from the ocean's edge. Even the Grand Sheikh of Mecca in his green-turbaned glory was present, braving the treacherous caravan route north from the peninsula. It was the first time the curly-bearded *sharif,* the head of the Prophet's tribe, had ventured outside the Holy City since Reginald's shocking attack. Emissaries from as far as India and the Mongolian steppes had come to play a part in the glorious liberation of Al-Quds, as Jerusalem was known to the Muslims. The entire Islamic world was represented, except for its titular head itself. The Caliph of Baghdad had not sent an ambassador to witness the city's surrender, pointedly reminding Saladin in a terse letter that the Sultan was his representative. In truth, Saladin was as independent a ruler as the caliph's rivals, the Almohads in Cordova, but it served little purpose to antagonize Baghdad openly. So Saladin would formally take control of the city in the caliph's name and keep the Abbasid armies away from his doorstep. For the time being.

A herald, a boy of not more than fifteen, sat on a brown-spotted pony at the head of the entourage. He seemed nervous and excited, as were the other men, but was still too young to camouflage his true feelings under the pretense of bravado. He fingered the bone horn he had been given for the momentous task of announcing the arrival of the Sultan. The herald glanced eagerly at Saladin, waiting for the signal.

Saladin sat astride al-Qudsiyyah, the ebony stallion's gold-streaked mane flowing in the desert wind. The horse stood almost eighteen hands high, one of the largest Maimonides had ever seen, and the rabbi marveled again at how such a powerful creature could stand easily upon such thin, finely crafted forelegs. The Creator was beyond a doubt a masterful artist. Saladin, himself not a particularly tall man, towered over his troops in the saddle, adding to the majesty of his appearance at this historic moment.

The heavy bronze doors of the Damascus gate swung open before the conquerors as they advanced on their most treasured prize.

Maimonides saw Saladin close his eyes and whisper a prayer of thanks to Allah before raising his head and gazing past the gates into the Holy City. The cobblestone streets were empty but safe. Al-Adil had led an advance guard of the Muslim army inside several days before, dispatching the last of the Crusader knights and restoring order to the terrified citizenry. While there were likely a few armed rebels waiting inside Jerusalem's gates for their moment, organized resistance had vanished.

Saladin raised his hand and spoke, his voice booming with authority.

"In the name of Allah, the Beneficent, the Merciful," he began. A hush fell on the caravan and all eyes fell upon the Sultan. "We enter the holy city of Al-Quds, my brothers, with humility, knowing that the earth belongs only to Allah, the Lord of the Worlds. It is by His mercy that we have defeated the sons of Satan and ended their reign of terror in the land of the prophets."

A raucous cheer erupted, but Saladin's face turned stern. He raised his hand, and the jubilation quickly died down.

"Remember always that the city is a sacred trust, and we are its vice-gerents," the Sultan said gravely. "If we act with justice and mercy toward its people, Allah will grant us a long reign. But if we become the very evil that we have defeated, then He shall raise a new people to take our place and our names will be written in the book of the tyrants."

The intensity of his words, the power of his moral conviction, seemed to penetrate the hearts of men hardened by the brutality of war. As he spoke, a blanket of peace descended upon the excited dignitaries, enveloping the entourage in a deep serenity, akin to the calm a man feels relaxing at home with his loved ones after a strenuous day. Their journey had taken a hundred years, but they had made it to their long-awaited destination, against all odds. Now was a time for reflection and thanks, not for the boastful pride of victory.

With Saladin's words echoing in their souls, the entourage slowly followed its master and entered the city walls. The soldiers broke out into spontaneous song, praising Allah and sending blessings upon His Messenger as they followed the path of the Rightly Guided Caliph Omar into the heart of God's city. Much blood had been spilled on the road to Jerusalem, but it was now the time to spill tears—of joy and wonder at the vagaries of time.

Time, Maimonides knew, was a mischievous trickster. Man journeyed long and hard through life and wearied over its relentless push, but time was, in truth, little more than a dream. The ages that had passed between Creation and this moment were beyond mortal comprehension, yet only a twinkle in the eye of God. And, as it often does at moments of great import, time seemed to slow down now. As Maimonides rode under the majestic arch, he felt as if he were being transported into the distant past. Two thousand years of his people's history fell away from him, like raindrops shaken from the hair of a maiden caught in a summer shower. With each fall of his horse's hooves, the sands of time flowed backward, lifting off the veils from the city's turbulent past.

Turning to look at the crumbling stone tower to his right—it was as if he could see the Jebusite sentries sounding the bells from its turret, alerting the pagan inhabitants to the oncoming juggernaut of David's army. Around every shadowed corner, the rabbi saw flashes of people, clad in primitive robes of bygone eras. He could hear the laughter of children as they celebrated the first feast of Tabernacles after the end of the Babylonian captivity. He caught glimpses of the workers who labored for years to erect the first Temple, their spirits basking in the glow of its virgin limestone. The air was thick with the dread and awe of the Prophets as they cried out against Baal and the denizens of Jezebel.

And he could hear the screams. So many screams. It was as if every worn stone in Jerusalem had absorbed the cries of the dead, the pleas for mercy that regularly greeted the hardened hearts of the city's conquerors—the Babylonians, the Persians, the Greeks, the Romans, the Arabs. The Franks. And now the great Saladin, master of Egypt and Syria, had added his name to the list of the city's masters, alongside Nebuchadnezzar and Caesar Augustus.

Then the screams faded into the shadowed regions of his mind, and the rabbi noticed the deathly quiet that blanketed the city. The winding streets were deserted, every window shut, as if Jerusalem had been abandoned to its troubled ghosts. But Maimonides knew that thousands of Christian citizens remained within Jerusalem's walls, locked inside their homes, praying for deliverance from a vengeance long in the making. Most were the descendants of the men from Europe who had invaded this land with such brutality a century before, and the memory of the atrocities their grandfathers committed weighed on them.

Forty thousand Jews had been killed during the first Crusader conquest in 1099. Many more Muslims, and Christians who had been loyal to the Seljuk sultans, had met their deaths in ways too frightening to contemplate. The legacy of fire, blood, and hate was written into the stones of the Holy City by the hands of the Franks and their forefathers. And the day of retribution, the time for repayment of their cruel debt, had finally dawned.

Of course, Saladin had sent advance word that he would spare the Christian citizens of Jerusalem and that a general amnesty would be declared upon his arrival. But the Franks, accustomed to empty promises and betrayal from their own leaders, put little stock in his words. If the kings who ruled in the name of Christ could not be trusted, how could they rely upon the forked tongue of a heathen? No, the simple folk of Jerusalem were certain that today would be the end. It was a day to be spent at home and at church, preparing themselves for a doom that would not come upon them unawares.

Good. Let them suffer and fear. The thought flashed through the rabbi's mind, despite his best efforts to suppress the cruel sentiment. These Franks, these settlers from Europe, were barbarians who had built their lives on the corpses of his people. The stone-and-mud homes that they barricaded themselves in had been built by the very men their forefathers had so mercilessly butchered. Saladin could extend them mercy, but Maimonides was allowed a moment of cold satisfaction, knowing that these interlopers would experience for a few hours the fear they had so casually inflicted on others for a century.

But, of course, such sentiments were wrong. Weren't they? Had he not taught his students that the Torah required men to love even their enemies? That a magnanimous victor sat at the right hand of God? Then why was it so hard for him, at the greatest moment in his life, the triumph of his people over their oppressors, to forgive? It was as if the memories imprinted in the city streets were flooding his soul, the conflicts that had torn Jerusalem apart for two thousand years were now raging inside his heart.

Then he saw the child. A little girl of three or four who had somehow slipped outside her home and wandered onto the deserted alleyway. The child was dressed in a simple yellow tunic, her curly brown hair tied back with a few strings. She stepped away from a stone cottage with a rickety iron door and looked up with wide eyes at the long train of stallions and camels riding directly toward her. She was too young to know who these people were. Too small to comprehend that she was looking upon a moment in history that would be memorialized for generations. Too innocent to know that these men were supposed to be her enemies. All she saw were the pretty horses and the gallant soldiers in shiny armor. The little girl with the mousy hair stood alone on the corner, waving her greetings at the approaching conquerors, when the door to her house flew open.

"Leave her alone!" A burly man with a pockmarked face and eyes glistening with terror burst out onto the road. He brandished an old sword, rusty in places, but with an edge still razor sharp. A blue-eyed woman, clearly the girl's mother, followed, a scream for mercy exploding from her lips as she saw her daughter standing in the midst of the conqueror's entourage.

At the sight of the man with the sword, one of Saladin's lieutenants raised a bow, ready to strike down this petty rebel, when the Sultan leaned over and put a stern hand on the soldier's arm.

The lieutenant lowered his weapon as Saladin dismounted and approached the little girl. Her father rushed toward her, still holding his sword high, but he froze in his tracks as he met Saladin's steely gaze.

"I can restrain my men only so much," the Sultan said. "I suggest you lower your blade, friend, before this little angel must mourn her beloved father." The frightened man looked to his wife, whose pleading eyes broke his resolve. He dropped his sword, his eyes focused with uncertainty on the Sultan as the older man knelt beside his daughter.

Saladin smiled and stroked the girl's hair. She looked up at him with sky-blue eyes filled with the divine light that clings to the young. In her hand was a tulip freshly picked from her neighbor's garden. The little girl offered her new friend the flower, her face breaking into a toothy smile. Saladin accepted the gift with a kiss to the girl's forehead. As her parents watched in shock and confusion, the Sultan removed an emerald chain from around his neck and placed it on the delighted child. He then turned to her parents.

"I was wondering whether I would receive a warm reception in Jerusalem. When I saw the streets were empty, my heart sorrowed that the people were estranged from me. But your daughter has given me a welcome more precious than the false devotion of a thousand fearful subjects." Saladin lifted the child in his arms and brought her to the trembling mother. She took the girl and hugged her close, as if she was afraid that the child would escape and fly away like a captive dove set free.

Saladin climbed back onto his horse, then reached into his belt, removing a bag of gold, which he tossed to the startled father. "Spread the word, my Christian brother, that Salah al-Din ibn Ayyub will host a grand feast this Sunday to celebrate the peace between our peoples. And your daughter shall sit beside me as the guest of honor, for it is she who first welcomed the Sultan to the city of God."

As the startled parents watched, Saladin and his companions rode on to the heart of Jerusalem. The inner torment that had plagued Maimonides was gone. God had shown him through that little Christian child the miracle of love and forgiveness. The horrors that had drenched Jerusalem in blood over the centuries could never be erased, but their victims could be honored by bringing the cycle of vengeance to an end. The poisonous fumes of hate could be replaced with the gentle autumn air of a new day without recrimination. As he thought this, the voices from the past seemed to fade with a sigh of release, the stones growing silent.

The company rounded a corner and the rabbi's musings came to an abrupt end. It was as if he had stepped out of pitch-black into the searing light of the noon sun. And he finally understood where he was. He had indeed returned to the navel of the world, and he gazed upon the sight before him like a son looking upon the face of a beloved mother he had not seen in years. In a lifetime.

The Temple Wall stood before him, towering in its solitude. The massive blocks of limestone seemed to emanate a light of their own, as if kindled by an internal fire. He realized that he was the first Jew to set eyes on his people's most sacred site in almost a century, and he felt unworthy. Dwarfed by the ancient wall, he realized the true insignificance of man before his Creator.

"Go, my friend. Worship the God of Moses, as your heart has longed to for all its years." Saladin was smiling at him. Maimonides knew the Sultan understood what he was feeling. Rising just beyond the wall, the Dome of the Rock glistened in the sunlight. The golden cross that the Franks had placed atop the Dome had been torn down by al-Adil when he first entered the city, and Saladin gazed upon the reclaimed Islamic monument with awe. For the Muslims, the mosques that sat upon the ruins of the Jewish Temple were as sacred as the sanctuaries in Mecca and Medina. Maimonides saw that Saladin's eyes were glistening, much like his own, as he looked upon the holy mountain of his own religion.

Two men of different faiths stood before the hill where Heaven wept as it met Earth. In that moment Maimonides realized the true power of the ancient city. Like a beautiful woman, Jerusalem could inspire passion and frenzy among her suitors, hatred that could lead to bitter rivalries and duels for her heart. But the doctor finally understood Jerusalem's secret. She was not a fickle tramp seeking to play men against each other. Her love was deeper than that, so intense that those in her thrall could not understand that it sprang from an everlasting well that could be shared by many and never run dry. She loved all men and welcomed every son of Adam to her embrace. It was the pettiness of her lovers that prevented them from seeing that her heart was bountiful and could never be monopolized or controlled, even as the earth could not hold the vastness of the heavens in its grasp.

So caught up were the two friends in their reverie that they barely noticed a small entourage of Frankish nobles approaching from the otherwise empty square in front of the Temple Wall. Heraclius, the Patriarch of the Holy Sepulchre, dressed in ebony and covered in a sea of crosses and ornaments, was followed by a gaggle of nervous Frankish lords hoping for clemency. Saladin moved his horse forward to greet his new subjects, while Maimonides dismounted and walked with a bowed head toward the wall. Diplomacy was best left to the statesmen.

As he knelt before the most sacred site on earth, tears of reverence streaming down his cheeks, Maimonides could not help but think how his people had toasted each other through the ages, promising "next year in Jerusalem." That promise had never felt real to him, no more than empty words said to provide comfort to a wayward folk. But, against all odds, a miracle had happened. The exile was over. And next year had become today.

A beautiful, wailing chant rose from a tower near the Temple Wall, a poignant reminder that while his people had returned as honored guests to Jerusalem, they were no longer its masters. And perhaps would never be again.

Allah is Most Great. Allah is Most Great.
I testify that there is no god but Allah.
I testify that Muhammad is the Messenger of Allah.
Come to Prayer. Come to Felicity.
Allah is Most Great.
There is no god but Allah.

As the Islamic prayer call echoed inside Jerusalem for the first time in a century, Maimonides felt a shiver, a premonition, run through him. God had brought His People back to Jerusalem for a reason, of that he was sure. But would He now grant them peace?

6 Royal Palace, Tours—AD 1187

Richard the Lionheart shifted uncomfortably under the gaze of yet another enamored noblewoman. The flaxen-haired maiden with the long lashes (Jolie was her name?) stared at him from across the ballroom, her clear blue eyes reminding him of a hawk focusing in on its prey. She was the daughter of the Viscount of Le Mans, if he remembered correctly. A minor court strumpet, someone his mother would have immediately dismissed as beneath his station. She would probably have been right, but the difference in social status wouldn't have mattered much if Richard had been sincerely interested. One of the privileges of being the Crown Prince of England was, of course, the right to bed any woman he desired. Indeed, most of the young men who had held his illustrious rank over the centuries had fully availed themselves of the advantages of their position. But Richard was different. He had little use for most women, particularly those raised in the stifling mediocrity of court culture.

A mediocrity that was very much on display tonight. Averting his gaze from Jolie, he looked around with a grimace at the pomp and circumstance of the evening's ceremonies. It was as if the entire aristocracy of western France had descended on the ball at Tours. The rumor that the reclusive King Henry was supposed to be in attendance had caught the attention of every fool with a claim to a hereditary title. They were all here in the hopes of garnering favor at the highest levels. And they had all brought their daughters, dressed in the finest silk gowns imported from Rome and Florence, hoping that one of them would at last catch the fancy of the notoriously impervious crown prince. Of course, most of these girls had never been inside one of the royal palaces, and Richard could see them looking around in awe at the ballroom, with its two-story, stained-glass lancet windows opening directly onto the moonlit balcony. Gothic clustered columns served as the base for the deep ribbed vaulting of the ceiling, fifty feet above. The walls were lined with large oak cabinets displaying the finest arms and weapons of the English and the French. And a hearty flame burned in the marble fireplace, thirty feet high and crowned with carved icons of cherubim and seraphim looking down benignly at their mortal charges.

Richard glanced back at Jolie, who was chatting away with some heavily rouged friends. While her companions seemed almost to tremble with excitement, their eyes flitting around the magnificent chamber in awe, Jolie appeared completely comfortable and at ease in the royal world. Well, at least that was a good sign. As he gazed upon her pale countenance from across the brightly lit ballroom, Richard wondered, in a detached way, what she would be like in bed. So prim, proper, her hair perfectly coiffed in the layered fashion of Paris. A screamer most likely. The restrained ones always were. Those rare times that Richard had scratched an itch with a palace maiden had served as a kind of intellectual exercise for the prince, a chance to analyze the fickle female mind when the veil of social propriety was let down. Richard had found that women inevitably revealed their true natures, the forbidden corners of their souls, while caught in the wild abandon of lovemaking. That discovery had only increased his general distaste for the fair sex.

Perhaps tonight would provide an opportunity for another experiment. Richard kept his concentration on the girl until the invisible force of his gaze made her look up from conversation with a buxom friend. Jolie blushed under his unwavering, carnal stare. She looked away briefly, and then returned to meet his eyes. That was it! He had her. Richard knew that the first look was just a test, the second a sign of victory. He looked away. Too easy.

"I agree. She's not your type." He could hear the amused smile behind his sister's words. Joanna had the most annoying habit of reading his innermost thoughts even when he hadn't spoken a word. He looked up to see her slip beside him on the royal dais, her golden braids shining like a row of daisies on a summer afternoon. The princess settled herself comfortably on the silken blue cushion and gave her brother a look of mock disapproval.

"You say that about every woman." Richard did not brook even the most minor criticism from most men, let alone women, but he had a soft spot in his heart for Joanna. She was the one person in the court, in his family, whom he trusted unconditionally. It was as if she were immune to the disease of intrigue that plagued the blood of the Angevin. He knew that any advice she gave came from sincere love and a desire to protect her older brother's interests, and not from some secret agenda of her own.

"And I am always right," she said playfully. "Look at her. Nice eyes, but flat-chested as a cricket. Worse, she will fail to provide you what you need most—a challenge. She will spend all of three days dutifully denying your attentions, then throw herself in your bed with little ceremony."

"Most men would be happy with that."

"Ah, but you are not like other men," Joanna said with a smile. "Still, she's probably better than some of the others you've let crawl into your bed. And there would probably be fewer repercussions."

Richard flushed at the memory she was alluding to. Some years back, when he had been a mere boy, he'd had a misadventure that haunted him to this day. An act of childish curiosity that had made him the laughingstock of the Angevin court. He had been best friends with the dashing young Philip, Crown Prince of France, who was known for a rather indiscriminate approach to affairs of the heart. Drawn by Philip's youthful exuberance and energy, Richard had allowed himself to be seduced by the handsome young prince. It had been a brief affair, one more about sealing the intimacy of their friendship than about any unnatural passion. But the rumors quickly spread and the boys were forcibly separated by their embarrassed families. Richard had endured the smirks and cruel jokes of the court gossips for years, until his prowess on the battlefield finally turned the nation's attention away from his bedroom habits. But the wound was still fresh in many ways, and he didn't like it probed too deeply, even by his beloved sister.

"You are so quick with advice on my love life, Joanna. Yet you seem determined to become a spinster yourself."

Joanna flinched and Richard immediately wanted to take his words back. She was still nursing a broken heart from three years past, when their father forbade her to marry Edmund of Glastonbury. King Henry had a long-standing feud with the Earl of Somerset and could not stomach the idea of his daughter joining with his rival's family. Joanna loved her father dearly, and his decision had torn her heart asunder. She had not spoken to him for almost two years, save formal greetings and cursory banter, but the two had finally reconciled after the royal doctors advised her of Henry's worsening heart ailment.

The king could be summoned to the bosom of Christ at any moment, they warned, and it was best for everyone that their estrangement be healed before that time. Joanna and her father had begun anew, although their relationship was never quite the same again. She was more sober, less prone to laughter or tears. And she had become a loner, no longer interested in the game of seduction played out by the young nobles.

"Forgive me. That was uncalled for." Richard never apologized to anyone as a rule. It was unnecessary for a prince and heralded a lack of confidence in his divine authority that could be used by an enemy. But for Joanna, he always made exceptions to the laws by which he governed his life.

"I merely seek to protect you from sorrow, brother," she said, a tinge of hurt evident in her voice. "I fear that the kind of woman you are drawn to will rain chaos upon your life."

"And what kind of woman would that be?" Richard smiled, seeking to turn the conversation away from her loss.

"In your heart, you seek a girl that will stand up to you. Someone who is not impressed with the 'future King of England.' And then, when she has your devotion and sits beside you on the throne, she will ride you like a pony and the kingdom will fall to the French." The playful tone was, thankfully, back in her voice.

"Show me a Frenchman that can wield a blade and I will gladly hand over the throne to him myself," he said with a laugh, running a hand through his thick, reddish gold curls.

A shadow fell over him.

"Don't crown yourself just yet, boy." Richard bit his lip to restrain himself, then looked up coldly at his father. King Henry, wiry, bearded, and dour, stood above him, his face a mask of scowls. "The throne is for real men who have tasted the fire of battle and death. Not children with toy lances."

A hush fell over the ballroom as Henry slowly walked over to the center of the royal dais. Joanna rose and helped the monarch to gingerly lower himself on to his throne.

"Good evening, Father." With a curt greeting, Richard turned away from the man he despised, the king in whose smothering shadow he had always lived. The two rarely spoke anymore, the distance between them growing greater even as the Angel of Death flew closer to his father's bed every night. Richard told himself that their estrangement was natural, even welcome, for it confirmed that he was on the path that all great men had followed since the beginning of time.

It was all quiet poetic, in fact. Richard was an avid student of the ancient myths, not only those of the Celts and Normans, his forefathers, but of the Greeks and Romans to the east. He believed that these richly embroidered fantasies, shunned by the clergy as pagan lies, were actually tales rich in wisdom regarding the human condition. Perhaps that was because he saw his own life reflected daily in the tales of Uranus and Kronos, father and son, locked in a perpetual struggle from which the cosmos was born. Richard wondered if Henry knew the outcome of all such legends—the son, at the height of his power, invariably defeated and castrated the arrogant father. The old must give way to the new— such was the law of both Heaven and Earth.

King Henry limped forward, his left leg supporting his increasingly arthritic right knee. The gray-haired monarch settled down into his throne, conspicuously refusing to look at his son or return his halfhearted greeting. The crotchety old man surveyed the nobles, who stood at formal attention at his arrival, with barely concealed distaste.

"Oh, get on with it. I'm too old for all that fuss," he said, his voice raspy but still rich with authority.

The music arose again and the nobles, men and women of gentle upbringing and cruel hearts, passed by his throne. A brief bow and curtsy, and the couples returned to the dance floor. Richard looked at the ceiling, avoiding meeting eyes with any of the sycophants lined up for favor. His father's presence always dampened his spirit, like a snowfall in the Scottish highlands that deadened the sapphire lakes into ice.

A side door to the ballroom, set in bronze and silver, opened and Richard's mood turned from sullen to openly angry. In the arch was framed the hated silhouette of his younger brother, John. The boy was not expected back from his mission to Spain for another week. The music stopped again and a murmur spread through the crowd as the dark-haired prince stepped inside, followed by an entourage of knights, all dusty and disheveled from a long ride. The procession moved to the royal dais, before which John and his soldiers bowed low.

"My son," Henry said. "The clouds part from before an old man and give him hope whenever you grace his presence."

Richard noted with chagrin that Henry's grim face was now all smiles and warmth. John had been the favorite son for years, a position he had earned through obsequiousness and honeyed words. Whereas Richard never failed to speak his mind and question his father's often overly cautious policies, John seemed content to flatter the old fool and let the kingdom fend for itself.

"I rejoice to bask in your holy glory, dear father, after weeks in the company of unclean infidels," John said. The prince had been sent to supervise trade negotiations with the Moorish invaders who held sway over much of Iberia. Richard had felt it was his duty as crown prince to conduct diplomacy with the heathens, but Henry had refused, bluntly stating that his hotheaded nature would end up pulling England into the quagmire of war with Arab Spain rather than open the bazaars of Cordova to Welsh pottery. The French had held back the Muslim invasion at this very city of Tours four hundred years before, and Henry said he would not risk his son providing a pretext for the Moors to launch a second *jihad*. In Richard's eyes, however, the decision was based less on his alleged failings as a diplomat and more on his father's efforts to raise John's standing among the nobles.

The raven-haired prince smiled at his father and at Joanna, but he pointedly failed to meet his elder brother's eyes. He stepped forward and handed his father a heavy scroll, which the old man unfurled with some effort.

"I have good news, Father," he said. "Our emissaries stood their ground against the infidels at the bargaining table, and we have secured an agreement that will bring much gold into our merchants' coffers."

Henry examined the document closely, and then smiled proudly at his son.

"We will discuss the details of your voyage to Cordova and the guarantees you have secured for our people in detail tomorrow," the king said. "But tonight is a time of song and dance. I bid you and your men to refresh yourselves with wine and good cheer among your fellow citizens."

The old man turned to the gathered nobles.

"I dedicate the evening's festivities to John and his brave knights, who journeyed far into the realms of our enemies and returned with the blessings of friendship and trade." Henry raised a shining goblet in toast to his successful son.

His statement was met with a loud cheer from the audience that easily drowned out Richard's derisive snort. The crown prince knew that the old man was deluding himself in thinking there could ever be peace with the Saracens. The dark-skinned invaders could wrap themselves in costly silks and finery, but they would always be mongrels from the desert. He knew a little about their religion and found it offensive and self-evidently preposterous.

A priest had told him as a child once that Satan speaks lies by hiding them inside truth in order to mislead men into serving him. The infidel's religion was a prime example. They claimed to worship God, but then denied the authenticity of the Holy Bible. They claimed to even believe that Jesus Christ was the Messiah, only to deny His divinity and even the fact of His crucifixion. And all based on the word of an illiterate camel herder. Richard had no doubt that Mahomet was the Beast of prophecy sent to test the valor of God's people. While his father could take shortsighted pride in his treaties with these evildoers, Richard knew that opening trade would only embolden the devils to spread their pestilence farther into the heart of Christendom.

John took a seat on the dais next to him, nodding only perfunctorily to his elder brother. Richard felt his bile rising. The minstrels began to play again and the revelers returned to the dance floor to celebrate the successful return of the young prince. Richard caught the eye of the pale Jolie again and forced himself to turn his attention away from the present situation. He got up and strode purposefully across the room, bowing smartly before the startled girl. A murmur spread among the gossipmongers, which was of course what he wanted. The girl was clearly beneath his station, but she could still help him cause a stir that would deflect the court's attention away from his brother John's unexpected arrival. And Richard knew that his father would soon be bristling with rage at his violation of princely etiquette; pricking the old man's temper was merely an added bonus.

Jolie took his outstretched hand, color rising to her pallid cheeks at the flattering offer of a dance with the crown prince. Richard took her by the arm, aware of his father's glower following him across the dance floor. A path opened immediately among the nobles, eager to give the prince comfortable room to sashay with the delighted daughter of a minor lord. He swept her in his arms despite the fact that the music was meant for more formal steps. After a moment of communal hesitation, the other dancers followed suit. It was always best to take their lead from the royals, even if the prince chose to break with tradition. The musicians quickly adapted, altering the tenor of their curved krummhorns, double-reeded shawms, and naker drums to accommodate the more informal and lively steps that now resonated through the dance hall.

Richard held Jolie close to him, whispered sweet nothings and princely lies into her ears. He could feel her excitement rising and he knew that if he had wanted, he could find release in her arms before the sun rose. He felt no real desire for her, but if he did choose to have his way with her, he knew that he would have to answer to his father the next day for whatever scandal followed. Richard felt the eyes of the entire room on him and he forced himself to ignore the stares. He had learned that the only way to preserve sanity in the court was to live in the moment. Consequences be damned. Which is perhaps why he acted the way he did shortly after the papal herald burst into the royal hall with news that would change all of their lives, indeed all of history, forever.

7

That boy will be the death of me," King Henry said. "And of my kingdom." The aging leader watched with increasing irritation as Richard danced away the evening with Jolie. He knew the girl's father, an annoyingly obsequious little man, and he was not interested in having to apologize to people so far beneath his rank on behalf of his wayward son. There would be the expectant cries of shock and dismay by the parents when they learned of the loss of their daughter's innocence at the hands of a lustful youth (although he guessed that the days of Jolie's virginity were a long-forgotten memory). There would be the inevitable demands for compensation for this blot on their family name. Still it was preferable to the vicious rumors circulated by his enemies of Richard's secret preference for boys. And it would be better for the legacy of the Angevin if his son bankrupted the kingdom through romantic indiscretion than with his foolish dreams of conquest.

As the hourglass of his life emptied, Henry was left with little patience for Richard's grandstanding. He harbored no illusions about his son's ambition, and of his reckless delusions of destiny. The redheaded boy had christened himself "the Lionheart" after a few victories on the battlefield, and the name had rapidly spread through the land, along with the tales of his bravery and cunning. Henry could only grudgingly admit that the reputation was not unfairly earned—the boy's natural prowess at warfare did border on genius. But, in truth, the king feared that Richard's skill with the blade would one day bring his people more tales of tragedy than of valor. Henry knew that his handsome son commanded a powerful following among the masses, who saw in his fiery locks and regal bearing the faint, pagan memories of Apollo. But if the lad were to ever reign on the throne of England, he would need to be disabused of his pretenses before he launched the kingdom on some ill-thought adventure to further his own myth.

"May I ask a question, Father?" Joanna's voice pulled him out of his worrisome thoughts.

"Ask, my pet, and all shall be revealed." He so loved this girl, this vision of gentle perfection. He often found it hard to believe that she had sprung from his loveless union with a vindictive, hateful woman.

"Why are you so hard on him?" For some inexplicable reason, his dear Joanna felt a bond with Richard and came to the boy's defense at every turn. Henry remembered how, as a little girl, she had wept when John and Richard had gone hunting for a wolf that was terrorizing the Welsh countryside. When the proud boys returned with the gray carcass of the monster in tow, she had cried for the slain beast as if it had been a beloved pet.

Joanna's heart went out to all, and that was both the source of her power and her most tragic flaw. It was her willingness to see the best in others, even when there was nothing truly there to see, that had led her into the arms of Edmund, a drunkard and a whoremonger who had promised to put his wild days behind him, just for her. Henry knew that such vows were easily made and broken, and he had no choice but to object. Of course, the fact that Henry hated Edmund's father with a passion had made his decree easier. He had never denied Joanna anything before, and a shadow fell between them that had never truly lifted again. Edmund had claimed a broken heart and soon left home to heal his alleged wound. Henry had little doubt that word would have soon come back to Joanna of his many trysts with the ladies of the French countryside had the fool not gotten himself killed in a tavern brawl outside of Nice. As it was, she would always remember Edmund as her one true love, and her father as the evil ogre who separated them for eternity.

Still, it was a fair question. Why would he not relent toward his son, the heir to the kingdom, when his heroism was sung throughout the land? Why the vast chasm between the two men? The truth was that if Henry was forced to look too closely across the divide, he might find himself staring not at his son, but at a dark mirror. In his pride and his vanity, in his fundamental insecurity, Richard was himself.

Henry had learned the hard way the true burdens of kings, and this knowledge had left him feeling hollow and alone. The throne was a prison. The palace a zoo with the petty nobles as its keepers, their never-ending intrigues the one thing that remained constant in an otherwise transient world. The long journey within his heart from adventurous prince to hardened king had left him weary, more so than any battle he had ever fought against men. The Prophet of the Saracens was alleged to have said that the greatest battle in life, the greatest *jihad*, was against oneself. Henry had learned that heretics sometimes knew the true nature of man better than the righteous, who pontificated smugly about ideals, secure in their own hypocrisy.

But these were thoughts that he would be unable to express to anyone in his lifetime, even his beloved daughter, whose very existence proved that there must still be a spark of virtue flowing through his blood.

Ah, he was an old man, for he could no longer control his ramblings, even within his own head. The girl had asked him a question. A stock answer should do.

"I seek to protect Richard from the nobles," he said at long last. "When they smell weakness, they attack. If Richard cannot be a man, then he will not be a king. He will wake one morning with a blade in his chest and the tender caresses of the ladies will be forgotten."

Joanna was looking at him strangely. Her sea-blue eyes seemed to penetrate deeper into his being than even the grasping claws of Azrael. Hmm, perhaps that was why he still lived, to the marked surprise of his physicians. The angel was looking for a soul to wrest from his worn body, but Henry doubted he still had one after all these years on the throne. But if he did, the girl would see its hiding place and undoubtedly keep its secret.

"Richard is indeed young," she said. "And perhaps reckless. But he would fare better if you expressed faith in him rather than denigrating him at every turn. Many men become the mirror of their father's expectations."

How did she get to be so wise? It certainly didn't come from that banshee of a mother. And he would not flatter himself as a man of natural insight. Whatever wisdom Henry had gained had been earned through the cruel lessons of fate and folly. But there was a spark in Joanna that seemed to originate from somewhere beyond the flow of his bloodline.

"My dear, sometimes I think that England would be served better if I set aside both Richard and John and placed the crown of succession on your head," he said, only half joking. The thought had crossed his mind in a few moments of private despair at his legacy, but he was aware that the nation was not ready for a woman to openly wield such power. Especially when everyone knew that it was the women of the court who truly controlled the kingdom anyway through the secret whispers of intrigue.

Joanna laughed, the first real merriment he had heard in her voice for a long time. Henry eyes sparkled at the forgotten sound.

"Keep the crown, Father," she said. "I would abdicate at a moment's notice. Power has no attraction for me." She paused and the laughter in her eyes faded. "I am not my mother."

Henry felt his blood rising at mention of Eleanor of Aquitaine, the woman who had shared his bed, whispered sweet words of love to him under the covers, while plotting to bring about his downfall. The treacherous queen had been imprisoned for the past fourteen years after her failed efforts to orchestrate a coup. He had, in essence, raised his children without a mother. Perhaps it was little wonder how sadly things had turned out.

But the thought was banished from his head and forgotten as the inescapable force of history intruded, seeking to turn his world upside down one last time. The heavy doors to the hall flew open unceremoniously and the music immediately died. Henry's view was blocked by the crowd for an instant, but he saw John rise from his seat at the dais, his eyes wide with concern. The sea of nobles parted to make clear the way to the throne. Henry saw someone whose presence filled him with dread.

In the doorway stood an Italian man dressed in black-and-red velvet robes emblazoned with the papal insignia. A messenger from the Vatican who had arrived unannounced. From the bearded man's somber expression, Henry surmised that he bore dark tidings.

The messenger strode forward across the long hall with the easy confidence of a man who was unimpressed by the presence of kings. He spent his days in the company of the Vicar of Christ. No earthly ruler could sway the heart of a man who dwelt at the very center of the Kingdom of Heaven. The envoy stopped before the regal dais and bowed in a perfunctory manner.

"Your Majesty, I bear a message from Rome. From the Holy Father," the man said, his voice cold and stark. The herald had dispensed with the protocol of long formal introductions and praises to the Almighty and was prepared to plunge straight into his news. A nervous jabbering rose among the worried nobles, and the rising clamor of fear and speculation threatened to drown out whatever he had come across Europe to say.

Henry struggled to his feet. Joanna put a gentle hand on his arm, allowing him to balance against her as he stood before this harbinger of tempest. Henry raised his hand and suddenly he was more than just a doddering old man. He was the King of England again, in deed and demeanor as well as in title.

"Silence!" His sharp command cracked through the crowd like a whip and the lords instantly snapped to attention. "Speak your word, Herald of the Vatican. The nation awaits."

The robed man hesitated, as if he was having difficulty finding the right words. Or could not believe himself the receptacle of the message he had been ordered to relay.

"His Holiness, the Pontiff of Rome, sends the blessings of Christ to Henry, Lord of the Angevin," the herald said, pausing for just one more moment. "It is with great grief and sorrow that I relate the news that Jerusalem has fallen to the Saracens . . ."

If the messenger had said any other words, Henry never heard them. The uproar that erupted through the banquet hall was like the thundering hooves of horses led into battle. Henry knew that image, which flashed through his mind as he tried to restore order, was more than likely a premonition of dark days to come. The king grabbed hold of his ivory walking stick, a gift from a long-forgotten ambassador of some savage country on the northern coast of Africa. He banged the staff hard against the oak floor of the dais until some semblance of order was restored. As Henry's eyes flashed across the faces of the outraged nobles, he met Richard's stare from across the room. There was something in that boy's look that unnerved him, a mixture of bitter anger and grim determination the old man had never seen before.

As the shouts died to a muted rustle of terror and despair, Henry found that his legs were giving way. Not due to the horror of the news, but to the ravages of age. He slowly lowered himself back on the dais, Joanna instinctively wrapping a protective arm around his shoulder.

"What news of King Guy and Reginald of Chatillon?" His thoughts flew automatically to his countrymen and fellow Christians, although he thought the latter description was unnecessarily flattering to that stone-hearted killer Reginald. Henry had known the cruel Frenchman as a boy and had been delighted when he chose to sail off to serve the kingdom of Jerusalem. It was better to have a man like that wreaking havoc abroad than devastation at home.

"King Guy has been deposed, yet lives at the mercy of the devil Saladin as a prisoner." The herald paused, as if even he could not bear to speak the bad news. "Reginald, I regret, has returned to our Lord a martyr."

More cries erupted from the crowd, particularly from Reginald's cousins and assorted relatives who feigned horror at his death. Henry knew that these same grieving family members would secretly toast to his demise tonight as they began the process of redistributing Reginald's land among themselves.

"This was an end long in the making," he said. "Guy was weak and Reginald a monster. Men such as this could not have held the Holy Land with God's blessings."

There. He had said the truth out loud. When he had learned that he was dying, Henry had vowed that he would speak his mind from that day on, for there was nothing left to be gained from the subtle lies by which men clung to the throne. Still, years of practice at diplomatic prevarication proved hard to erase, until this moment. The word that this herald had brought was a turning point for his nation. He knew what the Pope wanted. Another holy war. And, by God, Henry would deny it to him. If he had to offend every sensibility in the court to save his people from that madness, he would do so. And the first step was speaking the truth, even if the great and the good of the nation took exception.

And they did. The murmur that spread through the crowd was like the hissing of a snake that senses it is in new territory and must reexamine its hunting strategy. Henry's eyes flitted to John and Joanna. They were clearly confused at his unexpected condemnation of his martyred kinsman, but they would stand by his side. Then he heard a voice from the crowd that turned his blood red-hot.

"Father, surely it cannot be God's blessing that barbarians should hold sway where Christ died?" It was Richard, questioning him before all the nobles. He saw the lords glance between father and son, and the murmur increased. Tonight was shaping into fine drama indeed, much greater entertainment than was normally found at stuffy palace balls. Henry had to quench this fire before it spread.

"These so-called barbarians have left us in the dust," he said, his aged voice still ringing with authority. "As I'm sure your brother, John, witnessed for himself, a day in the schools of Cordova would shame the greatest scholars of the Christian courts. And for this, we have none to blame but ourselves."

Henry's eyes flitted over the nobles. His words rang hollow to them. But what did he expect from a bunch of inbred illiterates who could not bear to face the truth that the Muslims had far exceeded Europe in culture and science? It was easier to condemn others as infidels and barbarians rather than face the failure and stagnation within their own societies. Henry doubted he could reach most of their hearts, but he would not allow prideful delusions to drag his impoverished people into a confrontation with the most advanced civilization on earth.

Unfortunately, his son did not share his views, as usual.

"Surely, a king of England would not humble himself before the black heart of Saladin," Richard said, sensing that he was tapping into unspoken feelings among men in the room. The boy loved to be the center of attention, even if it were through open rebellion.

"Do not forget your place, boy, or your head shall adorn my mantelpiece," Henry said, his tone suggesting this was not an idle threat or hyperbole. Whatever discontented whispers were still flowing through the room were silenced immediately.

But, to Henry's increasing anger, Richard seemed to thrive on the challenge.

"I am but a humble servant," he said. "Yet even a servant knows what his duty is when the Lord calls him." With that, the proud Lionheart jumped on a polished table, his hands outstretched. The nobles flowed around him, caught up in the boy's passion. Henry saw that even the Vatican herald seemed enthralled by the performance.

"O, lords of England and France, hear me," his fiery son said. "I swear before all who gather at the court of the Angevin that this deed shall not go unpunished. The infidel shall not defile the sacred earth in which Christ lay. I am ready to take the sword back to the Holy Land, to cleanse our beloved Jerusalem of the Saracen pestilence." Richard paused, and then said the very words Henry had sought to quash when he first heard the news. The words that would damn his nation to failure and suffering. "In the name of God, and on behalf of my beloved father, I proclaim that I will lead the next Crusade!"

A wild cheer spread through the crowd like a brush fire. Henry caught the eye of the papal messenger and saw the triumph in his face. He would return to the Holy Father with encouraging news. Word that the nobles of England and France were willing to back the Pope despite the resistance of the king himself would strengthen the Vatican's hand in dealing with other intransigent monarchs. It might take months, but all of Europe would soon be mobilizing for war at the behest of the Church. Henry knew that such alleged men of God loved nothing more than killing others and stealing their property while declaring themselves blameless.

He would be dead soon and it would be out of his hands. Yet he could not help but look at his son, basking in the glory of the crowd's excitement. The boy would learn the hard way, just as he had.

"He is a fool," he said, to no one in particular.

"He seeks to please you," his daughter said in quick response. Even to the end, Henry knew that Joanna would not speak ill of her brother.

"Richard seeks to embarrass me in front of the court," he said to Joanna, his tone brooking no further argument on her part. "To seize my throne while I still sit upon it. But he will not lead any man down this path of madness while I still have breath in my body."

Joanna turned away, clearly realizing there was little she could do to protect a brother who did not have the wisdom of self-restraint in front of the throne. She rose quickly, excusing herself from the royal dais and the festering wound that was her family.

As the nobles congratulated Richard on his valor and toasted to the splendid excitement of a new Crusade, the king glanced at the quiet John sitting nearby. The boy was of a taciturn nature, so unlike his gregarious older brother. He rarely spoke, preferring to listen attentively and calculate his position. Henry knew that John was in many ways more like his mother than the outspoken Richard. Eleanor was most dangerous when she was silent, for her mind was invariably at work spinning webs so intricate that none could escape their grasp. Through all the excitement, John had said not a word. He was clearly analyzing the day's events rapidly, seeing how he could turn them to his advantage. Henry admired the boy, and had often thought he would make a fine king, but the nobles preferred the sunny, extravagant Richard. John had not yet developed a support base that would give him the strength to take his brother's position at the king's side. But now, more than ever, Henry knew that the issue of succession had to be settled. The world was rapidly changing, and England needed a steady hand guiding the rudder of the state through the oncoming storm. Henry locked eyes with John, his voice dropping to a soft whisper.

"My son, tonight we shall speak at length about the future of the kingdom, if you are willing to entertain an old man's thoughts."

John sat up, his eyes wide, as if he was finally hearing the words that he had anticipated for many years. Which was not far from the truth.

"I am ready, Father."

8 Jerusalem—AD 1189

"The heart of the world? More like the heart of a sewer," Miriam snorted.

Her aunt Rebecca gave her a chastising look, but Miriam ignored it. As usual.

She was unimpressed. All her life she had heard wondrous tales about the glory of Jerusalem, a city, paved with gold and diamonds mined by the angels for Solomon, where the evening sky glowed with the light of a hundred thousand saints. Rubbish, all of it. Quite literally, she thought as her carriage plowed through one of the dirty old streets of the Christian quarter. She knew that the Franks were unaccustomed to the rituals of hygiene, but the piles of refuse and camel dung that lined the cobbled alley made her want to vomit. Her uncle would have teased her, called her a snob. Not every city could be maintained in the manner of Cairo. Perhaps that was true, but as the carriage turned a corner and passed through a thick cloud of flies, Miriam found herself longing for the indoor gardens of Egypt.

Still, she realized that topography and necessity played a role in the city's rather stark and gloomy atmosphere. Set on a hill close to the wilderness, Jerusalem had begun as a military citadel in the days of the Jebusites. It had not originally been intended to serve as a living city, nor did it have the natural amenities to support a large and permanent population. She had noticed on the caravan ride north that the villages in its vicinity had plentiful springs, but Jerusalem itself was arid. True to its origins as a Canaanite fortress, the city was enclosed by strong walls of mortared stones, accessible only through a series of strategically located iron gates. As their escort had approached the grim walls, she noticed that there were few trees outside the city's imposing perimeter. The desolate terrain outside the Holy City was more reminiscent of the empty wastes of Sinai than of the lush fields she had encountered traveling through Palestine.

Inside the city walls, the stark emptiness continued. The streets were paved with slabs of gray stone. The smaller hills had been excavated over the centuries and made level. Their caravan driver, a normally quiet little man with an unfortunate series of moles on his face, had mentioned that the paved streets were structured so that rainfall would funnel down the heights and wash the entire city clean. Unfortunately for Miriam's overloaded senses, there had been little rain this season.

Still, from what Maimonides had written her, things had vastly improved in God's city over the past two years. She dreaded to imagine the state of affairs before the Sultan crushed the barbarians and restored Jerusalem to the Children of Abraham. Miriam knew all too well that the Franks were a throwback to the marauders of ancient Canaan who had faced Joshua when he first set foot in the Holy Land.

Her childhood teachers had said that the Franks had been set upon the Chosen as punishment for the people's sins, their failure to adhere to the Law. Which, as far as she was concerned, was a load of horse manure. Much like the rank pile that her carriage was sloshing through just at that moment. Miriam wasn't sure she believed in a divine being, but if there was one, she could not imagine that it would find the murder of thousands of innocents to be just retribution for the minor infractions of weak mortals. No, her people clung to such notions because it made them feel God was with them always, even though their sorry history seemed to indicate otherwise. Better to believe in an angry God who is nonetheless watching over you than to face the stark emptiness of the cosmos alone.

"You're awfully quiet, dear." Miriam's aunt Rebecca leaned over and placed a bony hand on her leg. "Are you feeling well? Do you need some water? It's so hot out today. Your uncle told me that it might get this bad in the summer, but I never imagined he was serious. Always exaggerating, you know him . . ."

Miriam smiled at the old woman who had served as her mother, sister, and counselor for almost a decade. It was impossible to get a word in edgewise when Rebecca started talking. Her uncle Maimonides was known for his wonderful skills as an orator, but even he found himself silenced in the presence of his loquacious wife.

"I'm fine, Aunt Rebecca," Miriam managed to squeeze in quickly while her elderly guardian paused for a rare breath. "Just taking in the sights." A sudden gust of wind blew her filmy head scarf aside, and Miriam allowed her ebony hair to flow freely in the wind for a few seconds. She loved the feel of the dry summer air on her curly locks. Then she saw the lecherous stares of men on the streets and decided to abide by the custom, no matter how irritating she found it. She slipped the light blue scarf around her head again, but found that she was still drawing attention. Perhaps it was her eyes—a brilliant sea green, unusual for this region. Or, more likely, her ample bosom, which the scarf never quite successfully hid from male gazes. Annoyed, she pulled the scarf closer over her breasts and looked away from the gawkers.

"I never thought I would live to see this day," Rebecca said. "To pray in the shadow of the Wall, to gaze upon the stones that still sparkle with the light of the Shekinah. But I shouldn't marvel. Life is filled with such wonders. Hashem's hand pushes us along every day toward destinies whose outcome only He can see. The twists and turns of fortune, the fate of nations, they are all part of His joyful dance with His people."

Miriam wasn't sure she agreed, but she respected her aunt's faith. Years ago, she had believed in the God of her people with the unquestioning acceptance of a child. Then the Franks had raped and killed her mother before her very eyes. She had found it hard to believe in anything after that.

"How far is uncle's home?" Miriam asked, mostly to get her mind off the direction her thoughts were taking.

"Actually, I have a surprise for you. We're not going to his house, at least not just yet," Rebecca said.

Miriam gave her a quizzical look. She was tired from the journey and wasn't interested in any detours right now.

"Your uncle has arranged to grant us an audience before the Sultan himself as part of our welcome to Jerusalem," Rebecca said, her eyes sparkling with the excitement of celebrity. Even a few moments with Saladin would grant her aunt months of bragging rights in her tight circle of society matrons.

The Sultan. Well, that would be interesting indeed. She had never met Saladin, but it was impossible to escape his shadow. Miriam had spent the last decade in Cairo, where talk of the man dominated all conversation. Every day she would hear stories about his chivalry and valor. For the Muslims, he was a reminder of the glorious days of their prophet and the Rightly Guided Caliphs. For the Jews, he was a savior of their people, the new Cyrus sent by God to return the wanderers to Jerusalem.

Her uncle had long worked in the Sultan's employ as his personal physician and adviser, but Maimonides had been careful to keep his family away from the court itself. For all the love he garnered among the common people, Saladin still had many enemies among the Egyptian lords, especially those associated with the former Fatimid regime that the Sultan had overthrown. The fact that her uncle was willing to bring his family into the inner circle suggested that Saladin felt more secure in his rule in Jerusalem. They would be protected from the intrigues of Cairo here.

The carriage turned a corner and moved toward the southeastern section of the city, and Miriam suddenly felt as if she had entered a completely different realm. The streets were whitewashed and covered in rows of roses, tulips, orchids, and lilies, glistening like the rainbow bridge in the myths of the desolate lands to the north. The square was lit by the reflected glow of the great Dome that covered the rock of Moriah. She heard her aunt catch her breath as the carriage rode past the grand wall, before which throngs of recently arrived Jewish worshippers bowed in a ritual that had been brutally interrupted during the century of Frankish rule. Miriam knew that Rebecca wanted to ask the driver to stop before the sacred site. But one did not keep the Sultan waiting. There would be a time for reverence to the heavenly power after proper due had been paid to the earthly one.

The carriage rode quickly up the hill toward the glistening minarets of the Sultan's palace. Originally built by the Umayyads in the early days of Islam, the structure had been devastated by an earthquake, and then suffered further depredations and neglect under Crusader rule. Her uncle had written that Saladin had begun an ambitious project to restore the old palace to its former glory. Even though construction was continuing, Miriam was impressed with what she saw. The palace covered an area of over twenty-five thousand square feet and was surrounded by a ten-foot-thick protective wall, constructed of large, trimmed bricks similar to the stones Miriam had glimpsed on Herod's Wall. She saw that two main gates, one facing east and one facing west, gave access to the palace. Soldiers and dignitaries were flowing in and out of the massive entranceways, like bees rushing to fulfill their queen's commands. Their carriage approached a broad, stone-paved courtyard in the center of the building, which was surrounded by rows of columns supporting the roofing of the porticoes. Miriam thought she glimpsed crosses carved into the columns, perhaps remnants of the Crusader era. No, their designs were too similar to the old Byzantine crosses she had seen on display in the museums of Egypt—probably leftovers from the initial Muslim conquest of Palestine under the caliph Omar five hundred years ago.

Her musings about architecture came to an abrupt end as she heard her name called in the distance.

"Miriam! Rebecca!" It was her uncle, waving excitedly from the western gate. Miriam climbed out of the carriage as the driver brought it to a slow halt. She rushed into her uncle's arms, felt the warmth and surprising strength still pulsing in his aging muscles.

"It's so good to see you again, Uncle," Miriam said, and meant it. He was more than a father to her. He was a mentor in whose company Miriam's mind felt truly challenged and alive. Since he had come to Jerusalem, her life had been remarkably dull and lonely. Well, not that lonely. Miriam had not had any difficulty attracting the company of men, a fact that she had skillfully hidden from her aunt's knowledge. Miriam did not wish to cause her family pain, even if she herself had no fear of scandal. After all she had been through, the opinions of polite society did not matter to her. And, in truth, Miriam preferred to be the hunter in the game of love rather than the prey. Still, her lovers had never been intellectually stimulating and she had longed for the rich conversations and debates that she and her uncle had engaged in over the years.

Rebecca came to Maimonides' side and the two smiled at each other wordlessly. He stroked his wife's cheek softly but said nothing. He didn't need to. There was no need for public displays of affection between her uncle and aunt, even though they had not seen each other in almost two years. Aside from traditional Egyptian notions of public propriety, Miriam knew their relationship was far deeper than any such demonstrations could reveal.

"By Hashem, how you've grown!" Her uncle was looking at her again in delight. Then he saw that other men in the plaza were looking at her as well, but with quite different expressions, and he frowned at her tight-fighting Cairene blouse, only barely covered by her rebellious scarf. "We need to get you more appropriate robes, my dear. Jerusalem is not Egypt."

Miriam rolled her eyes and was about to protest, when a loud gong echoed from within the palace. Maimonides spoke as he ushered the two most important women in his life inside the palace doors, "The Sultan is about to hold court and he is expecting you both."

9

A hush fell over the court chamber as Saladin stepped inside and took his place on the seat of judgment. The room, almost fifty feet long and thirty feet wide, sparkled with freshly laid marble and limestone, the walls covered with new murals of flowers and geometric shapes—these favorite motifs of Islamic art had been restored to the palace designs after the Crusader desecration. The Frankish rule over Palestine had been an aberration and Saladin was determined to erase all memory of this brief yet bitter interlude.

Miriam watched the Sultan closely as he sat upon the imposing judgment seat, with lions carved of gold serving as hand rests and scarlet cushions for a seat. The arched windows were carefully placed in the high ceiling so that the noon sun shone directly on the judgment seat, illuminating Saladin and lending him an almost divine aura, like the Pharaohs of ancient times. He surveyed his subjects with an air of confidence that exuded more inner strength than pride. His features were strong, his nose aquiline, his skin fairer than that of either his Arab or Jewish subjects. She remembered then that he was not a fellow Semite. Saladin was a Kurd from the Caucasus Mountains, born from a long line of nomadic warriors who had served as mercenaries to the various feuding lords of the caliphate. He was thus the most improbable of kings, a servant who had become the master. But she saw in his piercing eyes a nobility that seemed to emanate from deep within his being, one that made him appear to be more worthy than the sons of many aristocrats of "pure" blood to wield the scepter. Then those soulful brown eyes fell upon her.

Was it her imagination, or did he react? She had been accustomed to lusty stares and catcalls since her breasts first began to bloom at an early age, but she was startled by the intensity of the Sultan's gaze. For an instant she felt as if she knew him. Or, perhaps more accurate, that she *would* know him. Looking back, Miriam would come to understand that there are moments of destiny in life, when the divergent paths of mortals are brought together by a force greater than themselves. When people who will write a complex history together are first joined by the hand of *kismet*. It is at those moments that the senses are most alert, that a shiver runs down the spine, as the breath of God washes over the soul, gently sprinkling the heart with the tremors of premonition.

The Sultan turned to Maimonides, who stood by Miriam's side, and smiled warmly.

"My friend, I hear that you have good news," Saladin said.

"My family arrived from Cairo today, *sayyidi*. May I have the honor of presenting them to you?" Maimonides asked.

"By all means." Saladin's eyes rested on Miriam again briefly and she felt the same tingling.

As Maimonides hurriedly brought Rebecca before the throne, helping the old woman to bend down and touch the Sultan's sandals, Miriam realized that her uncle was anxious to complete the introductions and usher his family away from the court. While the Sultan was sheltered from the grand intrigues of Cairo here in Jerusalem, the old man had told her that petty jealousies still ran hot among nobles in his inner circle. Maimonides was a Jew and accustomed to rivals in the Sultan's entourage taking offense at even the slightest honor or attention bestowed upon him.

This had all been made quite clear to her before she even walked inside the royal chamber. After the warm but quick embrace from her uncle, Miriam had been taken aside and lectured on the rules of court decorum to prepare her for an audience with the most powerful man on earth. It had not been the rabbi's idea to bring his wife and niece before his master, but Saladin had insisted. Maimonides had no choice but to prepare his family and pray that the ordeal would end quickly.

And she now understood why. Even as her aunt bowed before the Sultan, she caught glances of distaste and bemusement passing among some of the turbaned lords. In their view, Saladin's respect for people of inferior religions was a political necessity to preserve peace among the common people. But they clearly could not see any reason why such courtesies had to be accorded these Jewish interlopers inside the royal court itself.

As Rebecca stepped back and Miriam moved to take her place of obeisance before the ruler, she felt the eyes of the room focus sharply on her. Miriam was aware that men thought her beautiful, with her ebony mane and eyes of a brilliant sea green. She did not seek out attention, but found that it could be used to her advantage when she received it.

"And this, *sayyidi*, is Miriam my niece. She has been like a daughter to Rebecca and myself. Miriam has longed to see Jerusalem since she was a child, and your valor has made that possible at last." Maimonides was sufficiently obsequious before his master. Saladin nodded to him briefly, his eyes never leaving the stunning figure draped in blue chiffon that bowed before him.

"Then I shall make sure that you are given a proper tour of the city," Saladin said.

Miriam raised her head and met the Sultan's gaze steadily.

"The Sultan honors me with his bounty."

"As you honor the court with your beauty."

A murmur rippled through the crowd. Surprise mixed with discomfort. Women rarely spoke in the Sultan's presence, and the electricity in their exchange was felt by everyone in the room. Maimonides shifted uncomfortably.

"*Sayyidi*, my niece is weary from the journey. I should take her to our home."

Saladin and Miriam continued to hold each other's gaze. She thought she saw something in his eyes. Was it a test? A challenge? Or something else? As she often did, and sometimes to her regret, she decided to press her luck.

"But, Uncle, is it not the hour of judgment? I have heard of our sultan's great wisdom and wish to see how he dispatches his cases." She paused. "If that pleases you, *sayyidi*."

She saw her uncle grow pale, heard the murmur among the court gossips. Let them be horrified, she thought. Miriam had spent her entire life confronting the limits that society tried to place upon her, both as a woman and as a Jew. Most men would tremble in fear of death to speak with such confidence before Saladin. But the girl had no fear of death. She had lost that fear, and much more, many years before on a desert road near Sinai.

Saladin, for his part, appeared amused, even delighted, at her courage.

"That would very much please me, young Miriam." He turned to one of his guards and nodded. "Bring in the first case."

Miriam stepped aside gracefully and returned to the company of her startled aunt and uncle. She knew that she was constantly shocking them with her boldness, but that was who she was. Who she had to be.

The carved silver doors to the judgment chamber opened, and Miriam was stunned to see a terrified woman dragged in by a guard, followed by a haughty man in a finely embroidered tunic and purple sash of nobility. Miriam guessed he must be her accuser. The woman was pale and gaunt, her dark brown hair drenched in sweat and her eyes red with tears. She did not look capable of committing any crime that would cause her to be brought before the Sultan himself.

Miriam glanced at Saladin and saw the perplexed look on his face. The Sultan was clearly thinking along similar lines. He turned to his unsmiling vizier, Qadi al-Fadil, who was seated on an ornate couch to his right, his back straight as an arrow, an aura of proud aristocracy hanging over him like a halo. Al-Fadil was examining a scroll that detailed the woman's case.

"Who is she and what is her crime?" Saladin's tone was now rigid and stern.

Al-Fadil closed the scroll and looked up at his master.

"The prisoner is named Zaynab bint Aqeel. She is the wife of a carpet merchant from Bethlehem, Yunus ibn Waraqa." The vizier's voice was high-pitched and nasal, grating on Miriam's ears. Al-Fadil acknowledged the richly dressed man who stood nearby. "She stands accused of adultery with an Abyssinian slave."

Zaynab bent her head in shame. Miriam felt the lurid stares on the humiliated woman as if they were daggers thrust into her own heart.

"Where is this slave?" Saladin was abrupt, to the point. His eyes never left the shaking woman.

"Her husband slew him when he found the brute in bed with her," the vizier said.

"How convenient. Are there any other witnesses?"

"Just the husband, *sayyidi*, but Ibn Waraqa is a highly respected man of the city. His word—"

"Alone has no weight. The Holy Qur'an requires four witnesses to the crime of adultery."

Miriam was surprised. She had a good working knowledge of Islamic law and was aware that the ideals of the Qur'an were usually lauded in the courts but rarely applied, especially in areas regarding women's rights. The requirement for four witnesses to the act of *zina,* unlawful inter-course, had been incorporated in the Qur'an after a scandal surrounding Muhammad's favorite wife, the fiery Aisha. When the teenage Aisha was lost in the desert after a caravan returning to Medina mistakenly left her behind, a handsome soldier had found her wandering alone and come to her aid. The man had escorted the Mother of the Believers back to the oasis that served as the Muslim capital, where she was greeted by scorn and gossip. Catty rivals, jealous of Muhammad's devotion to the proud beauty, spread rumors that she had been carrying on an affair with her protector.

The scandal threatened to tear apart the nascent religious community, or *ummah,* until the Prophet received a revelation from Allah exoner-ating his wife of adultery, and demanding that any accusation of *zina* be backed up with four witnesses to the actual act of intercourse. The requirement was meant to protect the honor of women, and was especially important considering the punishment for conviction—a public lashing, or even stoning to death, depending on which school of jurisprudence, or *fiqh,* was applied. Miriam respected the intent of the Qur'anic rules, but she knew that they were in practice conveniently ignored or misapplied by men seeking to control women. The fact that Saladin was adhering to a 550-year-old commandment was astounding in this day and age.

Her surprise was shared by the courtiers, as well as by the allegedly cuckolded husband. The carpet merchant stepped forward to press his case.

"*Sayyidi,* I swear by Allah that I—"

"I did not give you permission to speak!" Saladin's eyes were livid and the husband quickly fell back, bowing his head to indicate his immediate submission.

Saladin addressed the trembling girl, who was on her knees, prostrate before the throne.

"Woman, stand up. Look at me," he said.

She immediately complied, shaking, her legs appearing as if they would collapse under her at any moment. She tentatively raised her head, but did not quite meet the Sultan's eyes.

"Zaynab bint Aqeel, is the charge against you true?"

Tears streamed down her cheeks, but she did not speak. From where Miriam was standing, she could see the back of the woman's neck. Her fury rose. There was a clear scar, apparently recent from the discoloration, running down her neck and disappearing into her ruddy tunic. Miriam's indignation reaching a boiling point, she turned to whisper to her uncle, who had stood passively through the whole drama.

"Look at what they did to her."

Maimonides frantically gestured for her to be silent, but it was too late. The vizier saw them and was clearly shocked at the audacity of the young Jewess.

"How dare you converse while the Sultan passes judgment?!" Miriam was startled by the rebuke, and felt her cheeks flame. A rumble of shock ran through the chamber. Such brash disrespect for the decorum of the court was unheard of, especially from a disbeliever.

"*Sayyidi,* she is young . . . unschooled in the protocols of the court. I beg forgiveness for her youthful indiscretions." Maimonides spoke rapidly, hoping to put out the flame before further damage was done.

Miriam realized that Saladin was again looking at her. But he seemed more amused than outraged. One corner of his mouth twitched, as if he were forcing back a grin.

"Do not fear. I am interested in what you have to say about this case, young Miriam," the Sultan said.

Miriam was taken aback for a moment. The she glanced again at the sorry creature trembling in the center of the room and decided to speak her mind.

"*Sayyidi,* are the guards accustomed to beating women? Look what they have done to her back."

As courtiers gasped at her effrontery, Maimonides buried his face in his hands. Miriam knew what he was thinking. Even his loquacious Rebecca understood the time and place to let loose her tongue, and she stood rigidly silent. But his niece was hopeless. She would keep digging her grave until it was large enough to hold his entire family. Miriam should have been unnerved by the growing hostility in the court, but somehow she felt safe as long as Saladin seemed willing to indulge her. She had learned that men would tolerate much in a woman when they were overcome by her beauty. She hoped it was true today as well.

In any event, her words had the desired effect. Saladin rose from the seat of judgment and approached the prisoner. Zaynab stood frozen, unsure how to react as the Sultan circled her. His rough hands, weathered by battles and the desert life, examined her neck. Seeing the scar, obviously made by a whip, the Sultan pulled the clasp off the girl's tunic, revealing her upper back.

Miriam had to suppress the urge to retch. Zaynab's shoulders were heavily scarred, the skin twisted and growing as best it could around the injuries. Her pitiful secret revealed to the world at last, Zaynab could no longer hold back her sobs.

Miriam watched Saladin's face change, from the sobriety of the jurist to the outrage of a warrior. He turned to face the guard who had escorted the prisoner. The man was a head taller than the Sultan, but took a step back under the intensity of his master's gaze, his heavy brown mustache quivering nervously.

"Did you do this?" Saladin's tone was cold, his voice soft, almost a whisper. Miriam felt a chill go through her. There was more menace in that quiet tone than she had ever heard from the bark of an angry man.

"No, *sayyidi*. I swear by Allah, I would not strike a woman," the guard said.

Saladin looked closely at the man's face for a long moment, as if he could read a map to the man's soul in its contours. He then turn back to Zaynab.

"Who has done this to you?"

Zaynab's weeping grew and she shook violently, her hand covering her mouth.

"Answer your sultan!"

"My . . . my husband . . . with a horsewhip." Her voice was choked, her words muffled by sobs, but they cut deep into Miriam's heart. You did not need to be like Sinbad and travel to mystical islands to find monsters. They were with you every day, behind every face.

Saladin examined the bruises carefully, before closing the clasp of the prisoner's tunic and covering her shame from the world.

"Some of these wounds are not fresh. Were you whipped before this alleged incident with the slave?"

Zaynab no longer had the strength to speak, but she managed a feeble nod. Saladin turned to face Yunus ibn Waraqa, the "victim" of the crime now falling under the wrath of the arbiter.

"Tell me, carpet merchant. Does a bastion of society beat his wife like a mule?"

Ibn Waraqa blanched. This was clearly not how he had expected things to go.

"I merely discipline her once in a rare moon. It is my right."

Miriam wanted to scratch his eyes out there and then.

"I see." Saladin returned to his judgment seat, the edge back in his voice. "I have considered the matter before us. Since you cannot produce the four witnesses required by the Holy Qur'an to substantiate your allegations, I find Zaynab bint Aqeel innocent of the crime of adultery."

There was a murmur of surprise in the court, but a lethal glance from the vizier silenced any whispered conversation.

"And in accordance with the Divine Book, I find her accuser, Yunus ibn Waraqa, guilty of the crime of levying false charges against the honor of a chaste woman. You will be sentenced to eighty lashes. With a horse-whip."

Yunus cried out in protest, but was immediately seized by the guards and dragged out of the stunned chamber. Miriam was as surprised as everyone else. The penalty in the Qur'an for failure to produce the requisite witnesses in a *zina* case had also been instituted in response to the scandal surrounding Aisha. A final incentive to protect the reputation of women from gossipmongers and those seeking to dispose of their wives for gain. But the rule had fallen to the wayside over the centuries, as the value of a woman's honor dropped with the vagaries of culture and time.

She realized in that moment why Saladin held the loyalty of his subjects. He was a living example of the justice and moral character that Muhammad and his earliest Companions exhibited. Muslims always spoke of a golden age, the days of the Rightly Guided Caliphs, as if it were a bygone era to be eulogized. In Saladin, that golden age was alive and wonderfully present.

Zaynab seemed too stunned by the day's events to react. She had come expecting to be put to death as a criminal, not shown the compassion due a victim. The abused woman finally managed to lift her head and meet Saladin's eyes, as if seeking to confirm that this was not all some cruel jest to be revealed at the moment of her execution. Saladin met her gaze with a smile.

"I will arrange for your divorce, if you so wish it, and safe passage to your father's home," the Sultan said.

Zaynab dropped to her knees and touched her forehead to the ground.

"I am forever your grateful servant," she said.

Saladin rose again from his chair and went to the prostrate woman. He put an arm around her shoulder and helped her to stand.

"Serve Allah instead. I hope that you will put the past behind you, and that you will find true love someday. There is no greater moment in life then when you find your heart's companion."

A guard took the grateful Zaynab's hand and led her out of the judgment chamber. The woman locked eyes with Miriam as she walked by, but did not speak. She didn't need to. Miriam bowed her head slightly in acknowledgment of Zaynab's silent gratitude.

"So, my friend, are you pleased with how I handled this case?" Saladin was back on his throne and spoke to Maimonides, who had been deathly quiet, hoping that his niece would not bring further disrepute on his family.

"The Sultan is wise and merciful. Particularly in matters of the heart," the rabbi said.

"I think the ladies of the harem would take issue with that."

Nervous laughter erupted around the hall at the Sultan's self-deprecating joke. Miriam found herself again the subject of Saladin's study.

"And you, my lady. Did you find the Sultan's judgment to be just?"

Miriam raised her head proudly. If the court gossips wanted to talk, then let them. She was determined to preserve her dignity underneath a hundred jealous stares.

"The Sultan is all my uncle has proclaimed, and more."

"Then welcome to Jerusalem. I hope that you will grace our court again. And that you will pay heed to the words I spoke today. A woman of your beauty and intellect will find many suitors in the city of God, so choose wisely." He paused, and then locked eyes with her. "There is no greater moment in life than when you find your heart's companion."

The Sultan rose from his throne and all bowed to him as he exited the chamber. As she raised her head, Miriam felt her uncle's arm on hers, squeezing tightly.

"There is much about the court that you do not know, child," he said in an angry whisper. "Many enemies hide in the shadows. It is best if you do not draw attention to yourself again."

With that, her uncle took hold of Miriam and her aunt Rebecca, who had stood in mortified silence throughout the girl's performance, and hurried them out the silver doors to the judgment hall. Even as she departed, she felt the heavy gaze of the courtiers upon her from all sides. She caught the furtive whispering and fingers pointing in her direction through the corner of her eye. Miriam turned to face the crowd, her eyebrow rising in defiance. The whispers died under the intensity of her gaze

A soft smile on her lips, Miriam turned and followed her uncle into the heart of the palace.

10 Tours—AD 1189

So this is how a king dies," Richard said softly, staring down at the lined face of his father, who lingered between sleep and eternity. "Like everyone else. Cold and afraid."

Richard always thought his father's death would be a moment of freedom, when he would finally get to spread his wings and take flight from the old man's legacy. But now, as he stood by Henry's side, he found himself surprised at the torrent of emotions that the king's impending demise had unleashed. Perhaps, on some level, the Lionheart had never really believed that his father would pass away. The old man was proud and ornery, like the prize bulls in the royal stables, and had stubbornly held on to life for the past two years, despite predictions from every court physician to the contrary.

But every play must come to an end, and the drama of Henry Plantagenet had reached its finale. As a young boy, Richard had idolized his father, had imagined that the great and mighty warrior would meet an end that would be sung about for generations, like the ballads of the Greeks or the Normans. But it was not to be so. He would, as it turned out, die like any number of common men, shivering in his bed, nursing a heart filled with regrets. Richard looked down at the shriveled, trembling figure, eyes glazing over from delirium, and he felt the first stirrings of pity in years. As the perennially loyal Joanna wiped her father's drenched brow, Richard accepted that even if Henry's end would lack the majestic heroism of Odin's demise in the Ragnarok, he would at least die in the company of someone who loved him. Perhaps, in the end, that was all any man could ask for.

The door to the small stone chamber opened and a sturdy guard led in the person the prince had been waiting for all evening, someone who had not stepped inside the palace in sixteen years. Richard turned to face Eleanor of Aquitaine, his mother. It was not the first time he had seen her in all those years, of course. He visited her regularly in the various castles at Chinon and in England where she had been imprisoned, but he had been unable to secure her release until today. Her jailers had been informed of Henry's imminent passing, and they had quickly acquiesced to the command of the crown prince who would become their liege lord by the morning.

Eleanor stood proudly before her son, her honey-colored hair, now streaked with silver, held tightly back with an emerald-studded ringlet. Richard moved forward to embrace her. As a child, he had always been fascinated by the steely power of his mother's arms, more like a veteran soldier than a pampered noblewoman. The iron will was still present in her sinews, but Richard felt the tremor in her body, the surge of emotion that she was keeping locked inside. The prince admired her constant calm in the midst of crisis. She had withstood the humiliation of exile for years in patience, spending her time preparing her son to claim his rightful legacy. Richard knew that his support among the nobles was largely the result of her tireless lobbying from within the prison walls. Henry had once angrily remarked that the traffic of courtiers that came to meet Eleanor at Chinon made the fortress look more like a bustling marketplace than a jail. And he was right. For Chinon had become a bazaar of intrigue that had kept Henry's plans for the kingdom in constant check. She was a woman unlike any other, and Richard worshipped her. That was perhaps the main reason for his indifference to the fair sex. He had never met any woman whose intelligence and courage could match his mother's. And Richard doubted he ever would.

"Thank you, my son," Eleanor said, running her hand through his sandy hair, so much like her own, just as she'd done when he was a child and would bring her a fresh bouquet from the palace gardens.

"I am glad that you are with us at last, Mother," he said. "It has been far too long." As he escorted Eleanor toward the sturdy cot where his father lay dying, Richard caught Joanna's eye. She looked over at Eleanor coolly, before turning back to tend to the king. Joanna had refused to join Richard on his trips to Chinon, saying that she wanted nothing to do with their treasonous mother. Richard had hoped that their father's death would lead to reconciliation between the two women he loved the most in this world, but he saw that their wounds would take much longer to heal. Perhaps they never would.

Eleanor ignored her daughter as she took a seat beside the old man. His breathing was irregular, at times slow and steady, only to be interrupted by a harsh coughing fit followed by a spat of desperate wheezing. His eyes had been closed as he slipped in and out of consciousness, but they opened as his estranged wife sat down. He looked at her for a long moment, possibly unsure as to whether she was really there or was just another hallucination produced by his feverish mind. Henry glanced around the royal bedchamber in confusion. The doctors had ordered the lights be kept dim. Not that there was much to see. All the tapestries of florid hunting scenes, unicorns, and playful satyrs had been removed from the cold stone walls. Even the bearskin carpeting had been pulled from beneath their feet. Henry had become more austere, or perhaps more mad, in his final days and his servants simply acquiesced to his barked requests without troubling as to his reasons. The only sources of illumination in the room came from faint moonlight reflected off the windowsill on the east wall, and from a single, failing candle on an oak stand next to the cot. The weak flame shed just enough light to blanket the people who had been at the center of his life's grand drama in gloomy shadow. The king's eyes fell on Joanna, dressed in a black gown that presaged the mourning to come, and then at Richard, whose normally pale face seemed even whiter than usual in the flickering light.

"So the vultures circle at last," the king croaked. "Fear not, you will feast on my carcass before the sun rises."

"You're delirious." Eleanor was, as always, to the point.

The old man smiled at her, but there was no affection in the expression. His teeth were yellowing and cracked and a putrid stench emanated from his open lips.

"Perhaps," he said. "However did you come back from exile, my dear wife? I thought I had gotten rid of you for good."

Eleanor glanced at Richard. Henry nodded, clearly unsurprised.

"Of course. Your beloved son to the rescue," he said. "Does he still suck from your bosom, too?"

Henry suddenly coughed violently, spewing drops of blood on his already much-stained nightshirt. Eleanor grimaced in disgust as Joanna wiped the old man's wrinkled lips clean. She gave her mother an acid stare before turning to Henry again.

"Hush, Father," Joanna said. "You need your strength."

"Not anymore," Henry said, his voice raspy and grating. "But I am glad that you are here at least. Of all the things in my kingdom, I only loved you, my daughter."

He said these words to her, but his eyes were on Richard. The prince felt icicles cut into his breast. So this was how it was going to be, even at the very end.

"Then I shall make sure that she holds an honored place in my kingdom," Richard said, trying to keep the bitterness out of his voice. He wanted to say something to hurt the old man in return, but found he could not. It was strange how he was not able to remember any of the cruel and prideful things he had fantasized about saying to his father over the years.

"You presume too much, boy," the old man said. He glanced around the room again, his eyes coming into focus for a moment. "Where is John?"

Richard felt his heart grow cold. Even in his final moments, all Henry wanted were his beloved Joanna and that sycophant John.

"My brother has been summoned by a herald," Richard said. "His steed will bring him here in due time."

"Time is a luxury, and I am poor," the king said. Henry's eyes fell upon the broad-shouldered soldier who stood respectfully away from the royal family by the door. The man was dressed in the finest engraved cuirass over a hauberk forged for the elite Royal Guard. The dying monarch lifted a bony finger and pointed to the soldier. "You! Come here. I need a witness."

The guard was clearly startled at the king's sudden attention, but he stepped forward dutifully. Richard saw as he approached the candlelight that he was little more than a boy, nervous and awed to be in the presence of such notables.

"What are you doing?" Eleanor knew her husband better than anyone, and Richard caught the glint of alarm on her face at what was about to unfold.

"I, Henry, King of England, proclaim with my last breath my testament to our people," he said. "When John returns to the court, he will be crowned the next King of England."

What little color remained in Richard's face drained, and then came rushing back in a torrent of outrage.

"What are you saying?" Richard was only partially aware that his hand was on his sword, but the guard saw the gesture and blanched. The young man was trained to serve on the battlefield against the enemies of England. But he was not ready to be at the center of a familial struggle over succession.

"I have given you a gift, Richard—freedom," the king said, after another violent spout of coughing. "Go, frolic with your maidens and live a carefree life. The crown shall not burden your head."

Eleanor sprang to her feet, her usual control forgotten. Her hands clutched her ruby pendant, shaped in the form of a winged dragon, as if she was restraining herself from reaching over and strangling the king herself. Richard wondered if his own eyes were aflame with the venom he saw in hers.

"You cannot deny him!"

"My will is law," the king said, stating a simple, final truth.

"I despise the day I met you."

"As do I, my sweet." Henry's coughing suddenly became more intense, his whole body racked by desperate spasms. Richard turned away from his father, struggling to hold back tears of rage and defeat at his unexpected loss of the throne at the whim of a delirious fool. He could not bring himself to admit that at least a few of the tears came from a place outside of his own hurt pride. The tears of a child who had once looked upon his father as a god who could do no wrong, who was invincible. Immortal.

"Joanna, take my hand," Henry said at last, his voice barely audible. The weeping girl clasped her father's trembling hand, felt him squeeze one last time. Henry shivered, and then went still.

Joanna cried out in grief, her voice tearing through the otherwise stunned silence that permeated the little room, reeking with the sickening stench of decay and death. Eleanor ignored the girl, her eyes focused coldly on the anonymous guard who had been entrusted with the keys to the kingdom.

The shrill cry of a trumpet echoed somewhere below them. Richard was only vaguely aware that tears were rolling down his cheeks. He walked over to the window as if in a daze and gazed down. A cloaked rider raced past the gates a hundred feet below as the royal sentries announced his arrival with their horns.

Richard realized that the guard, the witness to their father's final decree, was standing nervously nearby. The boy was in far above his head and clearly had no desire to drown in the cesspool of court intrigue.

"Prince John arrives," the idiot guard said, helpfully stating the obvious. "Shall I bring him to the chamber, my lord?"

"He can find his own way." Without any warning, Richard grabbed the young soldier and flung him out the window to his death. The boy's terrified screams ended abruptly as he hit the rocks with a sickening thud. Richard held his head high and turned away, not bothering to watch the sentries race over to the guard's body.

The murderous prince saw his mother nodding approvingly. He had, in that instant, proven that he was the man she had raised, one who would seize his divine right with his own hands. Richard felt a swell of pride, adding to the complicated stew of emotions raging through his veins this night. Then he saw the horrified, accusatory look on Joanna's face and he felt anger rising. He did not need his sister's reproach. He would not take it anymore. From anyone. He was now the King of England.

"Not a word, Joanna," he said. There was a knife in his voice, an edge that had never been turned on his beloved sister. But tonight he had no choice. "In this matter, all who stand in my way will fall."

Joanna's eyes flashed. She was clearly stung by the implied threat, but Richard could not allow himself to be swayed by his love for her. The stability of the nation was at stake. He could not permit a civil war over the throne. Richard was aware that John had been working to develop his support among the lords over the past two years. Even if his father's last words were never made known to the nation, there would be those who would try to push John's cause forward in the months to come. The squabbles and suspicions of the Angevin court could still erupt into a bloody feud, unless Richard could unify his people behind him quickly. And he knew that the best way to unite a kingdom was to channel its inner turmoil outside, beyond its borders. The Lionheart realized in one instant that he had no choice. War was the only way to preserve the throne of England.

The heavy iron door to the chamber swung open, and John rushed in. His eyes took in everything at once. The unexpected presence of his exiled mother, the rage still hot on Richard's face. The fear and confusion on Joanna's countenance. And the quiet peace on his father's. Whatever John was thinking about the strange tableau, he kept it to himself. The dark-haired prince knelt over Henry's body, checking his neck for a pulse, before he turned to face his brother.

"I came as fast as I could," John said, his voice stoic, unreadable.

Richard locked eyes with his younger sibling.

"His last words were of you, my brother."

"Tell me."

"He said that he wished you were here, but he knew that you would honor his memory by serving your new king with valor." Richard watched his brother closely. The Lionheart had always been a good liar, and had won many a wager with a closely guarded face, but the stakes had never been as high as they were now.

John's eyes narrowed. He looked at his mother's cold, statuesque face, then at the reddened eyes of his sister. But they revealed nothing to challenge his brother's words. Finally, slowly, as if he was forcing himself against the pressure of his own pride, Prince John bowed down to Richard the Lionheart, King of England and France, Lord of the Angevin.

"The king is dead. Long live the king."

Richard held his breath for a moment. This was it. The destiny of his people lay in what he must do next.

"My brother, I shall need your help now, more than ever," he said. "Before he died, our father asked me to fulfill one last wish. To carry out a new Crusade in his name and free beloved Jerusalem from the grasp of the pagans."

John raised his head and met his brother's gaze. Did Richard sense a hint of cold amusement in the look?

"I shall gather the lords of the people," John said, his voice flat, betraying no hint of his true thoughts. "Together we will wrest the Holy City from the Saracens." He paused. "For our father."

Richard felt a chill go down his spine. His brother was acquiescing too easily. Richard had been gearing himself up for passionate resistance, but his brother appeared to have given in without the hint of a fight. As if, somehow, everything were playing out the way John wanted. A thought came unbidden and unwelcome to his mind. There was something in John's dark eyes that frightened the new king, as if he were looking into the heart of a spider waiting ever patiently for its prey to walk into a trap that had been set in place years before. Richard pushed the disturbing image from his mind, and glanced at Henry's corpse. This adventure would be his great revenge on his father. To conduct a war in the name of the man who had opposed it all his life. There was perhaps poetry and justice in the world after all.

"Yes. For our father," the King of England said.

11

Despite her initial distaste, Miriam was beginning to develop an affinity for the Holy City. This was a surprising development, considering how her entire visit so far had been burdened by the weight of scandal and gossipmongering among the palace crowd. Her aunt Rebecca had been scandalized by her most unladylike behavior in front of the Sultan. Maimonides had been less shrill in his admonitions, and more to the point. She was new to the city, and life in the court could be dangerous for those who did not understand the limits of social propriety. This was especially true for a beautiful woman who had clearly piqued the Sultan's interest. The intrigues of the harem were far more subtle—and far more deadly—than any war fought by men in the open. On the battlefield, the rabbi had warned her, men knew their allies and their enemies. In the harem, the enemies were rarely so obvious, and usually more cruel.

Miriam had taken his words to heart. She had been a loner much of her life, actively avoiding the company of other women for precisely this reason. Deprived of external power by men in society, women were forced to play ruthless mind games to assert their control from behind the scenes. The fact that Miriam was unusually attractive had made her both the center of attention among the girls of her family circle and the subject of much envy. She had quickly learned that few women could be trusted and she preferred the company of men whenever possible. Such interaction was rare, however, as the culture of gender segregation was the norm in both Jewish and Muslim society. While she had managed quite a few nightly excursions with enamored suitors, and had enjoyed the wonderful release in the arms of hungry lovers, it had all felt rather empty. None of the men in her life had challenged her mind, which she valued far above the charms of the flesh. Miriam had therefore found solace in the company of her uncle's books and the solitary pursuit of knowledge.

It was that quest which guided her through the worn streets of Jerusalem's *souk*, or marketplace, this Friday afternoon in the company of a young palace guard. Maimonides had insisted that she be accompanied by one of the Sultan's soldiers if she was planning to leave the rebuilt Jewish quarter where they were housed. She had grudgingly agreed to the escort, but had refused to comply with her uncle's requests that she don one of the Muslim veils when stepping out. She would wear the Egyptian head scarf, but anything more restrictive was out of the question.

In hindsight, Miriam thought her pride was foolish. She had never felt so many prying eyes upon her as she walked through the marketplace. A green-eyed Jew in stylish Egyptian robes was an unusual sight in Jerusalem, and the attention quickly became unwelcome. Miriam saw several unsavory men who appeared ready to accost her until their eyes fell upon Zaheer, her bodyguard. The Kurdish soldier with light brown hair and rippling muscles appeared to be itching for a fight and she noticed that his hand rarely left the hilt of his scimitar.

Still, when she ignored the stares of her fellow citizens, she found the walk through Jerusalem invigorating. The sun was shining and the stench of dung seemed more tolerable today. The main bazaar was not as large as that of Cairo, but contained a wider variety of goods. Rickety outdoor stalls were filled with a bountiful diversity of fruits and sweetmeats. Veiled women passionately haggled with bored proprietors over quinces and raisins of unusual colors, gold and beet red, as well as bananas imported from India, oranges, apples, cheese, and a seemingly endless supply of pine nuts. She had sampled some honey produced by local bees and was pleasantly surprised at its rich, intoxicating flavor. The Franks had kept up trade with their homelands in Europe, and she found some of their goods still available for purchase. The intricate French pottery and Italian jewelry was of particular interest. Not that the barbarians had more sophisticated wares than those produced in the caliphate. But even in their rudimentary designs she saw the beginnings of cultural awareness among the infidels. Perhaps the century of contact with Arab civilization would eventually serve as a catalyst to revitalize their stagnant societies. It was possible, she mused, but she did not expect any such European renaissance in her lifetime.

Miriam was less interested in the bauble stands than in the book dealers. Zaheer had dutifully stood by her as she entered various stores and leafed through dusty manuscripts and scrolls in Arabic, Greek, and French. She felt a little sorry for the young guard—Miriam was well versed in several languages, but she doubted he could read even his own. She saw him look over some heavy tome, nodding thoughtfully as he scanned its contents, oblivious to the fact that he was reading the book upside down.

The proprietor, a Christian man with a pronounced limp and a disconcerting tic, also noticed the guard's error but said nothing. While it was rare for a woman to enter his shop, it was unheard of for a soldier. She could tell that he was hoping the strange couple would leave soon. Feeling sorry for the nervous merchant, Miriam paid him several dinars for an Arabic text of Plato's *Republic* and stepped outside. Her guard followed, leaving behind the incomprehensible scroll he had been pretending to examine.

Miriam glanced up at the sound of the muezzin echoing through the city streets. It was time for 'Asr, the midafternoon prayer, and she saw turbaned Muslim men hurry in the direction of the Haram al-Sharif. Since the liberation of Jerusalem from the Franks, both Muslims and Jews made a point of regularly attending services at their respective holy sites. The loss of the Dome of the Rock and the Wailing Wall for ninety years had brought home to these believers the spiritual blessings that their ancestors had taken for granted. Miriam knew the sun would set in a few hours and she wanted to get back in time to light the Sabbath candles with her aunt. While she did not know for sure whether she believed in the God of the Covenant, the gentle rituals of her people still held an emotional sway over her.

"We should head back," she said to her escort. Zaheer nodded and led her through the maze of stands selling pomegranates and dates. They emerged onto the stone plaza just beyond the marketplace where her carriage was tethered. As she approached the wooden coach, she saw the hooded figure of a beggar seated nearby. His tattered clothes were those of a leper, and she fought off an automatic wave of revulsion.

"A dinar for an old man, my lady?" The beggar's voice was cracked; his features shadowed under the hood. She was glad she did not have to see how the disease had ravaged his face, and then felt an immediate pang of guilt over the thought.

Zaheer moved forward, a hand on his sword, ready to push the unsightly mendicant away. Watching the illiterate guard act on her unspoken disgust heightened Miriam's shame.

"No, it's all right," she said, reaching into her purse for a few coins.

Zaheer put a restraining hand on her. She winced as the coarse calluses of his palm scratched her skin.

"Leave him to die with the dogs. He is unclean."

Miriam pulled free of his grasp, irritated that he had touched her, and angry that part of her wanted to shoo the disease-ridden wretch away too.

"He smells better than you do," she said, and immediately regretted it. The young man had been kind to her, and she had paid him back with the sharp edge of her tongue. Then, to her surprise, the leper laughed.

"My lady is witty as a fox. And beautiful as a *houri* of Paradise," the beggar said. Miriam froze. The voice was no longer cracked, and sounded disturbingly familiar. Zaheer stepped forward before she could stop him, his blade drawn and aimed at the leper.

"Watch your tongue before you lose it. She is a guest of the Sultan," he said, his voice suggesting that there would be no further warnings on the matter.

"I know," the leper said in response.

She had no time to react as the beggar leaped to his feet and grabbed hold of the guard's sword arm. In one swift move, he twisted Zaheer's hand at the wrist. The surprised guard cried out in pain, dropping his weapon, then fell to his knees as the robed man applied further pressure.

Miriam's scream died in her throat as his hood fell back, revealing Saladin.

Zaheer appeared even more stunned, but his military training immediately fell into place. He remained on his knees, lowered his head, and stopped struggling.

"*Sayyidi*, I did not recognize you," the soldier said. Saladin let go of his hand, but Zaheer did not move from his position of submission.

"That was the idea. Give me a moment with my guest," the Sultan said.

The guard bowed low, then rose and stepped back. Saladin's eyes turned to the startled Miriam, who belatedly remembered to curtsy in a clumsy fashion.

"No need for that. You'll ruin my disguise. A lady does not bow to a leper," he said.

"I don't understand."

Saladin glanced at the bronze gate to a garden path not far from where her carriage stood.

"Walk with me and I'll explain."

12

Miriam glanced around her and saw that they were very alone. She would expect the plaza near the main bazaar to be bustling at this time of day, and the thought flashed through her mind that the Sultan had arranged for it to be conveniently empty. She glanced at Saladin's face but saw no sign of menace, although if he wished to have his way with her, there really was little she could do about it.

Miriam followed the Sultan inside the gardens, and her eyes widened in wonder. It was as if she had entered an entirely different world. As she strolled through the brightly paved paths lined with roses, the beloved native flower of Palestine, she felt as if she had glimpsed the fabled Eden from which her people believed mankind had sprung.

The garden was dotted with crumbling stone structures that looked as if they had stood untouched since the days of Herod. Near a cluster of grapevines, she saw a cracked stone grotto dug into the earth, the remains of an old winepress. The gentle cascade of a man-made waterfall down an old wall drew her attention to a small pool at its base. The water was crystal clear and she saw a school of blue-and-red-flecked fish swimming languorously in the afternoon sun amid reeds and lilies.

Saladin saw the wonder on her face and smiled. He stooped beneath a thick tree bearing pink blooms she had never seen before, then bent down to pick a white rose from the grass. To her surprise, the Sultan reached over and placed the bud in her hair. She felt a spark like lightning flash through her as his hands brushed a curly strand that fell in front of her eyes. Miriam wasn't sure what this was exactly, but she found herself willing to let it play out.

"Tell me, young Miriam, who is the most powerful man in the Islamic world?"

"That's a trick question."

Saladin's eyebrows rose at the quick response, but he seemed pleased.

"I know. But indulge me nonetheless."

Miriam turned away from him to look at the Dome of the Rock, shining in the light of the afternoon sun.

"If I were a Muslim, I would have to say the caliph in Baghdad, for fear of blaspheming."

"But you are a Jew. Blaspheme as much as you like." He was clearly enjoying this.

Miriam turned back to face him, her eyes meeting his. As she gazed into those dark pools, she had a strange feeling that she was looking into a soul as old as the firmament.

"Well then, as a heretic and as a student of politics, I would say you."

"Why?"

"You single-handedly united Egypt and Syria after a century of civil war. And you crushed the Franks against all odds." Suddenly Miriam felt very small. She had been a proud girl all her life, with a sense that she was meant to be more than just another rabbi's wife and mother to a brood of noisy children, the fate her aunt had expected for her. But now, standing in the presence of the Sultan, she felt foolish. Who was she to banter with a man of this stature? Long after her bones were ground to dust, his name would still be hallowed on the lips of millions.

Saladin waved his hand dismissively at her praise.

"That may be true. But all of that was an accident of history," he said. She could detect no hint of false modesty in his voice.

"I find that hard to believe," was all she could say in return.

A soberness entered Saladin's face at that moment, the timeless gleam in his eyes more intense.

"We are all slaves of history, Miriam. It is a river that no man can harness. We cannot swim against its power. Indeed, we drown in its torrent."

There was a moment of uncomfortable silence between the two. Miriam finally spoke, hoping to bring the Sultan's thoughts away from the crushing weight of his own legacy.

"You still have not told me why the most powerful man in the world walks in leper's robes?"

A smile returned to Saladin's face and the spell was broken.

"A leader cannot know his people's needs from lofty towers. But there are other reasons today," he said.

"Such as?"

Saladin turned his gaze away from the Dome and toward his citadel, whose towers were visible even from the garden.

"The palace is a gilded cage. I could not enjoy the company of a beautiful woman without tongues wagging."

Saladin moved close to Miriam. He reached inside his robes and produced a necklace of sapphires. The pendant was shaped in the form of the Roc, the mythical bird of the *Arabian Nights*, its wings outstretched in proud defiance. Miriam's eyes widened at the unexpected sight, and she felt herself stiffen in surprise as he proceeded to tie it around her neck with a finely linked chain.

"A gift. To welcome you to our city."

This was all moving a little too quickly for her.

"It's stunning . . . I cannot accept this," she said.

But Saladin would have none of it.

"Nonsense. Besides, it's radiance pales before your own."

Her uncle's warnings echoed in her mind. She was not ready to play this game.

"I should go home. My uncle is at the bazaar buying supplies for the Sabbath. He'll be back soon."

"Not for at least another hour. Or so my spies tell me," he said. Saladin looked at her closely, perhaps sensing her discomfort. He stepped away from her, giving her room to breathe, and looked out over the rows of tulips set beneath a lemon tree.

"Do you like the garden?"

Miriam was grateful for the respite from his amorous attentions.

"It's beautiful."

A strange look came over Saladin's face, as if he were caught in a memory that he had long suppressed.

"It is nothing compared with the oasis at Ascalon."

Miriam felt a chill run through her spine, as unwanted memories of her own arose.

"By Sinai?" She feigned ignorance. It was better that way.

Saladin nodded.

"I have spent most of my life in Cairo and Damascus. The jewels of the caliphate. But the gardens of Ascalon are unrivaled in all the world," he said.

Miriam tried not to look back, but she was unable to stop the memory. She was eleven years old when their caravan had stopped in Ascalon. The gardens were indeed unlike any she had seen before, or since. She remembered picking golden desert sunflowers as a present for her mother, Rachel. Her mother had been wearing one in her hair when the Frankish soldier pinned her to the ground . . .

No. No more memories. Miriam found herself removing the flower that Saladin had pinned in her own braid.

"The Sultan surprises me. I did not know that warriors found comfort in the growing things of the earth," she said, forcing her own thoughts from her mind.

Saladin was still wistful.

"I loved my first girl underneath a palm tree in Ascalon one moonlit night. It will always be a special place."

Other women would have blushed at such an intimate revelation, but she just watched him closely.

"It sounds like you still love her."

Saladin looked back at her and smiled. If he had noticed that she had removed the flower from her hair, he did not say anything.

"She was very beautiful." Was there a hint of teasing in his words? Miriam felt a sudden wave of irritation growing in her breast.

"Do you see nothing more than a woman's beauty, *sayyidi*?" She had hoped that he was truly as sophisticated as he initially appeared, but he was proving to be like any other man when it came to certain matters.

Saladin approached her until he was standing perhaps a little too close. He ran a hand across her cheek and she felt her heart skip a beat.

"I live a hard life, Miriam, filled with war and judgment. I find comfort in beauty."

Miriam took a step back. The strange tingling was rippling through her again, and it was beginning to frighten her. But she laughed, hoping to quell the storm that was building within.

"And when she ages and shrivels into a prune? Will her beauty comfort you then?"

Saladin leaned forward, as if to tell her a state secret.

"Then I will find comfort in her laugh."

Miriam found herself drawn inexorably toward him. A moth to a flame.

"*Sayyidi* . . ."

He bent forward, as if to kiss her. She felt her heart quicken. Then, unexpectedly, he stepped back.

"I was impressed by your courage the other day. Few have the spirit to speak openly in my presence," he said.

Miriam flushed. She found herself confused by this game, and confusion inevitably brought out her pride and her anger. She was not some illiterate peasant girl he could play with.

"Is it not your Prophet that said the greatest *jihad* is to speak the truth in front of a king?"

Saladin turned to her, startled at her quote from one of the prophetic oral traditions, or *hadith*. Few people, except the religious scholars in the *madrassas*, were fluent with the thousands of sayings of Muhammad. He certainly did not expect such knowledge from a young Jewess.

"You do not cease to amaze me," he said. She noted that his admiration appeared real.

"My aunt raised an educated girl," she said, unable to suppress the haughtiness in her voice.

Saladin suddenly moved closer to her again. She could feel the heat from his body as he took her hand in his.

"As well as a beautiful one," he said.

Confound him! She felt annoyance turn to desire again. In his presence Miriam felt strangely powerless, a sensation that both terrified and invigorated her.

"There's that word again," was all she was able to say before he leaned forward and kissed her. Miriam wanted to fight him, but she felt herself pulled inexorably into the flow of his destiny. None can swim against the river of history, he had said. Or of passion.

Their kiss was long and deep and, for an instant, time stood still. It was not, of course, the first time that Miriam had been kissed. Her aunt would have been horrified to know how experienced the girl really was in affairs of the heart. And the body. But there was something primordial in Saladin's embrace, a need that overwhelmed her, as if she were plunging down the garden waterfall into a river that flowed deep into the well of souls . . .

Miriam broke free, like a drowning girl climbing to the surface in the hopes of one final breath. She wanted to go on kissing him, losing herself in the ferocity of his passion, and that was what frightened her.

Saladin was looking at her, the color in his pale Kurdish face rising. Whatever force had swept through her, it had marred him as well.

"What would you say if I asked you to join my harem?"

This was too much, all too much for a gentle summer afternoon. She had to put a stop to this, before the madness consumed her.

"I would say that I am not worthy."

"And if I said you were?"

Miriam forced herself to look deep into his eyes. It was as if she were staring straight into the sun. But she did not flinch.

"But, *sayyidi,* you are already married to four of the most beautiful women in the caliphate. I understand that your religion does not permit you another."

Saladin paused, his eyes examining her face closely.

"That is true. But you do not need to be my wife to share my bed," he said.

The words cut into her like a knife, and she felt a rage rising in her that was wholly unsuitable for a liege in the presence of a king. She backed away from him, and he did not follow this time.

"My uncle said that you are a wise ruler and not a tyrant. May I then speak freely, as I did in court?"

Saladin smiled, his expression unreadable even to her skilled eyes. Was she signing her own death warrant with her words?

"By all means. I am surrounded by sycophants. It is refreshing to hear the truth," he said.

She took a breath, and then plunged forward.

"I cannot deny that the idea of being with you is a tempting proposal," she said. "But I am a free woman. I will not lock myself in any man's harem as a concubine. Not even the jeweled prison of the Sultan."

There. It was out at last.

Saladin stood frozen to the spot, his eyes locked on hers.

"You are indeed brave. No woman has ever spoken to me in such a fashion."

She felt something hit her in the pit of her stomach. Suddenly all the childhood fantasies of seducing princes and riding away on white horses to distant castles vanished. She had stood up to the most powerful man on earth, had declined his advances. Now she would learn the true nature of Saladin's power.

"Was my uncle wrong, then? Will my head be hanging from the palace walls this evening?" It was all she could manage to say. If she were to die, then Miriam wanted her executioner to say it to her face.

Saladin said nothing for a moment, and then burst out laughing. It was not the cold, humorless sound of an insulted man seeking to cover the wound of injured pride. No, it was the hearty laughter of an adult bested in a playful game by a beloved child.

"I admire your spirit, Miriam," he said. "If you come to me, you will do so willingly and not at the edge of a blade. Peace be upon you, daughter of Isaac."

Then, without another word, the most powerful man on earth turned and strolled out of the garden, leaving her to wade through the torrent of emotions that raged through her soul on a warm July afternoon in Jerusalem. As Miriam gathered her breath and followed the path back toward the carriage that would take her home for Sabbath dinner, she failed to see a cloaked man watching her from the lengthening shadows of the garden.

13

The Sultana sat nude in a steaming bath of inlaid marble, her flawless olive skin glistening, while a muscular African concubine massaged her shoulders with myrrh and scented oils. There were no windows in the bathhouse, but the room was brightly lit by a series of crystal lamps arranged in a semicircle around the pool, the glass etched with flawless Arabic calligraphy.

"Who is this girl?" Yasmeen bint Nur al-Din asked with cold fury. Her eyes, wide and oval-shaped, a remnant of her grandmother's Persian ancestry, were burning like the unforgiving desert sun.

The thin eunuch with strawberry hair and freckles, an Armenian named Estaphan, cautiously relayed the tidings of Saladin's encounter with Miriam.

"A niece of Maimonides, recently arrived from Cairo," Estaphan said, his voice even higher pitched than usual. This was not a pleasant task, and his normally nervous constitution was barely capable of withstanding the stress of his duty. Estaphan had, of course, conducted a discreet investigation before approaching his mistress, and had learned the identity of the girl he had spied with the Sultan. Yasmeen expected detailed information about any new developments in the court, and when she was dissatisfied, the purveyors of incomplete news would likely meet an unfortunate accident in the shadowed corners of the harem.

"A Jew?" Yasmeen's tone suggested a hint of outrage mixed with incredulity. She gestured to the concubine to stop. The African beauty stepped back as Yasmeen turned to face this messenger of ill tidings. The steaming bath rippled and churned, much like the emotional turmoil of its beautiful and regal resident.

"Yes, Sultana," the eunuch said, his voice trembling. Perhaps he should not have been so diligent in his investigation.

"And she turned down my husband? She must be mad."

"Undoubtedly." Estaphan had found that agreeing with powerful people rarely got him in trouble.

Yasmeen stepped out of the hot bath. Estaphan averted his eyes out of habit, although, with his ruined member, the sight of the Sultana's perfectly rounded curves would not occasion any threat. His mistress reached for a linen cloth and covered her abundant breasts as the African concubine began to brush her jet-black hair with an ivory comb.

Yasmeen looked at the ceiling, as she often did when her mind was calculating. She stared straight at the frescoed arches twenty feet above her, but her mind was too focused to pay attention to the exquisite murals of wildflowers, their petals encrusted with rubies and sapphires. In any event, she had seen far more beautiful art in her father's palace in

Damascus and had little respect for the rustic styles of the Levant. Her mind was very much on other matters right now.

The arrival of a pretty new girl into her husband's circle forced her to reexamine a thousand and one strategies she had devised for keeping the harem, and the court, under her control. On a certain level, she supposed she enjoyed the surprise twists of fate that inevitably kept her on her toes. Like her husband, she wearied quickly of easy victories.

"She is probably no more than a passing fancy," the Sultana said. "Still, I want you to keep an eye on her. If they meet again, I expect to know the details within the hour."

"As you command, my lady." The eunuch prostrated himself low before his queen.

She waved a hand in dismissal, and Estaphan quickly rose and scurried away, thankful to have emerged from the audience without the loss of any more body parts. Yasmeen turned her attention to Mihret, her alluring Abyssinian handmaiden. The girl approached stealthily, like a panther, and began to massage the Sultana's tense shoulders. Mihret always sensed exactly what she needed.

"I know my husband. He is like a child. If he is denied a toy, he will pine away for it," the Sultana said.

Mihret brushed aside a strand of her braided locks and stared into the Sultana's face in a bold manner that would have surprised any onlooker. It was a crime for anyone except Saladin to gaze directly upon the lovely Sultana's features. But then, Mihret and Yasmeen were guilty of far greater crimes than failure to adhere to court etiquette, if the Sultan but knew.

"You seem disturbed by word of this Jewess," Mihret said in the gentle voice that the Sultana had come to love. Yasmeen often thought that this concubine, with her tapered fingers and slender thighs, knew her better than anyone, including herself. The Sultana had grown accustomed to a solitary inner life, a private self that she was unable to share with others, especially her often-absent husband. But that had all changed when Saladin had purchased the Nubian beauty from a slave market in Alexandria and presented her to his wife as an anniversary present. The girl's rapid mind had provided her with hours of lively conversation. And her gentle touch had awakened in Yasmeen feelings that she had thought she was no longer capable of.

"I am just intrigued," the Sultana said. "No woman has ever turned down Salah al-Din ibn Ayyub. Except for one."

"Who?" Mihret retained a childlike pretense that Yasmeen knew was a complete façade, but which she always found endearing. The ebony-skinned girl was very much her intellectual equal, but never forgot the subtle graces, the daily acts of feigned ignorance, that allowed royalty to bask in the superiority of knowledge.

"Me, of course. That is why I once was his favored wife. A warrior thrives on challenge."

Yasmeen had a flash of unbidden memory, of strolling in her father's garden in Damascus. The grove, awash in oranges, jasmine, and citron, glistened in the light of the setting sun. Across a line of poplar trees rose the dome of the great Umayyad mosque, where five hundred years before, Muawiya had proclaimed himself caliph in opposition to the claims of the Prophet's son-in-law Ali. High upon its marble walls, she had watched the grand clock, its face taller than a man's height, the dial circled by bronze falcons that struck the hours. The bells pealed as the sun vanished, the face of the clock shining under the flickering light of crimson lamps. It was the last night of Ramadan and she had ventured out to see if she could glimpse the crescent of the new moon that would signal the start of the 'Eid festival.

As she scanned the eastern horizon, she had felt the prickly sensation that often touches the soul when it is watched from afar. The Syrian princess had turned and caught her first glimpse of the brash general who would one day sweep away both her heart and her father's kingdom. She had resisted Saladin's charms for longer than even she had believed possible, but he had been goaded on by the pursuit of the unattainable. For months, Saladin would shadow her footsteps, showering her with new jewelry from his conquests, or poetry from his lovelorn soul. Finally she had relented and taken him into her arms in the span of one wild, moonlit night on a beach with sugar white sand near the golden Barada River. She had never felt so alive as when his heart beat next to hers that night, his lips clinging to her trembling flesh as if he were sucking in her very life force.

No. Enough of memories. As the great Sufi masters taught their disciples in the *khanaqahs,* the past was an illusion, like a desert mirage tempting those who had strayed from the path of wisdom into eternal confusion and loss. All that existed was the omnipresent *now.* And the passion that had once bound Saladin and Yasmeen had no place in that now.

"You fear that this Jew has plans on the sultanate," Mihret said. It was a statement, not a question. Yasmeen emerged from her reverie. This was her now, her solitary moment in the present. The palace that was a luxurious prison, and a slave girl with full breasts and a soft tongue who served as her only true companion in life.

"Don't be ridiculous," Yasmeen said, closing the book on her unwanted memories. "Her ambitions will lead her only to a bed under the earth."

Mihret smiled and leaned forward.

"No woman is a match for you," she said.

Yasmeen would deal with this Jewess in due time. But she had more pressing matters to attend to at the moment. She set aside the burden of the throne for the evening and kissed the slave girl on her tender lips.

14 Lyons, France—AD 1190

Like God in the book of Genesis, Richard the Lionheart looked upon his work, and was pleased. He stood at the edge of the Rhône River in France surveying the massive army that had been brought together from all over Europe. Twenty thousand men had taken Richard's call for a new Crusade to heart. They had abandoned their fields and homes to participate in this sacred venture. Of course, Richard knew that many of his soldiers had far fewer spiritual motivations for participating in the campaign. His army was filled with young men who had been denied their inheritance in favor of elder brothers and were seeking to stake their own claim to land and wealth through conquest. And Richard could hazard to guess that more than a few were from the criminal ranks, escaping punishment in their home villages and hoping to return as heroes absolved of guilt through fighting in a holy war. Still, it mattered little to the Lionheart who these men had been before today. Nobleman or petty thief, they were all united under the banner of his glorious cause now.

Through much diplomatic haggling, supervised by the Holy Father himself in Rome, Richard had brought the reluctant kings of Europe in line with his grand vision. Now here, outside the wondrous city of Lyons, the armies of the Lionheart and those of his old compatriot in scandal, King Philip Augustus of Paris, had convened to cross the mighty river together. Their first step on a long, fateful journey toward the Holy Land and Paradise.

The world itself seemed poised for this grand adventure. The sky served as a perfect blue canopy above him, the sun rising to its zenith in heavenly salute to his glorious venture. The Rhône roared before the mighty host, as if applauding its courage from the very heart of the earth. The surrounding French hills were lush and alive, promising prosperity and bounty to those who crossed their paths for the glory of Christ. Even the birds, the joyful blue jays and robins, seemed to sing of their upcoming victories.

It was a good time for a speech. Riding out to the center of the massive wooden bridge that traversed the Rhône, Richard raised his sword and silence descended on the huge crowd of holy warriors.

"My brothers in the body of Christ, hear me!" he said. "Today we embark on a sacred mission that can have only one conclusion. We shall free Jerusalem from the heathens and shall sanctify the sepulchre of our Lord with their blood!"

A delighted cheer erupted through the crowd. Richard's words affirmed that these men, many of whom had never before left their quaint hamlets and farms, were about to set forth on a grand adventure to a far-off land at the end of which they would return home as heroes. Their grandchildren would marvel at their tales of the cruelty of the barbarian hordes they were sent to confront, and the valor of the servants of Christ in the face of the armies of Lucifer.

Richard, as always, drew strength from the crowd's adulation. He never felt more alive than when he commanded the attention of his subjects.

"There will be challenges," he said, his voice taking a sober tone. "Some of you will die, even before we set foot in Palestine. Heretics await us on land, and the sea is treacherous by her very nature. If any of you fear the road that lies ahead, go back to your farms now."

The king paused for dramatic effect. It worked. The men looked at each other and saw that no one moved to leave. It strengthened their sense of solidarity, their unity of purpose. They were in this enterprise together unto death, although most of the men did not really believe that they could actually die on the battlefield. Death is always a specter that haunts one's enemies, never oneself. Satisfied with the moment, Richard continued.

"I am proud to be one of you, and I shall be proud to fight by your side," he said. "In the name of the Father, and the Son, and the Holy Spirit—to Jerusalem!"

A thunderous roar of approval echoed, the sound magnified tenfold across the river, as twenty thousand men raised their weapons in salute.

To Jerusalem! To Paradise! Death to the infidels! Onward for the glory of Christ!

Richard felt a swell of emotion at the grandeur of the scene. Joanna had always said he was too easily swayed by pomp and glamour, but so be it. This was a moment that would be regaled in the history books for centuries to come. He would savor it to the last.

As cheers continued behind him, Richard rode across the long bridge. He could hear the tremendous footfall as the army began its trek across to join him. Thousands of brave soldiers from Brittany, Champagne, Languedoc, and Burgundy walked with their compatriots from England and Aquitaine across the Rhône River toward destiny.

As Richard crossed over to the east bank, he was met by a contingent of the joint army's best knights, who bowed their heads to their commander in chief. The Lionheart was delighted to see among them William Chinon, the most honored knight in his kingdom. If Richard viewed himself as the legendary Arthur, William was undoubtedly his Lancelot. With his flowing brown hair, piercing gray eyes, and chiseled features, William was much beloved of the ladies, but never seemed to return their interest. His handsome face was usually set in the stoic stone of duty, a fact for which Richard had often lovingly mocked him. But to no avail. William would never change. And in truth, his stability, his unwavering dedication, was his greatest asset to the throne. The king rode up to William and clasped his arm. William smiled politely, as was his wont, but Richard caught the troubled look in his friend's eyes.

The knight had counseled passionately against embarking on this military adventure over the past several months. He was always respectful of his king, and never aired his dissenting views in public, but he had not shied away from speaking his mind. William thought the Crusade was foolhardy and dangerous. While it had served Richard's immediate purpose of turning the nobles away from the simmering dispute around the throne, it could not be sustained in the knight's view. The Muslim forces were far superior to the European armies, in weapons, resources, and tactical genius, he had argued. The Christians of Jerusalem had only been able to hold them off for the past hundred years because of the Muslims' constant fratricidal infighting, not through any inherent military advantage. Now, with the inspiring leadership of Saladin, the unbelievers were united again.

Richard had listened to as much of this drivel as he could stand before finally silencing his premier knight. The petty band that had controlled Jerusalem for the past ninety years had become complacent and shortsighted, he argued. These nobles had forgotten their holy mission and responsibility, preferring wine and court intrigue to their duty to the Cross. But Richard would not allow a repeat of the mistakes of history. The mighty force that he led, perhaps the greatest army to have been brought together in Europe since the days of Caesar and Pompey, would crush the Saracen hordes like insects as they marched toward Jerusalem. He had no doubt at all. None. For Richard was a believer in destiny. *His* destiny. Like the heroes of the great myths, Perseus and Jason, he would triumph over all who stood in his way.

Richard turned away from his friend to face the army that slowly approached from the other end of the bridge. The king always marveled at the revolutionary design of such newer structures. The bridge was custom fit with projecting piers, triangular in shape, known as cutwaters. These were found on the upper side with the point toward the river. The cutwaters served to protect the pier from the force of the current and from the impact of trees and other objects borne along by the water. At the upper part of the piers, refuges for pedestrians were laid out across the roadway. The bridge was supported by wide arches connected to heavy stone and iron pillars that dug deep into the river, a remarkable feet of engineering considering the force of the mighty Rhône's current. The bridge spanned twenty feet across, running almost five hundred feet long from left to right bank, and was further supported by barrel vaults where the main weight was taken on ribs of stone.

Hundreds of men on foot and horseback were already midway across the great river, confidently striding across this wonder of modern Europe. Their colorful banners, golden and green, fluttered in the wind with the confidence that came with divine grace. The men strode forward, their heads held high, singing songs of joy and victory.

"Look at them, William," the king said. "Such pride. Such discipline. It augurs well for the Crusade."

William was not so easily convinced, however.

"Your father warned that a man should not seek auguries lest they foretell his own doom," the knight said.

Richard's face darkened at the memory of the late King Henry. Would he never emerge from the old man's shadow?

"My father was a fool."

"Perhaps." William shrugged. Anyone else would have trembled at questioning the king so bluntly, especially in his judgments about his own family. But the knight always spoke his mind, even if his opinions vexed the king. And the young monarch grudgingly respected him for it. Every ruler needed one man in his midst who was not in perpetual awe of him, who would speak the truth, even if it was unpleasant. Although Richard wished right now that his friend would allow him to enjoy his moment of glory, even if he did not agree with the campaign they were embarking upon.

Richard turned away from William and smiled at the approaching forward regiments. He had just raised his hand in salute of his men, when disaster struck.

At first Richard thought it was merely another of the myriad chaotic sounds that followed the march of an army, but then it became louder and more distinct. A cracking, tearing noise that froze the blood in his veins.

And then, without any further warning, the bridge across the Rhône River collapsed.

The central beams that held up the old passageway had been strained beyond their capacity under the armored footfalls of the crossing army, a massive parade the likes of which the bridge's designers had never anticipated. As the arched supports shattered, hundreds of men and horses plunged into the raging river. Richard watched in helpless horror as his brave men dropped straight down into the torrent. The horses kicked and screamed, but quickly went under, as did many of the men who either could not swim or were overly encumbered by heavy armor.

"My God," was all Richard could say, his mind refusing to believe the devastation that his eyes were cataloging.

William watched the whirlpool of drowning men and animals with a look of sad inevitability, as if he had expected as much.

"I believe, my lord, that you have received your augury."

Richard flashed his knight an outraged look. He would not be defeated, not this easily. The king jumped off his horse and rapidly stripped off his armor. William and the other knights followed his example. Richard dove into the river and swam into the vortex of flailing bodies. The current overwhelmed him and the king felt himself going under. He swallowed water, grimy with mud from the riverbed, and for a terrible instant he thought he would follow his drowning men to Neptune's depths. He willed himself to push his head above the surface and gasped for breath. Richard felt the blessed stirring of rage in his heart, his anger turning to defiance against the treacherous river. With a cry of bitter fury, the Lionheart fought against the churning water, his arm reaching out toward a soldier floating facedown in the chaos.

The king grabbed the man, an aging villager wearing a rusted breastplate that was probably an old heirloom from some forgotten battle waged by his grandfather against the Scots. As the man gasped for breath, Richard pulled him across the river to the bank. The king rested the old farmer on a grassy knoll, but it was too late. His body was worn from years of toil in the fields and was not able to survive the shock of the plunge into the icy river. Richard fought back tears of frustration as the brave peasant who had left his home to follow him looked up with dying eyes.

"To Jerusalem, my king . . ." The man coughed up water as he expended his last breath. Richard reached over with a gentle hand and closed the dead man's eyes.

The king looked up in grim determination as his men dragged to safety many caught in the embrace of the lethal river, while others vanished forever into the abyss. His eyes burned with anger at the injustice of the moment, but his heart hardened. He would not turn back. He could not.

Someone—he could not remember who—had once said to him that God favored irony. Perhaps the Deity found humor in the irony of this tragedy marring the start of his holy mission. Richard did not, in truth, know what kind of God would make a world as flawed and imperfect as the one mankind found itself in. A world with suffering and injustice coupled inextricably with joy and beauty, even as the screams of his dying men mixed with the song of birds soaring through the heavens above. But one thing he did know for sure. Richard had a destiny that would not be thwarted by death or disaster. And somewhere deep in his soul, the young king knew that his destiny would only be met when he faced the man who had brought shame and death into the heart of Christendom. When Richard the Lionheart stood before Saladin in battle, the world would at last come to know the true nature of both God and man.

15

Maimonides stood nervously outside the Sultan's study. The ever-present Egyptian twins towered on either side of the carved iron door, their brutal scimitars drawn and ready as usual. Maimonides vaguely remembered their names to be Hakeem and Saleem, the latter being slightly taller and more muscular than his otherwise identical brother. While Saladin treated him like any other close adviser, the rabbi had never quite won the trust of these gatekeepers, despite his many years of service.

"What is your business with the sultan?" The taller of the two lisped, his tone suggesting that, as far as he was concerned, the Jew was little more than another nameless petitioner seeking unwarranted access to the head of state.

"It is a private matter," Maimonides replied crisply. The men were unmoved.

"The Sultan is unavailable," the shorter one said. With that, both men turned their attention away from the rabbi and stared straight ahead.

Maimonides hesitated, and then decided it was not worth the effort. What he had to say could wait. In fact, as he turned away from the black-robed bodyguards, he felt a swell of relief rising in his chest. In truth, he was terrified of actually speaking to Saladin about the matter that was weighing on his mind. There were, after all, limits of propriety between a sultan and a lowly adviser, even if Saladin usually dispensed with the formalities of power. Maimonides did not relish testing his master's patience and pride, especially on the basis of court hearsay.

As he was about to retrace his steps down the brightly lit marble corridor toward the public quarter of the palace, the door to the study opened and Saladin emerged.

"Ah, I thought I heard your voice." The Sultan was beaming and looked remarkably youthful this afternoon. Maimonides cringed, guessing the reason for his friend's good spirits. Perhaps he could no longer avoid this conversation after all.

Maimonides turned back to face Saladin and bowed low.

"May I take a moment of your time, *sayyidi*?" Maimonides tried to sound casual, but his voice came out a little shrill.

Saladin looked at him carefully, and his smile faded slightly.

"Absolutely," he said, after a pause. "Come inside and we shall speak."

Maimonides rustled past the massive twins, who stood stoically, no indication of apology on their grim features for denying him passage just moments before.

Maimonides followed Saladin inside the chamber as the guards closed the iron door behind them. The room was spacious but sparsely furnished in accordance with Saladin's minimalist taste. The walls were of sparkling white limestone and mostly bare, except for a large tapestry opposite the arched windows that overlooked the palace garden.

Handwoven in striking shades of turquoise, crimson, and green, the tapestry depicted the fabled Night Journey in which Islam's prophet Muhammad was said to have flown from Mecca to Jerusalem on the back of his famous winged steed, the Buraq, and then upward through the Seven Heavens. Luxuriously drawn in the flowing style of the contemporary Persian masters, the tapestry showed the Prophet fully veiled in accordance with the strict prohibition against human imagery shared by the Semitic religions. The Prophet soared gloriously through the celestial spheres accompanied by Gabriel and a host of angels, all of whom were beardless and, to the rabbi's eyes, distinctly Chinese in their appearance. Maimonides was particularly impressed with the detail of the Buraq upon which the Prophet was seated—a lion's body with eagle's wings and the head of a beautiful woman. As a scholar of religion, Maimonides was aware that the Muslim legends of the Buraq were strikingly similar to the winged Sephardim who guarded the Ark of the Covenant. And as a citizen of Egypt, he could not escape the resemblance of both the Jewish and Muslim fables to the towering Sphinx that stood guard at the Pyramids. It was these remarkable similarities between religions and cultures over thousands of years that had long convinced him that faith in God, although expressed in infinitely diverse ways, was fundamentally the same worldwide.

"It is beautiful, isn't it?" Saladin's gentle voice broke the rabbi's inner musings. "It belonged to my father-in-law, Nur al-Din. Perhaps the most treasured item in his personal collection in Damascus. He gave it to me as a wedding present."

Mention of the Sultan's marriage to the exquisitely beautiful, and terrifyingly lethal, Princess Yasmeen brought Maimonides fully back to the present. He would have to broach his concerns now, and risk Saladin's wrath. The alternative, letting the situation draw to its inevitable and ruthless conclusion at the hand of the Sultana, was too disturbing to contemplate. Maimonides turned to face the Sultan directly, but he still found the words difficult.

"What brings you here, my friend?" Saladin was looking at him closely. He was no longer smiling, but was watching his adviser with the same focused intensity that he gave to heralds who had arrived with unexpected and potentially problematic news.

"It is a matter of some delicacy, *sayyidi*." Maimonides realized that he was sweating. Saladin's face was a carefully stern mask, impossible to read.

"Speak freely. I owe you my life several times over." There was a hint of strained patience in Saladin's voice. The Sultan had an intuitive understanding of human nature, and he probably sensed that Maimonides was planning to cross over the accepted boundaries of master and servant. The rabbi took a deep breath, hoping it would not be one of his last.

"It has come to my attention that you have taken a fancy to my niece, *sayyidi*." There. He had said it.

Whatever reaction Maimonides had been bracing for, he was unprepared for the explosion of laughter that followed. The Sultan threw his head back and roared, as if he had just heard one of Scheherazade's bawdy tales from *The Thousand and One Nights*. Maimonides found himself turning red with embarrassment, and then irritation. The Sultan steadied his mirth long enough to ask a question.

"You disapprove, old friend?"

Maimonides knew that he had to be careful.

"There is no man on earth greater than you, my sultan," the rabbi proceeded cautiously. "I fear that Miriam is a lowly rabbi's daughter, not worthy—"

The sultan interrupted. "That is not what is bothering you." His face was suddenly stone serious again, and Maimonides felt a chill go down his spine. "Say what is on your mind or leave."

An image of Miriam flashed through the rabbi's mind in that instant. Not Miriam as she was today—beautiful, impetuous, and haughty. But as a young girl who had somehow escaped the vicious murder of her parents at the hand of Frankish marauders. He saw her as she climbed slowly down from the back of a camel belonging to the Bedouin who had found her alone in the desert. Her hair stringy and unkempt, her face hard and unfeeling. But it was her eyes that he remembered the most. Unblinking, focused straight ahead, both dead and horrifyingly alive at the same time. It would be weeks before she spoke to any of them. Months before she laughed or played like a normal child. He never found out what she had seen or endured during the ordeal, and was quite certain he probably did not want to know, but he had vowed that Miriam would never suffer again. He had treated his niece like a queen, given her security and comfort. And more love than he had even known his heart to be capable of. But now his precious little girl stood poised at a chasm, staring down into a bottomless well of tears and betrayal. If she fell in, he would never be able to bring her back. While his beloved niece could survive the unforgiving desert, he knew that she would not withstand the wrath of a jealous and vindictive Sultana, whose empty heart made the wastes of Sinai look like the verdant hills of Eden.

"It is Sultana Yasmeen," Maimonides said with sudden courage. "Forgive me, *sayyidi,* but I fear for Miriam should the Sultana take offense at your intentions."

Saladin regarded his adviser for a long moment. The only sound in the room was the old man's labored breathing. Like the Roman emperor Justinian of old, Maimonides had crossed a river and burned the boats. There was no turning back now. He had inserted himself into the brutal intrigue of court politics, had spoken out against the Sultana, and the length of his life was now very uncertain. But if he was to die, he would rather it be protecting Miriam than succumbing to the inevitable ravages of age.

Then Saladin smiled with genuine warmth, and it was as if the sun had emerged from behind a thundercloud.

"You need not worry, old friend," Saladin said, his ivory teeth sparkling under his grin. "Your feisty niece turned down my advances most graciously. I'm sure the Sultana's spies have kept her abreast of the situation."

Maimonides suddenly felt like an old fool. The color, which had drained from his face during the confrontation with his master, returned in a rush of embarrassment, and he felt faintly dizzy. Miriam had told him flatly that there was nothing going on between the Sultan and herself, regardless of malicious court gossip, and he had chosen not to believe her. Of course, he knew that his niece was not always truthful about her personal affairs—he had heard too many rumors back in Cairo about her private life to dismiss it all as cruel innuendo—but he had been very quick to assume the worst here.

The Sultan clamped a loving hand on his adviser's shoulder.

"I admire your courage, Rabbi," he said. "It seems to be a quality that runs deep in the blood of your family."

"I apologize, *sayyidi*." Maimonides wanted to end the audience quickly and retire to his own study, where he could forget the ruthlessness of court intrigue and immerse himself in the safe world of books.

"You do not need to," Saladin said. The Sultan looked him over closely, and then added words that Maimonides would treasure for the rest of his life. "If you do not know it in your heart already, let me say it aloud. You are very dear to me, Rabbi. When I was a young man, I stood on the shoulders of my father, Ayyub, to find moral guidance in a cruel world that seemed to have no rules. Since my father returned to Allah, I have relied on you for that spiritual certainty. Do not ever change, my friend."

Maimonides beamed and felt his embarrassment and nervousness fade, like the morning dew when struck by the warming rays of the sun. Saladin was truly unlike any man who had walked the earth since the days of myth and fable. In a world where kings ruled with absolute authority and took pleasure in torturing their subjects for the least of infractions, here was a sultan who took reproach from his servants with equanimity and good humor. In a time when religion was the foundation of hate and division, here was a Muslim who embraced a Jew as a brother. In his heart, Maimonides thanked God for giving Saladin authority over the Holy Land. With Saladin, a man of such dignity and quiet strength to lead them, the Children of Abraham, Jews, Christians, and Muslims, could finally work together to create a world built on justice and peace, starting in the sacred city of Jerusalem. Perhaps, even as the Prophets had foreseen, the victory of good over evil was finally at hand.

But God was quick to remind the old man of His playful love of irony. Even as such grandiose thoughts flew through the rabbi's mind, the sound of urgent flapping at the window distracted him.

The Sultan turned and walked over to the arched windowsill, ten stories above the well-watered gardens below. He pulled open the carved oak shutters and let in a brown-and-white-flecked pigeon. Maimonides immediately recognized the bird as one of Saladin's trained carriers that relayed critical messages to him from all over the caliphate. A tiny iron tube was tied to one of the pigeon's legs and Saladin carefully removed it. He soothingly ran his fingers along the pigeon's down with one hand while he popped the tube open with another. A small piece of parchment was tightly wrapped inside, and the Sultan carefully removed it.

The sun disappeared behind a heavy cloud for a moment as Saladin read through the message, his eyebrows rising. Maimonides felt a tingling run through him, an electric sensation that he had not experienced since that day of the gloriously improbable victory at Hattin. But this time the feeling was clearly dark and foreboding. He felt his stomach twist in a knot. Maimonides knew somehow that he was about to be witness to history again, but he had the distinct feeling that it was a history that would be filled with dread and loss.

Saladin looked up from the note at long last. He smiled at his elderly doctor but there was no mirth in his expression.

"It seems we have greater things to be concerned about than the jealousies of the harem."

"What is happening, *sayyidi*?"

Saladin turned away from him and walked over to the open window. He stared out across the gardens to the platform of the Haram al-Sharif on the Temple Mount. The Dome of the Rock rose proudly against the Jerusalem sky, the symbol of a civilization reborn and reclaimed against all odds by the Children of Abraham from the desecration of the infidel hordes. Maimonides knew that Saladin considered the liberation of the Dome and the restoration of Jerusalem to Muslim control his life's sole purpose. Since his victory, he had often seen his master stare longingly at the mosque, like a child gazing upon his beloved mother after many years of forced separation. He saw that joy in Saladin's dark eyes again, but this time mixed with deep sadness.

"Some young fool named Richard is leading an army of Franks to retake our lands," Saladin said matter-of-factly. "The word from Europe is that these Crusaders are even now ransacking their way to Sicily. From there, they will sail to our coast."

No. Please God. Not once more.

Maimonides found it difficult to think. A wave of nausea was rising in his stomach and he struggled to keep from retching all over the pristine marble floors of the Sultan's study.

Saladin noticed the rabbi's discomfiture and smiled ruefully. He stepped away from the window and strode toward the iron doors of the chamber.

"Forgive me, my friend, but I have much to consider." With that, he walked through the gates and strode down the corridor, the two burly Egyptian guards following smartly at his heels.

Maimonides was left alone to ponder the dreadful news. A new Crusade. Thousands of ignorant, hate-filled vermin from the slums of Europe would soon be at their doorsteps again. Men who had no respect for God or moral law. Monsters who could roast little children alive for supper. They were on their way back to reclaim Jerusalem. And the world would never be the same again.

16 Port of Messina, Sicily—AD 1191

Sir William Chinon was a man of God, or at least he aspired to be. As he stood alone on the Sicilian hilltop, the knight mused bitterly about how the brutal realities of service to an earthly throne made it difficult at times to follow the commandments of his Heavenly Father. He knew that Christ bade the faithful to render unto Caesar his due, but to William's mind, the divine right of kings should not nullify the moral code of the sacred scriptures. The knight fervently believed that the Kingdom of Heaven was within the heart of man and could be made manifest on earth even as it was in the angelic realms. Unfortunately, he was rather alone in that regard within the court of his friend King Richard. The young ruler was too insecure in his recently acquired throne to pay much attention to talk of a "higher road" in governance, and his ear was filled with the schemes and machinations of the petty courtiers. William was a lone voice of moderation in an administration of wolves, and he had found himself swept up by the unstoppable force of pride and power that had brought him to this place.

He had always wanted to see Sicily, the jewel of the Mediterranean, but not in this way. William stood atop a lush promontory overlooking the Bay of Messina, which now served as host to his king's greatest folly. The crystal-green port was normally home to countless quaint fishing boats and larger merchant vessels conducting trade with the heathen world to the south and east. The private ships that were the lifeblood of Sicily's economy, bedecked in a rainbow array of standards from all over the known world, were nowhere to be seen now. In fact, the bay itself was barely visible under the dark crush of the Crusader warships that stretched out from the shoreline toward the misty horizon.

Over two hundred vessels covered the seascape like a rolling wave of black lichen. The Crusader galleons were mainly double-masted vessels bearing crimson sails with golden crosses. The *dromons* were descendants of the ancient triremes of the Roman Empire. Over 150 feet long and fitted with two rows of fifty-foot oars, similar in design to the Viking flagships, they were manned by the sturdiest sailors to be found in Christendom. Each *dromon* had recently been fitted with a heavy tube on its stem, from which issued a mysterious flaming substance that the sailors reverently called "liquid fire." The explosive was rumored to have been developed in China, but few facts about its origin or composition were known, even to William, as a result of the extreme secrecy with which the Italian traders guarded the material. The Arabs were believed to have access to the rare liquid fire, and their monopoly on the trade routes to Asia had thwarted European efforts to utilize this remarkable military technology for decades. But years of brilliant espionage work had allowed Byzantine and Italian infiltrators to secure some of the explosive material from the Turkmen tribes in eastern Anatolia. While their supply of the liquid fire was limited, when confronting a civilization as militarily advanced as that of the Muslims, William knew that every little advantage mattered.

The *dromons* were more stark and utilitarian than the elegant *buzzo* craft from nearby Venice. These galleons, with their extra levels of holds and their sweeping, crescent-moon design, towered above the smaller ships. They were beautiful but far less maneuverable in a sea battle. As such, they would sail to the rear and center of the armada, serving as command posts for the expedition leaders. William knew that the Frankish generals and their noble patrons would prefer to recline in ease and give orders from the safety of the luxurious *buzzo*s. The common men on the *dromons* and the tiny, one-masted cog ships would be sent to face death and worse at the hands of the Saracen captains. Such was the injustice of power, unchanged since the days of Cain and Abel.

William watched a flock of seagulls circle the crowded docks below. He envied the birds—their lives free of care, provided daily for by their Lord, even as the scriptures said. The knight was fluent in Latin and had read the Bible many times in the quiet of his personal study, away from the priests who jealously guarded interpretation of the Holy Writ. He wished more of his fellow believers would read the book themselves and not just mindlessly trumpet the doctrines of the Church. Of course, in this he was truly a loner, for most of his comrades could barely read their own native tongues, much less the alien language of the Revelation. And he knew that the Roman Church had a vested interest in maintaining the ignorance of the people. If the common man ever truly read and absorbed the words of the Lord, it would all end. The traditional power structures and relationships of the world—priest and laymen, master and serf, husband and wife, father and child, and perhaps even believer and heathen—would be thrown into disarray by the liberating power of Christ's simple teachings. Love was the antidote to power, and those in power would do anything to quell the flame of love, even as they had at Golgotha a thousand years before.

The knight's bitter musings were interrupted by the arrival of Richard. William had not seen the king look so happy since before that disastrous day at the Rhône months earlier.

Richard clapped a friendly hand on his knight's shoulder and gazed down the hilltop to his armada.

"Now, that is a sight that even your pessimism cannot sully," Richard said, his voice filled with a pride and confidence not shared by William.

"It has been a long march, my lord," the knight said with his usual frankness. "There is already much blood on the hands of our soldiers, none of it heathen."

Richard's face darkened for a moment. William knew that he had hit a nerve. After the chaos at the Rhône, Richard had gathered his shaken troops together for the journey to the coast. The long, exhausting trek through the French countryside had quickly turned the already poorly disciplined army of serfs and hooligans into a band of vicious thieves and marauders. William had watched with impotent horror as the men under his nominal command laid waste to village after village, plundering and looting their fellow Christians, attacking the girls and abusing the elderly. William had personally executed six criminals in their ranks for these atrocities before Richard sternly warned him to keep his avenging sword in check before the soldiers revolted.

"Most of these men are ignorant serfs looking for a chance to pillage and rape," Richard now said, with forced nonchalance. "What happened was to be expected. We cannot tame their natures, but we can harness their brutality against the Saracens."

William snorted with disdain. He knew that such men could not earn the blessings of Christ needed for victory. If these brigands could not be trusted to treat fellow believers with humanity, how could they fight an enemy according to the principles of just war?

"There are rules, my lord, even in war."

Richard's eyes went cold and his smile vanished.

"Yes," the king said quietly. "And they are made by the victors."

With that, Richard the Lionheart turned and left his friend William on the hilltop. The knight watched his liege lord walk determinedly down the slope toward the layered wooden docks below, where he would oversee preparations for the next stage in this madness. They would attack and conquer their fellow Christians who guarded the entryway to the land of the heathens and whose leader was committed to preserving the peace with the infidel hordes.

Cyprus would be the first true battle of the Crusade.

17

Al-Adil slammed his fist impatiently on the polished oak table, causing a goblet of snow water to overturn and spill on the lap of one of the Sultan's generals. The unintended victim of al-Adil's fury was a gray-haired Hejazi Bedouin whose face bore a long scar from his empty left eye socket down to his cheek. He winced with his good eye as the liquid chilled his crotch, but did not complain. It was an extremely bad idea to raise one's voice to Saladin's impetuous brother, whose temper was as legendary as the Sultan's patience.

"My sources are adamant that the Frankish ships are only days away, just off the coast of Cyprus," he said, his throaty voice rising above the din of argument that hung over the council of war. A dozen of the most powerful men in the land were seated at the carved oblong table, a surviving Seljuk relic from the pre-Crusader sultanate of Jerusalem. The private room, deep inside the bowels of Saladin's rebuilt palace, was sealed and heavily guarded by blue-veiled North Africans brandishing poisoned sabers. No windows shone in this most hidden chamber where state secrets could be discussed openly. The only light illuminating the secret hall came from three torches strategically placed in a triangular formation around the meeting table.

"What sources, if I may ask?" The high-pitched voice of the grand vizier, Qadi al-Fadil, was the first sound to penetrate the blanket of shock that had suddenly descended on the room.

"No. You may not ask," al-Adil said, barely restraining his fury. "When you bother to venture out of your perfumed study and fight on the front lines of a battlefield, then you may ask all that you wish, Qadi."

Saladin sat at the head of the ornate Turkish table and watched the exchange between his brother and his prime minister with a small smile.

"Tell us more of what your sources say, brother." The Sultan leaned forward, running a hand slowly through his ebony curls, a nervous gesture al-Adil knew well from childhood. And he also caught the slight tremor in Saladin's hand as he sipped water from a silver chalice. His brother was as tense as he had ever seen him, although the Sultan hid his anxiety expertly from most of his subjects. But al-Adil knew Saladin better than anyone else did. He loved him more passionately and genuinely than all the sycophants in the court combined, and he did not need to elevate Saladin to the level of myth to do so. No, his brother was very much a man, with fears and insecurities like any other. And al-Adil knew that word of the impending Crusader invasion had cut deep into Saladin's heart, bringing out all the uncertainty and self-doubt the great Sultan had wrestled with since he embarked on his life's mission to recapture Jerusalem. Saladin was as afraid as his nervous underlings, and only al-Adil grasped his turmoil.

"My *well-placed sources*," he said with emphasis, "inform me that this King Richard has rendezvoused with Italian troops sent by their Pope on the island of Sicily. From there, the Franks set off for Cyprus with a fleet numbering over two hundred ships." Al-Adil secretly hoped that the information he had gleaned from the Venetian traders was wildly exaggerated. He would prefer to be embarrassed by inaccurate intelligence than to allow his people to be caught unawares by a threat of this magnitude.

A collective gasp spread through the columned chamber where the secret meeting was being held. Word had not yet spread to the general public, although al-Adil knew that it was only a matter of time before the secrets of the council would be reported and distorted throughout Palestine. And the wave of terror that engulfed these pathetic courtiers would spread to the common people.

"What you say is impossible," the Qadi retorted, although his voice quavered with uncertainty. "The barbarians are viciously divided, even as the believers were before the great Sultan reunited us. They do not have the organizational ability or collective willpower to embark on a military expedition of that scale."

Saladin smiled, but al-Adil knew that there was no joy in his brother's heart.

"I wish that were true, my friend," the Sultan said, his voice calm and soothing, like a father talking to a distressed child. "However, I have heard that this Lionheart is a charismatic and intelligent foe, capable of moving the hearts of men to his cause. And he has the blessings of the Pontiff of Rome, who the unbelievers take far more seriously than the faithful do our own scholars."

Qadi al-Fadil, himself a respected scholar of Islamic theology and jurisprudence, winced at the veiled slight. Al-Adil found it difficult to restrain a grin at the vizier's discomfiture.

"But, *sayyidi*, the reports of this advance on Cyprus are problematic," the Qadi said, trying to regain credibility before the other courtiers without angering his master. "We know that these fanatics have no friends among the Cypriots, unless Comnenus has broken his pledge with us."

Al-Adil had also been troubled by the thought of Isaac Comnenus, the so-called Emperor of Cyprus, providing aid to the invaders. Comnenus was a Christian and a claimant to the imperial throne of Byzantium, but he had no love for the brutish thugs of Europe. He had always been a practical man who had sought to preserve and strengthen the trading relationships with the Muslim world that had made his island nation prosper. If the Crusaders were working with Comnenus, the threat was exponentially greater, as it would signal the unification of Byzantium and the west against the caliphate.

"Perhaps the Franks are not turning to Cyprus for aid." It was Maimonides who spoke up now, and al-Adil glowered. Seated to the left of the Sultan, the rabbi leaned forward, his hands steepled before him.

"What are you suggesting, Jew?" the Qadi snorted. Al-Adil knew that the vizier despised the rabbi even more than he did, if that were indeed possible.

Maimonides ignored the contempt in al-Fadil's tone and turned his attention to the Sultan, addressing his master directly as if there were no one else in the room.

"Cyprus guards the sea route to Palestine," the rabbi said. "A new war in the Levant will disrupt the flow of trade through the island, and Comnenus would be forced to intervene. It is not at all certain that he would side with his fellow Christians after his bitter experiences with King Guy and that demon Reginald. Perhaps the Franks are moving to eliminate a potential rival and turncoat rather than seeking the help of an ally."

Al-Adil grunted. The Jew had a point, he had to admit to himself grudgingly. Comnenus, a cultured and refined ruler, was not the kind of man to work with marauders whose brutal tactics would disrupt the recently restored flow of goods and gold from the caliphate into his coffers. And his warships would pose a serious threat for the Crusaders should he choose to throw his allegiance with his wealthy Muslim trading partners. Richard's armies would be trapped in Palestine between Saladin's forces and the Cypriot galleons blockading the coast. A two-pronged attack by land and sea would strangle the invading forces and crush the Crusade before it began. It made strategic sense for the Lionheart to eliminate a rival of uncertain loyalty before he set foot in the Holy Land.

Al-Adil had no doubt that he would have come to the same conclusion soon enough, but he was deeply irritated that a doctor with no training in military strategy voiced this theory before any of his great generals. To make things worse, the other councillors began to murmur their assent openly.

"I must agree with the rabbi, *sayyidi*," said the one-eyed general to al-Adil's right. "Isaac Comnenus will fight to the last man before he lets these marauders loot his island and use it as a way station for an invasion."

The Sultan steepled his fingers together, his mind racing as he considered various strategies.

"If Cyprus comes under attack, can we provide Comnenus with support?" Saladin turned to Junayd al-Askari, one of his naval commanders, a short and balding man with a prominent birth stain on his right cheek.

Al-Askari thought for a moment, and then shook his head.

"If al-Adil's intelligence is accurate, our ships would arrive too late to impact the outcome of any battle," he said in his trademark nasal drone. "And we face the risk that the Cypriots will consider our efforts as a pretext for expanding the caliphate into the Mediterranean. Muslim warships off their coast will not be greeted with the same enthusiasm as trading vessels from Alexandria. At worst, we would frighten them into the very alliance with the Franks that we are hoping to block."

Saladin looked at the faces of his other advisers. His eyes fell on al-Adil, who nodded his assent grimly.

"Then it appears that we must leave the fate of Cyprus in the hands of Allah," the Sultan said at last. "Let us pray that our friend Isaac Comnenus is able to hold his own against his Frankish brothers."

Saladin turned his attention to Keukburi, the broad-shouldered Egyptian commander who had masterminded the bloodless coup that ended the Fatimid caliphate.

"While we may hope that this Crusade will be thwarted before the Franks reach our coast, we must act on the assumption that Cyprus will fall." Saladin paused, and then sat up straight, his head held high in dignity. "Prepare the soldiers and the common people for the invasion."

The confidence in Saladin's tone could not dispel the shudder that swept through the room. Al-Adil looked at the cowardly councillors with contempt. He had spent his entire life on the battlefield and had, in truth, grown weary of an easy life in the shadowed gardens of Jerusalem.

Saladin rose, and the other councillors followed, ready to perform their duty. As the Sultan turned to leave, he stopped and addressed his commanders.

"Cyprus shall be the first battle of many in this new *jihad*," he said with a thoughtful smile. "Personally, I look forward to it. We shall see what kind of man this King Richard is in how he deals with his fellow Christians."

ichard the Lionheart surveyed the devastation he had wrought and smiled. Cyprus was on fire, it's once emerald hills blanketed in rolling clouds of smoke and flickering ashes. The battle raged on in the valley below, but the outcome was clear. Richard's knights would smash the Cypriots into submission. It was just a matter of time.

His ships had arrived a week earlier, covering the Bay of Amathus like a carpet of iron and steel. After a long journey through the treacherous, stormy sea, his double-banked galleys blocked out the setting sun as they converged on the island. The famed Cypriot war fleet was easily outnumbered by the Crusader onslaught. He had stood on the prow of his command ship, watching with satisfaction as his *dromons* surrounded the bay and hemmed in the Byzantine warships. Aside from a brief exchange of arrows from nervous archers on both sides, a dread silence had hung over the southern port as the Cypriots watched the horizon darken with a seemingly eternal parade of Frankish vessels.

Richard had, of course, sent word to Isaac Comnenus regarding his impending arrival. And he had made it clear that the Cypriots would be expected to join their Christian brothers in the holy war. But the King of England already knew where Comnenus stood. He was a traitor more interested in trading with the infidel than bringing him to his knees. Which suited Richard just fine. When Isaac was forced to show his true face to Christendom, when he betrayed the sacred cause at the hour of its greatest need, Richard would have no choice but to remove this pretender to the Byzantine throne from his island outpost. And in the process, his men would finally test their mettle on the battlefield against the highly trained and loyal Cypriot forces. In truth, Richard would have probably found a pretext to wage war against Cyprus even if Comnenus had agreed to support the Crusade. His men had proven themselves excellent poachers and highway robbers when faced with unarmed Italian peasants, but he needed to teach them to discipline themselves against a well-armed, committed foe.

When, predictably, Comnenus had sent heralds bearing gifts of golden chalices and beautiful local women, but no firm commitment to the military expedition, Richard had wasted no time in declaring Cyprus an enemy of Christ. His men had charged from their docked galleons with shouts of glee, embarking on their first true battle with the naive enthusiasm of all young soldiers. When no furious army awaited them in the deserted coastal towns, Richard found that it required every bit of his managerial skill to keep his men from looting the empty villages and stay focused on the march north to Nicosia. His friend William had proved invaluable in motivating the unruly troops and helping Richard to keep his temper on the long trek through the lush valleys of central Cyprus.

On the fifth day of their march, the Crusaders crossed a ruddy stream and found they could see the towering stone walls of the capital shimmering in the distance, apparently undefended. Richard had been uneasy, but he had little choice except to press forward. As they neared the seemingly deserted guard towers of the citadel, the Cypriot army, which had scattered and hidden in the surrounding hills, attacked from the rear. The surprise flank thrust had caused some of his men to panic, and Richard had ordered several deserters seen surrendering to the Cypriot troops shot by his archers. Richard knew that when a soldier had no choice but to fight the enemy or be killed by his own troops, he would quickly remember which side he was on.

The battle had gone poorly in its early stages. Richard had watched with growing alarm as the Cypriots formed a wall of spear-toting infantry to hold back the Crusader charge while their archers rained death on his men from hidden outposts in the surrounding hills. William and some of his best knights broke from the main mass of the Frankish army and launched themselves on a search-and-destroy mission, hoping to root out the invisible archers before morale plummeted further.

Frustrated with the timidity and confusion of his troops in the face of Byzantine resistance, Richard found he could not sit back and watch as his men flailed under the Cypriot attack. Against the hastily shouted advice of his generals, the king jumped on his glittering white stallion and charged straight across the rocky vale into the heart of Isaac's forces. Bearing the golden lion standard of his house in his left hand, a brutal broadsword in his right, Richard achieved the desired effect of his lonely and possibly mad attack on the enemy instantly. The Crusader troops rallied instinctively behind him, screaming guttural war cries and calling upon Christ to destroy the traitors. The Cypriots, for their part, were confused by the enemy king's unprecedented and suicidal ride into their forces. The front men of the Cypriot infantry, dressed in blue-and-white hauberks and carrying long, spiked pole arms, hesitated just an instant too long as the king's stallion bore down upon them. They did not live long enough to regret their momentary lapse. Richard's sword cleaved their heads from their shoulders as easily as if he were slicing loaves of French bread. His horse trampled the startled crowd as if enraged that these little men would deign to stand in the way of the King of England.

Emboldened by their monarch's courage, the Crusader soldiers charged after him, and the battle was joined with blood and fury. With his men tearing into the heart of the Cypriot defense lines, Richard dodged a volley of spears, arrows, and lethal darts as he rode back to the chaotic command tent atop a hill overlooking the Nicosia fortress. As the din of swords clashing and men dying filled the evergreen valley, Richard had given the order to set fire to the countryside. In the absence of a favorable wind, the thick smoke would be as blinding to his own troops as it was to his adversaries, but Richard knew the sight of their verdant hills disappearing under a rapidly spreading brush fire would skewer the Cypriot morale.

As Richard gazed down upon the battle below, he felt his heartbeat rise with pride as he watched his ragtag army of serfs tear through the center of the Byzantine corps. The tide of the battle had turned, and entire regiments of the heavily armored island natives were fleeing back into the wooded hills. He had achieved the impossible—yet again.

Then Richard saw something unexpected that caused him to laugh out loud. Perhaps rumor of his own mad dash into the heat of battle had spread through the Cypriot ranks. Perhaps his enemy was hoping to similarly rally support to regain the initiative in battle. Whatever the reason, the skirmish would soon be over. For into the midst of the heaviest fighting rode Isaac Comnenus, Emperor of Cyprus, himself. Clad in sparkling dress armor of bronze and steel, his skull covered in a helmet of plumed Roman design, similar to the headgear of his imperial ancestors, Isaac rode forward on a tall Arabian steed (a gift, no doubt, from his Saracen allies). The Cypriot troops were attempting to maintain a clear passage for their leader, a rather formidable task in the middle of the churning devastation that covered the battlefield.

Richard had met Isaac Comnenus only once before. In the days before he seized the throne of the island state, Comnenus had been an ambitious Byzantine nobleman who had visited Western Europe as part of an effort to resurrect ties between the estranged arms of the Christian Church. His message of reconciliation between the Latin and Greek churches had initially been well received by the courts of Italy and France, but his concomitant policy of reaching out to the Muslim hordes quickly brought the weight of the Vatican down upon him. Concert with Isaac Comnenus became anathema to the aristocrats who wished to keep the Holy Father's agents out of their own affairs. Only Richard's iconoclastic father had welcomed him with open arms as a man who represented the "future of Christendom."

Richard, who had opposed the audience on principle, had taken an immediate personal dislike to Isaac when he met him. His arrogant, pinched features and his supercilious voice that suggested he considered himself a representative of civilization on tour of a barbarian land, had made Richard immediately wish to knock the man off his feet.

Now gazing at the imperious, hawk-faced man from across the devastated landscape, Richard ran his hand across the jeweled hilt of his broadsword. Perhaps he would finally get to do just that. And more.

With a sudden cry of youthful glee, King Richard spurred his horse again into the storm below. He ignored the screams of dying men around him and charged forward. One of William's knights, a boyish-faced lad named Louis, saw the king placing himself again in peril and immediately rode to his side.

The smoke cleared for an instant and Richard could see Comnenus clearly. He sat on his stallion a hundred feet away, with only one bearded archer beside him. Instinctively, the men on both sides had cleared a path between the opponents, not wishing to be anywhere near a lethal duel between kings.

Richard beamed. This was what he lived for. The chance to take on a man who at least had a tolerable claim to be his equal, and best him in battle before his soldiers. Richard pulled out his sword and pointed it straight at his adversary in formal challenge. Comnenus did not move at first, a smirk playing across his tanned, skeletal features. Then he lifted his right hand as if he were signaling someone. The Cypriot archer next to him moved like lightning.

Richard heard the sharp whine of an arrow shoot across the field. He turned his head just barely in time, and felt the cold rush of air as the missile streaked past his ear. He felt his face go flush with anger. So Comnenus was a coward, unwilling to face him like a man; he would hide behind his servants. Richard reared his horse in defiance, ready to ride straight at his treacherous foes. He imagined ripping off the offending archer's head with his bare hands before skewering the so-called emperor with his blade.

The cry of surprise from behind him made Richard turn involuntarily. His faithful Louis had taken the arrow meant for him. It was a minor injury—the shaft was embedded in his left forearm and had not penetrated deep because of the knight's heavy armor. But Louis, who was perhaps one of the sturdiest men in William's honor guard, was screaming as if he were on fire. Richard watched in frozen horror as his knight began to convulse and a sickly white foam erupted from his mouth. As Louis fell off his horse and went still, Richard realized the truth.

Comnenus was using poisoned arrows.

"Coward!" he bellowed in offended rage. "Face me like a man!" The Church disapproved of the use of poisoned arrows as inhumane, and Christian warriors would only resort to such an extreme tactic in the most desperate of circumstances against the most evil of opponents. To attack the King of England, sent on a holy mission by the Vicar of Christ himself, with such a weapon was beyond insult.

Comnenus, however, did not seem to care that his honor was being sullied in such a public fashion. He had clearly succeeded in drawing out his adversary and now appeared intent on cutting off the head of the snake by any means necessary before his island paradise was reduced to rubbles and ashes. Richard instinctively dived as another volley shot through the smoky mist past him, striking and instantly killing a Crusader soldier who had just triumphantly beheaded a Cypriot guard. Richard could barely see Isaac and his villainous archer through the thick billowing smoke that now covered the plain like ghostly fog. Even with the low visibility, Richard knew that Isaac's man was a trained sharpshooter who would not likely miss a third time.

Rearing his horse back farther into the cover of smoke, Richard sheathed his sword. He looked around the firestorm that was the battlefield until he saw the body of one of his knights slumped lifeless on a confused and weary horse. The unlucky man still held a long, razor-tipped lance in his death grip. Richard rode over and in one swift movement ripped the pole arm from his deceased comrade's hand. Then he did the unexpected. Instead of retreating to the safety of his command pavilion in the hills above, Richard the Lionheart rode out to face death with honor.

The young king broke through the smoke cover like an eagle soaring through heavy clouds, his lance aimed straight at Comnenus. The startled emperor pulled heavily on the reins, trying to force his Arabian horse into a hasty retreat. Isaac's assassin let loose a volley of poisoned arrows that Richard dodged through the focused intensity of his rage. Realizing that the king could not be dissuaded from his vengeful charge, the archer rode forward, his iron shield raised high to protect his liege lord.

Richard's lance tore through the man's defenses, knocking the archer from his horse. But the distraction had served its purpose. Isaac Comnenus had vanished into a crowd of his cavalry that was bearing down hard upon the lone king. Richard hesitated for just one moment, long enough to skewer the treacherous archer through the neck, before riding back toward the Crusader line of defense.

Still trembling from the bloodlust running in his veins, Richard rode past his relieved commanders, who seemed stunned that he had returned alive from his second suicidal ride of the battle. He jumped off his horse, leaving it with a thin page who quickly rushed forward to examine the royal stallion for wounds. Tearing off his helmet, he took a deep breath to calm himself. But the air was acrid with blood and death, and it only intensified his anger. Richard stormed past a pair of nervous sentries and entered the crimson pavilion that served as his mobile base of operations. And then he stopped in his tracks.

Instead of the usual collection of generals and petty nobles seeking his attention, he found himself staring at a strikingly attractive girl. Her violet eyes were delicately oval, her chestnut hair bound by silk ribbons into a long series of twirling braids. She would have been even prettier had her face not been marred by a disdainful frown, a look of sheer contempt that reminded Richard for a moment of his mother's instinctive grimace whenever his father's name was brought up in conversation.

Beside her sat a terrified-looking girl who had clearly been crying, her mousy hair covered in a russet shawl. And behind the ladies, least expected of all, stood Sir William, who seemed remarkably embarrassed to be hosting these women in the midst of an ongoing battle. One of William's men, a short, stubby knight named Baldwin Something-or-other, seemed less bashful in the maidens' presence. He was looking at the violet-eyed girl with open lust, a fact that she was clearly aware of but making every effort to ignore.

"What is the meaning of this?" Richard was too tired and wound up from his recent brush with death to waste any time.

William coughed apologetically. He clearly did not wish to be here right now.

"My men were successful in raiding the enemy's command tent," William said, his tone suggesting that he regretted the extent of their success. "They found these ladies inside and brought them back as prisoners."

"Lovely as these girls are, William, in the future, perhaps you should instruct your men to bring back a general or someone else useful who could serve as a bargaining chip." Richard shook his head wearily. Was everyone on this mission incompetent? The king strode over to a carved oak table, bearing the royal insignia of a pouncing lion, and poured warm water from a crystal jug into a silver bowl. He drank in heavy gulps, and then splashed the remaining water on his grime-covered face.

"My lord, she claims to be the daughter of Isaac Comnenus," William said, after a moment of hesitation. Richard turned and saw that William was looking at the pretty girl with haughty features. Well, this *was* an interesting development. The other woman, clearly her handmaiden, looked ready to faint. Richard ignored the mousy servant's discomfort and strode over to her mistress. He took the girl's face in his right hand, running a finger across her proud cheekbones. Yes, he could see the resemblance to the man whom he had nearly killed a short time before.

"What is your name?"

The woman jerked her face away from his touch.

"Roxana, Princess of Cyprus," the girl said, rising to her feet. She was nearly as tall as Richard and she leaned dangerously close to him. "My father will hunt you down if any harm befalls me."

The king smiled as he looked into her eyes and saw a hint of fear buried beneath her pride. She was, all things considered, holding up quite well, certainly compared with her sniveling maid. Richard admired the girl's courage—at least her treacherous father had raised her with the right spirit. Had Joanna been in her predicament, he would have expected the same dignity. He also knew that his own father would have done anything to free Joanna from captivity at the hands of the enemy.

"I am counting on it," Richard said. He turned to William. "Please escort Lady Roxana to more appropriate quarters. I trust her stay with us will be brief."

William glanced at the weepy maid, but Richard shook his head slightly. William paled, but bowed and took Roxana's arm to lead her away. The princess refused to budge, her eyes on her handmaiden.

"I am not going anywhere without Louisa."

Richard turned to Roxana, putting on his most courteous mask.

"We have no use for her," he said. "Your lady-in-waiting will be returned forthwith to your father's camp."

A look of relief crossed Louisa's face, but the princess did not look convinced. William nudged her gently, and she finally moved away from him. Richard saw that William avoided looking at the handmaiden as he led the princess out of the command pavilion.

Louisa fell on her knees before the king and kissed his hand.

"Thank you, my lord," she gushed, her voice high-pitched and rambling. "I will make sure that the emperor hears of your compassion."

Richard ignored her and turned to Baldwin, his voice low and cold.

"You may enjoy the girl's company until sunset," he said. "When you've had your fill, have her head sent back to Isaac with word that the same will befall Roxana unless he surrenders by dawn."

Baldwin nodded, his eyes gleaming at the trembling girl on the floor, her face gone white with disbelief. Richard did not look at the unfortunate Louisa as he casually strolled out of the pavilion, but her screams followed him, rising above the cacophony of misery that emanated from the battlefield below.

19

Sir William stood at the edge of the Crusader base camp, his eyes following the half-moon as it emerged briefly before disappearing again into the cloud of haze and ash that hung over the valley. His chest felt like it had been crushed in one of the infamous vises used by Italian torturers. At the same time his shoulders slumped under the weight of his guilt and shame.

Of course, he had known that Richard intended to use the poor maid as an example to force Isaac's hand. Part of him had been gratified that his master had sent him away to chaperone the proud Roxana, leaving the dirty business to men more suited to such affairs. And he understood the reasons of state behind the king's ruthless actions. The battle had gone on long enough without a breakthrough. Hundreds of Christians were already dead at the hands of their brothers. Many more would die before the superior logic of numbers weighed conclusively in Richard's favor. Isaac Comnenus was a proud man who would rather watch his entire island go up in flames than reach an accord with his enemies. Richard needed to act decisively and bring the conflict to an immediate end so that the warriors could turn their attention toward their true goal—the liberation of the Holy Land.

Roxana's capture had been fortuitous, but Isaac would have likely wavered as long as he thought his daughter was protected under the code of royal honor. Only a drastic act, such as Louisa's execution, would send an unequivocal message that Richard would do whatever it took to bring the rebellious Cypriots to their knees. It was nasty, brutal work, more suited to a butcher than a king, but William knew that one woman's death could not be weighed equally against the lives of thousands of men.

Whatever the justification, his stomach still turned at the thought of the maid's final moments—pinned under the overweight, greasy Baldwin, knowing that each moment the rape was prolonged was another moment she could live.

The moon emerged again and this time it illuminated the valley enough to show a slow procession making its way toward the Crusader camp. A grim faced Isaac rode alongside several of his guards and a black-frocked priest of the Eastern Church. Their arrival was expected. Word had been sent an hour before from the Cypriots that Comnenus would meet with Richard and conclude a truce. William silently prayed that Christ would grant Louisa eternal love and peace in return for the tragic role she'd been forced to play in the games of kings.

Comnenus rode up to William, who lifted his visored helmet and bowed his head.

"You honor us with your company, Emperor," William said. He felt ridiculous keeping up the courteous façade after the events of the day, but he had little choice.

"Take me to my daughter," Isaac responded, his voice controlled and strong. William nonetheless saw the tremor in the proud Cypri- ot's cheek as he restrained the storm of emotions bubbling beneath the surface. With a curt nod, William turned his horse and led the impe- rial party toward the command pavilion. William could feel the gray- bearded priest's eyes on him, but he found he could not look at the man.

William dismounted and held his hand out to Comnenus, who grasped it with iron firmness as he slid off his Arabian steed. The rest of the Byzantine delegation followed suit. An honor guard was arrayed at the entrance to Richard's command center, knights in their finest dress hauberks, who held up their jeweled swords to form a corridor through which the party passed swiftly.

Inside, William saw Richard reclining on a velvet cushion, sipping wine from a sparkling goblet. A group of Richard's closest advisers, dressed in colorful formal tunics, stood behind him at attention. A hearty fire burned in the center of the pavilion, the smoke curling and escaping through a hole cut in the fabric fifty feet above. A roasted pig hung from a cooking rod above the flames, its rich scent filling the pavilion. Across from Richard sat Roxana, her eyes red, her statuesque features now cold with hate. She saw her father but did not move, tears welling in her eyes. William knew that Roxana blamed herself for her father's capitulation, but he saw no reproach on Isaac's face. Just profound relief at the sight of his unharmed child, and a sense of resignation.

Richard caught the look that passed between father and daughter. He smiled and rose to his feet, bowing elaborately before his adversary. The man who only a few hours before had tried to poison him.

"The emperor graces us with his presence," Richard said, a hint of mockery playing on his lips.

Isaac faced him, shoulders straight, head raised proudly. "Let my daughter go," he said simply. "You can have anything. My kingdom. Just do not harm her."

Richard laughed heartily.

"It is a poor negotiator that offers all of his wares on the first go-round," the king said. He turned his back on the emperor and took another sip from his goblet. With the exaggerated movements of a stage actor, Richard sat down on his cushion, reclining his feet arrogantly against the carved oak table. "But I will accommodate you. You will sur- render Cyprus to my men, and your daughter will be released."

The emperor did not hesitate.

"Done."

Richard looked at the man for a long moment, his face unreadable.

"But you, however, have waged war on the Plantagenets. You cannot go free." Richard watched him closely for a reaction, but Isaac Comnenus stood stoically, as if expecting this.

"I will go with you," he said, no hint of regret or shame in his voice. William hoped that he himself would have the same dignity should he ever find himself captured and at the mercy of the Saracens.

"No!" Roxana jumped up and rushed to her father's side. He embraced his daughter slowly, held her for a long time, and then wiped her tears, before turning to face Richard.

"I have only one request, as one king speaking to another," Isaac said. "Preserve my dignity. A ruler cannot be seen in iron chains by his people."

Richard watched him closely. William saw a moment of compassion flash across the young king's face. Then the monarch became aware of the smirks on the faces of his arrogant advisers. These men, who had long viewed Isaac Comnenus as a traitor for his peace overtures to the Muslims, were delighting in watching him beg for scraps of leniency. Seeing the ruthless, goading expression of his courtiers, Richard's features hardened. William looked away, knowing that his master did not feel secure enough in his power to shower his enemies—their enemies—with goodwill.

"You are quite right, Isaac Comnenus," Richard said at last. "For you I will forge chains of silver. But chains they will still be, my emperor."

Isaac shrugged, as if he had expected as much, but his daughter stepped forward unexpectedly and spit on Richard's face.

"You are a monster," Roxana said, her voice filling with venom.

Richard's guards stepped forward, their swords raised, to answer the insult, but the king lifted his hand to stop them. Richard wiped the spit from his face.

"You should tell your daughter that she is a very lucky girl," Richard said, his own voice becoming dangerously quiet. "I pray that she does not do anything further to bring her remarkable streak of fortune to an end."

Isaac paled and put a restraining hand on Roxana's shoulder. She stepped back, the fury still etched on her face, as Richard nodded to his guards. The bulky men moved in to arrest the now-deposed ruler of Cyprus. Comnenus did not resist as they led him out of the pavilion, his head bowed low so that he would not have to look at his own soldiers who had accompanied him on his final journey as emperor. A tearful and defeated Roxana looked at each of the men in the room with spite, her gaze lingering on Richard, before turning to follow her father.

William did not meet her eyes as she stormed past him. The Battle of Cyprus was over. For that he was thankful. But he was not in the mood to celebrate, as he knew his knights would soon be doing once word of Isaac's surrender spread through the Crusader camp.

"My lord, may I be excused?" William heard an unusual lilt in his normally strong voice, and realized that he was fighting back tears. He saw Richard look at him, and for a moment the hard king vanished and was replaced by the childhood friend.

"Of course, Sir William," Richard said, turning his attention to the Greek priest and the remaining Cypriot party. "I have much to discuss with these fine men of Cyprus to ensure a quick and stable transfer of power. Once we have restored peace to this beautiful island, we will turn our attention to the cause that unites all Christians . . ."

William walked out into the smoky moonlight before he had to hear the rest of the tired speech.

20

Miriam stood on the walls of Jerusalem, gazing at the glowing red aura that blanketed the western sky. The sun had set hours before, but it was not the last traces of a somnolent celestial body that shone so brightly now. No, there was nothing heavenly at all about the source of this light. As the flickering light grew brighter on the horizon, Miriam knew that the end was near.

She remembered a story her uncle had told her when she was a young girl. A legend that the end of the world would be foretold by the rising of the sun in the west. Miriam had dismissed such prophecies as fanciful tales her people used to frighten children who stubbornly refused to say their prayers. She now understood that there was great truth in the whispered forebodings of her nation. For the end of the world was truly upon them.

The Crusaders had arrived. She could smell their rank, diseased bodies from afar; the odor of barbarism carried easily on the wind. The horizon was on fire now as the light of ten thousand torches blotted out the stars, as if the constellations themselves were fleeing in the face of such a merciless foe.

Miriam gazed down from the abandoned guard tower into the chaos below. Hundreds of men stood inside the city wall, guarding the barricaded gates, scimitars raised in trembling hands. It would not be long before the Frankish hordes broke through the last of the city's defenses and stood face-to-face with the few surviving Muslim soldiers who bore the weight of history unsteadily on their shoulders.

Across the wall, she could see scattered archers on the parapets preparing to unleash their razor-tipped missiles on the sea of Crusaders covering the plain below. Miriam witnessed the turbaned marksmen dipping their arrows in naphtha and setting them aflame in a desperate attempt to inflict maximum damage on the heavily armored invaders. The Muslim Prophet had strictly prohibited the use of fire as a weapon, as only Allah had the right to punish with the flames of Hell. But the chief Mufti had given the soldiers a last-minute *fatwa* permitting defense of the Holy City by any means necessary. The old man had then locked himself inside the Dome of the Rock, preparing for the inevitable slaughter.

Miriam could see the Crusaders clearly now, their advance guard already within a hundred feet of the city's limestone walls. They wore long white-and-crimson tunics emblazoned with the Cross and many rode brutal stallions that looked even angrier than their masters. Their polished helmets glimmered in the torchlight as they descended on Jerusalem with hearts blackened by the fire of frenzy and hate. Miriam shuddered as she felt their unthinking rage penetrate the smoke-filled air like a whirlwind of daggers. These brutes were worse than animals, for even beasts only attacked to satisfy their hunger. The hunger of the Franks, however, could never be quenched, arising from a bottomless void where their souls had once been. No matter how much they killed and consumed, they would remain ever hungry for more.

The Muslim archers let loose their flaming arrows, their sparks cutting through the sky like enraged fireflies. The missiles hit man and beast and the screams of agony and death echoed from below. Miriam knew that once the wails began, they would continue until no other sound could penetrate the ear or reach the heart.

But the rain of fire could not hold back the armies of the damned. Even as their front lines fell to the desperate barrage, they were quickly replaced by new rows of steel-clad soldiers. Like an infestation of vermin, the Franks moved forward, unthinking creatures of the night focused on one goal—the gates of Jerusalem. For over 450 years, the sons of Christ had endured the shame of Muslim rule over the Holy City that had witnessed the Passion and the Resurrection. Now, at last, they would seize the sacred stones from the hands of the infidels and cleanse the streets with their blood. Miriam knew that men like this would never turn back. Their ears filled with empty promises of Paradise, these holy warriors would walk unflinchingly toward their deaths, all in the name of The Cause. Under the relentless push of such fanaticism, the exhausted Muslim forces would buckle and fall. Then all would be lost.

Behind the city walls the madness had died down and a lull of terrible expectation hung over Jerusalem, the dread silence that blanketed the heavens before the onslaught of the tempest. The women and children were off the streets and hidden in makeshift shelters beneath stone houses, churches, and mosques. The few hundred Jews still left in the city had taken refuge in the main synagogue west of Herod's Wall, praying for a deliverance that, as usual, would not come.

Time slowed as the world below descended into the steady rhythm of war and death. Then Miriam saw the battering ram and she knew that the battle was over, and the slaughter about to begin. An immense trunk of black oak, studded with collars of steel spikes, the battering ram had been hoisted on a fifty-foot platform that inched forward on an endless series of massive wheels—a giant centipede escaped from the bowels of Hell. The sawed-off forward section had been covered in tar and the Crusaders quickly set it on fire. Pillars of gray smoke rose defiantly toward the heavens, and Miriam could feel the intolerable heat of the burning log singe her hair from a hundred feet below.

BOOM. The walls rattled as the battering ram struck the iron gates. BOOM. Again and again, like the footfalls of a dragon escaped from myths of old. Steady. Determined. Patient. Sure of the outcome. BOOM.

The ancient doors buckled. Crumpled like a parchment in the hands of a frustrated scribe. The metal screaming like a tortured animal caught in a lethal snare. The dreadful BOOM of the battering ram stopped, to be replaced by an even more horrifying sound. The cruel clicking of armored boots on paved stone, much like the maddening cry of an onrushing cloud of locusts. The Franks crossed the threshold and the pestilence was finally upon them.

Miriam watched helplessly as the barbarian hordes stormed through the streets of Jerusalem. The few surviving Muslim soldiers inside the city walls put up a brave defense, flinging themselves with full force against the first wave of Frankish troops to cross through the breached walls. But they were cut down instantly, heads and other extremities flying in every direction. Watching the carnage below, Miriam was reminded of the dread moments in the book of Exodus when the Angel of Death crossed over Egypt, taking the lives of every firstborn who stood in his way. Like a dark wind that snuffed out the fire of men's souls, the angel was busy at work again this bitter evening.

The Franks were everywhere, their armor glinting with the reflections of a thousand fires that had been set throughout the Holy City. With brutal, focused efficiency, the Crusaders broke down every door, searched every house for signs of life. And when they found it, they took it. Terrible images, the likes of which she could not have imagined possible, were seared into her mind. Children flung from the roofs of buildings, women impaled on javelins, their bodies ravaged even after they breathed their last. Enraged soldiers sloshing through a flood of crimson as the streets ran with blood.

The screaming of thousands rose through the city streets and was transformed into a roaring wind of despair, a vortex from Gehenna unleashed on Miriam's overwhelmed senses. It penetrated her mind, her soul, and even deeper. She was being pulled into the tempest, lost forever in a whirlwind of terror and agony . . .

⟶ ⟶ ⟶

MIRIAM AWOKE WITH A start. Her heart was pounding so loudly she thought it would burst. She breathed deeply, trying to calm herself and regain her bearings. She was home in her house, safely tucked away in an affluent section of the rebuilt Jewish quarter. The gentle scent of lilacs and lemons wafted in from the small garden outside her window. There was no battle, no devastation. All around her, Jerusalem slept soundly, the horrors that had ravaged its inhabitants a forgotten memory. For now.

She climbed out of bed and threw a shawl over her bare shoulders. The stone floor was hard and cold beneath her feet. Miriam stepped quietly out of her bedroom and walked down the hall to check on her uncle and aunt.

Maimonides was sound asleep, his wife, Rebecca, curled up in a ball next to him, snoring loudly. Looking at them lying together, Miriam felt calm. Safe. Maimonides was the center of her aunt's world, and Rebecca was his Rock of Moriah. While her uncle regularly shifted in bed, Rebecca lay perfectly still. Miriam smiled at the sight. Her beloved aunt had always slept like a woman in her tomb, unmovable, oblivious to the world about her. Miriam had no doubt that should the Franks besiege the city again, Rebecca would slumber through the devastation and horror like a baby in its cradle. She would be spared the worst of it, tucked away in a world of soft dreams and gentle memories. And for that, Miriam was eternally grateful.

She should have left them to sleep in peace and returned to her bed, but Miriam was reluctant to go. She enjoyed seeing them together, for in truth she envied them. They had a bond that was deep, unbreakable. She had never experienced such a connection with another human being.

Not until she had met Saladin.

Since their stolen moment in the garden, she had only seen the Sultan in court, and never again in private. But he had quietly sent Miriam personal notes, delivered daily by one of his grim-faced bodyguards. They were rarely more than a few lines, and never contained any words that revealed his feelings. Usually his letters were simply comments on the day's events, stories from his life at the court, sometimes humorous, sometimes grim. Little anecdotes that detailed how the world appeared to him from the high perch of the throne. To any casual reader (or spy who might intercept the notes), they would seem to be minor musings about Jerusalem politics and the foibles of high society.

But Miriam knew these notes were more than they appeared. They were the most powerful symbol of the Sultan's feelings for her. Saladin was a deeply private man who had created a veil of mystery around his innermost thoughts, one that would be lifted only for those whom he trusted above all others. She could imagine him sharing his personal perceptions with only a few. His brother, al-Adil. His vizier, Qadi al-Fadil. Her uncle. And, in days long past, perhaps his wife, the Sultana.

Yasmeen. Miriam had seen her in passing only a few times in the court. The Sultana was usually present at important events of ceremony, such as a banquet in honor of the caliph's new ambassador to Jerusalem. Her face would always be covered by a silk veil that hid her famed beauty from the world. It was impossible to see Yasmeen's eyes clearly through the translucent screen, but each time Miriam had been in a room with Saladin's consort, she was certain that the Sultana's eyes were always on her. And she could feel the anger, the hate that lay beneath them.

Miriam forced the thought out of her mind. She left her uncle's room and walked slowly toward the kitchen to pour a glass of water. Her throat felt like it had been exposed to the raw sands of the Sinai desert that she had crossed as a child. The desert that had consumed her innocence and had revealed to her the true evil that hid behind the Cross. An evil that even now was gathering its forces for another attack.

Word had already come of the Frankish victory in Cyprus. With the fall of Isaac Comnenus and the subjugation of the Byzantines, the Crusaders were sailing to the Palestine coast. The barbarian hordes would set their feet on the sacred soil of Abraham's kingdom any day now. Her uncle had begged her to flee to Cairo, to save herself from this new danger. But she had refused. If the armies of Christ entered Jerusalem again, she would stand by the side of the people she loved.

Her uncle. Her aunt. And her sultan.

She put back the glass and returned to her small room. As she climbed back into bed, Miriam remembered flashes from her nightmare and shuddered. It had been so vivid, so real. It was as if she had been transported through time to witness the conquest of Jerusalem a century before, much as Muslims believed Muhammad had been transported on his Night Journey through the Heavens, where time and space lost all meaning.

But why? Her uncle might have said that she had been shown a vision from God. She was not sure if she believed in such things. But if dreams were indeed messages from a higher realm, what was the purpose of her vision? To prepare her for what was to come? Or to show Miriam that such evil could not, would not, be allowed to be repeated? Somehow, considering the miserable history of her people, she doubted it was the latter.

As she fell back into slumber, another image flashed through her mind. A vision of the Sultana watching her from across the throne room. As she slipped into another troubled dream, she saw Yasmeen raise her veil. For a second Miriam glimpsed the Sultana's face. But instead of the statuesque beauty of rumor, she saw a terrifying visage of an old crone, wrinkled and decrepit, smiling hungrily at her.

It was the face of death.

21

The supply vessel was trapped in a curtain of thick fog that billowed up from the sea. Like the angry breath of the mythic serpent that was rumored to encircle the world, the fog carried a warning: Turn back, foolish sailors, before you cross into realms from which terrors are spun. Samir ibn Arif had heard all the legends, from the fanciful tales of Sinbad's battles with sea monsters to the rumors of great lands beyond the western horizon where gold flowed like honey. He dismissed most of the stories as tall tales. But as he gazed out into the impenetrable clouds before him—the Devil's Mist, as his sailors called it—he wondered if some of the ancient warnings did not indeed have a basis in truth.

Samir was captain of the *Nur al-Bahr*, the Light of the River, a name that he wished was based on literal fact right now. His men stood on the deck of the fifty-foot-long galley, built from the finest cedars of Lebanon, holding lamps out as if they were offerings to the spirits that haunted the sea.

Samir wished for the thousandth time that he had not agreed to undertake this foolhardy venture. He was not a military man, nor was his ship equipped to fight a sea battle. Which is exactly why the Sultan's representative in Alexandria had commissioned the *Nur al-Bahr* to carry a clandestine payload of weapons past the small Frankish enclaves that remained in place on the northern coast of Palestine. Based just outside the beleaguered city of Acre, the Christian raiders were the last remnants of the former kingdom of Jerusalem. They were fanatics and madmen, willing to die en masse before they would give up the final Christian stronghold in the Holy Land. While Saladin had subdued the rest of the coast over the past year, the battles he had fought with the hardy Crusader regiment outside Acre proved inconclusive. The Sultan was rumored to be planning a full-scale offensive to wipe out these irritating leftovers of the previous regime, but news of a new Crusade had forced him to turn his attention elsewhere. Left alone for the time being, the Franks at Acre grew bolder, and had pirated two supply vessels in the past six weeks, forcing Saladin to come up with an alternative stratagem for keeping weapons flowing between his armies in Egypt and Jerusalem.

Samir was not convinced by the oily viceroy's promises that his ship would be ignored by the Franks because of its clearly commercial markings and design. But the Sultan's agent had offered him a fortune in gold dinars, enough to pay off the debt he had inherited from his father, a jovial, good-hearted fellow who had nonetheless been a terrible businessman. And he would have enough left over to secure a marriage with Sanaa, his childhood love. So he had agreed to this mad plan.

In order to disguise the vessel, its distinctive triangular sails, the *lateen* used exclusively by Muslim ships, were replaced by the square cloth used by Byzantine trading vessels, and a green-and-gold Cypriot flag was hoisted on the mainmast. The men discarded their turbans and distinctive Arab pantaloons for the oversize baggy trousers worn by sailors from the north. The holds below, normally filled with a bazaar of household goods ranging from Persian carpets to ivory utensils imported from Abyssinia, were now crammed with a vast array of weapons: razor-sharp scimitars, javelins longer than most men stood tall, suits of lamellar armor held together by small metal plates, oak bows and quivers filled with black-feathered arrows, axes that could cut through a human skull as easily as a knife through bread.

The Sultan's spy, a tiny Syrian with a long, curling mustache, had joked with him that, should the Franks actually decide to attack his ship, he would have all the resources necessary to defend himself. Samir did not appreciate the humor, but would not have dared say so to the little man. He knew enough about the machinations of the state to realize that this seemingly inconsequential fellow was a highly trained killer, chosen for his unremarkable appearance to serve the Sultan on the most important matters of espionage. Samir knew Saladin's reputation for honor and mercy toward his subjects, but he was not willing to test how far this philosophy had been accepted by those trained to do the Sultan's dirty work.

The first two nights of the voyage had been uneventful, the sea calm, a favorable wind guiding them toward the coast of Palestine at a healthy clip. Then, on the morning of the second day, he had been forced awake by the desperate clanging of the warning bell. Samir had run to the deck clad only in his nightshirt, a small sword gripped in his trembling hand. His first mate, Khalil ibn Musa, a freed slave from the Horn of Africa, stood by the bell, pointing a long finger to the horizon. A schooner was bearing down on them, a crimson flag fluttering from its single mast.

It was a Frankish patrol boat with probably no more than twenty armed men on board, but Samir knew that others would not be far behind. The Franks had learned from the Muslims how to use pigeons to carry messages from ship to shore, and the threat had to be neutralized before the Crusaders managed to inform their comrades in Acre.

Before he had departed, his beloved Sanaa had suggested a preposterous ruse for use in such a situation as he now faced. She had bitterly opposed his decision to get involved in a military venture, but once it became clear that his mind was set, Sanaa had made him promise to take on board a pen of pigs, to let loose on the deck if he came close to a Frankish vessel. Samir hated the disgusting animals, unclean before Allah, and his men had grumbled that their presence on the ship was a sin that would hold back the protection of the angels. But he had understood the reason. No Muslim ship would ever carry such vile cargo, and the sight of pigs on the deck could provide the cover necessary to deflect the attention of the simpleminded Franks.

Samir had signaled to the broad-shouldered Khalil to let the unclean animals loose from their pens. The monstrous, dirty creatures ran squealing over the main deck, and Samir had to hold back a retch as one of the pigs brushed up against him, defecating against his foot. But, remarkably, Sanaa's plan had worked. The schooner had come within a hundred feet of the merchant vessel, and he could see a sentry scanning their ship from atop its sole mast. The Frank apparently had a viewing lens, probably a prize from one of Saladin's supply ships that had been seized a few weeks before, and when he saw the pigs on the deck, he signaled to his men below. The schooner slowed and shifted direction, apparently satisfied that the galley was a trading vessel headed north toward Byzantium. Samir's terrified crew had breathed a collective sigh of relief as the schooner went on its way, and then grumbled loudly at the task of capturing the escaped pigs that were wreaking havoc all over the deck.

Then, on the fourth night, as they crept northward near the perilous rocks that signaled the border of Palestine and Lebanon, the temperature had dropped precipitously and the sea was soon covered by a chilly, dense fog. Samir felt as if the rain clouds themselves had descended on the ship, and the weak visibility had forced him to order the rowers on the lowest deck to stop, slowing his vessel to a worm's pace in the oddly windless night. The men on deck with the lanterns were unable to pierce the heavy veil that covered them, but he hoped that slivers of illumination would seep through and be enough to warn off any other vessels caught in the Devil's Mist. A collision this far from shore, and under such adverse weather, would be catastrophic.

His first mate strode up to Samir as he stood by the ship's now useless steering wheel. Khalil was fifteen years older than his captain, but looked at least twice that. From what little he had said of his past, Samir knew that Khalil had endured a difficult life. A farm boy in Yemen, he had been captured on a bandit raid in which much of his village died. Tall and strong for his age, Khalil had been sold into slavery to a merchant who sailed regularly between the Horn of Africa and India on spice runs. Samir, whose travels had not gone much beyond the trading posts of the eastern Mediterranean, was always fascinated by Khalil's tales of his adventures in India. Tigers and elephants abounded in these stories, as did a host of beauties that the man claimed to have bedded along the way.

Khalil's fortunes changed yet again after his trading vessel had been shipwrecked off the coast of Ceylon some seven years earlier. While Khalil, who was an excellent swimmer, could have used the capsizing as his moment to escape, as other slaves did, he had rescued his owner from the stormy sea and pulled him to safety. Grateful for his loyalty, his master had set Khalil free and given him enough gold to start a new life. The wiry-haired Yemeni had traveled to Alexandria, where he had fallen in with Samir's father, who had made him a steward on the *Nur al-Bahr*.

"The men are grumbling that the djinn have set loose this foul weather upon us," Khalil said, spitting some orange betel juice on to the deck. "Fools." Khalil was a man with little patience for fairy tales. He had lived a hard life and survived by accepting reality and molding it to his benefit.

"Do not dismiss their superstitions so quickly, my friend," Samir said, resting a hand on the older man's sinewy shoulders. "My stomach tells me that there is something evil lurking in this fog."

Samir turned to stare out again into the mist, as if willing the curtains to part and reveal the secret horror they had been hiding. Then the sea itself complied and Samir's worst nightmare came true.

Like a hawk thundering toward its prey, the bow of a massive Crusader *dromon* burst through the mist no more than fifty feet ahead. The vessel was on a direct course for the *Nur al-Bahr*. Samir heard the bronze warning bell go off on his deck, its frantic peals mixing with the shouts of terror from his sailors. But the military craft did not slow down.

"May Allah have mercy upon us," Samir said, feeling a wave of nausea rise up from his gut and tickle his throat. Khalil immediately ran to grab his sword, cursing at the terrified sailors to arm themselves and defend the ship. But Samir did not move. He knew that the end was at hand. The young man marveled at how, when death finally looms, stark and inescapable, the mind wanders to the small things of life that he would never have a chance to experience again. The spring blooms lining the walkways outside his house in Alexandria. The arguments of children jousting with wooden swords in the local park as to who should be the evil Frank this time. The smell of his mother's spinach pie wafting from the kitchen as the sun set, bringing the daily fast of Ramadan to a close. The taste of Sanaa's lips, moist and sweet like wild berries, trembling against his.

Sanaa. He realized that he would never have a chance to hold her in his arms, to make love to that sweet, lithe body he had fantasized about since he was a boy. To watch over a child in its crib, the fruit of their passion. Sanaa had been such a proper girl, refusing to even hold hands with him until their engagement was formally announced. She had wavered the night before he left on this mad voyage, and he would treasure that one sweet kiss as he traveled over the Sirat, the bridge into the afterlife. Although those who were slain in *jihad* were guaranteed seventy virgins to initiate in the arts of love, he made a silent promise to his soul to wait for Sanaa, even if it was until the Day of Resurrection.

A sharp memory of her face, its perfect angles and contours, filled his inner eye, even as a flaming arrow shot across the sea and struck him square in the chest.

22

Richard watched with delight from his command deck on the *dromon* as his archers let loose a volley of flaming arrows at the merchant ship less than thirty feet away. The king covered his ears instinctively as several of the men loaded a long tube at the bow of the ship. A roar like thunder echoed across the water as the Crusaders let loose their infamous "Greek fire." A line of blue flame exploded outward and struck the smaller vessel's sail, instantly turning it into a fiery ruin and consuming its forged Cypriot standards.

Richard's fleet was less than a mile from the coast of Palestine, and he knew that any vessel in the vicinity belonged either to the Saracens or their allies. While this ship carried the flag of Cyprus, he had spent enough time on the wretched island to recognize that its design was substantially different from other Byzantine merchant vessels. And a quick look at the swarthy sailors running for desperate cover from the Crusader onslaught was enough confirmation that, whoever these men were, they were aliens to his people and thus lawful targets.

Small fires were spreading across the merchant ship as the *dromon* pulled up alongside, but Richard noted how the infidels had covered much of the deck with raw hides that appeared to be deflecting most of his naphtha-covered arrows, and even the sparks from the Greek fire. He would order his men to bring him some of this material—the Saracens clearly had some unusual defenses that needed to be examined more closely.

Richard raised his right hand as a signal, and a wave of his soldiers swung on ropes across the divide. Within moments, they were on board, engaged in hand-to-hand combat with the unlucky sailors who had been the first to greet Richard's arrival in the waters of the Holy Land.

The king saw his armed warriors on the deck of the enemy ship slicing through the sailors, most of whom had stopped trying to fight and were on their knees, begging for mercy. But Richard had instructed that no quarter be given—he had neither the resources nor the patience to deal with prisoners of war at this stage of the campaign.

The merchant ship began to heave as rowers on the bottom deck frantically returned to their task, hoping to escape the looming behemoth. Seeing the stationary vessel starting to move away, Richard turned to shout across the deck at William.

"Release the divers!" Richard's voice was barely audible against the screams of the naval battle, but William nodded his comprehension. The knight stood next to a group of Richard's finest sailors, all of whom had stripped down to their undergarments. These men were holding long, thick ropes, and at William's signal, they jumped two by two into the Mediterranean.

Richard had developed the strategy some days earlier when they were speaking of possible ways to cripple any Saracen ships they came across without sinking the valuable vessels. The divers would swim underneath the enemy ship and tie the rudder, disabling its steering in such a fashion as to moor it temporarily. Once the battle was over, the ties could be released and the ship could be drafted for use by the Crusader fleet. It was an ingenious idea, but highly risky. If the Muslim ship gained speed or made any rapid change of course under battle conditions, the divers would likely be crushed to death under the lash of the shifting rudder. William had not been convinced of the wisdom of the idea, but he had bowed to his king's will. His knights had learned from practical experience that Richard's intuition and creativity in the game of war bordered on genius, and it was best to trust that his eyes could see farther than theirs.

The supply vessel that had fortuitously crossed their path tonight provided a perfect opportunity to test the plan. Richard peered into the depths, but could see no sign of his divers in the churning sea below. His friend William sighed, resigning himself to losing a cadre of good sailors to the king's mad plan. Richard held out for minutes that seemed to stretch into eternity. Finally, the king raised his hand in frustration, ready to signal the grubby Saxon at the steering wheel of his command vessel to pursue the escaping galley, when the merchant vessel lurched and shuddered. He saw the Saracen rowers desperately trying to push it forward, but the ship began to turn helplessly in the water. A smile spread across Richard's lips as he saw his divers resurface and swim toward the *dromon* as their comrades on the command deck waved to them in congratulation. It had worked. And his reputation as a miracle worker in the storm of war had been proven yet again in the eyes of his men.

The first sea battle of the Crusade was effectively over. Richard hoped that the rest of the war would proceed as smoothly, but in his heart he knew that Saladin was not a foe as easily overcome as a group of wayward sailors lost in the mist.

— ◆ —

THE RISING SUN CUT through the mist like a fiery dagger. Richard stood on his command deck and breathed in the crisp morning air, still acrid with the fumes of burning wood and flesh. The rout of the Saracen supply ship had been a greater victory than he had initially imagined. When his soldiers broke open the heavily locked hold, they had been stunned to discover a vast array of Egyptian weapons, clearly on their way to buttress Saladin's troops in the Holy Land. What had begun as little more than a training exercise meant to rehearse his soldiers for the long war ahead had turned into a magnificent plunder of his adversaries' resources.

As Richard watched the crimson disk of the morning sun float above the green hills of Palestine that dotted the horizon, he felt a deep swell of emotion in his breast. Although he had never been to the Holy Land, he felt just like Odysseus returning to Ithaca after an eternity in exile. More now than ever, he knew that this Crusade was his destiny, the adventure that would forever be inscribed alongside his name in the annals of history.

He felt, rather than saw, William come up next to him, and he turned to face his favorite knight.

"The men have finally spilled heathen blood," the king said. "Are you satisfied?"

William shrugged noncommittally.

"I take no satisfaction in war. It is a duty, not a passion."

Richard snorted and decided to change the subject lest his friend begin preaching again.

"Were we able to recover any of the Saracens' weapons before the ship sank?" Even though he had commanded his soldiers to capture the vessel intact, the infidel sailors had decided to flood its hull when it became clear that they would be unable to escape.

"A few swords, spears, and the like. We have distributed the Saracens' weapons among the soldiers of the command ships, sire," William said in his usual straightforward tone. "And the infidel sailors have been executed, all save one."

"Why was he spared?" Richard asked in a bored voice, turning back to gaze at the shoreline, which was rapidly becoming more distinct. He could see the foamy swells as the waves crashed on barrier reefs only a thousand feet away now.

"He was the first mate of the vessel," William said, following his master's gaze out toward their destination. "Apparently he speaks some French as well as Arabic. He may be a useful translator."

Richard considered this for a moment. He knew that the language barrier would be a critical issue when he eventually came into contact with Muslim forces. And demanded their surrender.

"Can we trust him?" The last thing Richard needed was a Muslim captive providing him false information under the guise of linguistic services.

"The first officer has sworn on Allah that he will provide us faithful service in return for sparing his life."

Richard laughed.

"Oaths on false gods hold little weight in this world or the next," the king said.

"I have found that the issue is not whether the oath taker's god is real, my lord, but that he believes in it." William's voice was still patient, although Richard sensed his knight's exasperation with his master's cynicism.

The white sands of the coast were sparkling under the sun. Richard could see a large tent city set up near the shore. Crimson flags with golden crosses flew atop the main pavilions. Ah, so the lucky bastards were still there.

"It appears that our brothers remain in control of the northern coast," Richard said with much delight. He had heard that a few Frankish knights had managed to survive Saladin's invasion and had holed themselves in an encampment outside Acre, but he had not given much credence to the reports. From the size of the sprawling compound, however, it appeared that a significant remnant of King Guy's forces had indeed escaped. If he had any lingering doubts about a swift victory, they vanished. With these forces, accustomed to fighting the Saracens on this terrain, combined with his own army, Saladin would be swept away into the dustbin of history. Assuming, of course, that these stalwart Franks accepted his leadership and vision and did not return to the petty infighting that had brought about the defeat of King Guy.

William seemed to be thinking similar thoughts.

"I will prepare a landing party and find out who is in charge," the knight said. "And gauge their willingness to cooperate with our forces."

He turned to walk away when Richard put a hand on his shoulder to stop him.

"These men have lived near the barbarians for years. They undoubtedly have sufficient translators," the king said.

William nodded.

"Then I will have the prisoner put to death," he said, his voice carrying just a slight hint of regret.

"Not just yet," Richard replied. "While I do not trust a Saracen to serve as an accurate go-between with Saladin, I do not know our brothers on the shore any better. You may keep the first mate alive and take lessons in their tongue if you so wish. I would prefer that my commanders be able to converse with the infidels directly if the occasion so arises."

William smiled at his lord's magnanimity. The ship shuddered as the anchors were let loose to prevent collision with the barrier reefs. Richard and William saw that the beach was covered with surprised soldiers, staring out at the incredible war fleet sent by God to their rescue. Some fell on their knees and wept; others just stood, their hands raised in prayers of gratitude. It was indeed a stirring moment.

As word spread through the beleaguered camp of the miraculous arrival of ships from the west, a cascade of trumpets and horns sounded from the beach, welcoming the victorious king and his legions into the alliance that was now sure to wrest control of Jerusalem from the infidels.

"The Holy Land awaits my king," William said. "You have fulfilled your vow to your father."

At the mention of Henry, Richard felt a cloud blot out the growing warmth in his heart.

"Not yet," he said, his smile fading. "When I hold Saladin's head in my hands."

23

Conrad of Montferrat, heir to the fallen kingdom of Jerusalem, gazed at the vast fleet that stretched out toward the western horizon with conflicting emotions. The rumors of his brothers in Europe gathering their finest troops together for a new Crusade had inspired desperately needed hope in his beleaguered troops for months. But now that they had arrived, a force far greater than he could have ever imagined, on hundreds of vessels carrying the flags of all the great nations of the papacy, he felt a chill go through his heart. An invasion of this scale had clearly been orchestrated by men of great valor and political skill. Such leaders, Conrad knew, had ambitions that rarely respected the rights of those in whose defense they claimed to serve.

Conrad could not, of course, reveal such misgivings to his men, who were rejoicing at the miracle that God had wrought in their darkest hour. For nearly two years, these dedicated warriors, the last remnant of the Frankish army that Saladin had destroyed at Hattin, had stood their ground against overwhelming odds. The infidels had pushed them relentlessly from the heart of Palestine to the very edges of the sea. His initial force, almost fifteen thousand strong, had been reduced by a third in that time, a result of starvation, disease, and the countless skirmishes that the Saracen hordes inflicted on them. Those who stood by him now were the most dedicated and hearty warriors of Christ, but Conrad knew that it was only a matter of time before the combined forces of Egypt and Syria would descend on their camp outside Acre, erasing the last memory of Christian rule over Palestine.

So the arrival of the western forces were seen by his exhausted soldiers as manna sent from Heaven. Twenty thousand men, dressed in the finest armor and bearing the latest weapons of France and Italy—an army of angels rising from the sea to reclaim the Holy Land for its rightful Christian king, Conrad of Montferrat. The nobleman knew that most of his fervently loyal men had not considered the possibility that the commanders of this wondrous rescuing force might have their own ideas as to who should retain that title.

Conrad rubbed the scar on his left cheek, as he often did when he was lost in thought. The jagged red line stretched from just underneath his eye to an inch above his lips, as if he had wept so hard one day that the tears had cut a permanent gash in his face. His men had spread many stories of his courage in battle against the infidels, and everyone assumed that he had earned that scar on a brave escapade against a mighty foe. The truth was a little more embarrassing, so he made no effort to contradict people's assumptions.

The King of Jerusalem stepped out of his worn command tent, its crimson trappings dulled by the ravages of the sun and wind to a ruddy hue. His base of operations was no longer a majestic ceremonial pavilion that was unfurled only in times of battle. For battle was no longer a momentous event that defined a brief but glorious moment in a young man's life. It had become the steady, dreary monotony of daily existence.

He found himself reaching inside his pocket and pulling out a jade necklace that he often fingered when he was deep in thought. An octagonal charm hung from the end of a series of sparkling beads. Had anyone bothered to look closely, they would have been startled to see a series of Hebrew letters etched into the jade. It was a souvenir from many years past, torn from the neck of a woman who had the honor of being the first infidel he had personally slain upon arriving in the Holy Land. She had been a beautiful, red-haired lady who had the misfortune of being caught in a Crusader raid on a caravan traveling on the outskirts of Sinai. That adventure had been a rite of passage, and he had kept the charm over the years to remind him of his sacred purpose—to cleanse the Holy Land of the pagan mongrels and their Christ-killing allies. The scar on his face was a more unfortunate souvenir of that day's events, but it also served as a necessary reminder of the price a believer must pay for the glory of victory.

Walking through the smoke-filled camp, the muddy earth covered in mounds of refuse and human excrement, Conrad ran a hand through his prematurely graying curls and remembered what brought him to these shores. The Lord of Montferrat had been raised in the finest palaces of Italy, his every whim catered to, the buxom maids in his father's castle ever ready and willing to scratch the itch in his loins. But a life filled with abundance inevitably satiates with boredom, giving rise to a youthful desire for freedom and adventure.

Against his father's passionate admonitions, or perhaps because of them, Conrad had left the shadowed groves of the manor and embarked on a quest to join his kinsmen in Palestine. Driven by dreams of conquest and glorious war against the infidels, the young Marquis of Montferrat had arrived in Jerusalem after cutting his teeth in minor battles between his Christian brothers in Byzantium and the Turkish hordes that encroached on their lands. He had been horrified to see the ennui and defeatism of the failing regime under King Baldwin and Guy of Lusignan. Instead of a life filled with heroic deeds against the barbarian hordes, Conrad had found that the only wars his fellow nobles interested in fighting were among themselves.

As a visiting nobleman, the marquis made the rounds of the distinguished families and quickly deduced the extent of the deteriorating political situation. Conrad had realized that most of the feuding nobles of Jerusalem were incompetent and a liability to the state's survival. Only Reginald of Kerak had the strength of will and the focused determination to stand up to the growing Muslim threat. Conrad had readily allied himself with the proud knight, despite warnings from King Baldwin and the distrust of the petty lords, and had even participated in some of his brave raids against the infidel caravans. It was on the first of these expeditions with Reginald that he had earned the scar on his face, although it was not by the hands of someone he would have deemed a worthy opponent.

Pushing that embarrassing memory from his mind, Conrad reflected on his alliance with the Lord of Kerak. He had known that Reginald's supporters were few, especially after his daring attack on Mecca and Medina, but Conrad had ignored the opinions of the naysayers in the court. The high families of Jerusalem could not appreciate Reginald's passion and commitment, did not realize that only a consistent show of strength and courage would hold back the infidel hordes. Frustrated by the constant infighting among the nobles, Conrad had seen the disaster coming long before his rivals in the court. And he had made preparations for a day that he had hoped would never come, but appeared to be inevitable.

As Conrad stepped over a dead rat covered in ants and walked proudly to greet the newcomers on the beach, he reflected on how much his life had changed in so short a time. The nobleman had spent the better part of the past decade watching his status degenerate from that of a pampered aristocrat lounging in the manors of Jerusalem to a desperate refugee leading a ragtag band of warriors surviving under the most primitive conditions. How he missed the warmth of his feathered bed, safe behind impenetrable stone walls, with the scent of lilacs bathing the warm summer breeze! Now he could smell only the rot of death and decay. The camp fever had recently subsided after killing another seventy men, but the odor of their disease-ravaged corpses still hung over the military settlement like a rank cloud.

With the fall of the kingdom of Jerusalem and the capture of King Guy, the surviving nobles had surrendered to Saladin in exchange for safe passage out of Palestine. The Sultan had been more than happy to let them go, realizing that executing his prominent captives would create martyrs and bring immediate retaliation from their families in Europe. Exile of the principal families whose machinations had brought down the Crusader government would be far more effective in quelling any residual resistance among the Christian population of Jerusalem. With their entire leadership rapidly fleeing to the safety of their ancestral homes in the west, the Christian masses would have no effective rallying point around which to organize resistance to the Muslim occupation.

Conrad had been one of the lucky ones. He had been on a diplomatic mission to Byzantium when Jerusalem fell. Word had not yet reached Constantinople of Guy's defeat at Hattin when he embarked on a pilgrim ship heading for Acre. Conrad would never forget the eerie silence that greeted the small vessel, teeming with awestruck Greeks who had spent their life savings for the journey to the Holy City, as it pulled into the abandoned port. There were no bells to greet them, no signs of human activity at all. He had disembarked with a terrible premonition that his life would never be the same again. A Saracen knight finally sauntered up to greet the new arrivals, who he had assumed were friendly traders because of the ship's neutral Cypriot flag. Conrad had been stunned to see the turbaned infidel walking unmolested on the beach, and he realized what had happened. Going along with the foolish Arab's misapprehension of his identity, he was able to garner the truth. Palestine had fallen and King Guy was imprisoned in Damascus. Jerusalem was then still under siege, but the infidel had boasted confidently that it would fall in a fortnight. That left only the Lebanese Christian stronghold of Tyre free of Saladin's dominion.

Perhaps it was something in Conrad's demeanor, perhaps he had failed to mask his true horror at the news, but the curly-bearded soldier became suspicious and eventually sounded the alarm against the "merchant" vessel. Conrad had only barely managed to return to the ship alive, ordering the stunned captain to fly toward Tyre before they were caught and enslaved by the infidels who had overrun the Holy Land.

Conrad's arrival at Tyre had been the beginning of a long, painful campaign to reverse the devastating loss his people had suffered at the hands of the unbelievers. The marquis had refused to accept the ignominy of defeat and expulsion. Outraged by Saladin's brutal murder of his friend Reginald, he had vowed revenge. But the exhausted commanders at Tyre were despairing and beginning preparations for surrender of the city to the Muslims. Realizing that his people needed a new rallying point, a new leader to inspire them, Conrad had forcibly married Isabella, sister of Sibylla, wife of the deposed King Guy. With his blood ties to the throne secured, Conrad proclaimed himself the new King of Jerusalem, giving the men a desperately needed symbol that the tide would turn.

And for a time, it had. Conrad had inspired the surviving Crusader troops to hold off a prolonged siege of Tyre by Saladin's army. When the unforgiving winter set in and Saladin was forced to break the siege, Conrad had mounted a daring expedition to retake Acre. And there he had found himself trapped between the unrelenting forces of the Sultan's nephew Taqi al-Din and the bottomless sea.

Battle after battle, defeat after defeat, had worn down his men. Conrad knew that the grumbling had begun, and he needed to boost the bleeding morale in his company before his titular kingship ended in bloody revolt.

So the arrival of the Frankish army should have been exactly the salve needed to heal the wounded hopes of his men. But when he had been wakened that morning by his nervous, jabbering page and led out to the beach to behold the stunning array of battleships crowded into the harbor, he had felt a blanket of dread come upon him. He could not shake the feeling that this new batch of Crusaders were neither saviors nor allies, but conquerors for whom the claims of a single noble weighed little against the ambitions of their own commander.

As he left the camp behind him and strode on the gray sands of the beach, the King of Jerusalem saw this commander at last. Richard's rowboat had just docked, carrying the Angevin king and his general, William Chinon, whom Conrad had met earlier in the morning as part of an advance delegation. Richard stepped confidently onto the soil of the Holy Land. Conrad had not seen the boy in a decade, not since his last visit to the court in London on an errand for his father. Richard had been an impetuous youth who hardly seemed fit to succeed the stately King Henry. Indeed, as he recalled, the old man had spoken quite openly about his weariness with his son's immature antics. Conrad wondered how much the young king, upon whose shoulders his fate now rested, had changed over the years. If at all.

Well, the boy's flair for drama remained evident. Richard knelt briefly and scooped up a handful of sand, kissing it dramatically, as his courtiers followed suit. Ah, such reverence for the Holy Land, Conrad thought grimly. The welcome home of Christians that played such a mythic role in the children's stories of Europe. Conrad wondered how long it would take for this cub to learn the dark truth, that this land was neither holy nor welcome, least of all to Christians.

Conrad lifted his head, trying to maintain a sense of dignity as he walked toward the new arrivals, but he was painfully aware of his stained and torn cloak, and its marked contrast to the flawless silk mantle that adorned Richard's shoulders. He saw that the other man had noticed the difference as well, and smirked. Bastard.

Conrad's page, the skeletally thin Jean Coudert, stepped forward in accordance with protocol, bowing low to the king. Conrad knew that, according to the code of aristocracy, Richard was an equal to himself. But it was clear to everyone present that, in practical reality, Richard was the greater of the two men. For now.

"Lord Richard, may I present King Conrad of Jerusalem, Lord of Montferrat and envoy of the Vicar of Christ to the Holy Land." Coudert spoke in his usual florid French, his voice trembling with practiced humility. But Richard did not bother to look at the page, or at Conrad. He turned his head to his left, then to his right, his eyes following the excited activity of Conrad's men as they scurried from the tents to catch a glimpse of their golden savior.

Richard's gaze traveled from the unkempt soldiers clad in muddy hauberks to the line of military tents that covered the beach and extended a thousand feet inland, toward the rocky hills that served as the de facto border between Frankish and infidel territory. In the distance, the stone towers of Acre were gleaming under the noon sun; emerald flags emblazoned with the hated gold crescent of the Muslim army fluttered from their turrets. The flowing standards were a constant and painful reminder to Conrad and his men of their failure to wrest the fortress from the Saracens and their humiliating existence as refugees in their own land.

It was a symbol that was not lost on the newly arrived king either. Richard shook his head and sighed, like a father expressing his disappointment with an incompetent son. The subtle contempt filled Conrad with hot rage. Then the King of England extended his hand toward the King of Jerusalem.

"I am impressed with your camp, Lord Conrad, and even more impressed to see that the fallen kingdom of Jerusalem still retains a claimant to the throne," he said, grasping Conrad's reluctant hand firmly at the wrist. "How long have you held sway against the Saracens?" His mocking tone suggested incredulity that this motley band had survived at all in the face of Saladin's invasion, much less under Conrad's leadership.

Conrad forced himself to take a deep breath before responding to the arrogant youth. He knew that his men were watching and were expecting him to form an alliance with the newcomers. He also knew that he had to restrain his anger, as he would likely be dead if he kindled Richard's. The young regent's brutal reputation had crossed the sea well in advance of his arrival.

"Eighteen months," Conrad said, swelling his chest with pride. Yes, it was a miracle they had lasted this long, with the land infested by Saladin's hordes and their backs trapped against the sea. But their endurance was a sign of his men's courage and tenacity, and he wanted to make sure this newcomer understood that he was in the company of the bravest soldiers in Christendom. "The infidels control the cities, but we retain the coast. My forces number only ten thousand, but we have held back the Saracens despite their vastly superior numbers."

Richard was looking straight into Conrad's eyes, unblinking, like an eagle staring at its prey from afar. Then he spoke loudly, as if to ensure that his words carried to the ears of Conrad's men gathering nearby.

"Impressive. These soldiers are clearly lions among men. They will serve as valued members of my army." Conrad heard the appreciative murmurs from the awed soldiers behind him, and knew with growing irritation that Richard was playing to the crowd and seeking to assert his authority over his men.

"They are indeed valiant, and I am proud to have such men serve under me, like the heroes who defended Charles Martel at Tours-Poitiers," Conrad said, matching Richard's loud voice. He knew he was stretching quite a bit in comparing himself to the Hammer of God, who had successful blocked the Muslim invasion of France four hundred years earlier. But he would be damned if he let this boy assume control of his army with little more than a crafty speech.

Richard smiled, but there was no good humor or friendship in his expression.

"Martel succeeded in driving the infidels from the heart of Christendom, not trapping his men against the sea," he said.

Conrad flushed, struggling to control his rage.

"A temporary setback," he said, without as much conviction as he would have liked. "But with your support, I do not doubt that I shall drive the idolaters out of our lands."

Richard scratched his cheek and looked away casually, as if already bored with the conversation.

"If you and your master, Guy, had held Jerusalem, you would not have needed my support."

Conrad felt a vein throb in his temple.

"Guy was a sniveling fool," he said. "You will find that I will be a true king in accordance with my family's divine right."

Richard stepped forward, his face close to Conrad's, his eyes focused on the older man with lethal intensity.

"Kings are made by deed, Conrad, not words. Even God's."

Conrad's temper was threatening to boil over, when he remembered. The cold blue eyes in which he was gazing belonged to the same errant boy he had seen regularly shamed by King Henry's tongue.

"That is very profound, Richard," he said, a cold smile playing on his lips. "I remember your father saying something like that to you. More than once, if I recall. And less tenderly."

Richard's controlled façade fell for a second and Conrad saw his true face, that of the ruthless killer, flash across his chiseled features. He knew his words had penetrated the underbelly of the dragon. And Conrad wondered whether his reign as the nominal King of Jerusalem was about to come to a swift end under the vengeful blade of an insulted monarch.

And then the spoiled, petulant child vanished, replaced again by the image of a calm, collected statesmen. Richard turned away from Conrad as if he had wasted enough time conversing with someone who was little more than a self-appointed king. He faced Conrad's trembling page, who had witnessed the tense confrontation between thrones with barely concealed terror.

"Bring me your best herald, one conversant in the tongue of the heathens," Richard said. "I have a message to send to the infidel Saladin."

Turning to William, who had stood by passively during the heated exchange, Richard lowered his voice, but Conrad still caught his words.

"You will accompany the herald," the king said. "And bring along that captured sailor to confirm what he claims is said. I want you to be privy to every word spoken in the company of the infidels."

Conrad stepped forward to protest. It was an insult to suggest that his heralds would mistranslate or conceal anything from their Christian brothers. But something in Richard's cold gaze made him hold back. Arrogant and brash, the Lionheart was nonetheless Conrad's last and only hope. He needed this man's help for the time being. Richard glanced back at Conrad as if he were an afterthought.

"My men are weary from a long and arduous journey," he said. "Perhaps you would be kind enough to arrange a feast to welcome your brothers to the Holy Land."

Then, without waiting for an answer, Richard walked toward the crowd of curious onlookers, who reached out their hands to him in excitement.

"It would be my honor," Conrad rasped as he watched Richard embrace his men as if they were his own. Conrad saw the light of joy in their eyes, as if the Lionheart were Christ Himself come to lead them to victory and Paradise. All their attention was on the valiant newcomer in the splendid crimson mantle. Conrad, their sole commander during the darkest days of the war, had been forgotten in an instant.

Conrad walked slowly back toward the camp. *His* camp. As he gazed at the torn and weathered tents that billowed around him in the sea breeze, he forced himself to regain control of his emotions. Yes, he needed the Lionheart for now. But when Saladin was defeated, there would be more than enough time to arrange for the boy king to meet an unfortunate accident.

24

Maimonides looked with trepidation at the three men dispatched by the king known as the Lionheart, whose ships had been first spotted off the coast of Palestine four nights before. Al-Adil's spies had reported over two hundred ships descending on the northern beaches, with between fifteen and twenty-five thousand men disembarking to join their beleaguered colleagues outside Acre. In the past few days, the Sultan had sent criers to every town in the Holy Land, summoning every able-bodied believer to join the army, but it would be weeks before the Muslim forces would be ready to face the invaders. And order in the region was rapidly breaking down already. The dull blanket of nervous expectation that had covered Jerusalem over the past several months now erupted into hysteria and chaos.

And then the heralds arrived. Bearing the hated Frankish standard, golden cross against crimson, that Maimonides had thought he would never see again, the three men had ridden into Jerusalem unarmed. Saladin's nervous archers would have cut them down at the city gates, but they were robed in the blue mantles of diplomats, and the Sultan's law prohibited them from being harmed. Maimonides had seen one of them before—a herald named Walter Algernon, with hair the color of straw and a flush of freckles dotting his ruddy cheeks. Walter was an attendant to the fugitive Frankish noble Conrad, who had refused Saladin's generous amnesty and joined the remnants of his people at Acre. Over the past eighteen months, Saladin's forces had fought several inconclusive battles with Conrad's men, but the skirmishes had died down into an unofficial truce as both sides became exhausted by the stalemate. Walter had served as Conrad's envoy and chief negotiator over those months, and had become a familiar if unwelcome figure at the court. Born and raised in a village by the Jordan River, near the border between the Crusader lands and Muslim Syria, Walter was a native Arabic speaker who had proven to be a faithful go-between and had earned Saladin's respect.

But the other two men with him were strangers. One was obviously a soldier from the European brigade that had just landed. Tall, with flowing dark hair and sad eyes, he looked remarkably like some of the icons of Jesus of Nazareth that were displayed in the churches in Jerusalem. While Walter seemed nervous and fidgety as he stood in the center of the great hall (the herald had never been surrounded by heavily armed soldiers when he delivered Conrad's messages in the past), the European was sublimely calm in the face of potential death. He stared straight ahead at the empty throne, waiting patiently.

Maimonides was intrigued. Even though the newcomer had likely never been in the presence of Arabs, or stood in such a palatial hall covered in what must have seemed very alien-looking frescoes and geometric designs, he seemed oblivious to everything around him except his mission. Although the man had not said a word since he was ushered into the hall by Saladin's twin bodyguards, Maimonides sensed no arrogance or bluster, the usual trappings of his people. Instead, the European radiated calm and serenity.

The third herald, if he could be called that, was the most unusual of all. With skin as dark as sunburned leather, woolly hair, a prominent hooked nose, and a pair of golden earrings that weighed heavily on his lobes, the man was clearly either Abyssinian or Yemeni. He was also obviously a slave, and stood two feet behind the European, head bowed and arms crossed before him. The dark slave was clearly terrified and Maimonides wondered why he had been brought on a mission of such critical diplomatic importance.

The powerful silver door to the great hall swung open, shattering the silence with a heavy metallic clang and driving all other thoughts from the rabbi's mind. A burly guard with a face half covered in swirling tattoos raised an ivory trumpet carved from an African elephant's tusk and let sound the horn announcing the Sultan's arrival.

Saladin entered, and everyone present fell to their knees, except for the honor guard, as well as Walter and the European. The slave, for his part, was utterly prostrate on the ground as Saladin walked past him, gazing down at the unexpected figure briefly before sitting on the lion-armed throne. At that moment a balding page standing beside the judgment seat raised a silver rod, carved with a spiraling design of leaves and flowers, and then tapped the ground three times. At the signal, everyone rose to their feet. The Crusaders then promptly bowed to the Sultan from the waist. The formalities of protocol completed, Saladin turned his attention to Conrad's aide.

"You are welcome to my court as always, Sir Walter," the Sultan said in Arabic. "And I see that you have brought colleagues. Please be so kind as to introduce them."

As Saladin spoke, Maimonides noticed the slave nervously whispering inside the unfamiliar European's ear. He was obviously a translator, which was odd, considering that Walter was more than capable of performing such a service for his comrade. The rabbi saw Saladin's dark eyebrows rise as he made a similar observation.

Walter ignored the whispering slave and spoke loudly in Arabic.

"We are honored by your hospitality as always, great Sultan," he said in his high-pitched, almost feminine voice. "Please allow me to introduce Sir William Chinon, recently arrived from the land of England, which lies on the outermost regions of the setting sun."

Saladin met William's eyes for a long moment. The Sultan appeared to be studying the young knight closely, as if he were trying to gauge the depths of his soul.

"We welcome you in the name of God to the land of Abraham, Sir William," the Sultan said, in his best French.

The young man's mouth dropped, and Maimonides saw the flicker of a smile on Walter's features. The courtiers, unfamiliar with the tongue of the infidel, shifted nervously. The rabbi, who was well versed in the barbarian language, followed the Sultan's words effortlessly, but he was surprised that Saladin would honor a mere herald by addressing him in his native language.

But the man named William recovered from his surprise quickly, bowing his head, but said nothing. Saladin turned his attention to the slave, his curiosity piqued.

"And who is this?" he asked Walter, returning to Arabic.

Walter tried to hide his distaste, but was unsuccessful.

"He is a slave of no import," he said. Then, with some hesitation, he stated the obvious. "He serves Sir William as a secondary translator."

Saladin smiled with genuine amusement.

"I see that the level of trust between the Franks has not improved much with the passage of time."

There was a rumble of laughter at the Sultan's remark.

Saladin's eyes passed across the sad but dignified face of the slave, then he returned his attention to the heralds.

"I assume you bring a message from my old friend Conrad," he said.

Walter shifted, with slight nervousness.

"The message is actually from the leader of the Frankish expedition which has recently arrived on these blessed shores, as you have undoubtedly heard, my lord."

Maimonides saw Saladin's face tighten. So this was it—the first official communication from the leader of the invasion force.

"Proceed."

Walter reached into his black velvet tunic and pulled out a scroll sealed with the wax image of a lion bathed in the light of the rising sun. The herald unfurled the scroll slowly. He cleared his throat and began to recite.

"'From Richard, King of England, to Saladin, Sultan of the Saracens. Greetings and God's peace be with you . . .'"

"A peace backed by swords." It was al-Adil who spoke, his words spit from his mouth like cobra venom.

"Silence!" Saladin rarely rebuked his brother in public, and the courtiers cringed at the uncharacteristic outburst. Al-Adil bowed his head in apology.

"Pray continue," the Sultan said to Walter.

The herald nodded, and read aloud.

"'Our nations are on the verge of a bitter and unnecessary conflict. Word of your compassion has reached even the halls of London. I beseech you to avert this war, which can only bring suffering to the innocent. I invite you to visit my camp at Acre, where you will be treated with utmost dignity.'"

Walter paused, as if he were having difficulty completing the message. Taking a deep breath, he finished rapidly.

"'And there we can arrange for a peaceful surrender of your forces as two men of honor.'"

There was a moment of absolute quiet so deep that Maimonides thought he could hear the waves of the sea from beyond the distant horizon. Then the hall erupted in the outraged cries of the courtiers and the generals. The rabbi glanced at the Sultan, who appeared to have retained his cool at the insulting communiqué, but he could see his eyes burn with barely contained anger.

Saladin's brother was, predictably, less restrained.

"We should send this herald's scalp back on a platter as our reply."

At his words, Walter paled and Maimonides thought he would faint. While it was not normally Saladin's custom to abuse messengers, such a practice had a long and honored tradition in this part of the world.

The rabbi saw that the newcomer, William, was watching the Sultan closely, as if judging his foe by his reaction to the offensive proposal.

Saladin let the hubbub continue for a moment, and then signaled his page, who struck the silver rod against the marble floor repeatedly to restore order in the hall. The tiles cracked in a spiderweb pattern under his repeated blows, until a semblance of silence returned.

Saladin turned to face the courtiers, his eyes passing over each of them as if willing them to feel the calm he exuded.

"Gently, my brothers," he said softly. "Only clear heads will prevail at this moment."

The Sultan turned to Maimonides.

"What have our spies learned of this Richard?"

The rabbi felt every eye on him in surprise, a few, including al-Adil's, in anger. The Sultan had come to trust Maimonides' judgment in matters of state as well as medicine. But his recent request, that the Jew interview al-Adil's spies and come to an independent conclusion about the danger posed by this new conqueror, had been unusual to say the least. And had earned him the enmity of the men in the court who were normally assigned to analyze intelligence. Saladin had dismissed Maimonides' concerns about his fitness for the task, saying that a doctor of men's bodies was the best person to diagnose the state of their souls.

"The Angevin king, who goes by the self-anointed title of Lionheart, is young and brash," he said, hoping that his estimation was accurate. "His men both love and fear him."

Maimonides saw the Yemeni slave whispering rapidly in William's ear. The newcomer's face hardened and he met the rabbi's eyes coldly.

"Is he a man of honor?"

"Of that I can attest, glorious Sultan." It was William Chinon who spoke now, in French. There was a startled rumble as courtiers turned to each other, trying to decipher the infidel's words.

Saladin smiled at him, like a father amused by the enthusiasm of a child.

"You are most kind, Sir William," he replied in French, to the continued frustration of the Arab nobles. "But I shall look into the matter from less interested sources."

William bowed his head, and then turned his attention on the now frightfully uncomfortable Maimonides, who had been one of the few men in the court to understand the brief exchange.

"His men have earned a fearsome reputation," the doctor continued, then paused, realizing that William, the apparent lapdog of the villainous Richard, would not like his next words. "They have ransacked and pillaged their way through Europe. Entire villages have been laid to waste. They have all the markings of the uncouth barbarians that descended like a plague on the Holy Land a hundred years ago."

While this harsh public judgment of the Crusaders likely earned him the respect, if not the admiration, of many of the nobles in the room, William was understandably outraged.

"I must protest . . ." he cried out in French.

Al-Adil stood up, towering above Saladin's page, who nervously stepped aside.

"Speak again unbidden and I will cut out your tongue." His words were hobbled together in crude French and lacked the sophisticated accent of the Sultan's trained speech. But they were effective quite the same.

Maimonides saw Walter tremble and put a restraining hand on William, who merely met al-Adil's eyes with a raised eyebrow.

The grumbling in the court was now a steady buzz, as the few court-iers who spoke French attempted to translate for their colleagues. Sala-din signaled his page to rap his staff and restore silence, but not before turning to his brother. Maimonides was close enough to hear.

"If you again treat a guest with disrespect, my brother, I will remove not only your tongue, but your eyes and ears as well."

Al-Adil sat down, his face red with embarrassment. A few of the courtiers were shocked to see the giant Kurd put so harshly in his place by his brother, but it was clear to most that Saladin was wise to handle the situation as delicately as possible. The arrival of the infidel forces on their shores was a reality that could not be wished away by bluster and rage. The barbarous forces of Richard the Lionheart could be thwarted only by the iron will and control the Sultan always demonstrated at moments of crisis. And this was the greatest crisis any of them had faced in their lifetimes.

"Pray forgive my brother's manners; they still reek of the untamed desert," the Sultan resumed in Arabic. "I have a reply for your king, if you would be kind enough to relay it."

Walter, obviously glad that Saladin appeared to have retained his control despite the fury of hot emotions swirling around him, removed a blank scroll and a feathered pen from his cloak and began to jot down the Sultan's response to Richard's message.

25

William read over the contents of Saladin's letter for a third time. He sighed and handed the note back to Walter, whose responsibility it was to relay formal communica-tions between monarchs. It was not a role William envied. Envoys who bore such tidings were often the victims of the misplaced wrath of their leaders.

The knight turned to the west and allowed himself a moment of relief as he gazed at the campfires of the Frankish base in the distance. Standing on a rocky path high in the hills surrounding the army camp, he gazed down at the waves of tents billowing in the sea breeze under the light of the full moon. His horse was exhausted from the journey back from Jerusalem, a feeling that he shared with the faithful steed. At least the return trip, which had taken three days and nights, had been largely uneventful. For that, he was grateful to the Muslim sultan for his generous offer of an honor guard to escort the heralds to Acre. The surly Arab soldiers wearing the colorful turbans and cloaks of their company had been obviously unhappy with the shameful task of accompanying the enemy to its base of operations, but they had acquiesced to their leader's command.

Traveling through Palestine with an armed force bearing Saladin's eagle standard had been far more convenient than merely reversing their initial journey to Jerusalem. William and the others had made that trip by skulking through the countryside at night, disguised in brown peasant robes and hiding in the hills from Muslim patrols who would likely execute them as spies despite their diplomatic papers. The quiet journey back under the warmth of the sun had allowed William to take in the Holy Land in all its beauty. The air was rich with the scent of dates and honey, the trees laden with bright oranges and dun-colored figs and olives. There was gentleness to the breeze, a sleepy peacefulness that belied the bloody history the land had endured for thousands of years.

While their initial journey into enemy territory had consisted of rapid rides through back roads under the cover of night, they had made more leisurely time on the way back. This was partly due to the slow and irascible donkey that had been conscripted by the Sultan's men to pull a wagon cart bearing two oak chests lined with gold and studded in emeralds. The boxes contained gifts and treasures from Saladin to Richard, an unusual gesture for a man communicating with his sworn enemy as war loomed. While William had been impressed by the largesse, Walter had dismissed the act of generosity as a carefully calculated ploy meant to signal the Sultan's supreme confidence that Richard would never pose a threat to Jerusalem.

Had he not met the enemy leader in person, William would normally have been inclined to agree. But the knight had watched the Lord of the Saracens carefully as he held court. He had seen the hate and fear in the eyes of the swarthy nobles dressed in outlandish robes, their hair covered in turbans of silver filigree, but he had not gotten the same sense from the Sultan. The infidel king had an aura that seemed to signal nobility. Watching the Sultan defend his guests' honor before the hostile courtiers, his eyes expressing his outrage at their rudeness toward the heralds, the knight had a strange feeling of familiarity. It was as if he saw for a moment a kindred spirit. But the man was an unbeliever—how could that be possible?

The young knight pushed the disturbing question from his mind and focused his attention on the evergreen countryside around him. William Chinon had always wanted to make a pilgrimage to the Holy Land, but he had never wished to enter it as a warrior. God apparently had a different plan for him. As he had ridden through the verdant hills near Bethlehem, the birthplace of the Lord, William wondered what would be left of the land's pristine beauty once the latest conflict was over. Precious little, he surmised.

Regardless of who won, the flower-laden groves that dotted the landscape would be gone. Fire and pestilence would ravage the quaint stone towns that his party crossed on their voyage north. Many of the curious villagers, who had come out to watch the foreigners pass through, would be dead soon enough. Such was the cruel nature of the world, unchanged since the days of Abel and Cain.

Their journey had been one of communal silence. The bearded Muslim guards did not dare speak except in hushed tones around the Franks for fear of letting slip information that could be used by the enemy in a war that was now inevitable. And his colleague Walter had not said a single word since they crossed through the massive iron gates of Jerusalem, despite William's efforts to engage him in polite conversation. But after a few comments about the weather and other irrelevant matters fell upon deaf ears, William had decided not to press the matter. Walter clearly trusted him less than he trusted Saladin's guards.

And perhaps with good reason. William knew that Conrad of Montferrat considered himself the rightful heir to the throne of Jerusalem, and Richard's forces as mere support troops sent by the papacy on his behalf. Of course, the proud King of England had a very different view of the situation, and it was inevitable that the two leaders would clash. William fervently hoped that their conflict could be contained and resolved, for what he had seen of the Muslim defenses around Jerusalem, with its heavily armored towers and circular array of fifty-foot-wide trenches, the war would be difficult enough to wage with a united Crusader force. Infighting between the kings at this stage would lead to a repeat of the ignominious defeat that had sent Guy into exile and Reginald to Hell.

And if William could not even earn the trust of a lowly page, he wondered how the kings would find common ground.

William had more success with the slave Khalil. The rescued sailor was fully aware that his life had been spared by William's intervention, and he had sworn an oath of loyalty before Allah to the young knight. Ever since Richard had entrusted the sole survivor of the *Nur al-Bahr* to William's care, the Yemeni with the sonorous voice and sad eyes had spent several hours each day teaching his new master the native tongue of the land. William had found the journey through the heart of Palestine a perfect opportunity to advance his Arabic training. While he was far from fluent, he could at least recite simple greetings, such as the ever-common *assalaamu 'alikum* (peace be upon you), and knew the basic words to describe the environment: *as-samaa* stood for the sky, *al-ard* meant the earth, *an-naar* was fire, etc. What William found most interesting in their lessons was the depth to which religious faith was intertwined with the language of the Arabs. Whenever Khalil spoke of the future, even to say obvious statements such as they would reach Acre tomorrow, he would add the phrase *insha'Allah,* if God wills. Apparently, this was a direct commandment from the Muslim Holy Book to remind men that every instant they were in the presence of the Divine, and not even the smallest matter of daily life could proceed without the permission of Allah. There was something very spiritually profound about this all-encompassing view of God, and William was intrigued that men he had been raised to view as ignorant savages had such intense faith. He resolved to find out more about these infidels and their beliefs. Perhaps his grasp of the language would advance to the point where he might even learn to read their Qur'an, even as he had privately become versed in the Latin Bible.

William's language lessons with Khalil drew suspicious stares from the bearded Muslims troops, who would break their silence every now and then to laugh and shout at the young knight phrases that Khalil was initially reluctant to translate, as they were obviously vulgarities. This had amused William greatly. He remembered when he was learning Italian from a boyhood friend whose mother was a lady from Rome. The first things the curly-haired Antony had sought to teach him were the vilest curses he knew. Perhaps this desire to spread obscenity in all of its rich linguistic forms was a primordial trait in all humanity.

William's growing camaraderie with the black slave also brought him withering stares from the arrogant Walter. Conrad's envoy had been barely able to mask his disgust when he had learned that William would be serving as Richard's representative to Saladin, and that he would bring a Muslim captive along as a cotranslator. The use of an infidel's services was beyond insult, but the freckled herald was clearly terrified of the newly arrived Richard and had kept his tongue in check. Still, that did not prevent him from sending William angry glances whenever the knight conversed with the woolly-haired savage. William wondered if Walter's outrage was less the result of Khalil's presence on the mission itself than of the fact of the slave's surprisingly good grasp of the French language. It was of course not all that completely unexpected that a merchant seaman whose profession required interaction with men of many nations should speak their tongue. But William had to admit that it was peculiar to hear French spilling from the lips of a black infidel.

But their conversation had slowed and eventually halted as their journey drew to an end. The rich fields of central Palestine vanished, replaced by the hard, gray earth of the coast. The well-groomed olive trees gave way to a few scattered acacias lined with razor-sharp thorns. They had reached the desolate frontier of the Holy Land, and William felt his heart grow heavy with the knowledge that his people had been driven out of such a beautiful, bountiful world to take refuge in the barren waste that surrounded Acre.

They had reached the towering walls of the Acre fortress by sundown on the third day. Their escorts had led them as far as a faint path at the foot of the hills, given them one flask of water each, then turned without another word in the direction of the Muslim outpost. The strong-willed donkey had moved to follow its Arab masters instinctively, but both William and Khalil had pulled on its leather reins until the ornery beast relented and began the slow trudge up the gravel path. As they climbed higher, William had taken a moment to gaze upon the dark towers of the fortress that had once been the pride of the Christian military. Its ramparts towered above the hills, every arched window lit from within by fireplaces and oil lamps, as if the walls encased the sun itself. The stone keep, with its raised belvedere turrets and crenellations, was designed to resemble the frontier castles that dotted the French landscape. The heavy gray-and-black ashlar walls were cut with loopholes and cross-shaped slits for archers, and sturdy logs supported hoardings, wooden platforms from which missiles could be dropped on any attacking force. In a land of domes and sloping roofs, the keep was the first familiar architecture William had seen. And it now belonged to the enemy.

The impenetrable fortress had been built to repel attack from both land and sea, and Walter, in one of his rare talkative moments, had mentioned that its storage rooms had been supplied with enough grain and water from an internal well to withstand a siege of up to two years. When the defeated Crusader forces escaped Jerusalem and fled Saladin's advance from the south and east, the citadel of Acre had been an obvious place of refuge. From there, the surviving generals of the Christian army had expected to hunker down in relative safety and comfort until support troops were dispatched from the papacy to reverse the barbarian invasion.

Unfortunately, by the time Conrad and his soldiers had arrived from the stronghold of Tyre, the corrupt and cowardly Frankish commanders had already delivered the fortress of Acre into the hands of the infidels. Rumor had it that Saladin had paid the Christians of Acre their weight in gold and precious gems for their betrayal of the Cause, and they were now living in Damascus as his honored guests.

Whatever truth lay in that account, the undisputable reality was that the keep had been evacuated by its garrison and in the possession of the Saracens by the time the newly proclaimed King of Jerusalem had arrived. Conrad's troops had been wholly unsuccessful at dislodging the infidels and had been pushed back by the Muslim troops over the western hills until their backs were against the murky sea.

As the sun vanished into that same sea beyond those hills, William caught sight of the twinkling lights of the nearby Arab settlement that had sprung up under the watchful protection of the fortress. The Muslim citadel had been expanding relentlessly during the past eighteen months, and the trapped Frankish troops had been powerless to hold back its advance. In the distance, the gentle scent of roasted lamb and spinach wafted from the hearths of thousands of Arab settlers who were even then sitting down for dinner. William felt his stomach rumble at the smell—he had been subsisting on dried goat-meat strips and other meager rations for the past three days. The night before they had left Jerusalem, Saladin had invited them to feast with the nobles of the court, but Walter had politely declined. The heralds had understood that despite the Sultan's hospitality, they would be unwelcome guests in the eyes of his courtiers. Their mission was to relay Saladin's response to their com-

manders at Acre as quickly as possible, although William secretly regretted not sampling the royal cuisine. While he was an ascetic man on many
levels, the knight had a weakness for good food. And he had rarely had
the pleasure of a well-prepared meal since they had left Europe months
before.

Turning his attention away from Acre, William followed Walter as
they led their horses and the unhappy donkey carefully along the rocky
path. Their torches provided just enough light to navigate the treacherous terrain as the sun vanished and Venus made her first appearance in
the heavens. The tent city below glowed red with the flames of hundreds
of campfires as they approached the first Crusader sentries at the crest
of the hill. Recognizing their crimson standards and diplomatic mantles,
the guards lowered their bows and saluted the heralds as they rode down
toward the worn command pavilion where Richard and Conrad awaited.

→ → →

WILLIAM WAS SHOCKED WHEN he saw Richard. Seated on a purple velvet cushion in the center of the tent, while Conrad sulked beside him
and the French leader Philip Augustus and commanders from both
forces milled about, the King of England was deathly pale. Beads of
sweat were rolling down his forehead, even though the shabby command
pavilion was already chilly with the evening breeze fluttering in through
the tears in the fabric. His master was clearly sick, but how could he have
contracted an illness in so short a time? They had been in Palestine for
only a fortnight, and William had been gone from Acre less than a week.

The two heralds bowed low to their respective masters. Khalil was
not present, and was currently waiting inside William's tent under heavy
guard by Conrad's men. As they rose, a group of sturdy Italian soldiers
who smelled distinctly like camel piss hauled in the chests of treasure
that Saladin had given the emissaries. At the sight of the shining boxes
lined with precious metals and gems, Conrad stepped forward, his eyes
gleaming. William ignored him and faced Richard, who seemed to have
difficulty keeping his eyes open.

"My lord, it is good to be back in the company of believers. May
God's grace shine upon you and the Christian cause," William said automatically, but his heart was not in the protocols of greeting. He wanted
to throw the other men out and tend to his ailing master.

Richard smiled weakly in welcome to his friend. He coughed heavily, and then raised his hand to point at Walter with a slightly trembling forefinger.

"You . . . Whatever your name is . . . Do you have an answer from the enemy?"

Walter bristled slightly at the rude tone of the monarch. Then he glanced at Conrad, who shook his head slightly as if signaling the herald to humor the arrogant newcomer. Drawing himself up proudly, he removed a scroll of parchment from a pocket in his dust-covered mantle. Breaking the seal on the document slowly, as if this were a laborious chore, Walter unfolded the letter containing Saladin's response to Richard's bold demand for surrender. Clearing his throat, he read aloud.

"The infidel replies: 'From Saladin, commander of the believers, to King Richard of England. Peace be upon you. While I am honored by your gracious invitation, I regret that I must decline. It is not fitting for kings to meet before peace has been arranged. But I welcome you to our land with a small gift.'"

Walter nodded to the guards while crinkling his nose at the rank odor that emanated from their rusty armor. The men moved forward and flung the larger of the two chests open first. There were several gasps from the startled soldiers, and William thought he saw the beginnings of drool shining on the greedy Conrad's parched lips. The chest was filled with gold coins from all over the Muslim empire. Dirhams from Egypt marked with the names of Saladin's family, thick dinars bearing the crescent seal of the Caliph of Baghdad, and strangely shaped coins from the east, some apparently hailing as far away as India. William caught the looks of disbelief on the faces of the Frankish generals. Saladin had inexplicably provided them with enough wealth to conscript hundreds of mercenaries, buy a cache of weapons from arms traders in Cyprus, or purchase more ships to strengthen their blockade of the Palestine coast. It made no sense. Unless Saladin held such stores of treasure that his own forces would be even better equipped and prepared for the war to come.

The guards then opened the smaller of the two chests, although with some difficulty. It was sealed with an unfamiliar gumlike resin. When they finally pried the box open, they saw that it contained a smaller box made of silvery metal the likes of which none of them had ever seen before. After the locks to the interior compartment were opened, the Crusaders witnessed a sight that made even less sense than the fortune of gold bestowed on them by an unrepentant enemy. The inner container was filled with a strange white powdery substance that sparkled in the lamplight. They all knew what it was—but it was impossible. It was *snow*. Somehow, in the blazing heat of the Palestine sun over several days, the mysterious box had kept the frost preserved and frozen. Who were these Muslims? Sorcerers? Demons? Or perhaps something even more terrifying—ordinary men, but possessed with unimaginable wealth and incomprehensible technology.

Aware that all eyes were back on him, but were now filled with confusion and trepidation, Walter nervously continued reading Saladin's response.

"'I present you with a small gift of gold from the treasuries of the caliphate, as well as snow from the mountains of my homeland in the Caucasus. I hope it will cool your brow in this intemperate clime . . .'" Walter looked up at his master, Conrad, and grimaced apologetically. The claim that this magical box could hold pure snow over a journey of months was both preposterous and unnerving, and the herald clearly did not enjoy bearing such strange tidings. He then reached into his cloak and brought out a small purple bottle studded with diamonds and capped in silver. He passed the bottle toward Conrad, but Richard's hand shot out and intervened. The English king, his hands trembling from whatever ailment plagued him, managed to pry it open and sniff its contents as Walter continued reading.

"'. . . a drink that is native to Palestine, which you may come to enjoy. It is called *sherbet*,'" Walter recited, and then stopped. Taking a deep breath, he finished reading the scroll.

"'May you enjoy a pleasant stay in our lands. I regret that it will be so brief.'"

Richard threw the bottle aside without drinking the foreign liquid, which everyone in the room assumed was poisoned. The flask rolled on the mud floor of the pavilion and spread a bloodred stain across the parched earth. Visibly gathering his strength, the young king stood up and turned his attention to William, who saw fury in his bloodshot eyes.

"He mocks me . . ."

William wasn't sure what to say to his master, but decided that his first priority was to calm him and get him to bed, where a doctor could tend to him. Confound these people—why wasn't there a physician there with him already?

"I do not think that was his intent, my lord," William said slowly, moving closer toward the sickly king. "From my dealings with him, he appears to be a man of honor."

Conrad of Montferrat, who managed to tear his eyes away from the treasure trove before him, laughed. It was a terrible throaty sound that combined incredulity with contempt.

"Heathens have no honor," he said, turning to address his commanders, who automatically cheered their assent. William felt color rising to his face and he spoke out before the restraint of wisdom could rein him back.

"Know your enemy sire for what he is, not for what you would prefer him to be," William said, the coldness in his eyes matched by his voice. "You cannot defeat that which you do not understand."

Conrad stepped forward, outraged, and for a moment William regretted his inability to hold his tongue. This man, at least in theory, was his superior, and even Richard might not be able to save his knight from the consequences of insulting someone of such rank.

But if Conrad and William were destined to come to blows, tonight would not be that night. Fate intervened, and all attention in the room shifted away from the confrontation between noblemen to the steadily worsening condition of the one undisputed monarch in their presence. Richard had stepped over to the smaller chest and was running his hands through the snow as if in a confused daze, when his legs gave way and he fell to his knees.

"My lord!" William was instantly at his side, cursing himself for wasting time arguing with an arrogant pretender while his master was clearly ill and in need of treatment. As the stunned commanders looked on, William knelt down and helped Richard lean against his body. The king felt limp in William's arms and he knew that his lord had fainted. The knight ran his hand across the king's perspiration-drenched forehead.

"He is on fire," William said, looking up desperately for help. But no one moved. Conrad met his eyes, and for a second William thought he saw the alleged king smile slightly. It was an expression that made his own blood boil with rage. What kind of men were these Franks, who would rejoice in ill fortune to their Christian brothers, their rescuers?

"It is the camp fever," Conrad said, turning away from William as if bored. "We have lost many men to it. Your king's days can be numbered on one hand." He turned his attention to the chest containing the Muslim gold and examined a hexagonal piece embossed with Arabic calligraphy and an array of geometric symbols.

William felt Richard stir and immediately turned his attention to helping his master.

"My lord, can you speak?" The king's pupils focused on William, and he smiled weakly.

"Help me up," Richard managed to croak. William shot a scathing glance at the idle soldiers standing about staring at the Lionheart's misfortune, and his reproachful look managed to stir some sense of duty on their parts. Two of the younger commanders moved forward and joined William in lifting Richard to his feet and guiding the king to a cushioned cot at the far end of the command pavilion. The knight helped Richard lie back, his hand pillowing the king's head.

Richard coughed violently, expelling a viscous green mist, and even William was forced to back away for fear of contracting the camp fever. The knight turned to one of the men who had helped him, a bushy-haired exile from Beersheba sporting a beard flecked with red henna.

"Find a doctor!" he all but shouted in the young Frank's face. The bushy-haired soldier turned to look questioningly at Conrad, who sighed in exasperation.

"Our doctors have no cure for this disease."

William heard a terrible cracking sound, like nutshells grated against a marble floor, coming from Richard's direction. He whirled, expecting the worst, then realized that the king was laughing like a lunatic.

"Life is a joke," Richard croaked. "I crossed the world seeking battle, only to die in my bed . . ."

William stepped back and knelt by his master's side. He held Richard's trembling, burning hand in his.

"Not on my watch, sire."

Then he rose, and with a final withering glance at the collection of nobles who had stood by and impassively watched his friend's suffering, the young knight stormed out of the pavilion in the direction of his own tent. Even though the sky was awash with twinkling stars and most of the soldiers in the camp were already lost in their troubled dreams, there would be no rest for William Chinon tonight.

Pushing away the guards in front of his striped white-and-red tent,

William stormed inside and found the man he was looking for. The slave named Khalil sat patiently on the floor, his arms shackled, despite William's order to the guards to leave him free.

Cursing under his breath, William summoned one of the guards inside and demanded that the slave be unchained. When the Welshman with the bad teeth and foul body odor complied, William dismissed him. Once the guard had departed, William turned to Khalil, who had sat impassively through the entire scene.

"My lord has been struck with the camp fever that has plagued Acre. Tell me what you know about medicine," he said in French, trying but failing to keep the desperation out of his voice. The man with the woolly hair and sunburned skin stared at William for a moment, and then replied.

"I know only what is necessary for survival at the sea," Khalil said in French that was acceptable if not perfect. "How to cure a bout of vomiting from the tremulous motions of the waves. How to soothe bowels loosened by unclean water. I even know how to stem the bleeding from a shark bite that has torn off a man's foot. But the disease that inflicts your people is not from my world. Its home is deep within the desert where water finds no refuge. Its allies are the slinking, vile creatures of the earth, who spread the pestilence in the dead of the night."

"But is there a cure?" William said, uninterested in the slave's poetic responses.

Khalil shrugged.

"I heard once on a trading stop in Alexandria that the doctors of Egypt had found a remedy that saved many lives from the plague four years ago," he said. "It is said that the medical colleges of Cairo now train doctors to easily cure the fever."

William collapsed, feeling defeated. Egypt! The distance from Acre to Cairo was roughly equivalent to the span between the earth and the moon, except that a trip through the celestial spheres was less dangerous to a Christian Frank than a journey through the realms of the fanatical Bedouin of Sinai.

"Then my king will die," he said after a long, painful silence. He felt hollow inside. He had failed his master, even before the war could begin.

Khalil looked at William as if gaining new insight into his master's soul.

"There may be a way, but you will need to swallow your pride."

William looked at him in surprise, and then stood up, his face hardened in determination.

"Pride is of no value to me, when I would trade my very life for my king," the knight said.

Khalil chuckled, a high-pitched wheezing sound that contrasted with his normally sonorous voice.

"Once your brother Christians learn what you have done, my lord, they may indeed demand such a trade."

26

Maimonides walked rapidly through the paved marble hallway of the palace, his heart pounding. He had been wakened from a deep sleep by the heavy pounding on the sturdy cedar door of his modest family apartment in the Jewish quarter. The thunderous banging had even managed to stir his beloved wife, Rebecca, who had woken with a startled cry. Maimonides threw on an old striped robe and walked barefoot into the main chamber. It was well past midnight, and his imagination had run wild with dark possibilities regarding the caller's identity and intent. He was not alone in his fears. Miriam stood by the door in her thin cotton dressing gown, holding a sharp meat cleaver Rebecca used to prepare his favorite lamb dish, ready to take on any intruder who threatened the sanctity of their home. There was an intensity in her eyes that he had seen once before many years ago, and it frightened him.

Even as the banging increased in volume and intensity, Maimonides had gently stepped forward and put a hand on Miriam's shoulder. She had jumped in surprise, and there was a terrifying moment when he thought she would hit him square in the chest with her kitchen blade. But recognition dawned with merciful speed, and he had been spared death, at least by the hand of his niece. Whether his insistent caller would complete the task, he could only wonder.

When Maimonides finally opened the door a crack, he saw that outside stood the twin banes of his daily life at the court, the two Egyptian brutes who served as Saladin's personal guard. Their presence at such a late hour at his home meant only grave tidings.

"The Sultan?" It was Miriam who had spoken, and Maimonides saw in her fearful expression that she shared his thoughts. Perhaps Saladin was gravely ill, which seemed unlikely, since he had seemed in the best of health earlier that evening, or had been injured in some accident. Or perhaps even poisoned by one of the myriad jealous courtiers in Jerusalem.

The twins had ignored the girl and turned to Maimonides, telling him only that he was needed at the palace at once. The impatient soldiers had given him just enough time to throw on a dark mantle that Rebecca had recently woven to keep him warm during his chilly morning walks to the palace. As he bound the little wooden clasp around his neck, he saw the twin brothers eyeing the loosely clad Miriam with obvious interest. Instead of being unnerved by the presence of these hulking warriors, his niece had stood defiantly, meeting their eyes, her hand still on her cleaver. She left only after a frightened Rebecca literally pulled her into their bedroom. Whatever madness had been unleashed tonight, neither of them wanted the headstrong Miriam to be pulled into its vortex.

Maimonides had shuffled the guards out, hesitating for a moment to find his leather medical pouch, but the taller of the two had shaken his head ominously. He would not need it tonight. The rabbi had felt the color drain from his face. Perhaps the Sultan was already dead, and Maimonides was being summoned merely to witness his passing. Silly as it sounded, the idea that Saladin could die had never really occurred to the rabbi. The Sultan had been such an all-encompassing part of his life for so many years that he could no more imagine his friend gone than he could believe that the sun would not rise tomorrow.

The guards had led the doctor outside, where two pitch-black Arabian stallions waited patiently. The shorter twin, the one named Hakeem, hoisted Maimonides up unceremoniously on to the saddle of one of the horses, then climbed on as well. The rabbi had been forced to hold on to Hakeem's waist as the two brothers rode off like lightning toward the palace. Despite the rabbi's repeated attempts at gleaning information from them, they remained silent. Maimonides kept speaking, if for no other reason than to keep his mind focused on anything except the hair-raising ride through the cobbled streets of Jerusalem.

Even though the city appeared to be dead, and there were no lights except for the twinkling constellations above, the guards chose a strange and haphazard route through the souk and the Christian quarter, as if

they were trying to confuse anyone hoping to follow them. Maimonides
had found this thought very disconcerting.

But now they were in the palace halls, dark except for a few scattered
candles that shed strange and foreboding shadows. Trying to steady his
breathing, Maimonides limped the last few steps to the gates of the
grand hall where Saladin kept court. The taller twin, named Saleem,
swung open the grand silver doors to the chamber. Maimonides blinked
incredulously as he finally saw who awaited him in the grand chamber.
His mind reeled. What was this all about?

Gathered in the center of the room was a small crowd of Saladin's
family and top advisers, while the Sultan sat upon his throne looking
tense. Al-Adil towered above the rest, his permanent scowl more grim
than usual. Beside him stood Qadi al-Fadil, who was wearing an unflat-
tering brown robe rather than his usual gold-ribboned finery. The chief
minister looked like he too had just been dragged out of bed. Beside him
was the perpetually sad-faced Keukburi, the brilliant Egyptian commander whose support Saladin credited for his relatively bloodless over-
throw of the Fatimid dynasty in Cairo.

And beside Keukburi was someone Maimonides had not expected
to see in Jerusalem. Taqi al-Din, the Sultan's legendary nephew, had
returned from the critical task of leading the skirmishes against the
Crusader encampment outside Acre. Strikingly handsome with a thin
beard clipped into a goatee, Taqi al-Din was said to combine the best
of both sons of Ayyub. His prowess in battle and utter contempt for
death rivaled al-Adil's reputation for courage, but he retained his uncle's
sense of restraint and diplomacy in matters of state. There were many in
the realm who expected Saladin to bypass his own young sons, al-Afdal
and al-Zahir, and pass the sultanate on to Taqi al-Din, and the courtiers
endeavored to stay in his good favor. The warrior, for his part, made little
secret of his own ambitions. He had counseled Saladin for months to let
him lead an expedition to conquer the lands west of Egypt and bring the
Almohad sultans of the Maghreb under the Ayyubid flag. But news of
the impending Frankish invasion had caused those plans to be scrapped,
and Taqi al-Din had been assigned along with seven hundred of his finest horsemen to support the citadel at Acre. He was their first defense
against the newly arrived European hordes, and only a matter of grave
concern for the sultanate would compel him to leave his post.

As Maimonides stepped into the dimly lit chamber, he saw two men in dark robes, their faces hidden behind shadowed hoods, turn to face him. At the sight of the approaching doctor, the men lifted their hoods and revealed their identities. Maimonides gasped. It was the young Crusader knight William Chinon, who arrived as Richard's herald only a few days before. Beside him stood the Yemeni slave with the bushy hair and gold earrings who apparently served as his interpreter. Feeling every eye on him as he bowed before the Sultan, the rabbi got the distinct impression that this secret meeting with the enemy had something to do with him. He met Saladin's gaze uncertainly. The Sultan smiled thinly, and then turned his attention to the Christian knight.

"Do your men know that you are here?" Saladin spoke in Arabic, his voice carefully measured, his eyes watching William's face closely in the flickering torchlight.

"Only a few that I trust," William responded in French after the interpreter passed along the Sultan's words. Saladin politely waited for the Yemeni to repeat his master's statements in Arabic for the benefit of the other courtiers, even though he and Maimonides were able to follow the knight's speech.

"How bad is he?" Saladin asked, his eyes darting to the doctor.

"He is alive, but he will not open his eyes," William replied, after a moment of hesitation. The truth began to dawn on Maimonides. The Lionheart was ill, probably with the camp fever that had plagued the Franks.

Al-Adil laughed contemptuously.

"It seems Allah has taken care of the Lion's Ass for us." He sneered at the stone-faced William. "I assume that you are here to negotiate the surrender of your pitiful band of mercenaries to our sultan?"

Maimonides saw William's eyes flash even before he heard the translation. Al-Adil's tone spoke volumes by itself. But before William could compose an unwise retort to the bad-tempered giant, Taqi al-Din stepped forward.

"Sir William approached me at Acre under the flag of truce," the young man said steadily, his voice laced with ice. "He is under my protection, Uncle, and I will not permit him to be subjected to any disrespect."

Al-Adil bristled, but caught the warning glance from his brother and stepped back, muttering curses against the Franks. William took a deep breath and faced the Sultan.

"I have no authority to undertake any arrangements for a cessation of hostilities between our peoples," he said. "I have come here to speak not as your enemy, but as a knight who throws himself upon the mercy of the great Sultan."

This was unexpected. Maimonides caught the glances of disbelief passing among the courtiers, and the look of deep suspicion on al-Adil's face. Saladin alone seemed unperturbed. He leaned back, his fingers steepled before him, as he often did before passing judgment on complex matters. After a long pause in which the only sound in the chamber was the passing buzz of mosquitoes, Saladin addressed the knight, his voice neutral, his face impossible to read.

"How can I be of service to you, Sir William?"

The knight raised his head proudly.

"I swore an oath to protect the king, but I am at a loss to help him now," he said, his voice registering his regret that he had to resort to this last, humiliating measure. "Our doctors cannot cure this fever, but I have heard that your physicians are more advanced."

"Do you jest?" al-Adil thundered. "Why would the Sultan help his greatest enemy?"

William met Saladin's unblinking eyes.

"Because it is said that Saladin's chivalry knows no bounds," he said. "I cannot believe that a man of honor such as yourself would let a king fall out of common pettiness."

Saladin smiled graciously, then turned to his friend the rabbi.

"What say you, Maimonides?"

The old man was stunned. He had served as the Sultan's adviser on many matters of state, but none as important as this. What he said now to his friend could change the course of history. It was not a burden that Maimonides wanted, nor one he could avoid. The rabbi knew what the right answer was, even if it went against every survival instinct he possessed. In his heart, he had secretly hoped that some such misfortune would befall the newly arrived invaders, a crisis that would cut off the head of the snake before it could strangle Jerusalem. And the God of irony had granted his wish, only to place him in the position of undoing the very outcome that he had prayed for.

"I am a doctor, and I cannot permit any man to die of disease when he may be cured," Maimonides said at long last, his voiced laced with regret. "But there is a greater issue at stake than my ideals."

Saladin raised an eyebrow.

"Name it."

"Should the Frankish king die, his men would be leaderless and desperate in a strange land," the old man said. "Without him, we will have thousands of angry marauders on our coast and no master to rein them in."

"I see," Saladin said, his tone flat and controlled, giving no hint as to where he himself stood on the issue. "My brother, what is your view of this matter?"

Al-Adil ran his hand through his beard, tugging at it forcefully, as if he was about to voice something he did not really want to say.

"For once, the Jew speaks with wisdom," he said, to the rabbi's great surprise. "While I have no love for this Frank, we cannot negotiate peace with a corpse."

Saladin turned to each of his courtiers. Qadi al-Fadil reluctantly chimed in with his agreement. Taqi al-Din nodded, but said nothing.

"Then the matter is settled," Saladin said. He turned his attention again to the doctor. "Maimonides, you will accompany Sir William as my ambassador to the Angevin and see what you can do for our adversary."

William released his breath in a rush, as if he had forgotten to exhale for the past few moments. He had obviously not expected the Sultan to acquiesce with such little resistance.

"You are a true gentlemen, Sultan," the knight said, bowing low from the waist. "Perhaps in another time and place, I would have been honored to call you lord."

Saladin smiled, and this time it was not merely a polite gesture.

"And I would have been doubly honored to call you liege," he said. "Any man that would risk his life and his honor to save his master walks upon the Straight Path of the Holy Prophet, peace be upon him, even if he bears the label of an infidel."

William wasn't sure how to take the compliment, but he bowed again stiffly. He was startled when Saladin spoke again, this time in French, his voice suddenly cold.

"Sir William, carry a message to your lord when he awakes."

The courtiers looked to the Yemeni interpreter, but one glance at Saladin's hard features signaled to the slave to keep this part of the dialogue private.

"What word, Sultan?" William replied cautiously, sensing the sudden change in the air.

"Tell your Richard that I will spare him the demise of a sickly dog," Saladin said softly. "But I will not hesitate to give him an honorable death on the battlefield should he pursue this war against me."

The color drained from William's face, but he nodded in understanding. Saladin rose and departed from the chamber without another word. All eyes then fell on the Sultan's newly appointed ambassador to the Franks. The man on whose aged shoulders the future of the war now rested.

"Go and get your medicines, Rabbi," Taqi al-Din said. "We leave before sunrise."

27

Miriam was not about take no for an answer. She had sat up with her terrified aunt worrying for several hours until the sound of a distant muezzin announced the arrival of first light and the time for the *fajr* prayer. The thudding drone of approaching hoofbeats had caused her to run to a small window and look below as the mysterious twin guards who had thrown their lives upside down rode up to the gate of their apartment. Maimonides, looking pale and flustered, dismounted and hurriedly walked up the stone path toward the door. Miriam was disturbed to notice that the two soldiers, who remained seated on their midnight-black steeds, had been joined by several horsemen. One was handsome and thin-bearded, dressed in the lamellar armor worn at the front lines by soldiers facing down the remnants of the Frankish scourge. The other two were more sinister, dressed in black robes, their faces cowled and hidden. Whoever these people were, she had wanted them away from her family as soon as possible.

Maimonides had rushed inside, kissed her on the cheek, and embraced his wife briefly before gathering his medical bag. Despite their persistent and frantic questioning, her uncle kept claiming that everything was all right, just a small medical emergency he needed to take care of, and would they all just go back to sleep? Only when he heard Rebecca sobbing in fear, something his strong-willed wife rarely ever did, did his resolve break. With glistening eyes, he had told the women just enough to truly terrify them both. He was being dispatched to the enemy camp to save the life of the barbarian king.

Rebecca had shouted at him that he was a fool for embarking on such a mission, to save the life of an enemy to their people. He had responded firmly that he had no choice.

"It is the will of the Sultan," he had said, as if that alone would sanctify a misguided plan to save the leader of the murderous Franks.

"Then the Sultan is a madman!" Rebecca had shouted before she could stop herself. A deadly pall had fallen over the house. Maimonides gave her a terrified look, then glanced out the window at his impatient escorts. They assiduously avoided meeting his gaze. Apparently they had not heard her treasonous outburst, or had decided to ignore it given the pressing urgency of his mission.

Maimonides had turned to face his wife, and they embraced for a long moment, his tears mingling with hers. Then Rebecca ran into her bedroom and slammed the door shut, leaving Miriam to help her uncle pack his leather satchel with the necessary vials of medicine. And to convince him to let her accompany him on his suicidal journey into the belly of the Leviathan.

"Out of the question," he said yet again.

"If I were a boy, you would not protest," she retorted angrily, after having found that honeyed pleading was having little effect.

Maimonides lifted a long, sharp knife he kept for surgery and gingerly placed it in its special sheath inside the medical satchel.

"You are correct," he said, not meeting her eyes.

"You need my help," she said, trying to keep her fury in check. He could be so damned stubborn!

"Nonsense." Maimonides continued filling the satchel with delicate crystal vials of healing ointments and camphors.

Miriam put a gentle hand on his arm, trying to put a soothing lilt to her voice.

"Uncle, you are entering a wolf's den. Do not go alone."

"The Franks will not harm me," he said, although she did not hear much conviction in his voice.

Miriam took a deep breath, knowing that she was about to broach an uncomfortable subject.

"You have been ill," she said. "If your hand slips, they will think you are trying to kill their king."

He jerked his arm away from her, his eyes flashing with wounded pride. Maimonides stormed over to an old cedar chest in a corner and pulled out a heavy glass bowl he used for mixing medicines. Even as he lifted it toward the worn satchel, Miriam could see the strain on his face as he fought the arthritis that had worsened over the past several months.

"My hand is as steady . . ." Her uncle's grip weakened and he dropped the bowl. It shattered into a thousand fragments against the cold stone floor of their apartment.

Betrayed by his own body even as he spoke, Maimonides knelt down to clean the shards from the ground, his head bowed in shame and fury. Miriam crouched beside him and wordlessly swept the glass fragments into a thistle bucket that was used for waste. Even though he would not face her, she saw the gleam of tears welling at the side of his eyes, and felt her heart break. How she loved this man! She cursed herself for hurting him, for pouring salt on the wounds of his soul, but she knew that she had no choice. She would not let him face the Franks alone. Her uncle was a man of God who did not know the depths of evil lurking in the hearts of the filthy European invaders. Miriam, however, had seen that evil up close on the road through Sinai. The Franks respected neither age nor wisdom, and should this King Richard die, as he probably would, they would not think twice about unleashing their anger on a weak old man. Miriam had failed to protect her mother and father from the barbarians; she would not allow them to take Maimonides from her as well.

Miriam leaned over and took her uncle's face in her hands, as he had often taken hers when she was a child and he wanted to comfort her in her grief. He finally met her eyes and saw that tears were flowing down her cheeks as well.

"Uncle, please. You trained me in your healing arts in preparation for this day. Do not let your pride stand in the way of doing the right thing for yourself. And your patient."

Maimonides looked down at the glass shards in his shaky hands.

"All a man has is his pride," he said softly. Miriam took his hand and gently squeezed it.

"You still have your pride," she said. "And mine along with it."

Maimonides embraced her for a long moment.

"Stay close to me, my dear," he said. "I will not lose another loved one to the Franks."

Miriam smiled at him. She did not allow him to see the growing panic that was filling her heart at the thought of facing the enemy again.

28

Miriam tried to pinch her nose shut, but the rancid odor of the Crusader camp had already overwhelmed her and was threatening to make her retch in a most unladylike fashion. The tent city that served as the base camp for thirty thousand Frankish soldiers looked and smelled like a sprawling nest of cockroaches. Miriam stared with barely disguised horror at the vast array of unkempt, spittle-and-blood-stained barbarians lumbering around the rocky coast of Acre.

She chose to ignore the grim looks of Saladin's guards, who believed the presence of a woman on such a dangerous mission was not only foolhardy but a harbinger of bad luck. She had ridden on a mare that had been hastily taken from Saladin's stables after Taqi al-Din had failed to change her uncle's mind about bringing her along. The Sultan's nephew had cursed, threatened, and cajoled Maimonides, but found his resistance infuriatingly obstinate. He had only acquiesced after one of the cloaked men, whom Miriam had been stunned to discover was a long-haired Frank, had pleaded with the young soldier to hasten. The man, whose name was apparently William, had spoken in French and his cloaked companion, who looked to be an African (or a very dark-skinned Arab, she couldn't be sure), translated his words for Taqi al-Din. Maimonides had schooled Miriam in several of the barbarians' languages, but she liked French the most. It was melodious and flowing, like her native Arabic. But she kept silent, not wishing to let the enemy realize that she understood his tongue, even though her uncle freely conversed with the knight in French. She preferred that he did not know about her fluency. Men who felt secure that they could not be understood inevitably let their guard down and spoke unwise words in the presence of their enemy.

As the motley and improbable crew of travelers—Arabs, Franks, and Jews—prepared to set off, Taqi al-Din had ordered them all to don drab peasant robes to hide their identities. In addition, he had demanded that Miriam cover her face with a full veil. She was about to protest, until she saw in her uncle's eyes that she would get no support from him on the issue. Muttering to herself, she endured the indignity and blanketed her mouth with the dark gauze. The riders then set off from Jerusalem through its northern gate. Taqi al-Din and William rode in front, the black interpreter constantly at the knight's side, with Miriam and Maimonides closely following, along with the Sultan's twin bodyguards, who covered the rear.

The journey to Acre would normally have taken three days, but Taqi al-Din had insisted that they follow a roundabout route on poorly traveled roads. At the first sign of approaching company, be it one of Saladin's routine patrol garrisons or a lonely farmer riding a donkey, the Sultan's nephew ordered them to take refuge behind trees, boulders, anything that would shield them from view, while he and one of the Egyptian bodyguards rode out to investigate. Invariably, there would be no threat, and they would be able to continue on after the interlopers had gone their way. Taqi al-Din stuck to this cautious strategy, despite William's pleas that they were losing precious time. Miriam had grumbled once to her uncle about the situation, but he counseled patience—the armies of war were gathering and there was no way to know when the Franks would send their first reconnaissance missions into Muslim territory. Maimonides had reminded her that, for all they knew, the Lionheart was already dead and his leaderless thugs were on their way in waves of thousands to loot and pillage the land. It was not a comforting thought.

But the journey had been uneventful. Miriam had spent the days listening carefully to William's conversations with Taqi al-Din. Most of their talks were about their personal histories and the culture of their respective homelands, but both men were assiduous in avoiding saying anything that would give tactical advantage to the other should their nations find themselves at war. She found it to be mostly a boasting contest, as often happens between men, with each soldier glorifying his own deeds and the valor of his people. But she was a natural student of body language and the secrets buried in the tenor of men's voices, so Miriam ignored the content of their words in place of analyzing their characters through how they spoke.

Taqi al-Din was everything she had heard—proud, brash, and confident. He seemed sincerely convinced that he was on a mission from

Allah, much like his revered uncle, and that he would play a pivotal role in pushing the Crusader scourge into the sea for all time. William appeared amused by the young man's grandiose sense of destiny, as if he had seen many such men in his own ranks, all of whom were inevitably humbled by forces far greater than their sense of self-importance. Miriam found the knight puzzling. He did not fit her image (and painful experience) of Frankish crudity. In fact, the chiseled-featured William reminded her of some of the refined young men of Cairo with whom she had dallied over the years. Surprisingly well educated (she had been shocked to hear him make a reference to Aristotle) and decently mannered, William Chinon had shattered every well-earned stereotype of the unclean barbarians that had filled her mind since that terrible day in Ascalon.

But now, standing in the midst of the unwashed Frankish hordes, she realized that the handsome knight was an exception. A rare exception. They had arrived on the outskirts of Acre in the middle of the fourth night of their journey. Taqi al-Din and the Egyptian brothers had led them to the hillside beyond the armored fortress and citadel that marked the extent of Muslim power. They were on their own from here. Miriam had glanced nervously at her uncle, and saw that he was as worried as she. William had sworn to them on the blood of Christ that he would protect their lives with his own when they entered the Crusader camp, but when they crossed over the hills and looked down upon the vast tent city that sprawled all the way out to the distant sea, she realized that his oath was empty. If the Franks wished to harm them, they would assuredly die. Or worse.

The Christian guards at the pass had appeared like ghosts in the wind from their hiding places behind the trees, their crossbows aimed at the newcomers. But they lowered their weapons when William's face became clear under the yellow light of the waning moon rising above the hills. The men had stared at the newcomers with surprise, but had asked their commander no questions.

She held her uncle's trembling hand as William strode forward through the gaping crowd of soldiers, his head raised with the confidence of command. And as they crossed the sea of enemy warriors, dressed in heavy hauberk armor underneath long flowing surcoats emblazoned with the Cross, she saw that the men did indeed fall aside, opening a path for the knight and his strange guests. But while they obviously acknowledged William's authority and none moved forward to harass them, every bloodshot eye in the camp was on the newcomers. On her. For the first time she was grateful for the veil that covered her face and the baggy robes that hid her ample curves. But even with only her green eyes and forehead visible through her heavy *niqab,* she could feel the horrible swell of lust. These men had been without the company of women for months and her very presence was bringing out their animal instincts.

It was disgusting and terrifying all at once. And it was bringing back awful memories that she had carefully locked away since she was a girl. Miriam felt her throat constricting and she struggled to breathe. Sweat trickled from her hair and her heart began to race uncontrollably. As the dreadful sounds of the enemy camp closed in around her like a prison, she wanted desperately to go home. This had been a dreadful mistake. She felt tears welling in her eyes. Miriam was not, in truth, the woman she pretended to be in the safety of her uncle's home—proud, courageous, invincible. Now faced with real danger, she was a frightened child again, the same terrified girl who had watched helplessly as her mother was thrust to the ground by a crazed Frank, his penis obscenely emerging like a dagger as his armored trousers fell to his pasty-looking knees. She was no more in control now than she had been that terrible day when she had seen . . .

NO.

Miriam stopped her thoughts with brutal finality. With an incredible force of willpower, she took control again. There was no past. No horrible violations, no torture, no deaths. There was only NOW. And in this moment her uncle needed a brave, competent protector, not a sniveling girl caught up in memories of events long past.

Miriam locked out all other images and sensations. The chaotic army camp, with its foul sights, sounds, and smells, vanished from her attention. Her consciousness was focused solely on the mission, like a lens gathering the far-flung light of the sun into a single, unstoppable beam of light. She stared straight ahead, her hand tightly clutching her uncle, as their guardian, William, led them toward a large crimson pavilion. The tent was massive, soaring almost fifty feet above them, but its trappings were muddied and worn. Outside the main entrance, she saw two grim-faced guards carrying drawn broadswords in one hand and holding eight-foot-long pikes in the other. She noticed that they were wearing faded leather cuirasses of the type worn by the native Frankish fighters, in contrast to the shining breastplates donned by William and the newer arrivals from Europe.

Miriam concluded that these men were part of the contingent that had been holed up in Acre, and were likely loyal to the one whom William had called Conrad during the long trek. From what snippets she had gleaned from William's guarded conversations with Taqi al-Din, Miriam deduced that Conrad had not yet accepted the Lionheart's full authority over the forces of both east and west. But if these men answered to Conrad, it seemed doubtful that they would acquiesce to William's stratagem.

Miriam was right. There was a long and uncomfortable moment in which the guards looked over the newly arrived visitors, their dark eyes scanning them with a combination of disbelief and suspicion. They did not seem impressed or intimidated by William, who she gathered was likely their superior.

"Stand aside," William finally said, when it became obvious that they were not prepared to do anything of the sort.

One of the guards, a tall Italian with bronzed skin and a long, twirling mustache, moved forward. He was standing toe-to-toe with William, his brown eyes locked on the knight's face. His companion, a shorter man with a pale face and curly black beard, kept his cold focus on William's guests.

"Why have you brought infidels into the sanctuary of the believers?" The soldier's voice was low, but rumbled like a tiger preparing to roar.

William stared straight back at the Italian, his face showing no fear, but Miriam saw that his hand was already on the pommel of his blade.

"They are healers," William said, enunciating every syllable as if speaking to an imbecile. "I have brought them to tend to the king."

"The Lionheart is beyond their help," the guard replied, his tone suggesting indifference to Richard's fate. He glanced with distaste at Khalil, the black interpreter, before turning his attention back to William. "I have been ordered by King Conrad to let no one pass, save a priest to administer the last rites."

"The king will have no need for last rites, my friend," William said, his voice soft but deadly. "But you will, if you continue to stand in my way."

The Italian guard laughed contemptuously.

"You forget your place, *Sir* William," the tanned warrior said, adding mocking emphasis on the nobleman's title. "You are not standing in the luxurious halls of London or Tours, where your word before the pampered knights of the Angevin is divine writ. You are a guest of King Conrad in his realm, and threatening his men will only bring you a swift burial under the sands of Acre."

The Italian glanced at his bearded friend for support. The man merely nodded his assent, his eyes never leaving Miriam or her uncle.

William considered the guard's words for a long moment, then nodded and took a step back. He bowed from his waist as if apologizing for an embarrassing faux pas at a dinner party, and then turned to face his Jewish wards behind him.

"Forgive me," he whispered to Miriam in his rudimentary Arabic. Before her mind could comprehend his words, he leaned forward and ripped her veil from her face. Her long, ebony curls flew free in the sea breeze, her face pallid from fear and confusion, the moonlight highlighting her sharp, startled features.

The guard's glance involuntarily fell on Miriam's beautiful face for a second and lingered just an instant too long on her startling emerald eyes. That was a mistake. William suddenly whirled, his sword whipped from its scabbard like a streak of lightning.

Before the guard or his shorter partner could react, William had sliced through the man's pike with one flowing move, like a leaf gliding in the current of a gentle stream. With the same blow, he cut deep into the Italian guard's right gauntlet, severing his hand at the wrist. The soldier screamed like a wild animal being tortured in some cruel hunter's trap. As the Italian fell to his knees, his bearded compatriot swung wildly at William with his blade. The knight jerked his neck back and barely missed the sharp edge that was meant to decapitate him.

Seeing his master in danger, the tall Yemeni slave rushed forward. Weaponless, he used his body to protect William. With a sharp kick to the knee, Khalil sent the attacker tumbling back even as he grabbed the pike from the falling guard. Honoring the prohibition against slaves bearing arms, Khalil instantly passed the long spear to William. The bearded guard tried to lift his sword again, but William skewered his sword arm with the deadly point of the pike.

Miriam pulled Maimonides back as far as she could from the dueling Christians. These men were supposed to be allies? They were all insane!

She had allowed herself to be lulled by William's gentle demeanor on their voyage into thinking that she had perhaps misjudged the nation of Franks, that there might be wise and peace-loving men among them. But here, watching the charming knight suddenly decimate his foes with ruthless efficiency, she realized that they all shared the same blood, even if some hid their true natures better than others. These Christians were all animals.

Miriam wanted to run, to escape this den of lunatics. She would rather brave the dark, leopard-infested hills surrounding the camp than spend another moment in this demons' lair. But even as she turned, her arm pulling her uncle toward her, she saw that they were surrounded. Hundreds of Crusaders were pouring out of their tents at the sound of the commotion around the command pavilion. And she stood before them with her face and hair uncovered. Naked, for all intents and purposes.

The men were moving toward Miriam, their grubby arms reaching out for her like the djinn from her childhood nightmares, faceless monsters that hid under her bed and were waiting to pull her into their soul-crushing embrace as she plummeted to a fiery doom beneath the earth . . .

"NO!"

It was William's voice. She felt rather than saw him move between her and the voracious, lust-driven crowd. His sword was still covered in the blood of his Christian brothers and it gleamed with crimson fire under the moonlight. She saw him toss something on the ground before him, then felt faint as she realized what it was. It was the severed hand of the Italian guard, its fingers still twitching in horrifying spasms.

"Anyone who lays a hand on them will lose it," he said. "They are under the protection of the House of Chinon."

She saw the men step back as a group, almost as if they were propelled by something more than the fire in William's voice. It was if an invisible force of angels had come to shield the Jews from the angry mob with their wings. She knew that the Muslims loved such fairy tales, and indeed their Prophet had used such powerful images to inspire many victories on the battlefield, but she never believed it was anything more than wishful thinking. Perhaps she had been too quick to dismiss the unseen world as a figment of the imagination. Whatever power was the source of the sudden field of calm that descended on the windy beach of

Acre at that moment, she thanked it profusely in her heavily pounding heart.

Without another word, William turned and hurried them toward the crimson tent, its guards still lying on the ground weeping like children from their injuries. Miriam forced herself to ignore the pool of blood that covered the threshold as she followed Maimonides inside the royal pavilion.

The interior was sparsely furnished, although the sandy ground had been covered with bearskin rugs. A man lay on a simple cot made of finely tied ropes. His hair was matted from sweat but still shone golden red, like the first colors of heaven as the sun vanished beneath the sea. His eyes were closed and he did not appear to be aware of their presence, but she did not think he was asleep, as he shivered violently.

So this was the great Richard of Aquitaine, known as the *Coeur de Lion* to the delusional French, and as a merciless killer to the rest of the civilized world. She could not suppress a moment of contemptuous satisfaction at the pathetic sight of the man who had arrived with the intent of murdering her people and driving them from the Holy Land. She shot Maimonides a glance, but she could not read his features. He seemed completely focused on the task at hand, examining the dying king even as he fumbled in his leather satchel for his ointments. Her uncle was such a pious man that she doubted evil thoughts of revenge ever arose in his heart. That was all well and good—she could think enough dark thoughts for the both of them.

"What is the meaning of this?!"

Miriam spun toward the booming voice behind her. A man with graying hair and a nasty scar on his left cheek was standing at the entrance to the tent. Three massive soldiers in silvery hauberks, their heads covered in coifs forged of interlocking rings, stood behind him, their lethal crossbows aimed directly at Maimonides and his niece.

William stepped forward and put himself in between the archers and their targets.

"They are healers, Lord Conrad," he said, his voice controlled, betraying no fear. "I am duty bound to save my king."

So, this was the infamous Conrad, Richard's rival for the loyalties of the Crusader forces. Miriam watched him closely as he moved toward William, his hands balled into fists at his side. Her eyes flew to the red scar underneath his left eye. She felt a heavy weight in her stomach.

There was something horribly familiar about him. Her gut told her she had seen him once before, but she couldn't remember when. Or, more accurate, some part of her didn't want to remember.

Conrad seemed like a pent-up thundercloud, ready to unleash a storm of invective in William's stoic face. Then Miriam saw him glance at her uncle, and all color drained from his face. When she saw what he was looking at, the same happened to her.

Maimonides had removed the heavy peasant robes when he entered the pavilion in order to afford more easy movement as he examined his royal patient. He was dressed in a simple tunic with baggy trousers underneath, no more dignified than the clothes of a farmer or a cabbage merchant at the souk. But, for some utterly incomprehensible, foolhardy, insane reason, he was also wearing a simple bronze charm on his neck. Shaped in the form of the Star of David.

Miriam wanted to reach over and strangle Maimonides herself. She could not imagine what would cause him to bring such an obvious trinket that identified them as the one thing the Franks hated more than Muslims. Jews.

"He is . . . he . . ." Conrad seemed utterly baffled, at a complete loss for words. Then the storm broke and he unsheathed his sword. "How dare you bring this Judas here! Answer me!"

Even as the situation spiraled down into the pit of Gehenna, William became calmer, his voice taking on a soothing tone.

"You are not the King of Jerusalem yet, my lord," he said, apparently unafraid of inciting Conrad's rage further with insult. "Not in the eyes of my men, who, I must remind you, outnumber your exhausted forces by double. Richard is my lord and theirs, and as long as my master breathes, I answer only to him."

There was something dangerous lurking underneath William's calm, a cold fury that Miriam had seen unleashed only moments before against the hapless guards who'd stood in his way. Perhaps Conrad sensed this as well, for he took one step back. But his weapon remained firmly grasped in his hand, and William made no move to arm himself. Yet.

Conrad stared at Miriam for a second, and she felt a terrible shiver go down her spine. There was something so familiar about those terrible gray eyes. But he broke her gaze and turned his attention to her uncle again. Throughout all the commotion Maimonides had continued about his business, removing particular vials and medicinal aides from his satchel. All doubt and fear were gone. He was in his element now. He was a doctor before a patient, and no man would come between him and his sacred duty.

Conrad stepped toward Maimonides, his sword still held before him. Miriam felt her heart leap into her throat. She noticed that William's hand was now edging closer to his own hilt.

Conrad looked over Maimonides with a mixture of curiosity and disgust.

"Where did you find this Jew who claims to be a healer?"

Miriam's eyes pleaded with William to make up a story, any tale that would preserve her uncle's life.

"He is the personal physician of the Sultan," the knight said, as if his connection with the hated king of the infidels was a matter of small import.

Conrad whirled to face William, his face contorting into an ugly look of outraged disbelief.

"Do you think Saladin would send a doctor and not an assassin?"

William stepped forward and placed a firm hand on Conrad's sword arm. The archers grew tense, readying to fire if the knight posed a threat to their king.

"If this man is an assassin, the king will die," he said slowly, his eyes locked on Conrad's face. "And if he is truly a doctor and you slay him, the king will die. So what is the harm in letting him go about his business?"

Perhaps Conrad sensed the darkness lurking behind William's perfectly calm exterior, for he lowered and finally sheathed his weapon. He walked back toward the archers, who were unsure as to whether they should drop their crossbows. The thick air of blood and danger had not lifted inside the royal tent. Conrad turned to face William again.

"Richard will not live to see the morning. Then I will be commander of the Crusade."

William shrugged, as if he could not care less.

"Perhaps."

"Know that I shall bury you in the same grave as your arrogant king."

William went to stand beside his gravely ill regent. He touched Richard's arm and gently squeezed his trembling hand.

"If the king dies tonight, I shall dig that grave myself," he said.

Not knowing how to respond, Conrad gave Miriam a final cold look before storming out of the tent, his archers following quickly on the putative king's heels.

William placed a comforting hand on the rabbi's shoulder, and then looked over at Miriam with a smile. The fire of wrath gone, his face was now haggard and exhausted.

"Please pardon his lack of chivalry," he said, and Khalil translated.

Maimonides laughed, a deep throaty sound that finally put Miriam at ease. As long as he could laugh like that, rich and mirthful, she felt safe, even in a den of scorpions.

"Do not fear," her uncle responded to William in French. "Conrad's reputation as a scoundrel long precedes him."

Miriam stepped over to the dying king's side. She ran her hand across his forehead. It was like touching a live coal.

"The fever is consuming him," she said in French before she could stop herself.

William looked at her in shock as the realization that this woman had understood every word he had said for the past four days hit him. She saw that the interpreter, Khalil, was grinning at her as if he was not surprised at all.

But, whatever else he was, the Frank was indeed a gentleman. Without making any reference to her rudeness in hiding her linguistic abilities from him, he continued speaking with her in his native tongue.

"Can you save him?"

"My uncle has been called a miracle worker by Jews and Muslims alike."

Maimonides looked at her like a father who was both proud and embarrassed to be the recipient of a child's unquestioning devotion.

"God works miracles, not I," he said piously. "If it is the will of God, Sir William, your king will be restored to the life of this world." Then his voice became somber. "When he chooses to do with that life, however, will be up to him."

Maimonides lifted a small wooden bowl that had replaced the larger one he had shattered in his pride at the onset of their journey. He poured water into the bowl and began to mix in herbs with droplets of a syrupy black tonic.

Miriam leaned forward and wiped Richard's brow with a wet towel. Although not exactly sure what motivated her to do it, she bent down and whispered in the unconscious man's ear.

"Do not leave us just yet, Your Majesty."

ichard the Lionheart stood in the heart of Jerusalem as its conqueror. Before him sprawled the burning remains of the once-majestic Dome of the Rock, its glittering cupola shattered. Thick black smoke poured out of the ruined edifice of the pagan temple and soared toward the crimson sky.

Richard stepped forward and gazed upon the righteous devastation he had wrought. The heavens above him churned with billowing clouds and crackled with bolts of fiery lightning that streaked across the earth, bringing swift retribution to the ungodly.

As he moved forward, he heard a terrible crack beneath his feet and looked down. The limestone platform upon which the heathen mosques had once stood was now carpeted with bodies and he had stepped on the exposed bones of a man. It was difficult to tell whether the unfortunate fellow had been friend or foe, as his body and clothes had been incinerated, the foul stench of burning flesh fuming from his charred remains. Richard tried to avoid stepping on other bodies, but it was impossible. There was not an inch of clear ground visible underneath the waves of severed limbs, heads, and torsos.

He had done this. Somehow, he knew in his heart that all these men were dead because of him. Their lives had been the price of victory. Yet somehow the thought of his triumph did not fill the terrible void that seemed to be enveloping his heart. He had seen dead men before, lying sprawled on a battlefield, their corpses soaked in blood and urine. But he had not felt empty, as he did now. Richard Plantagenet had never allowed weak emotions of remorse or guilt to haunt him after a day's slaughter. So why should such feelings disturb him now, at the moment of his crowning achievement? Jerusalem was his! The name of Richard the Lionheart would be inscribed in history alongside Alexander of Macedon, Julius Caesar, and Charles Martel. He wanted to cry out to the flaming heavens that he had proven the might and glory of Christ before the world, but no sound emerged from his parched lips.

Richard turned to look up on Jerusalem from the heart of Mount Zion. But he could see nothing. A wall of fire and sulfurous smoke covered the city. Richard thought he could see faces in the billowing clouds of pitch. The faces of the damned, the souls whom he had sent to oblivion in his quest for ultimate power. The wind rose and he thought he could hear their voices calling out to him, beckoning him to join them in the rotten pits of Hades.

"I told you that this was madness," a chilling voice spoke from somewhere behind him.

Richard knew who it was. He didn't want to turn around to face him. The thought of seeing the source of that terrible voice again, dripping as always with shame and embarrassment, was too much for him. But whatever power had brought him here knew no mercy. Richard felt himself turning around against his will to face the man whom he loved and hated more than any other in the world.

His father, Henry, stood behind him, dressed in gray robes of mourning, tears flowing down his cheeks.

"You wanted me to be a man, forged in battle." Richard's voice sounded hollow, distant.

Henry shook his head. His eyes were red with grief. Richard wanted to turn away, but found his legs frozen to the spot as if they had been encased in bronze.

"A real man chooses his battles," Henry said. "He does not let them choose him."

"I will save the Holy Land," Richard said.

Henry looked around at the carnage before them in disbelief.

"By destroying it?"

Damn him! Why could he not just rest beneath the earth, feeding the worms like other dead men? Why did he have to return to torture his son, to rub salt in the open wounds of his boy's soul?

"If need be," Richard said coldly. "I am a warrior."

His father's words entered his memory. *The throne is for real men who have tasted the fire of battle and death, not children with toy lances.* Henry had said that. It was his father's fault that this had happened, that he had taken this dark and foul path to Jerusalem. Surely the whole world and all the angels in Heaven knew that!

Richard wanted to absolve himself, to free his soul of the terrible bonds of blood and guilt, but the screams from the flaming city still tore through his mind. Henry was looking at him, no longer with horror, but with something worse, an expression that hit Richard like a razor-tipped lance skewering through his gut. Pity.

"Come, let me show you a true warrior," Henry said. He glided over the bodies that lined the devastated courtyard of the Dome, passing through them as if splashing through a thin puddle. Richard found himself following against his will, each footfall crushing the face or arm of a fallen warrior beneath him. Every body he stepped upon sent a shiver of disgust through his spine. Not the natural revulsion of the living toward the dead. But something much more horrifying. With every step, he felt their dying pain. The fear that had coursed through their veins as Azrael came to wrench their souls from their bodies. The Angel of Death, like a proud artist, always took a different form, never repeating himself. For some, he came as an arrow rushing straight at the terrified eye of the doomed man. For others, it was the blow of a curved sword cutting deep into the jugular. Or a bolt of fire that consumed the flesh of the man, every nerve feeling the coursing agony distinctly.

Please God, end this! Richard desperately hoped that one of the multitudes of tortures he was being forced to endure would claim him as well, freeing his soul from his tormented body. But the torture continued as his armored boots sloshed of their own accord through a river of blood that ran through the main street of Jerusalem. He knew even as he stepped into the sea of death that it was neither the blood of martyred Christian soldiers nor that of the infidel warriors. It was the blood of women and children, of innocents whose cries for mercy had been ignored by the frenzy of battle. And it burned him like boiling water as his legs forced him to travel beyond the fallen walls of the city into the fire-ravaged hills just beyond.

Then suddenly, just as swiftly as it had overcome him, the agony lifted. He felt no pain, no horror. The sky above him turned black as the sun vanished into eclipse. But a single ray of light descended from the heavens, illuminating the wondrous scene before him.

They were standing on a hilltop. Even though he had never been here before, Richard knew exactly where they were.

Golgotha. Three men hung from crosses before him. The two on either side appeared long dead, vultures feasting on the flesh of their eyes and skulls. But a small crowd was gathered before the tortured man hanging in the center. Richard gazed with reverence and wonder upon the emaciated figure, His head bowed under the weight of a blood-soaked crown of thorns.

CHRIST.

"It is for Him I fight," Richard said.

Henry looked at him with both compassion and resignation.

"You cannot fight for Him, my son. He has already won."

A mist passed between father and son, and when it lifted, King Henry was gone. Richard found himself moving toward the site of the Crucifixion. Tears welled in his eyes as he beheld the weeping disciples bowing before their dying master. A tall Roman centurion wielding an ugly spear pushed them back forcefully, all except a lone woman, who sat on the ground, rocking back and forth as if in prayer. Her hair was covered with a shimmering blue veil, and though he could not see her face, Richard knew in his heart who she was.

Mary. The Holy Virgin wept for her agonized son, her cries tearing through Richard's heart like a dagger. The King of England found himself kneeling in awe before the figure of Christ Himself.

"My Lord, please help me," Richard found himself saying to this figment of his feverish imagination. "You healed the blind and the leper. I left my home seeking Your glory. And it is for You that I am now dying."

The wind rose mournfully. And then the figure on the Cross began to stir.

"No, my son," Christ said in a soft voice. "It is I who die for you."

The figure raised his head, and Richard saw his blood-soaked, bearded face. A sudden cold terror gripped Richard's heart. This was not his Lord, Jesus of Nazareth. Although he had never met the man in person, one look in his dark, ancient eyes revealed the truth.

The figure on the Cross was Saladin.

Richard stared in horror at the obscene, blasphemous vision, only to feel himself pushed aside by the fast moving centurion. The Roman soldier stepped forward and, with one brutal blow, thrust his spear deep into Saladin's side. As the Sultan screamed in agony, the centurion turned to face the young king, a horrifying smile frozen on his golden face.

The centurion was Richard.

Richard screamed. He tried to flee, but his eyes would not leave the terrible sight. At that instant one of the disciples who bowed before Christ turned to face him, his face strangely peaceful, filled with forgiveness.

Richard knew the man instantly, wanted to cry out to him for help, but it was too late. With a mighty rumble, the earth shook and the ground beneath him gave way. He was falling backward, being sucked into the flaming vortex that had erupted from the bowels of Hell. As he plummeted downward, deeper into the all-encompassing darkness, he saw the Virgin Mary turn to look at him from above, her face shining with a light brighter than a thousand suns.

She was the most beautiful woman he had ever seen. Her curly black hair was visible as the roaring wind pushed her blue scarf back. Her eyes, green as the emerald waters of the sea, looked down upon him with an ethereal sadness as he was pulled deeper into the void.

"Holy Mother . . . please forgive me . . ." Richard's scream echoed as darkness took him . . .

* * *

RICHARD AWOKE WITH A start. He was not trapped inside a fiery lake, nor pinned beneath the claws of a demon. But he was in Hell nonetheless. Richard looked around at the torn fabric of the wretched command pavilion that signified his return from the land of the dead to a realm almost as unwelcoming—the bitter shores of Acre.

He could see the sunlight hitting the threshold, and found that it hurt his eyes. The king blinked and tried to get up, but his weak knees were stubbornly resistant. His hands fumbled against the sweat-stained woolen blanket that covered him from his feet to his neck. Richard felt like a man who had been mistaken for dead, only to awaken midway through the embalming process. He managed to raise himself up slightly from his waist, only to be overwhelmed by a sudden surge of nausea. He was barely able to bend over the side of the bed when an explosion of vomit erupted from his stomach.

At the sound of the king retching, a young woman dressed in evening blue appeared at his side. He did not know her name, but he felt as if he had seen her before. Her ebony curls were visible under a light head scarf, her sea-green eyes focused on him with concern. She bent down and helped the ailing king to lie back down, gingerly stepping around the nasty pool of vomit on the floor.

"Gently, Your Majesty," she said, in oddly accented French. "You are still weak."

Richard stared at this blue angel in confusion. Then he remembered. The dream . . . or was it?

"Are you the Virgin?" His voice sounded hoarse, as if he were an old man plagued with a disease of the throat.

The beautiful woman with the sharp cheekbones looked at him in surprise, as if perhaps she had misunderstood him. Then he saw rich color rise to her pallid cheeks.

"A gentleman does not ask such things of a lady, sir."

Richard the Lionheart, King of England and France, Master of the Third Crusade, felt like a blithering idiot.

"No, I mean . . . Who are you?"

The young woman brought a silver goblet filled with cold water. She held it to his lips, and he sipped it. He found that it burned his throat and he could swallow only a few drops at a time.

"A healer," she replied in that strange accent.

Richard looked into her soft face and saw the intelligence and strength in her eyes. She could not have been more than a girl, but there was wisdom in those orbs. And sadness.

"I have seen you before," he said, even as the intense images of his nightmare vanished from his waking memory.

"I doubt it, Your Majesty," she said softly.

Richard felt his strength returning even as he gazed into those crystalline eyes. And he felt an unusual flush in his cheeks that was not the product of fever.

"Your beauty is such that I cannot remember ever not knowing you," he said before he could stop himself. It sounded preposterous even as he spoke. Richard had little patience for most women, and usually thought flattery of the feminine heart beneath him. Still, he meant every word, although he could not explain why. The blue angel threw her head back and laughed heartily. It was a wondrous sound, like the gentle roar of the river water cascading down Les Cascades du Hérisson, the waterfalls that had awed him in his youth.

"You are clearly feeling much better," she said, with an amused smile that pierced Richard's heart.

30

The warm afternoon sun had vanished beneath the sea and twilight was setting in. It had been several days since he awakened and Richard was able to sit up in bed now, the muscles in his waist and thighs regaining their strength. He watched without expression as Maimonides approached his bed with a steaming bowl of some broth. Even from afar, it reeked of vinegar and camphor, and the king struggled to hold back a retch.

Richard had learned over the course of the past few days what had happened. William had successfully enlisted the gray-bearded doctor (and his beautiful niece), to come to his aid even as his soul prepared to fly free from its earthly bonds. His life had been saved, not by an ally, but by a Christ-killer who was in service to his sworn enemy. Richard would have laughed balefully at the irony, but he was loath to bring on another coughing fit.

Richard had not said more than a few words to this rabbi in whose hands his life had rested, but he realized that at least an expression of gratitude was in order. Maimonides had placed the steaming bowl on an oak stand beside the bed and was turning to leave, when Richard reached over and grasped his worn gray cloak weakly in his hand.

The rabbi turned to face the king, but before he could speak, a pair of visitors passed the threshold and approached. A delighted William came in wearing a sunny smile, which seemed so out of place on his usually stoic features. Beside him stood Conrad, who was decidedly less enthusiastic about his rival's unexpected return from the grave.

"You are improving rapidly, my lord. It is truly a miracle of God," William said. The king smiled at him softly, and then turned his attention back to the old unbeliever at his side.

"My liege tells me that I owe my life to you," Richard said, his voice strained but no longer hoarse.

"Not to me, but to my master, Saladin," the man said. "He is a man of honor, even to his enemies."

Conrad's eyes flashed.

"Careful, Your Majesty," he said in a voice that sounded remarkably like a snake's hiss. "The Jew seeks to sway your resolve against the heathen with honeyed words."

William moved to stand between the Lord of Montferrat and the doctor.

"Forgive him, Rabbi," the knight said. "You speak of honor, a concept foreign to Lord Conrad."

Conrad's face took on a murderous hue, but Richard raised his hand in warning. The nobleman looked like a rabid dog being held back only by the thinnest of chains.

"I do owe your master a debt," Richard said. "Tell him that I shall show him mercy when Jerusalem falls. He will be allowed to live, albeit in chains of gold."

Maimonides stood up straight and proud, an obviously difficult maneuver for his slightly hunched back.

"I believe he would prefer to die."

Conrad laughed unpleasantly.

"Then we will be glad to give him his heart's desire," the Lord of Montferrat said. William's fury at Conrad's rudeness to his guest was growing evident, and Richard decided to change the subject before the two men found themselves locked in a duel. He hesitated, and then posed the question that was weighing on his mind.

"Where is the lady Miriam?" the king asked, to everyone's surprise.

Maimonides shifted on his feet nervously.

"My niece has gone to answer the call of nature," he said uncomfortably. "Women's bodies are not well suited to the desert heat."

Richard smiled to himself softly. The call of nature, eh? Perhaps. But he hoped the girl was doing something different altogether at the moment. Something that would help him turn the tide of war even before a single arrow was fired.

Richard the Lionheart had seen a foreshadowing of the hell to come in his vision, and he was going to make sure that the devastation he had witnessed would not come to pass. And the only way to ensure that outcome would be to defeat Saladin before the Crusader army was forced to lay siege to Jerusalem.

If he had read her soul properly over the past few days, and had placed his chess pieces properly on the board, the green-eyed Jewess was about to bring about the fall of her master, the Sultan.

31

Miriam followed the gruff French guard through the maze of faded tents built from red-striped canvas, and past cruder refuges made from the hide of slaughtered camels and goats. She was keenly aware of hundreds of hungry male eyes on her as she walked through the Crusader camp. She was fully covered in the black Bedouin veil and baggy Persian robe known as a *burka,* and she was thankful for the protection afforded by the concealing gown. The surly guard, appointed by William after their dramatic arrival earlier in the week, growled at the spectators through his shaggy brown beard. His broadsword was unsheathed and held before him in ready position should a soldier's lust compel him to make an unwise move.

But they were unmolested. Word had spread through the camp that the infidel woman had helped save King Richard's life, and no man, at least among those who had sailed with the Lionheart, would risk dishonor by laying a hand on her.

The sun had long vanished beneath the western waters by the time they reached the large, filthy tent that served as one of the main latrines in the army base. It was made of heavy black cloth and held up by thick wood posts that crawled with an array of vile insects. Miriam waited outside while the guard poked his head in to check if there were any soldiers going about their business. She slipped her right hand underneath the veil, pinching her nose shut to stave off the overwhelming stench that wafted from the pits inside.

With the guard distracted for a moment, Miriam turned her attention to a blue-striped tent not far away, its cloth flaps waving mournfully in the sea breeze. It was unguarded and there was no sign of soldiers in the vicinity. Although her French guard did not know this, that little shelter was her true destination tonight.

The soldier returned to the mouth of the latrine tent. He appeared utterly oblivious to the sickening smells that permeated the area. Perhaps his nose was accustomed to the stench, because his own sweat-stained cuirass gave off a charming scent not altogether dissimilar.

"Hurry up, Jewess," he grunted. "Empty your bowels and then leave us."

The soldier took his position outside the tent, his legs firmly planted on the ground, his weapon ready to intercept any intruder. Miriam nodded and stepped inside, pulling a worn curtain over the entryway. This was a new addition, hastily arranged by an embarrassed William to accommodate her privacy, but it served a second purpose tonight.

The interior of the tent was almost pitch-black, with only a few shards of faint moonlight coming in through small tears in the roof above. It was just barely enough for her to see the rows of pits that had been gouged out of the earth and which served as the repository for the soldiers' bodily wastes. Miriam lifted her robes and carefully stepped around the holes that dotted the earth. She could hear skittering sounds from within some of the pits and knew they were infested with cockroaches, beetles, and other vermin.

Even though she tried to be careful, she felt the sickening slush as her wooden sandals sank into a pile of excrement that some drunken solider had left on the ground between the designated holes. She bit her tongue and suppressed a shudder as she pulled her foot back, rubbing it quickly against the dry earth in the hopes of getting most of the refuse off her toes.

Easing her way through the latrine tent, she found what she was looking for—a small slit in the tenth's cloth on the far side that she herself had carved with her sharp fingernails the night before. She pulled it open with her fingers, creating a hole just large enough for her to poke her head through and look around. No one in sight.

This was as she had expected. Over the past few days, Miriam had watched the camp carefully and had come to recognize the strict schedule followed by the army commanders. A half hour past sunset, the soldiers would gather on the center of the beach under large open fires to eat and commiserate, singing songs glorifying their past exploits and their future conquests against the evil Saracens. She could hear the sound now of thousands of voices echoing up from the coast to the base of the hills where this particular latrine tent was located. This was her moment.

Taking a deep breath and silently mouthing a prayer to a God she did not know for sure could hear her, Miriam dropped to her knees and crawled through the hole in the tent. The moment she was out, she looked right and left, but saw no one. With a heart beating like thunder, she ran in the direction of the solitary tent she had eyed earlier. From the corner of her eye she could see the sentry standing firm outside the latrine, his back to her. She realized that he might turn his head at any moment and see her. Miriam hurried, knowing she would not likely live long enough to use one of the many excuses she had concocted should she be caught wandering around the camp alone.

Through careful observation, Miriam had learned that the tent served as a meeting place for Richard and Conrad's generals. She had watched William and other top commanders gather inside, apparently to discuss matters of strategy, and was hoping beyond hope to find something inside that could help her people's cause.

As she approached the tent's small opening, Miriam froze. She could see a faint light glowing just beyond the portal, then she heard something that caused her heart to skip a beat. Voices! She felt all blood rush from her face. Over the past several days, Miriam had noted that the tent was always empty at the time of the evening repast, as the commanders would join their men's feasting and walk among them in the spirit of camaraderie. But tonight, apparently, a few had lagged behind to continue concocting their never-ending plots against the sultanate.

Her legs felt frozen to the spot in fear, even as she heard voices approaching. Just as the shadow of one of the men fell upon the threshold, Miriam's instinct for self-preservation kicked in. Like a fly managing to tear itself from a sticky line of tree sap, she fell back and hid behind the side of the tent even as two men emerged. One she had seen with William a few times before; he was an officer of some rank in Richard's military, fair-haired and beardless, his bulbous nose protruding prominently from his ruddy face. The other man was deeply tanned from long exposure to the sun and sported a bushy red mustache. She guessed he was one of Conrad's men, and from the looks of his complexion, probably a native of Palestine, a descendant of one of the marauders who had invaded a century before.

The men were arguing vociferously, but Miriam was too focused on avoiding detection to care about the content of their debate. She leaned back against the tent, painfully aware that her dark robes contrasted sharp with the brightly striped tent fabric. If they looked to their right just a little bit more, she would be exposed and likely put to death on the spot as a spy.

Which, of course, was what she was aiming to be, at least this one time. But she realized with growing trepidation that she was worse than a novice at this game—she was a fool. Miriam had read too many stories in adventure books she purchased in the markets of Cairo. But unlike the wonderful tales of Ali Baba's exploits, no magical bird or dutiful genie was going to come to her aid now. And now her impetuousness was about to bring about a very painful demise.

But, remarkably, the men continued on, absorbed in their machinations and stratagems. Soon she saw their outlines fading into the distance as they joined their fellow soldiers for a feast of unclean boar and other disgusting Frankish delicacies. Relieved but still conscious of the danger and the importance of her mission, Miriam glanced across the rocky plain to the latrine tent, still visible a hundred feet away. The guard remained at his post, but she knew that his own stomach would be rumbling soon as he smelled the wafting aroma of cooked meat. The Frenchman had not struck her as a very patient man.

Miriam slipped inside the tent. It was, as it appeared to be from without, a small pavilion with few furnishings. A rectangular cedar table stood near the entryway, with a few chairs scattered about, some with obviously broken legs. A bronze oil lamp hung from a rope tied to a pockmarked pole that supported the center of the tent.

Miriam walked slowly over to the table and froze, her heartbeat rising again. Arrayed across its polished flat surface was a dizzying collection of military documents in a variety of languages. She recognized the French and Italian scripts, but others seemed to be in a curvy alphabet that she thought might be a form of Byzantine Greek. A long parchment map was stretched out across the table, depicting the borders of Palestine, Syria, and Egypt with relative accuracy. The map was skewered with different colored quills that she guessed must represent the Crusaders' estimates of enemy forces and their locations.

Miriam felt both jubilation and panic rising in her heart. There was a wealth of information here, all of which could provide critical clues to the military plans of the Franks. But she was not a soldier and had no idea what was really of value. And time was running against her.

Realizing that she had tempted fate for far too long, Miriam resolved to grab something, anything, that she could bring back to Saladin's generals, and hope that it would be of some strategic value. Her eyes fell on a sheaf of parchments in French and she felt excitement turn to awe. She did not have time to read the document in whole, but a quick glance told her all she needed to know.

Grabbing the papers, she rolled them up and slipped them inside her long *burka*. Stepping carefully back to the entryway, she scanned outside. Still no sign of other soldiers, but she could see the guard at the latrine tent pacing back and forth impatiently. When he turned away from her direction for an instant, Miriam burst out of the tent and ran toward the rear of the latrine tent. As she flew like the wind toward the stinking pit holes that now seemed more welcoming to her than the gardens of Paradise, she realized that she was grinning like a schoolgirl underneath her veil.

32

Maimonides walked carefully on the sands of Acre. He was trying to keep the gray silt of the coast out of his leather sandals, but was failing miserably. As a younger fellow, he would have barely noticed the grating of the fine pebbles against the soles of his feet. But now even such minor irritations could inflame his tired muscles.

As he grimaced under the growing irritation of the sand, he looked up to see William beside him. Maimonides had come to know this young man over the past few days, and found that he was not at all what was to be expected of an enemy warrior. William was neither cruel nor arrogant. He appeared to be well read, and could quote the Bible as well as some of the classical Greek philosophers by heart. This was truly shocking considering that most of the Frankish soldiers could barely speak properly, much less read or write.

In William, the rabbi had found a glimmer of hope for Christendom. If such men, who valued knowledge and peace among the tribes of Adam over conquest and dominion, were allowed to speak their minds freely and touch the hearts of their brothers with their words, there was hope for the future of Europe. But Maimonides was doubtful. The days of the west were long past, and there was little hope that the likes of Socrates and Aristotle would ever rise again in those dark hinterlands.

Maimonides stumbled as his foot stuck a sharp rock too large to slip inside the tiny crevices of his sandals, and William grabbed him by the arm before he fell. The older man smiled in gratitude, and the knight nodded. They had not said much on this walk toward the beach, where the evening feast was fully under way. Maimonides and Miriam had not been allowed to eat with the Crusader soldiers, which was perfectly fine with them, and had taken their meals together in the dimly lit (and heavily guarded) storage tent that served as their hostel in the camp of the unbelievers. But tonight was likely their last evening in the company of the Franks, and William had chivalrously volunteered to take the rabbi out of his cramped lodgings and away from the ever-probing eyes of Conrad's guards.

Here on the beach, with the melody of crashing waves echoing in his ears, the rabbi felt almost at peace. Which was, of course, an illusion. Maimonides had succeeded in saving the life of the enemy king, but he had already surmised that Richard would repay the favor with blood and iron. It was obvious that the youthful king viewed the complete destruction of his foes as the only way to erase the dishonor of the life debt he now owed. It was the cost of injured pride, of course, which was not really a surprise. Pride was the very first sin, predating even man, when Lucifer refused to acknowledge the Lordship of the One. It was pride that exiled Adam to this wretched earth, filled with wrenching sorrow as well as terrible beauty. Pride was in the very essence of man, running in his veins thicker and more forcefully than blood itself.

Maimonides stopped as he looked ahead and saw the guard whom William had sent to watch over Miriam. The brown-bearded man paced back and forth with obvious irritation in front of a billowing black tent that the rabbi knew marked the latrine pits. Was his niece still inside? He felt his chest constrict with alarm. Perhaps Miriam was ill, having contracted one of the many diseases that seemed to sweep through the filthy camp continually.

William also saw the man and hurried in his direction. The guard, who had not yet noticed either William or Maimonides, finally strode up to the curtain that guarded the girl's privacy, obviously intent on flinging it aside to investigate her long absence.

"You have had enough time in there, Jewess!" he called out as he reached for the makeshift barrier. Watching him, Maimonides felt anger and shame rising in his breast. He did not wish to see his niece humiliated by this smelly lout, but he felt powerless to intervene.

He did not need to. William stormed up to the guard and grabbed him with a firm hand.

"What do you think you're doing?" William's voice was cold. The threat in the knight's voice was not lost on the startled soldier.

"My lord, the Jewess tarries," he said, his voice trembling. "I was afraid that she might be plotting—"

So rapidly that even Maimonides did not see it coming, William slapped the man hard across the face with his right hand, which was still protected by a shining gauntlet.

"While she squats over a hole? You disgust me."

The guard was bleeding from the side of his mouth, but he did not move in any way to defend himself from another onslaught.

"My lord . . ."

William grabbed the terrified fellow by his soiled crimson cloak.

"Another word, and I shall make you defecate in public before the whole army. Now get out of here!"

The embarrassed guard bowed low to William. He was so thrown by the incident that he even bowed to Maimonides, forgetting that the man was an infidel and an enemy. Then he hurried off in the direction of the campfires, where he would likely find more sympathetic companions.

William watched him go, his head shaking to and fro. He turned to face the rabbi beside him.

"I apologize, Rabbi," he said softly. "I am ashamed to call such men Christians."

Maimonides looked into the young man's storm-gray eyes that showed maturity and depth of character well beyond his years. He decided it was time to explore a mystery that had weighed heavily on his soul since he had come to see William as friend rather than foe. And perhaps, standing here alone, away from the ears of his fellow Franks, the knight would answer from the heart.

"May I be bold enough to ask you a personal question, Sir William?"

The knight seemed startled by the request. He looked into the rabbi's kindly face for a long moment before responding.

"You saved my master's life," William said. "Ask and it shall be answered."

"You are a decent man. Why do you take part in this war?"

It was a simple question, true, but Maimonides knew that the answer was likely far more complex than the knight could give in an easy reply.

The young man stood proud for a moment, his long brown hair flowing in the evening breeze. And then his shoulders slumped, as if he had been lifting a heavy burden for far too long.

"May I speak in confidence? As one man of honor to another?"

Maimonides nodded.

"This war is inevitable," William said, his voice sorrowful. "But it is my responsibility to make sure that my people remain true to the best of Christ's teachings, even in the midst of blood and death."

The rabbi nodded in understanding. He had heard the Sultan lecture his troops about strict obedience to the Islamic *sharia* before they entered battle. The Qur'an forbade the slaughter of civilians, women, children, and the elderly. It prohibited the destruction of trees and the poisoning of wells. And the moment an enemy combatant proclaimed the *shahadah*, the testimony of faith, *la ilaha il-Allah, Muhammadun rasul-Allah* (there is no deity but God and Muhammad is the Messenger of God), the opponent became a Muslim and could not be killed. In practice, these rules often fell by the wayside in the heat of battle, but the rabbi appreciated the fact that there were still men in the world who sought to restrain the horror of slaughter by following moral precepts. But it was unfortunate that such rules were even needed.

"It saddens me that so much death is administered in the name of God," Maimonides said.

William's eyes flashed and for a moment the rabbi thought the knight had taken offense somehow. But William seemed aflame with the passion of conviction rather than the heat of anger.

"This conflict is not about Christ or Allah," he said, his voice rising as if to proclaim the painful truth to be carried on the sea winds to the four corners of the world. "It is about wealth and power. About a civilization that was once the center of the world and is now reduced to a humiliated and impoverished backwater."

Maimonides was startled at the young man's depth of perception. He would have assumed that no Frank, no matter how well educated and thoughtful, could admit to himself the shameful reality behind a conflict that was cloaked in the sacred banner of Christ. And he felt compassion for William. How truly difficult it must be to know such a horrible truth, and yet be forced by the bonds of honor to further such an evil end.

"It must be hard for the sons of the Romans to watch camel herders rule the earth," the rabbi said sympathetically. And, yes, he truly did understand. While he had been raised in the company of Arabs all his life, had been accepted into the innermost circles of Muslim power as an ally, Maimonides would always be a stranger. He was a Jew living in Jerusalem as a guest of another people, not as a native son come to pitch his tent in the sacred groves of his father Abraham. Seeing the glory of Muslim might, whether it be in the majestic Court of Lions in Cordova, or the towering minarets of Cairo, or the shining Dome that stood over what had once been the Jewish Temple, Maimonides was always reminded of his status as an inferior alien in a world ruled by men of a different tribe, a separate creed.

Living perennially in the shadow of the Muslim Prophet, he had been forced to accept that the days of Jewish might and power were long over. His people had once ruled this land where he now stood, from the emerald sea to the sparkling waters of the Jordan, and beyond. The kingdom of David and Solomon had been a shining realm of power and glory in the ancient world, rivaling the grandeur of the shahs of Persia, the majesty of the pharaohs. And it was gone forever. His people would travel the world until the end of time as lonely wanderers, despised and persecuted in the Christian west, despised but sullenly tolerated in the lands of Islam.

Yes, he knew what it was like to live in the grip of a lost time, days of victory and pride. And while he still hated the Franks, he understood that this vicious war came from a place of humiliation and loss. Pride indeed ran thick through the veins of man. Including his own.

"Perhaps there will come a time when the West will be powerful again and the Arabs will fight to restore their lost glory," William said simply.

Maimonides smiled. For all his wisdom, the knight was still a boy.

"You can always dream, my friend. You can always dream." No, the era of the Christians was at an end, even as the day of the Jews were long concluded in the scrolls of history. The fire of Islam had risen from the empty desert of Arabia like a sandstorm, sweeping away everything in its path. For almost six hundred years, the sons of Ishmael had been unstoppable, and they still showed no signs of losing their remarkable energy for conquest and expansion. Even now, facing a Frankish invasion into the very heart of their territory, they would ultimately prove victorious, although likely at a terrible cost. Of that Maimonides was sure. God had promised Ishmael that he would be a great nation alongside his cousins of the blood of Isaac, and the Lord had never broken His word to the Children of Abraham.

The rabbi's inner musings were interrupted by the sudden emergence of Miriam from inside the latrine tent. She looked at the two men with surprise, but managed a sheepish smile.

"There you are," the rabbi said. "I was beginning to get worried."

Looking at her closely, he felt an instant flash of concern. She was sweating heavily and her breathing was labored. Perhaps she had indeed contracted the camp fever. He would need to get her back to their quarters and examine her at length.

Miriam laughed, her voice sounding unusually high-pitched and strained.

"Just a nasty case of the runs, Uncle." She grimaced under the old man's embarrassed glare. The girl really needed to learn what was a proper topic of conversation in the company of men.

But William smiled at her and bowed formally from his waist as if greeting a queen, not an uncouth girl with the manners of a Bedouin horse trader.

"Then, at last, we share something in common, my lady."

Maimonides saw a flush of color rise in his niece's cheeks and felt his heartbeat quicken with alarm as she met the eyes of the inordinately handsome young knight. Taking her hand in his, he quickly pulled Miriam away from William and started down the sandy path back to the main campsite.

They were leaving this mad world tomorrow. God be praised.

33

Richard was strong enough now to walk about, although he chose to sit in the gilded royal chair that had recently been off-loaded from one of his command ships docked in the Acre harbor. He ran his hand across the purple velvet, took in its tingling softness with a small sigh of pleasure. His senses felt as if they had been heightened since his return from the shadowy realm on the border of death, or perhaps he was just now more aware of the little joys of life, having come so close to losing his own. A soldier with a heavily pockmarked face and half a nose missing from an old arrow wound, entered the sparsely furnished tent. Bowing low before his resurrected king, the guard brought the news for which Richard had been waiting all morning.

"Have the Jews left?" the king asked.

"Yes, Your Majesty."

Richard nodded, feeling a sense of relief wash over him. He had found the presence of the doctor and his splendid niece discomfiting, but for different reasons. The rabbi had been an embarrassing reminder of Richard's humiliating salvation at the hand of the infidels, and he was glad to have him gone. But the girl was another matter. There was something about her presence that made his heart beat faster. She was attractive enough, but it was her unusually sharp mind, her rapier tongue, that intrigued him. In all his years, he had never met a woman who seemed so utterly unimpressed by the male species. No, actually, that wasn't true. He had known only one other woman who walked with such fearlessness and dignity in the midst of male power. His mother, Eleanor. In his rare moments of reflection on the matter, Richard had surmised that his general disdain for the opposite sex had been inherited from Eleanor, who had no patience for the frivolity and weakness of her kind. In Eleanor, Richard had come to love and admire the very qualities that other woman feared to develop—strength, courage, ingenuity. No man had been a match for her, not even her husband. King Henry could defeat her in battle and imprison her, yet he could not quash her indomitable spirit.

It was that same fire that he had been surprised to see in the young Jewess. He had watched her closely and had been truly fascinated by her rapid mind and cunning sense of humor. She struck him as the rare kind of woman whom a man could make love to, and then lie awake with, discussing matters of state and court intrigue. He had indulged these thoughts as she had bathed him nightly. He would lie naked on his cot save for a cloth over his loins, and she would rinse his grimy and sweat-stained body with a wet rag. She obviously knew that men underestimated her because of her gender and her religion, but Richard realized that rather than being insulted, Miriam enjoyed this cloak of misunderstanding. It permitted her to feel superior to the men around her, allowed her to manipulate and control them without ever revealing to the puppets who the true master was. In that respect, she was very much like Eleanor. He had seen the resemblance most clearly in her coquettish smiles and flattering words, which softened even the most virulent Jew haters among his troops. Whether or not Saladin had sent Miriam with that purpose in mind, the healer's aide obviously saw her own role as that of an informal spy who would try to bring back enough information to her master to change the outcome of the war. It was clearly a girlish delusion, but Richard had decided to see if he could use it to his advantage.

"And the girl? You're sure that she has the plans?"

The guard straightened, as if in mild reproach that his veracity would be in any doubt.

"We did as you commanded, sire."

Richard sighed. On one level, he was quite delighted that the pretty Jewess had walked so easily into his trap. Having seen her pretend not to listen to his men when they spoke in hushed tones to him of military strategy and plans for the impending invasion, he had decided to test his intuition. Richard had instructed his guards to take her regularly near one of the pavilions that normally served as a meeting place for his commanders and let slip enough information about the existence of critical war plans kept in that tent to whet her appetite. As expected, she had found the time to sneak in and steal some forged materials that he had ordered left there for exactly this purpose. Now she was on her way back to his enemies with documents that, if everything went right, would mislead the Saracens about his true intentions.

It had worked perfectly, but Richard was disappointed in Miriam. His mother would not have fallen so easily for the ruse.

His conflicted emotions must have been evident on his face, as the guard raised an eyebrow.

"You seem dissatisfied, my lord."

"I understand why Saladin would use her as a spy," Richard said, even though he was not completely convinced that the girl had been acting on the Sultan's orders. "Still, I expected more from him."

Or Richard had come to hope more from *her*? The woman who had saved his life, who had guided his soul back from the clutches of death, ultimately used and betrayed him the moment she was given the opportunity. It was a thought that made him feel, even in the midst of thirty thousand loyal men, very alone.

The guard snorted.

"Saladin is in truth a pagan, my lord. Any man who would use a woman's guile as a means to win a war has no honor."

Indeed, Richard thought uncomfortably. How true.

34

*M*iriam waited in the ornate antechamber. She stared down at the black marble floor inscribed with a series of complex geometric forms in silvery paint. Eight-pointed stars interconnected with hexagrams and dodecahedrons in whose segmented centers were drawn circles of orange blossoms and roses. All around her the walls were covered in lush Persian tapestries depicting scenes from the *Shahnameh,* the massive epic of Iranian royal history that synthesized legend, myth, and fact spanning thousands of years of oral tradition. Woven in threads of vibrant scarlet, emerald, and vermilion, the tapestries depicted hunting scenes featuring the great kings of the region, men like Cyrus, Darius, and Xerxes, who had founded a civilization that had outlasted that of the Greeks and the pharaohs. The noble warrior Rustam seated on his valiant steed Rakush battled a scaly dragon, while fair maidens wept tears of spun gold at his feet, thanking him profusely for once again saving their lives.

It was always the women who were being rescued by the heroism of brave, confident men in such stories, Miriam thought. Ever since she was a little girl, she had wanted to turn the tables and weave a tale in which the maiden saved the foolhardy warriors from their own self-destructive follies. Perhaps that was what motivated her to put her life at considerable risk and achieve what none of Saladin's trained spies had accomplished—stealing Richard's war plans from under his very nose.

She had kept the folded parchments hidden between her breasts the entire trip back to Jerusalem. William had accompanied them only as far as the hills of Acre, where they met Taqi al-Din and an honor guard to take them back to Saladin. The Frankish knight had been polite and gentle toward Miriam and her uncle until the very end, and she had felt a tinge of real sadness at the farewell.

William had shown her that not every Frank was a monster, even if her experience at the camp reaffirmed that most of them truly were. As she pondered the course of the impending war, Miriam had a terrible feeling that her surreptitious efforts to aid the Sultan could ultimately be responsible for William's death. Defeating the Franks had been a primary driving force in her heart, but now that the enemy had at least one human face, she had been surprised at the surge of regret she felt when the handsome young man with the sad eyes turned to climb back down to the tent city. But she had forced the doubt out of her mind. William had chosen to fight on the side of evil, and whatever fate befell him was the product of his own will.

On the long journey back, Miriam had been unusually silent. Even when her uncle spoke to her about his perceptions of the Frankish military power and their chances of mounting a sustained assault from Acre, she had simply listened and kept her own opinions to herself. Maimonides had been surprised by her distant demeanor, and had regularly checked her forehead for signs of the camp fever. She loved talking politics and military strategy, everything a young woman should not be interested in, and now that he was indulging her interests, she had remained aloof.

It was only when they had arrived inside the confines of Jerusalem itself that she told the rabbi her secret. Maimonides was about to send her off to their home, where a relieved Rebecca was waiting, when she revealed to him what she had done. Her uncle had initially not quite comprehended her words. But then she produced the papers from inside her blue woolen robe, and witnessed the blood drain entirely from his aged face.

Not knowing what else to do, Maimonides had numbly passed the material along to Taqi al-Din as they stood outside the high stone walls of Saladin's palace. The young commander had read the materials with a look of complete shock and bewilderment, his eyes rising to stare at Miriam in both disbelief and awe. Then, against the rabbi's protestations, Saladin's nephew ordered Miriam brought to the diplomatic chamber alone while he himself spoke with the Sultan of this surprising development.

Saladin's ever-present Egyptian bodyguards had led Miriam inside, and then locked the door ominously. Now, after an hour of diligent waiting, Miriam was beginning to feel like a prisoner rather than a hero of the realm. All kinds of dark thoughts flashed through her mind. Perhaps the men of the court were so embarrassed at her daring espionage that they sought to detain her for fear of public scandal. Or perhaps she had foolishly violated some obscure Arab code of military honor that prohibited spying on an enemy during a period of truce. Maybe the Sultan would have no choice but to punish her for bringing his reputation as a man of honest dealing in disrepute.

Miriam heard the lock on the door click and she felt her heart leap. She looked up and was surprised to see the Sultan himself standing in the doorway.

Miriam almost gasped. Saladin looked remarkably different than when she had seen him last, many months ago on the shaded garden path in the outskirts of Jerusalem. He looked as if he had aged almost ten years. His eyes. Those dark pools that she had once seen lit by passion and desire now appeared dull and troubled. His shoulders were slightly stooped, as if a terrible weight were pressing in on him. He smiled at her, but it was tinged with sadness and exhaustion. Miriam wondered if he had slept at all since Richard's ships had dropped their anchors off the coast of Acre.

Miriam realized that she was staring rudely at the most powerful man in the land, and she quickly averted her eyes, bowing in her usually clumsy fashion. Saladin approached and, to her surprise, took her hand in his.

"Your message caught me by surprise," he said. "But it was the most pleasant surprise I have had in a long time." Saladin was holding her fingers tight, almost as if he were afraid that she would vanish. She looked up and stared into his eyes. Miriam saw in his sadness, felt in his touch, a deep need to connect with her, with anyone. And it suddenly struck her how lonely it must truly be to a leader among men at a time of great tumult.

"Sayyidi . . ." Miriam wasn't sure what to say as the strange electricity rose between them again. She forced herself to focus and speak. "I know that I acted without your authority, but I could not let the opportunity pass."

Saladin released her hand, but his eyes never left hers. He reached into his black velvet tunic and removed a sheaf of parchment. She immediately recognized the documents as the secret plans she had stolen from the Crusader tent. So Taqi al-Din had indeed taken the matter to the highest levels. But then, why did the Sultan look embarrassed rather than excited? Was it because it was a simple woman, a Jewess no less, who had the courage to do what none of his brilliantly trained spies were able to accomplish? She felt herself flush with anger at the thought. Miriam tried to hold her head up with dignity. Saladin should have been proud of her demonstrating such cunning in the face of almost certain death. Then why did she feel as if he was looking at her as if she were a wayward child he was loath to discipline?

"These documents are quite remarkable," the Sultan said slowly, as if carefully selecting every word. "What you have here would be critical to our defense of Jerusalem . . ."

He paused. Miriam felt like she was a condemned prisoner waiting for the blade to fall.

". . . if it weren't such an obvious forgery."

Miriam stepped back, as if he had slapped her.

"I don't understand," was all she could say. She felt her stomach plummeting and a wave of nausea rose into her throat.

Saladin smiled apologetically.

"This document purports to discuss some of Richard's strategy for the conquest of Palestine," the Sultan said. "But I believe he left it there for you to find."

"That's not possible," she said stubbornly, hoping that she would believe her own words. "He was deathly ill."

"Did he know that you were aware of this command tent where his generals conferred?"

Miriam forced herself to think back. Finally, she managed a feeble nod.

"His commanders spoke of it in my presence, but they always appeared to ignore me."

"I'm afraid that he would have known that few servants of his adversary could have passed up the chance to steal secrets under such circumstances, and so he prepared for that possibility," Saladin said. He paused. "It was what I would have done as well."

Miriam felt a flush of red in her cheeks as the truth of the situation dawned on her. All that time she had treated the Frankish king as a young, ignorant colt. She had laughed in her heart at how easily she had manipulated him. And yet it was Richard who had been pulling her strings all along.

Saladin met her eyes again. Instead of mocking her delusions of intrigue, he seemed full of admiration, and this surprised her.

"Do not fear," the Sultan said. "My generals will study this document to address my suspicions. It may be that we will be able to deduce the Lionheart's true strategy from the lies he has presented us."

"I feel like a fool." Miriam's sharpest tone, used only for those whom she held in the greatest contempt, was now turned against her own self.

The Sultan took Miriam's hand in his again, and this time his grip was softer. She felt the strange buzzing in her heart again, the wonderful dizzy intoxication that his presence seemed to produce.

"What you did was courageous. You put your life at risk for the sake of the Sultan. But why?"

It was a question that she had asked herself over the past several days since they left the enemy camp. She had not truly known the answer until this moment.

"You have been kind to my people," Miriam said. "I fear that should the Franks win, they will kill us all as their forefathers did."

Saladin's mouth curled in grim determination. The cold fire was back in his eyes.

"I will not let that happen. The Children of Abraham are bound together in Palestine, Miriam. Forever."

As he said this, Saladin stepped closer to her. Miriam tried not to let the growing tension between them cloud her thoughts, but it was a true challenge.

"I hope that once the Franks are defeated, our peoples will not turn on each other in search of a new enemy."

Saladin smiled, as if she were a child expressing fear that the sun would not rise tomorrow. The Arabs and Jews had been brothers for almost five hundred years. They had worked together ceaselessly to expand the civilizing influence of the caliphate and to beat back the ignorant hordes of Europe. How could it ever be otherwise?

"I cannot imagine that will ever happen," he said. Saladin was much closer to her now. She could almost feel his hot breath on her lips. And they tingled in anticipation.

"So you don't think I am mad for having tried my clumsy hand at spying?" She was trying to fight it, but his body was drawing her like a magnet.

"Oh, I have no doubt that you are mad," he said, his voice soft, almost inaudible. "But then, I too have lost my senses."

Saladin kissed Miriam, and this time she did not resist.

35

Miriam trembled as Saladin's lips caressed her neck. This cannot be happening, her mind screamed out. But her flesh paid no attention. All doubts, all fear, vanished as Saladin took her in his arms. She felt herself falling back against the silk cushions of his bed. Found herself disappearing into the all-encompassing otherness that was him.

His hands trembled as he unlaced her linen undergarments. She ran a finger across his chest, felt the line of a scar running from just above his heart down almost to his navel. Saladin shuddered as if the wound, which must have been years old, was now rendered raw again under her silky touch.

They did not speak, as if they both knew that words would somehow shatter the dream, break the illusion that they were indeed here together. The only sounds that came from their lips were stolen sighs, gentle gasps as their bodies flowed together effortlessly.

She ran her hand through his dark, curly hair as he kissed her neck, then her collarbone. Then her breasts. Saladin stroked her soft curves slowly, languorously. He ran a finger across her rosy nipples, cupped them in his palm as they hardened with excitement.

Miriam gasped as he bent down to suckle on her breasts. Fire raced up her spine as his tongue traced wet circles against her flesh. He clung to her like a child, seeking comfort and warmth. She wrapped her arms around his shoulders, drawing him closer as tears welled in her eyes. She could feel his need, his terrible aching need, and she desperately wanted to give herself to him in entirety. Body, soul, and all that lay beyond.

Her back arched as she poured herself into him. The iron muscles of his legs pinned her down, but she struggled to meet him. Her body was screaming for him now. She felt his manhood brush against her inner thigh and she let out a cry.

Saladin kissed her again, long and deep. He ran his hands along the side of her face, tracing the contours of her cheeks as if he were a blind man seeing her for the first time through his touch. She felt her own hands trace the sinewy flesh of his back, his thighs. Every now and then, she would pass over an ancient wound, and he would tense, then release with an excited moan.

She bit his lower lip softly and felt his heartbeat race against hers. Her bosom was pressed deep into his chest and she no longer knew where she ended and he began.

Then, as the rhythm of their love grew to a frenzied pitch, she wrapped her legs around his hips, locking him in. He lifted himself and thrust against her, and in that moment he was the warrior again. Forceful, strong, unstoppable. She screamed through gritted teeth as he entered her moist, scorching sheath, her most private flesh wrapping him and clinging as if she would never let him go.

The fire rose in their wildly beating hearts. Their blood itself was aflame with the joy of forbidden union. They were together, entwined in a void from which came the first and the last, and *I* and *thou* lost all meaning.

→ → →

ESTAPHAN STOOD OUTSIDE THE Sultan's private chamber deep in the bowels of the palace. He stepped slowly away from the door. He had seen enough, heard enough, to report back to his mistress. The eunuch had spent the past several months discreetly looking into the matter of the Jewess, and although he had never spoken even one word to her, he had come to admire the girl's spirit and courage. She had quickly gained a reputation in the court as a dangerously intelligent and independent young woman, but she exuded a genuine kindness and warmth that Estaphan found refreshing.

He had been gratified to report to the Sultana that Saladin appeared to be keeping his distance. Yasmeen had eventually grown bored of his uneventful updates and had let the matter drop. Then the girl had left with Maimonides to tend to the infidel king, and Estaphan had secretly sorrowed, believing that Miriam would be unlikely to return.

Yet not only did she come back unharmed, she had apparently caused some kind of stir in the upper echelons of the court. He had tried to uncover the exact nature of her activity, but had found that there were some things hidden even from his masterful investigations. Whatever she had done, she was being spoken of in admiring tones in the hushed councils of the nobility.

But then he had seen the Sultan emerge with her from his study and lead the girl up a private set of stairs. Estaphan knew that the dark passage the couple turned down went to only one place, unguarded and hidden from all save a very few who knew the secrets of the palace. Estaphan had followed in silence, praying that he would miraculously not find what, of course, he knew he would.

He had no choice but to report this unfortunate development to the Sultana. He realized that her paranoia ran deep and he had no doubt that she had her spies followed by other spies. The truth would come out, and if it did not roll first from his tongue, she would cut it out of his mouth with a knife.

Estaphan regretted the task before him, but he would perform his duty. And the lovely Miriam would die.

36

Mihret watched her mistress turn a distinct shade of crimson as she heard Estaphan's report. The trembling eunuch laced his account with a plethora of apologies, which only infuriated Yasmeen more. For a moment Mihret thought that the Sultana was going to pull one of the many daggers hidden throughout her chambers and plunge it into the heart of the unfortunate eunuch. That would have been regrettable, mused the sultry Nubian, as she had grown rather fond of the little man over the past few years. He had proven a good listener who kept her confidences when she was looking for a friend. And he had been surprisingly adept at giving her pleasure, despite his unfortunate mutilation, when she grew bored with the soft and scented touch of her mistress.

But Estaphan managed to live that day, if for no other reason than that the Sultana's pressing need for information ultimately outweighed her blinding rage. Yasmeen ordered the eunuch to conduct a more thorough investigation into the life of the Jewess. She needed all the information she could possibly gather if she were to eliminate this new rival in a fashion that raised the least suspicion. And caused the most suffering.

Estaphan hastily bowed and ran out of the private chamber, leaving Yasmeen alone with Mihret. The Sultana was wearing a long, flowing robe that Saladin had recently imported from China through his trading contacts in Tashkent. Made of the softest crimson silk and lined in rich brocade, the gown was layered in rich colors that swirled around the Sultana like a flowing rainbow. Mihret could tell from the gentle points of Yasmeen's dark nipples peeking through the cloth that she was naked underneath. Despite the seriousness of the current matter, and her queen's murderous mood, Mihret found herself getting aroused.

But if she wanted to scratch that itch, she needed to calm her mistress. Not too much, of course—anger easily led to wondrous passion—but just enough so that the Sultana would seek the release from her pent-up frustration that the concubine was more than happy to provide.

"She is just a passing fancy, my lady," Mihret said in a smooth voice. "He will return to your bed in time."

Yasmeen whirled, her hands clawing into fists. She appeared insulted and embarrassed at the same time. Mihret knew this could be a lethal combination in her mistress, and decided to proceed carefully.

"I care not if he touches me!" Yasmeen screamed, like a petulant child who fervently denies that a broken toy has any meaning for her. "The Sultan's caresses awaken nothing in my body anymore."

Mihret knew her lover well enough to realize that this was not true. While she did not doubt that Yasmeen enjoyed the soft pleasures of a woman's touch that Mihret had introduced into her life, the concubine had no illusions about where her mistress's heart really lay.

Yasmeen bint Nur al-Din loved Saladin ibn Ayyub more than anything in the world. Her soul was consumed by the man, every moment she spent in his towering shadow filled her with joy. Mihret knew that for all the proud lies the Sultana told herself, she would fall to her knees and weep at Saladin's feet if she thought there was any way to rekindle the flame that had once consumed both their hearts. In truth, the concubine felt sorry for her mistress. The Sultana had really lost her husband many years before he had dallied with this Jewess or any of his other conquests. Saladin's first mistress had always been Jerusalem, and the *jihad* to conquer the Holy City had aroused a thirst far more powerful and all-consuming than any fountain of human love could ever quench.

"But you cannot think that this Jew has ambitions to take your place on the throne?" Mihret chose her words carefully, allowed Yasmeen to deceive herself into believing that she was only threatened by the presumptuous girl's proximity to the seat of power.

Yasmeen stiffened and calmed slightly, her mind obviously beginning to work through what needed to be done.

"She is wily, like all her people," she said, her voice now smooth and sharp as ice. "But she is a novice playing against a master."

"How will you handle her? If the Sultan finds out . . ."

Yasmeen's perfectly manicured eyebrows rose defiantly.

"Do you think I am a fool?!" She hissed like a snake.

Mihret pretended to cringe at the very outburst she had carefully engineered. The Nubian pouted in fake dismay at the Sultana's wrath, twisting a strand of her long, curly hair around her right index finger. It was a practiced maneuver, one that she knew always evoked her mistress's desire.

Yasmeen took a deep breath to calm herself. With that last outburst, she was finally at a place where her rage was locked up and controlled, like a bull in a steel pen. Mihret knew that her queen could now focus and do what needed to be done without undue brashness or foolhardy risk taking. Mission accomplished, Mihret thought with an inner smile. Now it was time to reap her reward.

"I am sorry," the Sultana said, reaching out to take Mihret's henna-dyed hand in her own. "You are the only thing in my life I care about."

Mihret moved forward and kissed the Sultana softly on the lips.

"And you are the center of my world."

Yasmeen's face was flushed, not with rage toward her husband but with desire for her servant girl. She led the tall African beauty by the hand back toward the bed where they would spend a delightful evening under the soft caresses of velvet sheets and moist tongues.

"Come, let us not mention palace intrigue," Yasmeen said as she undid the sash on her robe. Her perfectly rounded breasts broke free and Mihret stroked them with her hands, enjoying the feeling of her nipples hardening against her palms. "The moon is full tonight and the crickets sing of love."

37

*R*ichard surveyed the chaos of battle from his post on the hills outside Acre. Once he had fully recovered, the King of England had wasted no time in concentrating the combined Crusader and native Frankish forces into an all-out onslaught of the infidel stronghold. After conducting extensive discussions with Conrad's generals about their failed efforts to besiege the citadel, Richard had consulted with William and his old ally King Philip Augustus of France. The final strategy that emerged was both bold and untested, and as such would likely catch the complacent Saracens off guard.

So far it had worked. Richard had ordered the construction of a series of specialized siege engines. Over Conrad's protests that traditional siege towers had proved useless against the fortified walls of Acre, Richard had focused on developing a diverse group of weapons. Individually, these siege engines would likely have had little impact on the city's defensive barriers, but Richard hoped that, in combination, they would prove lethal. His primary focus was to develop a series of massive slings known as mangonels, of sewn leather and raw hides, which would be used to pummel the city's massive steel-enforced gates with rocks almost as high as a man stood tall. His soldiers found such boulders scattered throughout the hills that served as the de facto boundary between the Frankish camp and the Muslim army. Teams of thirty to forty men worked around the clock to load the huge rocks onto wooden carts and carry them across the precarious hillside and down to the waiting catapults.

Even as the Crusaders pummeled the city gates, Richard had ordered his men to build several trenches that were slowly encroaching upon the walls of Acre. Earlier attempts to dig under the walls had failed because of the constant barrage of arrows that rained down upon any Frankish soldier who came close enough to try. So the Lionheart had ordered an earthen dike built on the outskirts of the Frankish camp. The dike had a fortified wall in the fore and was surrounded by round stone towers meant to deflect any missile barrage unleashed by the Arab soldiers hiding in the city ramparts. Using the dike as a shield, his men dug a long trench that crawled daily closer to Acre. After naphtha-laced arrows failed to halt the slow-moving dike, the Saracens had been forced to reveal their secret weapon. On the fifth day of the siege, they unleashed a terrifying round of Greek fire on the trench diggers. Long lines of flame thundered from tubes placed atop Acre's defense towers, like the breath of an enraged dragon. The green earth outside the coastal city was burned to ash, and rows of olive trees were reduced to smoking rubble. But the dike survived the onslaught, inching ever closer to its target, with the lethargic ease of a spider that knows its prey is trapped in the web and cannot escape.

Richard was glad that he had acted upon the assumption that the Saracens possessed the Greek fire, and had strengthened his men's defenses against it. His own stores of the miraculous Byzantine explosive were limited and he chose not to use them against the impregnable walls. But knowing that the enemy possessed what was an obviously large supply of the flaming substance was critical information for his strategists. And it also made the capture of the city and its weapons stores even more important. Richard hoped that enough of the Muslims' supply would survive after the battle that he could use it against them in the more critical fights that were bound to ensue once the Crusaders penetrated the interior of the Holy Land.

Which looked more and more like an inevitable reality than a warrior's hopeful fantasy. While the Muslim defenders worried about the pounding of Richard's slings, and the danger posed to the walls by his approaching diggers, they found themselves distracted by the regular efforts of Richard's men to scale the walls. Using every technique available, the Franks beset the stone barrier from all sides. Wooden towers worked alongside scaling ladders. Some of his braver men even attempted to climb the ramparts with ropes, although this placed them in the direct line of a Saracen arrow or a javelin dropped from above.

The combined efforts were achieving exactly what Richard had hoped for. He was confusing and wearying his adversaries. Even though they could handle any of the siege tactics individually with relative ease, the never-ending onslaught of such a diverse and unpredictable series of threats was beginning to sap their morale.

As the trench diggers came within a hundred feet of the Acre walls by the second week of the siege, the Saracens realized they had no choice. They threw the gates open briefly to allow several hundred of their soldiers to flood onto the field in the hope of eliminating the diggers before they reached their target. Richard had anticipated this attack and had hidden five hundred of his own troops inside the long line of the trench itself. The Muslim attackers were met by an explosion of crossbow bolts from within the bowels of the earth. Many died without ever seeing their killers' faces.

With the Muslim army now engaging his men directly, Richard had sent William into the field with a contingent of his finest knights. The resulting clash of sword upon scimitar had been a welcome sound to the king's ears. He had grown weary of the slow methodical approach that he knew was vital to the success of the siege, and he had felt his blood surge with excitement at the sight of his brave soldiers taking on the pagan fighters in hand-to-hand combat.

And now Richard stood on the hill, witness to the moment of his impending triumph. The initial skirmishes had ended in stalemates, but he realized that this was about to change. Despite continued Saracen charges against the heavily guarded dike, his diggers were finally at the wall itself, chipping away steadily at its foundations. It would not be long before they dug deep enough to expose its vulnerable base and create a breach.

The Muslims had, of course, realized this as well, and they now launched the greatest offensive of the fortnight-old battle. From within the city walls, and the surrounding Muslim tent camps to the east, emerged a force of three thousand heavily armored Saracens, led by over six hundred mounted horsemen. This massive force, which had been reinforced steadily over the past several days by battalions sent from Jerusalem, descended on the plain outside Acre like an army of rats thundering hungrily toward a freshly killed carcass. They were led by Saladin's nephew Taqi al-Din, one of the infidels who had aided William in his embarrassing but necessary mission to save Richard's life. The king had sent word through a herald that he was willing to take into account Taqi al-Din's chivalry in aiding him, and would spare his men should he surrender. The pale-faced messenger had returned with Richard's note pinned to his hand with a dagger.

Richard watched Taqi al-Din now from his command station atop the Acre hills. The crimson-turbaned youth was clearly valiant, if somewhat reckless, in his decision to participate directly in the battle, but Richard understood his motivation. The king himself had waded into combat when it was necessary to boost the morale of his soldiers. Men, he had discovered, were more willing to die for you if you showed that you were willing to die for them. And Taqi al-Din's presence on the plain was certainly having a dramatic effect on the Muslim soldiers. He charged forward apparently without a second thought directly into the shields of Richard's infantry, lopping off heads with a single blow of his curved sword. This red-robed warrior with the seemingly unstoppable blade caused panic wherever he rode on his gray stallion. Though he should have been felled by a storm of crossbow bolts fired in his direction, Taqi al-Din seemed protected by an invisible force. He seemed completely unaware of the arrows and other missiles flying at him from all sides, and Richard noted that the warrior's apparent invincibility was fueling the Muslims' courage and his own men's cowardice. The king knew that myths were more powerful than facts, and he could not permit the legend of Saladin's nephew to grow any larger this day.

Even as Richard girded his long sword to his waist with a leather belt, William rode up, his face bloodied from the fight and blackened from the smoke that covered the battlefield like a dense fog.

"Are your knights prepared?" the king asked without looking up as he donned a mail coif and hauberk.

William looked him over as Richard tightened the straps of his shining breastplate, obviously realizing what the king intended to do.

"They have waited their entire lives for this moment."

Conrad suddenly appeared astride a perfectly groomed white horse, which Richard guessed had never set foot on a battlefield. He decided to ignore the pompous nobleman who persisted in clinging to his delusions of kingship.

"Once Acre falls, we will have a secure base from which to launch the final sweep of our campaign," Richard said to William, who also appeared to be ignoring the Marquis of Montferrat.

"It will not be that easy," Conrad hissed. "Do not underestimate the resistance of the Saracens."

Richard sighed, forcing himself to hold back his temper. For better or worse, Conrad still commanded the loyalty of the native Frankish troops who made up almost half of his combined army. He wanted nothing more than to pierce the annoying pretender's heart with his sword right there and then, but he did not wish to deal with the consequences. Not at that moment, at least.

"You are always ready for failure, Conrad," Richard said with scorn. "Sit back and watch how the Angevin conduct battle."

With that, Richard stormed over to his own stallion and jumped onto the saddle in one practiced move. He nodded to William, who pulled a trumpet to his lips and blew a thunderous blast, which, despite the terrible din of the battle below, echoed through the hills. The sound would carry across the bloodstained field and penetrate deep into the hearts of his brave men. And they would know that their king would soon be among them.

The sound of the horn was immediately followed by the clamor of hooves as five hundred of William's finest knights rode up the pass and exploded from the hills, charging straight at the Muslim hordes below.

It was an awe-inspiring sight. The armored stallions rode like a flood straight into the center of the battle, the horses trampling over any man who stood in their way, regardless of which side he fought for. These knights were focused on one goal alone—to confront Taqi al-Din's legendary horsemen and smash them into muddy graves before the eyes of both armies. Their unrelenting push through bodies and weapons was met by terror and panic, and quickly unleashed the fury of their turbaned counterparts. The two cavalries met in the center of the battlefield in a sandstorm of agony and death.

While Richard proudly watched the carnage below, Conrad could only scream in outrage.

"Those are our best knights and you have sent them in to die like expendable foot soldiers!" His voice was growing shrill to the point of hysteria. "If they are slaughtered, we will suffer a loss that could mean the end to this campaign."

"You should not underestimate my men," Richard said through gritted teeth.

And then he saw what he had been waiting for. There was a tremendous explosion from the base of the Acre walls where his diggers were valiantly continuing their efforts. They had clearly breached the foundations and had used Richard's limited supply of Greek fire to tear down the barrier at its roots. And it had worked! With a terrible shudder, a portion of the wall collapsed, sending the Saracen archers on its ramparts plummeting a hundred feet to their deaths. Heavy stones fell like titanic raindrops on the fighters below, killing both the infidels and many of Richard's men. But the loss was acceptable. As the smoke and dust cleared from the collapsing structure, Richard could already see a group of his soldiers tearing through the breach and entering the city' perimeter.

Richard could have sat back and watched what was now an inevitable victory, but the fire of conquest that raged in his blood compelled him into action. Even from the distance, he could see the red-robed warrior Taqi al-Din continuing his now desperate defense of the falling city, refusing to retreat, and he would not be upstaged by an infidel's courage.

Richard turned a joyous face to William, who watched the devastation below stone-faced, without registering either glee or sorrow. War, his friend had once said, was a duty, not a passion. Richard knew William had been fighting nobly and without stop on the front lines for several days. He would not compel him to risk his life again, when it was unnecessary, and victory was assured. But he felt duty bound to present the knight with the option.

"Are you ready to die for God?" he asked William.

"I am," the knight replied with the utmost serenity.

"Then come. Let us show the Saracens the valor of kings."

Conrad stared at the two commanders as their horses charged down the hill, away from the safety of the command center and straight into the heart of the battle.

"Where are you going?" Conrad cried out in shock. "This is madness!"

Madness it was, but Richard loved every moment of it. He swept down onto the mass of infidel soldiers like a hawk descending on its prey. His shining blade was instantly covered in the blood of his enemies. All around him, men fought with courage, facing their opponents in hand-to-hand combat. Axes, spears, and daggers were all in use, and the most frenzied fighters, their eyes red with bloodlust, continued attacking their adversaries with hands and teeth even when they had been completely disarmed. It was primal and glorious, and Richard felt more alive, standing in the center of a melee of hate, blood, and fire, than he ever felt safely ensconced on the throne.

Richard swung his broadsword and felt the blade tear through metal and flesh. His sword ripped through the neck tendons of a swarthy opponent and sliced into his windpipe. The king caught the look of horror in the eyes of his enemy before his head was detached from his torso and vanished underneath a horse's hooves. Blood erupted like a fountain from the stump that was all that remained of the Arab's neck, and Richard was showered by the hot liquid. Arab soldiers saw the king, covered in gore and entrails, his eyes burning with the madness of murder, and tried to flee from his charge. To little avail. The bloodlust had taken possession of Richard and turned him into a whirlwind of death.

He wanted to find Taqi al-Din and take on the Muslim commander in direct combat, but in the mass of fighters that surged all around him, it was impossible to locate the crimson-robed warrior. No matter. Each of the lesser infidels whom he dispatched to Hell this day would receive the brunt of his rage, and that was fine with him.

Then Richard heard a cry in Arabic spreading among the struggling troops. He did not need a translator to understand the call for retreat. The Muslims knew that Acre was lost, and it made no sense for them to sacrifice their men in the defense of a city that was even now swarming with Richard's men who had crossed the breach. The king managed to cut off a few more heads and limbs of the fleeing infidels before Taqi al-Din's entire army reversed course and went tearing up the sides of the eastern hills from which they had descended.

Richard saw William's knights pursuing the enemy, and he would have gone to join them, but he needed all of his men focused on subduing Acre and eliminating whatever resistance remained inside the citadel. The king called out to William to summon his troops back, even as he caught a final glimpse of the red-robed Taqi al-Din standing on the hill above, watching the loss of the city with shame and rage. And then Saladin's nephew was gone.

Richard turned to gaze upon a vanquished Acre. For eighteen months, his predecessors had been unable to dislodge the desert invaders from this verdant coastal city that had once been the pride of Christendom. And he had accomplished the task in only a few weeks.

Watching the dense cloud of smoke that was rising from behind Acre's now-ineffective walls, Richard knew that it was only a matter of time before he liberated Jerusalem from Saladin.

Soaked in the blood of his defeated opponents, he turned back and rode over mountains of dead bodies and severed limbs, heading toward the safety of the command tent in the western heights. From here he would coordinate the city's surrender and he needed to speak with his generals about the resources necessary to successfully occupy and rebuild the damaged stronghold. No longer would his forces have to camp out in the harsh wilderness surrounded by Muslim invaders. With the fall of

Acre, Richard had acquired a new and well-provisioned base of operations from which to turn the Crusade into a war of conquest that he
would take straight into the heart of the Holy Land. To Saladin himself.

As he rode up to the command pavilion, where he was met by the
applause and cheers of his generals and the loyal King Philip Augustus,
Richard saw a pale-faced Conrad looking at the fallen city beneath them
in disbelief.

"May I present to you, Lord Conrad, the city of Acre," Richard said,
making no effort to hide the sneer in his voice. "The first domain in the
new kingdom of Jerusalem."

He did not specify, of course, who would be the king of this reconquered realm.

38

A l-Adil wanted to get up from his seat beside Saladin and tear
the mealymouthed herald's head off with his bare hands. But
he managed to restrain himself on the off chance that his
brother might take offense at such disrespect toward a visitor. Even if
the man was a filthy liar.

Walter's words still hung over the throne room like a cloud. Nobody
believed him. Nobody wanted to believe him.

"Acre has returned to the bosom of Christ. My lord bids you to surrender now and spare the Holy City further suffering."

Saladin continued to stare at the messenger with a perplexed look, as
if he could not understand how Walter would dare to come into his presence and baldly state such an obvious falsehood. They had received regular reports from Taqi al-Din, who had led the Muslim defense of the city,
and there had been no indication that the situation at Acre had radically
worsened in the past few days. The dispatches noted Richard's renewed
efforts at besieging the city, but indicated that the Muslim commanders
viewed these as nothing more than the usual irritants that were the price
of keeping the Crusaders trapped against the sea. Taqi al-Din's men had
withstood ten thousand of Conrad's soldiers camped on the shore for
almost eighteen months. How could this puny man who served as a

mouthpiece for the unbelievers really expect the Sultan to believe that his best warriors had been decisively defeated without any warning?

Al-Adil could no longer keep his silence in the face of such delusions.

"It is impossible. The boy king could not have advanced that quickly," he said forcefully, as if hoping that the conviction of his tone would make his words true.

Walter Algernon smiled as if in sympathy.

"I assure you that I witnessed the battle myself."

He reached into his robe and pulled out a silver medallion, about the size of a man's hand if all the fingers were outstretched. Al-Adil felt his stomach plummet and his head spin at the same time. Even from across the room, he recognized the amulet.

A muscled guard snatched the medallion from the hands of the herald and brought it to the Sultan. Saladin looked at it carefully, as if searching for any evidence of a forgery. On one side was an engraving of a royal eagle, Saladin's personal symbol, and on the other were inscribed the Sultan's favorite verses from the Holy Qur'an proclaiming that the abode of the righteous was in "gardens beneath which rivers flow." At last he raised his head, and spoke with grim acceptance.

"The seal of the town. So it is true."

His words were followed by a thunderous burst of disbelief, outrage, and despair. Al-Adil watched his brother, who sat motionless, the amulet still clutched in his right hand. For once Saladin did nothing to quiet the excited crowd, letting them express collectively all the personal emotions he was not allowed to show.

Al-Adil remembered that Saladin himself had ordered the seal to be minted upon the fall of Acre during the initial conquest of Palestine. The Sultan had presented the seal to his trusted envoy, the Egyptian general Karakush, whom he had placed as governor of the city. Karakush had hung the seal directly above his seat of judgment in the governor's mansion at the center of the city. A city that was now in the hands of the barbarians.

Al-Adil felt a wave of nausea blanket him as he thought about a second tragedy that was facing the court. No word had been received from Taqi al-Din in days. It was now appearing likely that his heroic nephew had died protecting the city, along with most of his men, the prized horsemen of the realm. The Muslim army had lost one of its most revered figures and a troop of its finest soldiers. The blow to morale would be immeasurable.

Walter attempted to speak up again, but his voice was drowned out by the cacophony of cries echoing throughout the chamber. He closed his mouth and waited patiently, as if he had all the time in the world now that Palestine's first defense against invasion had been broken. Saladin watched him with narrowed eyes, as if trying to read his body language, before finally shouting to an aide to restore order. After several long raps of the servant's staff on the marble floor, the din finally dropped to a bitter murmur and the herald was able to speak again.

"My lord says that he will not forget your kindness in dispatching a doctor to his aid," Walter said. "You will not be mistreated if you surrender."

All attention was now on the Sultan. Now that Acre had fallen, the threat to Jerusalem had become imminent. Every courtier knew that it was not beyond the realm of possibility for the Sultan to negotiate terms under such conditions.

Saladin turned to look at his brother, and then at the crowd of assembled dignitaries. His face was unreadable. Al-Adil knew that if the Sultan were looking for support among his cowardly retinue, he would be disappointed. Most were probably already making plans in their heads for a quick escape to Damascus. It was at that moment that the towering Kurd realized how lonely his brother's position really was. Al-Adil had watched Saladin rally a crew of untrained rabble and lead them to incredible victories, first against the Fatimid caliph in Cairo, and then against the once-invincible Franks of Jerusalem. And he had done so without any support from the titled schemers who had flooded his court after his victory. And now, with the possibility of a reversal of fortune on the horizon, these fair-weather allies would likely desert him to save their own necks. The Sultan had been alone at the start of his journey, and he was alone again as it appeared to draw to a close.

If Saladin knew the truth of his isolation in his heart, he chose not to show it. The Sultan sat ramrod straight, his eyebrows arched as he stared with focused intensity into the eyes of the overconfident herald. When he spoke, his voice sounded calmer and more relaxed than al-Adil had ever heard, but he sensed it was the terrifying calm that preceded a tempest.

"Tell your king that I will not rest until the Frankish scourge has been driven out of Palestine forever."

In that instant al-Adil knew that his brother would fight to the death to protect the Holy City.

Saladin's words seemed to stir the souls of the terrified men around him, and several of the nobles broke out into cheers and cries of defiance. But most remained quiet, obviously calculating whether their lord was speaking a viable truth or a hopeful fantasy.

The herald, for his part, seemed unperturbed by the Sultan's lethal gaze.

"My lord has one more message."

Saladin raised his fingers and steepled them in front of his face. He watched the pale-faced messenger carefully.

"Speak it."

Even al-Adil detected a slight hint of reticence on Walter's part to relay this final word. But the man cleared his throat and continued.

"Our soldiers hold three thousand of the good citizens of Acre as guests."

This was utterly unbelievable.

"You mean hostages," al-Adil snarled, uninterested in the niceties of diplomatic language.

The herald ignored these words and kept all of his attention on the Sultan, as if doing a quick mental analysis of how best to proceed with his delicate news.

"In war, it is difficult to guarantee the comfort and safety of guests," Walter continued, as if he were apologizing for an obvious but painful truth. "We are in a foreign land with limited resources."

Ah, so that was what this was all about. Al-Adil allowed a measure of hope to creep into his heart. If this Lionheart was a man whose soul was dominated by greed rather than by faith, then he could be dealt with. The prospect of sufficient compensation might just be enough to prevent a bloody and destructive invasion.

Saladin appeared to be thinking along the same lines.

"Your lord seeks a ransom. Name it."

The herald removed a piece of rolled parchment from inside his blue cloak. He slowly unfurled the document, which al-Adil guessed contained his written instructions. The man undoubtedly knew the exact sum by heart, but the activity allowed him to lower his eyes and not have to face the Sultan as he made his exorbitant claim.

"One hundred thousand gold bezants."

If al-Adil had any doubts that he had heard the Frank correctly, they immediately vanished in the tumult of collective disbelief. Even Saladin appeared stupefied.

"If Richard cannot take the sultanate by force, he wishes to bankrupt its treasury instead."

The herald attempted a small, embarrassed smile, meant to indicate that he was merely a messenger.

"My lord asks that you not tarry in meeting his request," Walter said quickly, again glancing unnecessarily at his instructions in order to keep his eyes lowered. "After one week, he will no longer be able to guarantee the safety of his guests."

Al-Adil felt his anger turn white-hot. His hand was gripped firmly on the hilt of his sword. It took every bit of his self-restraint to keep from decapitating the pompous messenger and sending his head back as a fitting reply to the villainous King of England.

And to al-Adil's surprise, he was for once not alone in his open display of rage. His brother seemed to have finally discarded his carefully maintained air of detachment, cultivated over decades of diplomacy. The Sultan stood up from his throne, his hands clenched at his side, and the entire room fell silent. The herald looked truly afraid for the first time.

When Saladin spoke, the polite and emotionally controlled statesmen was gone. His voice thundered with the fury of his Kurdish warrior blood.

"Your king is a pig-eating son of a whore," he seethed. "I should have let him die."

And without another word, without even a glance at the assembly of shocked courtiers, the Sultan turned and stormed out of the judgment hall.

39

Miriam watched Saladin pace around the chamber, his head bowed in heavy thought. A muscle in his left cheek twitched as it always did when he tried to rein in the savage emotions that stormed through his soul. As the daily reality of the war had sunk in, the nervous twitch had become more noticeable.

They were in his private room, hidden deep within the bowels of the palace. There were no windows and the only light that fell upon them this evening came from the flickering of a single candle.

Miriam had found herself spending more and more time with the Sultan in this secret chamber, but not in the way she had imagined. Yes, they had enjoyed a few nights of passionate love since their first tryst, but she found herself serving more the role of sympathetic listener than of lustful mistress. She would find herself roused awake at odd hours by a tapping at her window, only to peer out and see Zaheer, the Kurdish guard whom Saladin had assigned to escort her when she first arrived in Jerusalem. The hapless young man was now burdened with the duty of discreetly bringing her to Saladin for their trysts. He was clearly most uncomfortable with the task, and would never come to her front door. Rather, he stood below her window and threw pebbles at the glass to signal his arrival. Miriam would quickly throw on a robe and tiptoe out, although she knew that both her uncle and aunt had deduced what was going on. She was unsure why she remained so secretive, but she guessed it was probably her old sense of Cairene propriety rearing its disapproving head.

Maimonides and Rebecca never spoke a word to her about her nightly disappearances, although she knew that they were both embarrassed and more than a little frightened about her affair with the Sultan. While her uncle had warned her loudly to stay clear of Saladin's bed after their initial flirtations, he apparently realized that there was little he could do to stop his headstrong niece now that matters had taken their own course. And she had no doubt that he was afraid of Saladin's wrath should he intervene. The knowledge that the man whom she loved as a father would live in such mortal fear of the man in whose arms she slept disturbed her greatly, but she did not know what she could do to remedy the situation. So Miriam went on pretending that nothing was going on, and that there was no cloud of terror and court intrigue hanging over her simple little home in the Jewish quarter.

In truth, Miriam was frightened herself. She knew that tongues were already beginning to wag, despite her and Saladin's discretion, and the thought that word of their affair would reach the imperious Sultana filled her with dread. Over the past year in Jerusalem, she had heard myriad tales from court gossips about Yasmeen's ruthless cruelty toward rivals for the Sultan's heart. While she hoped that such stories were little more than the usual fare of bored matrons, she did not relish the idea of making such an enemy.

Normally, the threat of discovery loomed heavily in her mind during their meetings, but tonight the tragedy of the situation at Acre pushed all other concerns from her thoughts. She had heard from Maimonides about the defeat of Taqi al-Din's forces and the terrible situation with the hostages of Acre. It was hard to believe that only a few weeks before, she had actually stood within the heart of the Crusader army, nursing to health the very man who had repaid her and her ruler's courtesy with war and terror.

Saladin had not spoken a word to her since her arrival. She knew well enough to leave him be when he was lost in thought, but she found the utter silence oppressive and nerve-racking. Miriam shifted uncomfortably on the hard-backed wood chair that was placed opposite the silk-cushioned bed that would likely remain unrumpled tonight. She knew intuitively that she was here to serve as adviser and confidante this evening, not as lover.

Saladin stopped his pacing at last and looked at her. He suddenly seemed very old and tired, the light in his eyes totally extinguished.

"I learned this evening what became of Taqi al-Din," he said slowly.

Miriam tensed. She knew that the young man who had served as her escort to the Frankish camp was closer to Saladin than even his own sons. His death would be a crushing blow to the Sultan, and she wondered if she could even find the right words of condolence to ease his grief.

"Tell me," was all she could say.

Saladin seemed to be struggling with the words, as if he could not believe how his world had been turned upside down so suddenly.

"He survived the fall of Acre, but he has fled."

Miriam's jaw dropped.

"I don't understand."

"Taqi al-Din blamed himself for the loss of the city and the capture of its residents," Saladin said bitterly. "I have received word that he has taken his surviving horsemen north, toward the Caucuses."

"But he would not abandon you, not when you need him the most!"

"The blood of Ayyub runs through his veins," Saladin said. "He was too ashamed to face me. My nephew apparently feels his dishonor is so great that he must journey to the land of my forefathers to do penance at their graves. I only pray that their spirits will counsel him to return, for in my eyes there is nothing to forgive. Even if Jerusalem itself fell under his watch, I would offer my life in his place at a moment's notice."

Miriam was rendered utterly speechless. This strange world of mountain warriors, with its incomprehensible codes of honor, was beyond her experience. Unable to process this desertion of Saladin's most valued general at the worst possible time, she tried to steer the conversation to the Lionheart, whose straightforward venality she could at least understand.

"What of King Richard? Will you meet his demands?"

The Sultan sighed.

"I have little choice. Three thousand lives hang in the balance."

"But one hundred thousand bezants. I have never even imagined such a sum!"

Saladin sat on the edge of the bed, but made no indication that he wanted Miriam to join him.

"I have sent a message to the caliph in Baghdad for both the funds and the support of his army, but I am not hopeful."

His gesture made sense, but she could not understand why he was so pessimistic. Baghdad possessed a treasury that made the coffers of Syria and Egypt look like a pauper's wallet, and the caliph was, at least nominally, the supreme leader of the entire Muslim world, including Palestine. She thought that he would readily make his resources available to protect the Holy Land from falling so soon after its miraculous liberation.

"But surely the Commander of the Faithful will not abandon you," she said, trying to instill hope in his heart.

Saladin put his head in his hands, as if he were a man who had been running all his life until he found that the road culminated in a pointless dead end.

"The caliph despises me more than he hates the Franks," he said. "He sees me as a direct threat to his rule."

Of course Miriam knew that Baghdad was nervous about Saladin's power and prestige, but she could not imagine that petty rivalries would stand in the way of unity against the much greater threat posed by the barbarian invasion.

"But he would not let Jerusalem fall just to keep you in line," she said, but the words were beginning to sound hollow even to her.

Saladin ran his hand through his hair. She saw several streaks of gray where there had been glistening black only weeks before.

"Have you ever seen a *khat* addict, Miriam?"

It was an unusual question, but she had learned that the Sultan often spoke in riddles and figures of speech during their private conversations.

"Yes," she said, her mind flashing back to that day in the souk before the Sultan had disguised himself to woo her. "In the bazaar. They are like beggars with dead eyes."

Saladin nodded.

"I was once asked to judge the case of a woman who killed her own son under the haze of *khat*," he said, his voice trembling as if the memory of the incident still caused him pain. "He had tried to save her by destroying her stores of the drug. She slit his throat in revenge."

"My God," Miriam said in sincere horror. She saw the Sultan's eyes glisten and she felt a tremor in her own being. She had never seen Saladin cry. He was always perfectly controlled, aware of the impression he was creating on others and his solemn responsibility to the office he held. Obviously the events of the past few days had pushed him to a place of intense vulnerability. And it terrified her to behold.

She stood up and went to his side, embracing him, letting Saladin place his head against her shoulder like an injured child. She held him tightly, hoping to transfer whatever strength she possessed to him. She did not want to see him break down; she would not be able to bear it. If he could not stand under the onslaught of these terrible world events, how could the rest of them hold together?

Saladin's trembling slowed as she stroked his hair, and he seemed to regain some composure. He finally looked up at her, his face no longer contorted with emotion. The dam was back in place, the illusion of detached calm restored.

"Power is like *khat*, Miriam," he said in the serene voice that he often used when playing the role of teacher. "Once you have tasted it, you crave more, until its desire consumes you. You will kill even your loved ones if they stand in your way. Such is the caliph."

Miriam stroked his cheek. She saw that the twitch was gone.

"I hate the world of men, with its wars and power games," she said.

For the first time in a very long while, a smile appeared on Saladin's face.

"You are beginning to sound like the Sultana," he said. "But I suspect she does not love men for another reason."

Then, to her utter amazement, he burst out laughing. A wild, infectious bray that resounded like a clap of thunder announcing the end of a bitter drought.

Miriam found herself laughing along with him, shocked that he would make such an open reference to the whispered rumors of his wife's predilection for slave girls. It was hard to believe that this was the same man who had only moments before appeared on the verge of collapse, the terrible weight of the world crushing his shoulders.

In most men, Miriam would have found such rapid and extreme change in mood a worrying indication of instability. Perhaps even the onset of madness. But she was so delighted to see joy in Saladin's features again that she brushed the thought out of her mind like an annoying gnat.

It would not be long, however, before the thought returned. And it would not be so easily dismissed at that moment.

40

Richard looked over the gray-turbaned messenger with interest. He had just arrived in Acre, along with a retinue of muscular Arab guards carrying several iron chests that presumably held the ransom that Richard had demanded for the lives of the city's denizens. Saladin's herald was dressed in a flowing white robe cut with vertical green stripes, and his curly beard had an unnatural reddish tinge that must have been the result of some dye. The guards behind him stood at attention, the chests at their feet, as the Sultan's representative bowed with an exaggerated flourish of his hand.

Richard was seated in a fortified stone building that had formerly belonged to Saladin's governor Karakush, who had found a new home in a windowless cell, chained to the wall in a room reserved for petty thieves and cattle poachers. The king had little doubt that the ex-governor's accommodations did not quite live up to the grand executive chamber that he now used as his base of operations. The room was luxuriously decorated, with sparkling chandeliers above, plush velvet carpeting below, and the walls around them covered in rich tapestries and murals depicting Saracen battles against the Franks. While it was not quite the throne room of London, the chamber served as a more worthy seat of power for the conqueror of Palestine than a mud-covered tent in the middle of a rocky beach.

To Richard's side stood William, suited in his best dress armor, as befitted a diplomatic exchange of this importance. His nemesis, Conrad, on the other hand, sulked in a corner of the room, his dust-stained tunic blanketed in a ruddy cloak. The Marquis of Montferrat saw little use in diplomacy, and he felt no need to don his best attire for his enemy's minions, regardless of traditional protocol. Richard, of course, did not care at all whether Conrad was present or, for that matter, whether he chose to stand naked at an audience with Saladin's emissary. The king had finally reached a point where he found it most effective to simply forget the presence of the arrogant nobleman altogether. There were more than enough courtiers and generals present in the room to allow him to ignore the irritating little man without having to seem especially rude.

The only person missing from Richard's senior council was King Philip of Paris, who had regrettably fallen prey to the same camp fever that had nearly killed the Lionheart weeks before. While Philip was slowly recovering, his retinue was already suggesting that the French king had played as much of a role in the conquest of the Holy Land as honor demanded. With the fall of Acre and Richard's march to Jerusalem now only a matter of time, Philip would likely return to Europe within a fortnight. Which, of course, served the Lionheart well. While Philip had been a trustworthy ally over the past several months during their long trek over land and sea, Richard had no desire to share the glorious title of Conqueror of Jerusalem with anyone. It was best that Philip returned and left him alone to focus on fulfilling his destiny, which now seemed so clearly within Richard's grasp. And it also served to finally curtail the secret jokes that he knew some of his men had been making at his expense. There had been times when Richard believed his youthful dalliance with the handsome Philip would haunt him throughout eternity.

After the ambassador had finished an extended salutation of greetings in remarkably fluent French, Richard went straight to business.

"Has your lord complied with my request?"

Saladin's herald nodded to his retinue, and the Arab soldiers unlocked and flung open the chests. The boxes were filled with sparkling gold dinars emblazoned with Arabic calligraphy that Richard had learned recently contained blasphemous verses from the infidel's sacred book. No matter. When the coins were melted down in the forge and refined into ingots, all traces of the heathen sacrilege would vanish.

But even as his officers stared at the marvelous bounty procured from the enemy's coffers, Richard knew that the sum presented was nowhere near the hundred thousand pieces he had demanded. That figure had been derived from estimates of Saladin's holdings, as provided under duress by the luckless former governor of Acre.

The herald bowed his neck in an act of diplomatic contrition that confirmed Richard's suspicions that the booty fell far short of the expected ransom.

"The Sultan regrets that he is not yet able to gather such a large sum in its entirety," the herald said in his peculiar nasal accent. "But as a sign of his good faith, he sends this treasure, which amounts to a tenth of what Your Majesty requested in his last communiqué."

Richard glanced at his courtiers, who were almost salivating at the sight of the gold. He could tell that they were quite satisfied with what had been proffered, and he felt his bile rising in contempt. It was this greed and short-term thinking that had brought the former Crusader kingdom to its knees. Richard knew that in order for the new regime to develop momentum against the Muslim invaders, he had to show both Saladin's men, and his own, that he was a man who meant what he said.

"I appreciate your sultan's generosity, but I made my terms clear. This paltry sum shall not suffice," Richard said, watching the herald's face fall as his hopes for a settlement of the affair were dashed. The king nodded to his own heavily armed guards, who moved in front of the Muslim delegation. "If you will excuse us for a moment, lord ambassador. I wish to confer with my counselors."

The turbaned emissary bowed his head. He and his soldiers were led outside, into a small anteroom. When the oak door closed, Richard turned, his eyes falling on William.

"Let us at least release the women and children from among the prisoners," William said in his usual righteous one. "We should meet his act of faith with one of our own."

Conrad spat a betel leaf he had been chewing at William's feet.

"The infidels have no faith," he growled. "That is the meaning of the word."

Richard watched with amusement as William struggled to keep his rising anger in check.

"Lord Conrad, you surprise me with the breadth of your education," William hissed. "Can you read and write as well?"

"I shall write your name on a gravestone one day!"

Bravo! For once, Conrad had managed to come up with a worthy reply to the king's chief knight. But no matter how much it amused him, Richard knew he had to put their bickering to a stop and return to the matter at hand.

"Enough!" he said, and both men stopped glaring at each other and turned to face him. Conrad was the first to speak.

"Your Majesty, we have only begun this campaign. You must stand firm now or the heathens will become bold."

Of course, that was exactly what Richard wanted to do, but he found it irritating that he was receiving such counsel from a snail like Conrad, rather than from his finest advisers.

"And slay thousands of innocents over an impossible ransom?" William's indignation, while obviously passionately felt, was clearly the minority view in the room. Richard looked at each of his courtiers, who shifted uncomfortably. Clearly they did not wish to be seen as supporting the arrogant Conrad over one of Richard's own men, but he knew where their hearts lay nonetheless.

"There are no innocents among unbelievers," Conrad said, echoing the unspoken beliefs of the others in the room.

William seemed utterly taken aback by Conrad's pitiless, albeit popular, approach to dealing with the Saracens.

"You are a monster."

Conrad shrugged, as if undisturbed by the label.

"I seek only to spare the soldiers of Christ further bloodshed," he said. Conrad turned his attention fully to the king. "If we spread terror through the hearts of the Saracens, they will buckle without a fight."

A murmur of assent ran through the room. A look of desperation was becoming apparent on William's face as the tide of opinion appeared to be turning against him.

"Reginald of Kerak thought like you, and he brought about the downfall of Jerusalem."

Conrad turned beet red at the mention of his old ally and mentor.

"Reginald did not have at his disposal thousands of Europe's best troops!" the nobleman shouted. "Your Majesty, it is time to show your resolve. A king must be feared before he can be loved." He paused. "Your father understood that."

Ah, nice touch, Richard thought. The marquis clearly still believed he could manipulate the king's heart with poignant references to his long-deceased father. But Richard no longer felt as if he were drowning inside Henry's shadow. Ever since he had returned from his tussle with death, Richard's heart felt remarkably free. He knew that his legacy was his own to create, regardless of whether the outcome pleased or enraged a dead spirit. Richard's rapid victory at Acre had solidified his belief that his name would outshine that of his father in the annals of history. He would become Alexander, and his father little more than Philip of Macedon, a passing reference in the tale of the son.

Richard had already made his decision on the matter, and now that he had provided the opportunity for dissenting views to be voiced and silenced, he knew he needed to act.

"A war cannot be won with pleasantries," Richard said. He found that he could not look at William as he spoke the judgment he knew was necessary. "As the enemy has only provided us with ten percent of the expected ransom, we will accordingly spare one tenth of the captives, including their leaders and men of wealth." He paused. "The rest of the hostages will be put to death."

◆   ◆   ◆

WILLIAM WATCHED THE MASSACRE with unabated horror. A massive trench had been dug outside the newly rebuilt walls of Acre. A long line of terrified and shackled prisoners was made to kneel side by side as the Crusader soldiers methodically walked down the length of the trench, decapitating the hostages with double-bladed battle-axes. Their severed heads would fall into the trench below, to be quickly followed by their still-writhing corpses, which were kicked in immediately after the execution. And then the next line would be brought forward, weeping in terror, until their wails abruptly came to an end.

All in all, twenty-seven hundred men, women, and children were to meet their Maker that day.

The knight had never seen anything like this. He could not have imagined that his brothers in Christ were capable of such abomination. It had to be an evil nightmare, from which he would wake up any moment screaming into the night. But no. The screams he heard all around him were not his own. They were the heart-piercing wails of the women, the screeching cries of the little ones.

Women and children.

A prayer rose from his shredded heart and exploded from his lips, flying with desperate speed toward Heaven. He did not know if God could hear him against the cacophony of such suffering. But it was all his impoverished soul had left to offer.

O Christ, dear beloved Lord, save us from ourselves . . .

41

atred and fear mix dangerously in the hearts of men.
This was another of his father's wise old sayings. And the rabbi had learned the truth of this aphorism over many years of tending to the victims of war and violence. All human conflict was fundamentally premised on those two emotions, hatred and fear, bound painfully together and forced to dance to a grim tune played forever on the Reaper's flute.

And the dance continued before him yet again, consuming the hearts and souls of the terrified citizens of Jerusalem. Word of the massacre at Acre had spread through Palestine like an uncontainable brush fire that now threatened to consume the fragile harmony that Saladin had built in the realm over the past two years.

Maimonides was seated on a gray-flecked mare that had been provided him on the direct command of the Sultan. He sat uncomfortably in the leather saddle, but he kept his grimaces and groans to a minimum, knowing full well that al-Adil was watching him like a hawk. The Sultan's brother had gathered together the finest horsemen in the Jerusalem guard and now awaited the arrival of Saladin to lead the expedition.

The hastily convened party stood at the western gates of the palace, and from their position high on the hills of Moriah, the rabbi could see the extent of the devastation. A billowing cloud of gray haze covered

Jerusalem, the result of dozens of fires that were now raging throughout the Christian quarter of the city.

When the ashen-faced emissary had returned with news of the horrendous atrocity perpetrated by Richard's troops, a horror he had been compelled to witness, it was impossible for Saladin to stop the immediate response. Youths had flooded the streets of Jerusalem, seeking out someone, anyone, to avenge this crime.

Christian churches and shops were the first to be set aflame. Soon the mobs descended on anyone who even vaguely looked like they carried Frankish blood. The lucky ones were just beaten and left for dead. Others were pummeled with stones until their faces were no longer recognizable. Some Christians were impaled with makeshift spears or nailed to wooden posts in mockery of their sacred Crucifixion. The least fortunate were doused in oil and set on fire.

The rioters showed no mercy to old or young. When word of the riot reached the Jewish quarter, Maimonides and Miriam had quickly run out to save someone, anyone, from the mindless hate of the mob. The first victim they found was an elderly man who had been hacked to pieces, a cross carved in his chest with a scimitar. Then a woman whose eyes had been gouged out by a dagger. And a dying child, who could not even cry out in agony, for his tongue had been cut out.

Maimonides had seen such things in war, but never among the innocent. And never by the hand of his Arab brethren. These were unspeakable crimes that he had once imagined only the barbarous Franks were capable of.

He and Miriam had made their way as far into the madness as they could, but it quickly became clear that they would be unable to proceed into the heart of the chaotic quarter without the protection of Saladin's guards. Somehow, in the midst of the bloodshed and rioting, they had managed to get to the palace gates, where stunned troops were trying to hold back a wave of residents fleeing the devastation all around them. The turbaned soldiers had pushed them back with their razor-edged spears, until one of Saladin's personal guards apparently recognized Miriam and ushered her and her uncle inside. Maimonides was not surprised. He knew, of course, about what was going on between the Sultan and his niece, and while he would never approve of the relationship, he had been thankful this one time for the access it provided.

Once they were inside the complex, however, Miriam had been spir-

ited away by one of Saladin's twin Egyptians, despite her vociferous protests. Maimonides was told that the Sultan wanted her taken to safety
outside the embattled city while he dealt with the bloody task of restoring order. Maimonides had pleaded with the stoic guard to arrange for
the transport of Rebecca as well, until the hulking giant named Saleem
finally grunted in acquiescence. The rabbi's wife had holed herself inside
their apartment, and although the rioting had not spread yet to the Jewish quarter, Maimonides knew that bloodlust, when kindled, knew no
boundaries.

The rabbi remained inside the tense confines of the palace, staring down from an arched window at the chaos. He stood in sad silence
for what felt like hours, ignored by the army of attendants and petty
ministers who ran around desperately trying to make themselves useful as the city burned. The Sultan himself was nowhere to be seen, and
for a moment Maimonides had wondered whether he too had fled for
the safety of the hills beyond the Damascus Gate. And then a massive
hand had gripped his shoulders and he found himself face-to-face with
al-Adil, who grimly advised him that the Sultan expected him to join
him in his effort to restore order to the Christian quarter.

And so he waited here, as the setting sun competed with the crimson
hue of the burning souk for his attention. Maimonides knew that the massacre of the Christians was a terrible blow to Saladin, both as a king and
as a man. The Sultan had promised his Christian subjects that he would
not repeat the atrocities of the Crusaders. Yet from what the rabbi had
witnessed this afternoon, the rioting Muslims were doing a remarkable
job of imitating the very people they despised. They were now criminals
condemned by their own faith, having flung aside all the proclamations of
their Qur'an to protect the innocent and curb the lust for revenge.

But in truth, the rabbi knew that the marauders had ceased to think
in terms of God or religion. They were like men possessed, driven by
their own fears of death to kill anyone who might one day do to them
what the Franks had done to their brothers at Acre. It was not about
right or wrong, or the well-considered arguments of religious scholars.
Terror was its own kind of madness and no reason, no faith, could shine
a light into that darkest region of the human soul.

Even as he thought this, the gates to the palace were flung open and
the Defender of the Faith rode out on his mighty black steed. Saladin
was dressed in full battle regalia and had on the same suit of plated

lamellar armor that he had worn on the fateful day at Hattin. It was clear
to all who saw the fire in his eyes that he was here to wage a new *jihad*,
which the rabbi's fickle and ironic God had destined to be one in which
he would fight his fellow Muslims to save the Christian infidels.

Without a word to his men, the Sultan raced forward on al-
Qudsiyyah, his prized Arabian stallion, and the party followed. They tore
through the streets of Jerusalem, and Saladin's archers were quick to dis-
patch any rioter who had the misfortune of crossing their path as they
rode down the cobbled and bloodstained streets into the eye of the storm.

Maimonides saw their destination. Towering above the nearby
buildings with its massive gray dome, second only to the grand cupola
that covered the Sakhra on the Temple Mount, the shrine was the most
sacred site in all Christendom. The Church of the Holy Sepulchre, where
Christians believed their "Messiah" had been buried after his rather
embarrassing and unforeseen death at the hands of the Roman centurions. Maimonides had always looked with distaste at the tomb, as it
reminded him of the thousand years of terrible persecution his brothers
had faced for their alleged complicity in the death of Jesus.

But today he felt no rancor in his heart. As the horses tore through
the streets in the direction of the holy building, Maimonides could only
feel sympathy and sorrow for those now caught in the terrible madness
that his own people had endured on a regular basis throughout much of
the world.

As they rounded a corner, Maimonides saw a large and angry
crowd armed with torches and farming tools that had been turned into
weapons—rakes, gardening shears, hoes with razor-sharp blades, crude
but as effective as any soldier's sword when it came to the business of
killing other men.

The rioters were being held back by a small contingent of Saladin's
soldiers, who appeared confused and nervous. They were obviously not
used to fighting against their brother Muslims in defense of unbelievers.
Saladin bore his horse straight for the front gate of the stone building,
yet even the sound of thundering hooves about to crush them to death
did not persuade the enraged crowd to move aside.

"Make way for the Sultan, or by Allah, you will all die!" Al-Adil's
booming voice and lethal gaze was enough to terrify the angry men, who
scurried out of the way just as the Sultan's riding party was upon them.

Saladin jumped off his horse and ran up the ancient cracked steps to the black iron gate of the Sepulchre. Just outside the door, surrounded by several soldiers armed with spears and bows, stood a gray-bearded man dressed in a black robe and wearing a conical hat. Silver chains dangled from his neck and he wore a massive cross, embedded with priceless rubies. This was Heraclius, Latin Patriarch of Jerusalem and last remnant of the powerful elite of the Crusader kingdom of Jerusalem. The patriarch had sullenly acquiesced to the surrender of the city two years before, on the condition that he would be allowed to remain in his position as shepherd of the Christians who chose to live under Saladin's rule. He had never been especially friendly with the Sultan, but it was clear to everyone that each man needed the other to keep the peace between the religious communities in Jerusalem. A peace that was now shattered, possibly beyond repair.

Saladin walked up to the Christian leader and shocked the angry crowd by bowing and kissing his hand.

"Holy Father, have you been harmed?"

The patriarch shook his head. His usual insouciant arrogance was gone and there was very real terror in his eyes.

"A madness has possessed them," he said. "If by the grace of Christ you had not arrived . . ."

Saladin's face hardened. He turned and spoke loudly enough for all to hear.

"No harm shall befall you while I breathe."

Maimonides gazed with astonishment as the Sultan took the patriarch's right hand in his and held it aloft before the entire crowd. At that moment the years of distrust and enmity between the two men vanished, and they appeared like old friends, gratified for each other's company.

"In the name of Allah, the Compassionate, the Merciful," the Sultan proclaimed, "I declare all the Christians of Jerusalem my brothers. Any man who harms a Christian shall be treated as having attacked the Sultan himself."

A stunned murmur spread through the crowd. A few of the would-be arsonists stepped back, lowering their torches in reluctant submission to their leader. But one young man, brown-haired and freckled, moved to the front of the crowd. His eyes were filled with the fire of righteous anger.

"Of course you are his brother," he cried out unwisely. "You befriend the infidels and you let the Franks murder believers. You are no brother to the martyrs!"

A terrible hush fell over the crowd at that instant. No one had dared speak like this to Saladin in years. There was a moment of utter silence, when all Maimonides could hear was the thunderous beating of his own heart.

Then Saladin reacted with ruthless, terrifying efficiency. The Sultan pulled an emerald-encrusted dagger from his belt and flung it straight at the offending rebel. The boy stared down in stunned shock at the hilt protruding from the center of his chest, then fell to his knees with a muted gasp.

An obese little woman in a red head scarf, who was obviously the unfortunate youth's mother, screamed in abject horror. She rushed to his side and cradled the dead boy's head in her arms, her wails so heart-wrenching that even Maimonides, whose medical training had made him accustomed to endure grief, found it difficult to hold back tears. He glanced up at Saladin, whose face remained a mask of iron.

"Any who question the Sultan will meet a similar fate," he said, his voice steady and unmoved by the tragedy that he himself had wrought. But Maimonides saw that his dark eyes were glistening. "I know that you grieve for our brothers at Acre. As do I. But these men are not responsible."

Saladin nodded to his horsemen, who raised their bows and arrows, ready to strike down any who repeated the dead boy's folly. The crowd began to back away from the church, a storm of fear overwhelming any flames of revenge still burning in their hearts. But one person moved forward. An elderly woman in a shapeless black *abaya* rested her hand on the shoulder of the still-grieving mother, before turning her wrinkled face to stare directly at the Sultan.

"Will you kill me for speaking as well?"

Saladin looked at her closely, and then signaled to his archers to leave her alone.

"No, old mother. Say what is in your heart."

"I have lived many years on this earth and have seen countless men die at the hands of these Franks," she said. "There is only one way to respond to these animals. Blood demands blood."

Saladin appeared taken aback at such cruel words coming from the mouth of someone who seemed like a tender old matron.

"Mother, I sorrow that you have seen so much death," he said slowly, as if trying to find the right words. "But in your years, have you not learned this? Blood never rests."

The old woman did not appear convinced, but she turned her full attention to the grieving mother, embracing her and whispering words of support in her ear. The woman in the head scarf looked up at last, her crimson eyes burning with unspoken hatred for the grand liberator of Jerusalem, a man whom she would always remember simply as the murderer of her boy.

Saladin turned away from her unforgiving gaze. He reached into his belt, and then gently tossed on the ground a wallet that Maimonides was sure contained more gold than the dead boy or his mother had ever seen in their lives.

"Make sure he has a proper burial," Saladin said. And for the first time on that terrible, chaotic day, his voice cracked.

42

*T*he Sultana wanted to strangle the Jewess with her own hands, but she realized that such a brutal act was entirely inappropriate for a woman of her stature. Her spies had followed the affair as it blossomed over the past several weeks, to the point that Saladin now appeared to be spending almost every night in that whore's arms. This was clearly no mere dalliance, no paltry itch that the Sultan needed to scratch and then move on. This girl was threatening to take Yasmeen's place not only in his bed, but beside his throne.

No. She would not allow that to happen.

The Sultana turned her attention to the nervous soldier who stood before her. She struggled to remember his name.

Zaheer. Yes, that was it.

Her loyal eunuch Estaphan had performed his task ably, gathering information not only about Miriam, but also regarding others in the court who could prove useful to the Sultana's plans. When she learned of the Kurdish soldier whom the Sultan had assigned to be Miriam's personal guard, Yasmeen had investigated further. And she had hit the rich vein of gold she had been digging for.

The Sultana's voice rang out after a long silence. "You are wondering why I have summoned you here." It was not a question but a statement of fact, a reading of the man's soul.

"Yes, Your Majesty." His eyes remained downcast and she enjoyed hearing the tremor of fear in his voice.

"I have heard about your feelings for the Jew."

Whatever the tall soldier was expecting from this audience, this was clearly not it. He broke protocol and raised his head to look upon Yasmeen in shock, all color draining from his ruddy cheeks. She was wearing a translucent silk veil, so he did not technically break the law. Had he actually gazed upon the features of the Sultana, he would have been condemned to death. Remembering this, he averted his eyes again.

"Do not be surprised," she said, smiling at his consternation. "There is little that happens inside the court that does not come to my attention. Particularly with regard to matters of the heart."

Zaheer lowered his head again, obviously unsure of what to say. She persisted.

"Fear not. You may speak openly."

Not knowing what else to do under these unusual circumstances, the Kurdish warrior spoke plainly, as was the custom of his people.

"Her beauty is like the sunrise over a crystal lake."

Yasmeen felt a flare of anger, although she knew that the poor boy was only doing what she asked.

"Apparently the Sultan thinks so as well," she said, unable to keep the rancor out of her voice.

Zaheer could no longer hide his terror.

"I had no choice, my lady," he stammered. "The Sultan commanded me—"

"It is no matter," she interrupted. "Your loyalty and discretion are to be commended."

Zaheer appeared terribly confused, but he nodded meekly. He nervously cast his eyes down at the marble tiled floor. Yasmeen ran her fingers across the sheer silk robe that rested lightly against her soft skin as she put her plan into motion.

"But, alas, this situation cannot be allowed to continue," she said. "Their affair is not in the interests of the sultanate. If word were to get out that my husband was carrying on with an unbeliever, it would foment unrest among our more devout subjects. The caliph in Baghdad himself would be forced to intervene."

The guard squared his shoulders and raised his head, although he was careful to stare at a spot on the wall over her shoulder.

"What would you have me do, my lady?"

The Sultana reached into the folds of her robe and produced a crystal vial containing a clear liquid.

"In my father's harem in Damascus, the women long ago perfected an elixir that can shift the heart of any man—or woman, for that matter—to its possessor."

She held aloft the potion to the Kurd, who tentatively reached for it, his fingers careful to avoid any contact with the forbidden hand of the Sultana. He stared at the vial in superstitious wonder.

"But why do you wish me to do this?"

"You have been a faithful retainer to my husband for many years. Think of it as your just reward."

The guard shifted uncomfortably.

"But if the Sultan finds out . . ."

"He will not," she snapped.

Zaheer took an involuntary step back at the dangerous tone in her voice.

"When shall I act?

Yasmeen smiled. That was more like it.

"Tonight. And by tomorrow, the Jewess will have forgotten the Sultan. The only man she will be able to think about is you."

43

Zaheer felt the tension building inside his chest as he stood outside the heavy oak door to the Sultan's chamber. He was not sure why he was really there. Was it just because he feared disobeying the Sultana's orders? Or did some part of him truly wish to do this deed?

Zaheer had served as Miriam's guard and protector for months. He was one of the few men who was able to spend time with her under the strict gender segregation of the court. Except of course for the Sultan.

The young soldier had always revered Saladin. The man was a living legend, a source of pride not only to the Arabs and Muslims he commanded, but also to the Kurdish tribesmen who were his brethren. Saladin's incredible series of victories, and his noble disposition, had raised the standing of the Kurdish people in the eyes of the entire Muslim *ummah*. No longer were they uncouth mountain men who served as lowly mercenaries in the armies of the believers. They had been elevated to the position of a sacred tribe, like the Prophet's clan of Quraysh before them, whose courage, valor, and moral decency was held up as a shining example of the best of the Muslim community. And it had all been due to one man.

The tales of Saladin's heroism had filled Zaheer's youthful heart with fire and longing, and he had run away from his home and life as a goat herder in the Caucasus Mountains seeking to join the *jihad* against the Franks. That had been four years ago. And, through his focused intensity and courage in battle after battle, the boy had garnered favor with his Syrian commanders, rising steadily through the ranks until he had achieved the pinnacle of success in the army—attachment to the retinue of the Sultan himself.

Zaheer had fought to hold back tears when he first met the famed warrior in person. The man was everything he had ever imagined—kind, honorable, and just. The flesh-and-blood Saladin became in that instant more of a myth than he had been when he was just a name spoken reverently on the lips of the common people.

And then Zaheer had learned, over the past several months, to his crushing disappointment, that the Sultan was a man after all. The young soldier had watched with complete shock as Saladin pursued a passionate and inappropriate affair with a girl half his age. A girl who, Zaheer was terrified to discover, was also haunting his dreams every night.

Miriam was unlike any woman he had ever met. Granted, his experience with the fairer sex was rather limited. Yes, he had enjoyed more than a few sweaty couplings with village girls awed by his status as a personal guard of the Sultan. But he had never met a woman whose mind excited him more than her body. To be sure, Miriam had been endowed with more than her share of physical attributes. But during the moments of their secret rides out to the palace when she would converse with him, he discovered that her wit and perceptiveness stirred him more than any stolen glance at her voluptuous curves.

Of course, Miriam was far above his status, even as an unbeliever. She came from a prominent family of the People of the Book. Her uncle was a close adviser and friend to the Sultan, as well as a religious leader of his community. And she was obviously highly educated. Miriam probably spoke more languages than Zaheer was aware existed, and her regular trips to the booksellers in the souk served as humiliating reminders of his own illiteracy.

In all the time they had spent together, she had very likely never once looked upon his youthful features and seen a man, much less a worthy partner. The thought filled him with fury, fury at God for granting him this wretched lot in life, which made him forever bound to witness the luxury and privilege of the upper classes. And fury at himself for his weakness of character, which trapped him in a servile role when he should have had the courage to seize the world with his right hand, as Saladin had done. And, finally, fury at Miriam, for entering his life and making Zaheer realize that no matter how far he had risen in the hierarchy of the court, he would always be nothing more than a dirty, uneducated mountain boy.

Using that righteous anger as a shield to keep himself focused on the task at hand, Zaheer raised his knuckles and rapped hard against the polished wooden door. "It is Zaheer, my lady."

There was a pause, and then Miriam's soft voice echoed from within with a single word.

"Enter."

Zaheer opened the door and stepped inside. Miriam sat on a velvet-backed chair, brushing her luxurious curls. She was dressed in a robe of black silk, covered in shimmering red and white flowers—a recent gift from the Sultan. One of her legs was visible through a slit in the garment, slender and sleek, with perfectly toned muscles flowing from calf to knee. Zaheer was immediately aroused and any hesitation vanished with the sudden flow of excitement.

"Forgive the intrusion. I bring a message from the Sultan."

Miriam continued looking into the silver mirror before her, her eyes never even rising to acknowledge him.

"Yes?"

Zaheer remembered the specific instructions given by his mistress, Yasmeen.

"The Sultan wishes you to dine with him this evening in his private chambers."

Miriam looked up at that, surprise on her chiseled features. Zaheer knew that since the onset of the war, Saladin almost always dined with his generals. In fact, there was rarely a moment in the day when he was not discussing military strategy. The Sultana, who had a deep grasp of human nature, had explained to Zaheer that it would require a special occasion for Saladin to break away from the pressing matters of state to spend a quiet meal with this girl. Obviously, the Jewess came to the expected conclusion. The Sultan was clearly taking their affair to a new level, a thought, Zaheer was jealously sure, would fill her with much anticipation.

"I'd best get ready, then," she said.

This was it. His moment of truth. As he gazed at her soft, lovely face, knowing that even as she looked in his direction, she did not see him, only the memory of the Sultan in her mind's eye, Zaheer's heart hardened to the task at hand.

"He also sends a gift," the guard said. He pulled from his leather tunic the clear vial that the Sultana had provided him. Miriam took the bottle in her hand. As her long fingers brushed his own rough hands, Zaheer felt a tingle run up his spine.

"What is it?"

"Sherbet from Armenia," the young Kurd said quickly. "He wanted you to try it. If it pleases you, he will order a cask for your meal together."

Miriam looked at him for a moment with an unreadable expression. He felt a knot of fear in his stomach. Had he raised her suspicions? Would she decline to drink, and then perhaps bring up the incident with the Sultan himself? If the Sultan were to discover the truth, Zaheer would likely suffer a punishment so excruciating that death would be a welcome release.

But his fears proved unfounded. She suddenly reddened and smiled at him bashfully. Zaheer instinctively realized that she had truly noticed him for the first time in that instant. Yes, he had served as her escort many an evening, and he had stood guard outside the Sultan's private chambers while his ears burned with the noisy sounds of their lovemaking, but it suddenly dawned on Zaheer that Miriam had probably not allowed herself to admit that he knew the true nature of her trysts with the Sultan.

Miriam met his eyes briefly, and then drank from the bottle as Zaheer held his breath.

"Does it please you?"

Miriam wrinkled her nose as if experiencing an unexpected aftertaste.

"It's a little sweet for my taste," she said, putting the now empty vial aside. She got up and began to walk toward the bed, where several beautiful gowns were laid out. "Now, if you'll wait outside, I'll get ready."

Zaheer was unsure what to do. Had the love potion worked? If so, why was she dismissing him like a servant boy rather than embracing him with desire? Was this all some kind of ruse? A joke played on him by the Sultana? Was he to become the laughingstock of the harem?

Even as his mind raced with images of his imminent humiliation, he saw Miriam stop at the foot of the bed. She grasped her stomach as if in pain, then reached for one of the carved bedposts to steady herself.

"Are you feeling well, my lady?" He felt a genuine wave of concern, followed by a rush of terrifying scenarios in his mind. Had the Sultana lied to him? Was the "love potion" in truth poison? Zaheer went pale at the thought that he could be held responsible for Miriam's death.

Miriam turned toward him, her face filled with confusion. She stumbled, and Zaheer grabbed her by the shoulders.

"Just a little light-headed," Miriam said, her voice sounding oddly distant. "It must be the heat."

Zaheer did not know what else to do but maintain the ruse.

"Should I send the Sultan your regrets?"

Miriam shook her head. Her eyes were growing unfocused.

"No, I'll be fine . . ."

And with that, she fainted into Zaheer's arms. He quickly dragged her limp form to the bed and checked the vein in her neck. Her pulse felt steady, and her body was not in any way convulsing or showing any of the other signs that Zaheer had been trained to recognize in poison victims.

Laying her down on the silk bed, he loosened her robe to ensure that she could breathe. The silk cloth fell aside, revealing the gentle curves of her breasts. Zaheer suddenly felt an irresistible urge that both frightened and exhilarated him. He knew the Sultan would be at a council of war until late tonight. And he himself was here, alone with the most beautiful girl he had ever seen.

Zaheer did not know if the Sultana's love potion had worked, nor did he care anymore. The lust that was stirring inside his loins was all he could think about. He slowly pulled open the girl's robes and caught his breath at the first sight of her rosy, pointed nipples.

Feeling like a child left alone in a marketplace full of sweets, Zaheer bent down and kissed the sleeping Miriam's lips while his fingers caressed her bosom. Even if she woke up and still loved only Saladin, Zaheer did not care. The Sultana had given him this gift, and he was going to enjoy every moment of it.

44

There were many pleasant duties that a grand vizier, right-hand man to the Sultan, was required to perform. This was not one of them.

Qadi al-Fadil backed away from the door to Saladin's private chamber, feeling his heart race. Not from any puerile excitement at glimpsing the raw carnal acts through a crack in the oak panel, but from the dread realization of what he must do next.

Normally the Qadi would keep the matter discreetly to himself. After all, there were far more pressing things to deal with as the war with the Franks intensified. Such antics should be the last thing on the mind of the Sultan, or of his prime minister.

But unfortunately, the situation between Saladin and the Jewess had reached a point where he had no choice except to intervene. Like much of the court, al-Fadil had been aware of the embarrassing affair between the Sultan and the niece of Maimonides. Normally, tales of the sexual exploits of kings were fodder for delighted gossip among the nobles, but this time the news had filled everyone in the court with shock and dread. Saladin had always been a moral exemplar to the court, and while nearly every petty noble in Jerusalem kept a girl (or, occasionally, a boy) as a plaything, the idea that their noble sultan possessed similar lusts was incomprehensible to the members of the court.

Saladin had acquired a legendary aura of piety and sainthood that had rallied his armies to achieve the impossible. In the eyes of his men, he was the last shining remnant of a bygone time, when the Rightly Guided Caliphs still walked on earth and there were men who held power without the slightest hint of corruption. But now, with Jerusalem yet again threatened by the Frankish hordes, when the people desperately needed to believe in the myth of the Sultan's perfection, the illusion had been shattered.

Al-Fadil had known the man for years, but he had been terrified of approaching the Sultan with his concerns. His fear was that the affair with the girl would undercut Saladin's standing in the realm at exactly the moment when he needed to bring together the people for a unified defense. He knew that he was not alone in thinking this. Even the girl's uncle, for whom al-Fadil generally had little regard, appeared to be uncomfortable with the situation, although his worries clearly centered more on possible repercussions to his niece. Typical of a Jew, al-Fadil had thought bitterly. The self-appointed "Chosen People" were always seeing everything in the universe through self-centered lenses, as if the fate of one foolish harlot in any way mattered against the needs of an empire. Yet even Maimonides could not bring himself to confront the Sultan about the affair.

But Saladin was always good at reading men's hearts, even when they worked hard at hiding their innermost thoughts. Al-Fadil had nonetheless been startled when Saladin had called him into his study one evening and demanded to know his feelings on the matter of the girl.

Al-Fadil had been both terrified and flabbergasted that his master had deduced his hostility to the Jewess, despite his efforts not to mention his thoughts out loud, except to a few trusted advisers. But he forced himself to look the Sultan in the eye and tell him what he didn't want to hear. The Qadi was well trained in Islamic law and knew that the Holy Prophet considered the greatest *jihad* to be the courage in speaking an undesirable truth to the king. He had prided himself over the years in giving his master straightforward advice, even when it caused discomfort.

And the Sultan had always listened, whether it was with regard to punishing cowardly allies who had failed Saladin on the battlefield, or pardoning his enemies for the sake of political expediency, as he did when he replaced the Fatimid caliph with Sunni rule in Cairo. Qadi al-Fadil had risen to his rank of grand vizier exactly because the Sultan could trust him to keep the ship of state on course.

The old man walked slowly along the dimly lit corridor, tugging at his finely groomed beard, his head bowed with the gravity of the situation. He would do as he always did and speak the truth. Of course, he had warned Saladin of exactly this possibility. That the girl was merely using him for his wealth and power, as young girls always did with older men who climbed into their bed. But he took no pleasure in the knowledge that he had been right about the presumptuous maiden. For his master clearly had developed deep feelings for the Jewess. The Sultan had even inquired with him as to whether it would be politically feasible to divorce one of his wives and marry the girl in her place. Al-Fadil had told him that such an action would cause consternation among the common Muslims, many of whom still resented his friendliness toward the Jews. With the Lionheart's forces poised to launch a massive attack from their new stronghold at Acre, the last thing the Sultan needed was controversy surrounding his private affairs.

Saladin had nodded in understanding, and had never brought the issue up again. But neither did he shun the girl, as the prime minister had advised. Instead Saladin seemed to be taking greater solace in her company as the clouds of war grew darker. Al-Fadil knew that the Sultan found comfort in the girl, and the news of her betrayal, with a common soldier no less, would shatter his heart.

He would have let the matter drop, except that it had been brought to his attention by someone who he knew would reveal the truth through other means if al-Fadil kept the secret.

The Sultana had told him of the girl's affair with the young Kurd, no doubt uncovered by her army of spies that seemed to be hiding in every corner of the palace. She had sent him to observe the truth for himself, with the implicit understanding that the Sultan must be made aware of his lover's treachery. The Sultana had claimed that she was motivated not by jealousy, but by concern for the state. If the Jewess was a traitor, then any information she had gleaned from the Sultan could easily be passed along to less friendly parties.

Regardless of the Sultana's motives, the situation was clear. Miriam had betrayed Saladin, and the truth must be brought out before disaster struck.

- - -

QADI AL-FADIL NERVOUSLY RAISED his eyes from the floor. He had finished telling Saladin in a halting manner what he had witnessed, but the Sultan had said not a word for what seemed like an eternity.

They were alone in his master's private study. Al-Fadil had interrupted a strategy session in which Saladin, his brother al-Adil, and the top generals of the army were poring over maps and arguing heatedly about their enemy's likely next move. The prime minister had pulled his master into the secluded silence of the little chamber and told him the story in a few clipped and nervous sentences that had been met with utter silence.

Gazing upon his master's face, al-Fadil saw that the Sultan's dark eyes gleamed with murder. The Qadi wondered if he had made a serious miscalculation. Maybe he had overestimated the bonds of friendship and loyalty with his master, and he would now pay the ultimate penalty.

"I know that you have taken a fancy to this Jew, *sayyidi* . . . but she is no different from the rest . . . Treachery is in their blood . . ."

Saladin stood up from the simple wooden seat that he kept in his study, and al-Fadil fell back as if ducking a blow.

"If you are mistaken, I will put your eyes out with my own hands."

The vizier felt all the blood drain out of his face. He had heard the Sultan use that tone of voice on rare occasions, and the outcome had never been good for its recipient.

"I swear by Allah! Even now she lies in the arms of a palace guard."

Saladin grabbed him by the shoulders and peered into his eyes as if looking for any telltale sign of deceit. Then he pushed al-Fadil aside as if he were kicking away a stray dog.

"I shall investigate for myself," he said, his voice as cold as mountain snow. "Take a good look around you, my friend. This room may be the last thing you ever see."

45

Miriam walked through a thick mist illuminated by a sickly green phosphorescence. But she could see no moon or stars in the pitch darkness that might serve as the source of the pale light. She was not alone, of that she was sure. There were creatures hiding in the mist, terrible beings that knew everything about her and from whom there could be no escape. Every now and again, she would see flashes of movement through the corner of her eye, but wherever she turned, she found only billowing clouds covering a vast emptiness.

She wanted to cry out, to scream for help, but she was afraid of bringing out the demons that she knew were looking for her. And then she saw the little girl. Dressed in a pale blue frock that looked hauntingly familiar, she stood alone, her hands outstretched, beckoning Miriam to her side.

Miriam did not want to go, but she felt her legs pulled by an invisible force, as if she were a marionette. Yes, she remembered now—she had loved marionettes when she was a little girl with long ebony braids and large green eyes, just like the child who was calling her . . . the child who she knew in her terrified heart *was* her.

As she glided forward, the mist lifted and the phantom that was her younger self pointed to a terrible tableau, one that Miriam had locked deep inside the shadowed corners of her soul but had now been set free.

Please, no! Her mind screamed, but no sound emerged from her throat. She did not wish to see this again. But she had no choice. Miriam knew she would be condemned to relive this vision throughout her life, and if her soul indeed survived death, this would be the Hell that awaited her in the embrace of eternity.

Her beautiful mother was on the ground, kicking and screaming, as a tall man held her down with one brutal hand. He was covered in shiny metal but had removed a plate that covered his crotch. His uncircumcised penis, bloated and purple, stood erect like a fleshy spear, ready to inflict its terrible damage.

Then her mother saw her from the corner of her eye and she stopped fighting. She surrendered utterly to the brutal thrusts of the angry man with the curly beard. Miriam knew that she had done this to save her daughter's life. If the knight looked up just a little to the left, he would see the little girl with the pretty braids hiding underneath an overturned carriage. Her mother was giving her the chance to run, escape into the howling sandstorm that had descended on them on the heels of the Frankish raiding party. But even now, as then, she could not move.

She watched through blinding tears as the Frank beat her mother, then ravaged her body, and then beat her again. Blood poured down her mother's thighs and formed a pool around her knees. But her mother just lay there, surrendering to the terrible fate that was the lot of captured women in war.

Then, when he had spilled his virulent seed, the man stood up, his privates soaked in her mother's blood. He reached with one forceful hand and tore from her neck a jade necklace containing the Tetragrammaton, the four Hebrew letters that made up the unpronounceable name of God. Her mother avoided wearing jewelry out of pious dislike for adornment, but she always wore that necklace. It had been a wedding gift from her beloved brother Maimonides, and Miriam could not remember it ever leaving its place near her heart. Miriam wanted to scream, to cry out in rage at the Frank's desecration of her mother's body and soul, but no sound came out of her mouth.

And then he pulled a dagger from his side, bent down, and slashed her mother's throat.

Please stop. O God of my people. Please stop this.

The scream that had been locked away in her throat finally erupted and rose above the cacophony of misery that swirled around the devastated caravan. The man raised his head, a look of boredom on his face, and then she saw him. But he was not young anymore. He had aged before her eyes, and streaks of gray now ran through his curly hair and beard. Yes, he was still the man who had raped and killed her mother, but he was also someone else. A man whom she had seen again, and recently.

The man saw her and a terrible smile covered his face. He began walking toward Miriam, his bloody penis jutting out obscenely before him, already yearning for a second conquest.

She screamed . . .

+ + +

MIRIAM AWOKE FROM ONE nightmare to find herself in another.

She was lying naked in the Sultan's bed, but the man next to her was not Saladin.

No. She was still dreaming. This could not be happening.

The young Kurdish solider, whom she had affectionately thought of as a little brother, was at her side, his head resting against the pillows. Zaheer stirred and opened his eyes. And then he smiled at her, the same embarrassed grin that had always endeared him to her but now repulsed her at the deepest core of her soul.

She leaped up as if lightning had struck her bed.

"Hashem preserve me!"

And, true to His nature, the God of irony chose to respond to her terrified supplication. The wooden door to the chamber burst open. But instead of the blue-winged angel Michael, avenger of her people and protector of the innocent, she found herself staring into the unbelieving eyes of Saladin.

Zaheer flew out of the bed as if he were on fire. But the Sultan moved forward and with one brutal sweep of his scimitar sent the unfortunate boy's head flying across the room.

Miriam screamed. And screamed. She felt like she would never stop screaming until the earth shattered and fell to oblivion under the keening vibrations of her horror.

And then the Sultan turned to her, his eyes filled with a mad fire that was more frightening than anything she had already witnessed. Even more terrifying than the cruel brutality of the Franks as they killed her family before her eyes. But the Franks were monsters—such was their nature. To watch the man she loved, the only fundamentally good man she had ever known, turn into a bloodthirsty demon—that was more than her heart could take.

As she scrambled to cover her breasts with the now bloodstained sheets, Saladin moved toward her slowly, like a mindless golem from the stories her people told their children. A monster with no soul who lived only to fulfill its mission of vengeance and death.

"You dare betray me!" His voice sounded hoarse and thick, like a lion's roar. His eyes were filled with fury and madness. The Saladin she had known was gone, and an *ifreet* from the bowels of Gehenna stood before her now.

"*Sayyidi*, please listen to me . . ."

He struck her then with his fist. Miriam fell back against the bed, tasting the iron warmth of blood in her mouth.

"Your honeyed tongue will not spare you tonight."

Saladin loomed atop her, his jeweled scimitar raised above him. Miriam found she had forgotten how to breathe. Not that it mattered, as she would never draw another breath.

And then she saw the tears falling from his eyes. The dark pools were flooding with grief and the Sultan made no effort to hold them back. And in his shimmering eyes, she saw Saladin again. Not the possessed demon bent on avenging his honor. But the man whom she loved more than anyone else in the world. He was still there, struggling to get out, to rein in the beast that had temporarily taken over his soul.

Miriam rose from the bed and found her footing on the marble floor.

She held her head up high, ready to take the deathblow with dignity, her eyes locked with his.

"Where are your witnesses?" Her voice was utterly calm. She felt as if she had been possessed by something else, a gentle force greater than herself. A counterpart to the dark spirit that had taken control of her beloved's soul.

"What?" He sounded tentative, confused.

"Your Qur'an says you need four witnesses to the crime of fornication."

Saladin stared at her in disbelief. She could see the struggle on his face, as his unrelenting rage fought the powerful faith that was core to his being.

"You dare cite the Holy Book, you . . ."

Miriam leaned into Saladin's face.

"Infidel? Jew? Christ-killer? Say it!"

Saladin lowered his sword at last. She saw his true nature triumph, his features racked with shame and horror at what he was about to do. He turned away from her and collapsed on the bed, his face buried in his hands.

Miriam leaned forward and embraced his trembling form and said the only words that mattered to her anymore.

"I love you."

And she truly did. But she wondered after the events of tonight whether her love would ever mean anything again. Saladin broke free of her arms and stood up. He did not look at her as he slowly walked out of the chamber, stepping silently over the decapitated body of the boy who had drugged and raped her. The door closed behind him and she felt her heart leap into her throat as she heard the dreaded click of the lock falling into place.

46

Miriam sat in the lonely cell, her tortured thoughts turning again and again to her betrayal. The room lacked any windows and she had difficulty keeping track of time. But assuming that the food the grim-faced guards brought was coming at normal intervals, she had been trapped here for a little over five days. She had been allowed no visitors and had no idea what was happening in the outside world.

All this time she thought she had known Saladin's heart. She had convinced herself that he was more than a tribal despot who ruled by his passions rather than by a code of honor. What a fool she had been! Now each time the door to the chamber opened, she prepared herself for the arrival of her executioner. Such would be the just deserts of a young girl caught up in romantic fantasies and delusions. Miriam had once prided herself on her willpower, her commitment to the life of the mind rather than to the childish romances and affairs of other young girls. And now, like the endless stream of idiotic women before her, from Eve to Helen of Troy, she had allowed her heart to rule her mind, and it was a mistake that would deservedly cost Miriam her life.

Even as she allowed despair to fill the last available spaces of her soul, the heavy iron door to her cell swung inward. And like the sun bursting out of the devouring blackness of an eclipse, Maimonides entered.

He appeared older than she had ever seen him, his back bent with the terrible weight of worry that her shame had only made heavier. Oh, how she despised herself! Not for falling in love with a man who had turned out to be a heartless tyrant. Not for allowing herself to become the victim of a young soldier's depraved fantasies. But for bringing heartache into the life of this sweet angel of a man.

Miriam did not move at first, shame and grief rooting her to the spot. But he held out his arms, just as he used to when she was a child, and the well of emotion churning within her was released.

"Uncle!" The word erupted from her parched lips unbidden. It was the first word she had said aloud since she had been locked inside this dark hole. She propelled herself from the fiber cot that served as the only furnishing in her cell, and then she was in his arms, embracing him.

He held her shaking body for a long while, then lifted her face and wiped away long-repressed tears.

"Have you been mistreated?"

She tried to breathe, to calm herself.

"No," she said at last, not wishing to worry him beyond the torment she was sure he had already endured. "I am well fed and spoken to courteously, but I am still a prisoner."

Maimonides nodded, his face sagging with weariness. He looked as if he had not slept since she had been imprisoned. And then, for no reason she could explain even to herself, she thought of Saladin, and found she could not hold back the question.

"How is the Sultan?"

Maimonides stared at her, utterly taken aback.

"How can you think of him when he has done this injustice to you?"

But she knew why. It was a truth that was always there, just beneath the surface of the rage and hurt that covered her heart. Somehow, being in her uncle's presence, the storm stopped raging and she could think clearly at last.

"He was lied to." Miriam knew that everything that had transpired, the terrible tragedy of the past few days, had been the result of one woman and her jealous machinations.

Maimonides shook his head in a combination of sadness and resignation.

"My dear, I warned you that the harem intrigues are more ruthless than any schemes concocted by the Franks in this war."

Yes. And far more deadly, Miriam realized.

"Will I be executed?" It felt so strange to hear those words coming from her own lips. But she needed to know the truth. She needed to prepare for the inevitable.

"No."

It was not Maimonides who spoke now. It was the Sultan.

Saladin stood in the doorway to the cell, his face sadder than she had ever seen it. Miriam found she could not look at him. Her own hurt was too great, too raw.

Maimonides turned to face his old friend with righteous fury in his eyes.

"You have betrayed your honor, Ibn Ayyub. I thought I knew you."

Coming from another, such disrespect toward the Sultan would likely have resulted in immediate death. But Saladin did not flinch, nor did he show any sign of offense.

"And you still do," he said. His face had a pleading look on it that Miriam had never seen before, as if he were asking his old friend for a moment of understanding so that he could try to justify that which was unforgivable. "This was the one place where I could watch over Miriam and guarantee her protection from her enemies in the court.

She was kept here for her own safety until I investigated this incident."

"And what have you learned from your investigation?" Miriam had found her voice again, but she still could not face him.

Saladin sighed.

"I suspected the hand of the Sultana, and I was correct."

There was something in his tone that made Miriam look up. There was a terrible emptiness in his eyes, as if he had purged himself of whatever emotions would prevent him from handling this situation.

"What will become of her?" She had no idea why she cared, considering the horrible trap the woman had sprung on her. But perhaps it was because Miriam understood the Sultana and her grim motivations. At the end of the day, they shared one thing in common. They loved this man. Despite his flaws and failings, they both loved him.

Saladin looked to the floor.

"The matter has been taken care of," he said, and stopped. Then, as if forcing the words out of his mouth, he went on. "She and her female lover were executed this morning for their unnatural crimes."

Miriam felt her heart grow cold. This was madness. All of it. She saw the look of utter disbelief on her uncle's face, and surmised that she probably wore a similar expression on her own. Yasmeen bint Nur al-Din, the most powerful woman in the land, was dead. And because of her. Miriam suddenly wanted to vomit.

"Love is not a crime, *sayyidi*." Tears of horror were welling in her eyes. This was all too much for her.

"For kings and sultans, it is."

Maimonides broke in, his mind obviously focused on only one thing—Miriam's fate in this terrible, unfolding drama.

"What will become of my niece?"

Saladin raised his head and looked straight at her.

"She has made many enemies in the realm. It is best that she leave."

So that was it. She would live, but be forced to endure exile. Compared with the terrible end for the Sultana, she had been practically offered a chest of gold dinars as reward for her illicit affair. Then why did she feel so empty at the thought of leaving this wretched nest of scorpions known as Jerusalem?

"Is that what you want?"

Saladin stood tall now, his shoulders squared. The hard part was over. Everything that needed to be said had been said.

"I want you to live, and you will not do so if you remain in the harem's grasp."

Maimonides took Miriam's hand in hers. She could see the relief on his lined face mixing with new worries.

"She is an unmarried girl. Where can she go at a time of war?"

"I have arranged a military escort to Cairo," Saladin said, then turned his attention to Miriam. "Once this war is over, I will join you there, if you still wish to be with me."

Miriam could see the look of horror pass across her uncle's face. The last thing he wanted was for his niece to have anything more to do with the Sultan. And, in truth, she herself was torn. The terrible experience she had just endured had scarred her heart deeply. She could not go through it a second time. Miriam hesitated before answering, gazing into Saladin's soulful brown eyes. Then she made her decision.

"I will await you," she said, to the rabbi's obvious despair. "But on one condition."

"Name it."

Miriam took a deep breath.

"I shall not be your concubine or playmate any longer," she said, not looking at her uncle's face, which she was sure would be red with embarrassment at her words. "If you enter my bed again, it will be as my husband."

Saladin smiled and bowed his head.

"I would not have it otherwise." The Sultan took her hands in his and kissed her gently. "Go with God, daughter of Isaac."

She held Saladin close to her, felt his heart beat against her bosom. Maimonides turned away, instinctively stepping outside of the prison cell to give them a few moments to say their farewells.

Miriam clung to Saladin fiercely. She did not know if she would ever see him again, and she wished they could have more time to say all that was bottled up inside. But, alas, she had learned that they were both slaves to destiny. Her fate, as she had perhaps always known, was to be found in the sheltered safety of Cairo, away from the madness of war and the piercing hatred of women's souls. And Saladin's fate, for good or ill, would meet him on the battlefield.

She found herself mouthing a silent prayer to whatever God or force commanded this vale of tears. *Please, grant him the strength to do what he must. To face the evil that even now is rising on the horizon.*

onrad of Montferrat stared in utter disbelief at the carnage that was spread across the battlefield. The corpses of over seven thousand infidels carpeted the earth, stretching from the bloodstained river to the dark confines of the forest that marked the borders of the coastal city of Arsuf.

Over the past several hours, he had witnessed what he was now convinced would be remembered as the decisive victory of the Crusade. And he reluctantly had to admit to himself that the credit was mainly due to Richard.

The Lionheart had carefully studied the terrain of the reconquered city of Acre and had determined that a direct attack on Jerusalem would be impossible. Saladin's forces covered the inland regions in ringed layers by the thousands. He therefore devised a strategy to conquer the relatively undefended coast. With access to the sea and the supply ports of Egypt blocked off, Saladin's empire would be effectively cut in half. Richard in essence was seeking to trap the infidels against the desert, even as they had trapped Conrad's forces against the sea.

The first major target of the Lionheart's plan was the coastal fortress of Arsuf, which was directly northwest of Jerusalem. The united Crusader forces had set out in full regalia, supported by the fleet of warships moored just off the coast that shadowed their move south. They easily crushed the poorly defended citadel at Caesarea and continued on past what came to be known as the "Dead River" about three miles south of the port. Here Saladin's horsemen had launched a series of irritating raids on their left flank, serving to enrage the Franks more than cause substantial damage. The river itself had been camouflaged by an elaborate web of reeds and rushes and a dozen horses fell in and drowned before the ruse was discovered.

Still, such defenses were laughably weak, and the Crusaders had grown increasingly confident that they would be able to cover the full swath of the coast without much resistance. The army's morale was high during that march south. Five battalions consisting of almost twenty thousand men moved proudly forward, singing with joy and confidence. The Knights Templar led the advance, followed by Richard's Angevins and Bretons, then the Normans and French. The rear guard was protected by the legendary Hospitallers, survivors of the terrible massacre at Hattin and thirsting for revenge. But there had been no sign of significant Muslim troops during the entire trek, and the soldiers were left alone to pillage and ransack villages along the coastal route with impunity.

Richard had waxed proud, proclaiming that the infidel army had likely deserted to Syria and Mesopotamia after news of their incredible victory at Acre. But Conrad had warned him not to underestimate Saladin. He sensed with growing dread that the quiet on the roads of the coast were little more than the deceptive calm that always precedes a tempest.

And he had been right. As the Crusader army marched in step through the olive gardens that lined the outskirts of Arsuf, Saladin had sprung his surprise. A Saracen force numbering over thirty thousand men came thundering out of the hills to the east of the citadel.

Saladin's forces had attacked from the rear, seeking to drive a wedge between the Hospitallers and the main body of the army. The holy warriors had been forced to march backward, firing crossbows at their attackers even as Richard commanded the advance soldiers to keep moving toward Arsuf. The king had ordered the Hospitallers to remain in place defending the rear, and ignore the temptation to break ranks and charge against the wave of Muslim cavalry that was steadily cutting them down from behind. It was a true credit to the men's training that they obeyed what to Conrad had seemed suicidal orders. The Hospitallers had held their position, and the rest of the army had been able to attain higher ground near Arsuf.

From there, Richard had turned the tables against the Muslim attackers. Without any warning, the full army turned about-face and launched a massive charge straight into the heart of the Muslim forces. The French knights tore through gaps in the Saracen infantry and decimated the center and left wings of the Muslim army. The brave Crusader soldiers had created a wave of fury that rode right over men and horses, crushing everything that stood in their way. The Lionheart, displaying his usual insanity in battle, was at the forefront of the charge. His flashing blade and utter fearlessness in the face of the Muslim hordes inspired incredible passion in his men, and terror in the enemy.

With their center and the left wing smashed in less than an hour of bloody clashes, the surviving Muslim warriors fled back to the safety of the hills, leaving behind their dead. Realizing that further pursuit of the infidels into their better-defended territory would lead the Crusaders from victory to crushing defeat, Richard had restrained his eager soldiers by proclaiming that any man was free to seize booty from the dead, and could keep all that he could carry, rather than accept only a strict share allocated by the commanders. Conrad had to give the boy his due— he understood his men well. While their hunger for Saracen blood ran deep, their lust for the spoils of war was even stronger.

So Conrad stood, shaking his head in utter amazement, as thousands of his soldiers bent over the bodies of the dead, collecting swords, gold, and whatever other items of value could be found on their persons. Every now and then one of his men would find a Saracen who was still alive, lying stunned on the field, or pretending to be dead in the hopes of escaping under the cover of nightfall. The ruse would, of course, be quickly detected and the infidel dispatched.

Conrad raised his head to see Richard and his ever-present knight William ride up to him. Richard smiled broadly as he surveyed the devastation his outnumbered and surrounded men had wrought on the enemy. William, on the other hand, remained as grim and sad as ever. Conrad had noticed that while he remained loyal to his master, the dark-haired knight had become increasingly silent and distant since the execution of the captives at Acre. The Marquis of Montferrat wondered yet again what this man, who clung to foolish ideals, was doing in the midst of a war that by necessity would have to be bloody and cruel. Perhaps the reason for the boy's perpetual gloom was that he was asking himself the very same question.

"The Muslim commander at Arsuf is prepared to surrender," William said, his tone flat and lacking any joy in their incredible and improbable victory. "The citadel gates will be open before the moon rises."

Conrad decided he could not stand to look at this sourpuss any longer. Still feeling the wonderful exaltation of victory, he turned to Richard, who at least was in similar spirits.

"With the fall of Arsuf, the coast belongs to us," Conrad said. "It is only a matter of time before Jerusalem is ours."

Richard shrugged nonchalantly.

"I do not celebrate a victory until it is behind me."

Conrad looked east. The Holy City was only a day's ride away from their new base of operations. It was as good a time as any to clear up certain matters before the siege of Jerusalem commenced.

"With Jerusalem looming on the horizon, it is now time that we begin discussions."

Richard's eyebrows rose in surprise.

"Regarding what?"

Conrad suddenly felt the first stirrings of unease eat away at the joy of victory in his heart.

"The administration of the new kingdom," Conrad said. "As heir to Guy's throne, it is my responsibility to ensure the stability of the regime."

To Conrad's shock and outrage, Richard threw his head back and laughed heartily.

"Ah yes, I forgot that I was addressing the King of Jerusalem."

Conrad felt his face turning beet red.

"You dare mock me?"

Richard did not look at him. Instead he kept his eyes on the sea of soldiers robbing the corpses of the enemy.

"As I have said, kingdoms are not held by words, but by deeds. Your forces cannot capture the throne without my men."

Conrad felt as if every nightmare that he had secretly suppressed were coming true before him in the waking world.

"What are you saying?"

Richard finally deigned to look at him. There was more contempt in that glance than in any act of butchery he had witnessed in war that day.

"There will be a king in Jerusalem, Conrad, but he will not be appointed by committee," Richard said proudly. "He will seize the city in his right hand."

With that, the King of England rode away, leaving Conrad standing at the edge of the battlefield with his mouth open. And then he caught sight of William, and his rage boiled over. For the first time in many days, the knight was smiling. Laughing at Richard's betrayal of the sacred cause. At Conrad's humiliation.

As William Chinon chuckled and rode after his master, Conrad stared in impotent fury at the bodies that lined the coast. *He* was the King of the Holy Land. And if Richard the Lionheart sought to steal his realm from him, he would soon learn that Conrad of Montferrat was a man who could not easily be trifled with.

48

iriam sat in discomfort in the covered carriage on the camel's back. The wooden howdah was small and cramped, and the red-and-green curtains that covered the box were incapable of keeping out the sand and the insects. And the dromedary beast itself moved in rumbling lurches that made her stomach feel queasy, as if she had been floating at sea for days.

It had been four days since she had bid farewell to Jerusalem and the comforts of the court, but it felt like a year. Her military escort was taking a circuitous route toward the Sinai through the barren wasteland of the Negev. Word had come that the Crusaders were on the march down the coast and a more direct journey through Ascalon would have invited trouble. Which was fine with her. She never again wanted to see that wretched oasis where her parents had been killed.

Still, she found the trek through the barren dunes depressing. The escort had blended in with a Bedouin trading caravan two days before, and she had been warned by the captain of the guard to stay inside the howdah for the remainder of the trip. While the soldiers had been handpicked by the Sultan and would die to protect her, the illiterate tribesmen whose company they now shared were not used to traveling with women and might have shown less restraint.

She had felt terrible fury at the warning, even though it was given with the best of intentions. Were all men slave to their penises? It seemed as if the entirety of human history revolved around men and their single-minded quest for an orgasm. Perhaps it should not surprise her that Islam, with its usual wry practicality, went out of its way to promise eternal sexual gratification to those who died on the battlefield. It appeared that the early Muslims had understood that nothing was a greater motivation for men than an opportunity to spill their seed.

Perhaps that was why intelligent women like the Sultana turned to their own gender for companionship and gratification. Miriam had not been shocked by word of her now-deceased rival's proclivities. She had met more than a few girls in Cairo, among both the Jews and the Muslims, who found the tender female touch far more comforting than the grunting, sweating, and brutal force that accompanied love in the arms of men. Miriam amused herself with the thought that if, as was likely, she and Saladin could never truly be together, she would eventually end up in the embrace of some sympathetic maidservant. In truth, the idea that she would ever hold any other man in her arms seemed incomprehensible to her. After her torrid passion with the Sultan, she doubted that any man would ever fill that void in her heart.

Her grim musings about her coming days as a spinster were abruptly ended by shouts from outside. Ignoring the captain's strict orders, she ripped open the curtain and gazed out at the blinding desert sands. All she could see was the long line of camels and horses that stretched through the desert, leaving behind a brief trail of footprints that quickly vanished in the shifting dunes.

Then her eyes followed the direction in which a young Bedouin boy wearing a purple skullcap was pointing excitedly. In the distance, behind two massive dunes that stood like golden mountains, she saw a line of dust rising from the horizon. She felt her heart skip a beat. Perhaps it was just a sandstorm, one of the many that rose unexpectedly and swept through the desert like a cleansing fire. Or perhaps . . .

One of the Sultan's soldiers had pulled out a telescope and was staring directly at the rising column of dust that seemed to be getting closer by the second. Then he shouted the very words she had hoped not to hear.

"Horses!"

The caravan erupted into a volley of defensive activity as men unsheathed scimitars and prepared their bows. Miriam desperately tried to convince herself that it was all just a precaution. They were still well within the Sultan's territory. At worst, it was a group of bandits who saw the caravan as easy prey. Such marauders would be unprepared to face fifty of Saladin's best-trained soldiers. She would not allow herself to consider the other possibility.

But the God of irony was clearly not going to pass up such a rich opportunity so easily. The sentry who was watching through his lens the horses rapidly approaching in the distance would soon be able to identify their surprised guests. Miriam felt her stomach turn as he now raised his fist to sound the alarm.

"They bear the Cross! It's the Franks!"

The Sultan's guards instantly went to work. The horsemen surrounded the caravan in an outward facing circle, their arrows ready. The Frankish cavalry descended from the parched sand dunes like a swarm of scarabs whose nest had been foolishly disturbed. They were instantly met by a barrage of missiles on all sides, but they kept coming.

Staring out from a small corner of her howdah's protective curtain, Miriam watched with disbelief as the quiet desert turned into a storm of agony and death. Her guards were outnumbered four to one, but they put up a valiant fight. Distant arrows quickly gave way to hand-to-hand combat with scimitars, maces, and battle-axes. But to no avail. The golden dunes were soon covered in sickening crimson pools of blood and entrails as Saladin's men returned to their Maker. It was over in a matter of minutes.

Realizing that they were lost, the Bedouin merchants fell to their knees before the Frankish regiment. She heard one of the men, a gnarled old sheikh who was probably the tribal chieftain, shouting something to the approaching Crusader knights. He was pointing in the direction of her camel.

Her heart sank as the terrible realization sank in. She had been betrayed. At the first sign of trouble, Miriam had pulled a dagger from a hidden compartment in one of her bags. She held it tightly as she heard the knights' horses bearing down on her terrified camel. Miriam had no expectation of escape—they were in the middle of the vast Negev on the borders of the desolate Sinai. There was nowhere to run. But flight was not the only way out of this predicament, and she had vowed to herself that she would never be captured by a Crusader. They would not have the pleasure of doing to her what they did to her mother.

The curtain was flung open and Miriam found herself face-to-face with a grinning, black-bearded knight with sparkling blue eyes. Without allowing herself a chance to think, she struck out and embedded her blade in the man's left eyeball. His scream was earsplitting, like the strangled sound of a woman dying in the midst of a tortured childbirth. The blinded Frank fell backward off his horse.

Miriam had managed to rip the bloodied knife from his punctured eye socket before he collapsed. She told herself that she had to do it now, before she lost her nerve. Miriam raised the dagger and aimed it directly at her own heart, praying to the God of her people to give her the courage to follow in the path of the martyrs of Masada.

She never found out whether she would have actually done it. At that instant her howdah gave way as the terrified camel on which she sat was hit by a slew of arrows. The dagger fell from her grasp as she tumbled out of the carriage. Miriam fell hard against the sandy earth and rolled down a gray dune. She tried to grab onto something, but her hand clutched only the shifting, empty sand.

She tossed and tumbled, crying out in despair. She was falling down into the caverns of Hades, past the gates of Persephone and Cerberus, toward an oblivion that had no name as blackness engulfed her . . .

49

ichard had been stunned when word came back of the raiding party's unprecedented success. The expedition had been sent from the Crusaders' new base of operations at Arsuf into the heart of Palestine to test the extent of Saladin's defenses. They had successfully penetrated as far south as the Negev with little resistance. Apparently the Sultan had pulled most of his forces into a shield formation around Jerusalem after his humiliating defeat at Arsuf, leaving the passes to the south relatively unprotected. Which was exactly what the Lionheart had wanted.

And then word came back that the raiding party had captured a member of Saladin's entourage, and Richard had been delighted. According to the Bedouin who had surrendered to his men, the girl was a favorite in Saladin's harem and was being sent to Egypt for her own protection (of course Saladin did not know yet that Egypt was about to lose its status as a safe haven in the war, but he would find out soon enough). The capture of this lover was like manna from Heaven. While Saladin might have been reluctant to pay an exorbitant ransom for thousands of faceless subjects at Acre, he would likely be more pliable when it came to a member of his inner circle, especially someone who shared his own bed. Such was the nature of all men—they would move Heaven and earth to protect their loved ones, but would rarely raise a finger to save a stranger, even if they were bound by all the laws of God and men.

So Richard had whistled with delight at the news of the unexpected prize as he entered his command pavilion to confront the tramp who spread her legs for the infidel. But when the prisoner had been brought before him, bound and bleeding, he had been taken aback. It was the stunning Jewess, the same girl who had nursed him back to health when his soul seemed determined to take flight. He had thought about the girl a great deal in his private moments since her departure, but he never expected to see her again. Or to learn that her service to the Sultan extended as far as his bed.

Looking at the ebony-maned girl kneeling before him, her arms tied with rough cords, her face heavily bruised, he was surprised at the sudden flash of anger that rose in his heart. He told himself that it was righteous indignation at the mistreatment of a lady of high birth. He would not admit to himself, except in a small corner of his heart, that a streak of jealousy at the thought of her in Saladin's arms played some role in his fury. In truth, Richard had so little experience with romantic envy that he probably would not have recognized it even if its green talons had torn apart his heart.

"Release her!" he shouted at the Templar captain who brought in the captive. "Bring the lady water."

The overanxious soldier who had hoped to earn good favor with his king was obviously startled by Richard's outrage. But he quickly bowed and moved to comply. With one quick slash of his knife, the sweaty Breton cut the cords that bound the girl's wrists and then handed her a gilded cup from a small table to Richard's left.

Miriam grabbed the silver goblet in trembling hands and drank with ferocity. Richard felt his bile rising at the sight of her desperation and it took every bit of restraint he possessed not to decapitate the Templar on the spot. The soldier apparently sensed that his capture of one of the ladies of Saladin's court had not been the triumph he would have liked, and he backed out of the tent, bowing his head several times in apology, although clearly unsure about his crime.

The Lionheart stared at the girl whose face had been burned into his mind since that first moment he'd awoken from fever. Even with her bruised eye and mud-scratched cheeks, her beauty remained ethereal.

"I apologize, my lady," he said, extending his hand to help her stand up. "My men are brutes."

Miriam watched him for a long moment. He could see both fear and confusion in her emerald eyes.

"Do you remember me?" She spoke in the strangely accented French that Richard found inexplicably enticing.

He smiled softly. More than she knew.

"How could I forget? You saved my life, Miriam."

The Jewess managed to stand tall, although Richard could see that the effort caused her pain. He had been told that the girl had fallen from her camel and been injured during the attack on the caravan. But if he found out that any of her wounds had been caused by his men, there would be a terrible retribution.

Miriam squared her shoulders and met his eyes with as much dignity as she could muster under the circumstances.

"Then perhaps you will return the favor."

Richard knew that she thought him a murderer and a barbarian. Perhaps that assessment was not altogether unfair. But he hoped that he would be able to show her another facet to his soul.

"No harm will come to you," he said, with a bow that he hoped was gallant, but was probably seen by the girl as unnecessary theatrics. "I swear upon Christ."

Miriam gripped a wooden chair beside the table as her weakened legs trembled beneath her. But her voice remained strong and confident.

"Let me go."

Ah, if only things were so easy—in love and war.

"That I cannot do, my lady," he said. "You are a wonderful healer, but a terrible spy."

Miriam went pale.

"I don't know what you mean."

Richard turned his back on her protestations to look outside the tent. The pavilion had been set up just outside the walls of Arsuf, in the midst of an olive garden that was even now being uprooted by dozens of his soldiers as they dug a new defensive trench around the citadel.

"I believe you do. But that is all in the past."

He felt Miriam come up behind him. She rested a tentative hand on his shoulder. Quite a brave move for a captive, but Richard knew her game.

"Please, let me send word to my family in Jerusalem." Her voice had risen an octave and taken on an especially feminine lilt. She was obviously trying to manipulate him with a show of female helplessness. He wondered if she played such games with the Sultan.

Richard bit his lip, feeling the jealous anger rising again.

"And to your lover, Saladin?"

Miriam did not respond. Richard turned to face her. Her face had gone rigid and her eyes were now as cold as snow. It was not the look of surprise at the ludicrousness of such a suggestion. Rather it was the steel gaze of a woman insulted by a gentleman's discourteous airing of her private affairs. Ah, so it *was* true.

Well, at least that would explain the strange rumors that his spies had garnered from their Bedouin captives about tumult in Saladin's court.

"The whole realm is buzzing with news of a mysterious girl who brought about the downfall of the Sultana," Richard said. "I must say, I never expected that vixen to be the same lady who so sweetly tended me back from the dead."

Miriam flinched, and then he saw control return to her face. She should have been frightened of him, of this entire situation, but the Jewess was doing a remarkable job of keeping her composure.

"If you know of my relationship with the Sultan, then you should realize that he will be outraged when he hears of this."

Richard laughed, although without malice. Her fiery nature had not changed in the months since she departed the camp. If anything, her romantic escapades with the Sultan appeared to have emboldened her.

"I hope he is," Richard said truthfully. "Angry men, especially those in love, rarely think straight. In a war, a distracted enemy is easily defeated."

Miriam's mask of haughty indifference broke for a second and he saw hot rage boiling in her eyes. Richard had no intention of handing over such a remarkable captive, regardless of the ransom, and her rapid mind had obviously grasped that reality. The Lionheart wondered if she would have the courage to strike him in her outrage, but the girl commendably restrained herself. If only barely.

"Come, let us attend to your living arrangements during your stay with us," Richard said, taking her by the arm. When she did not move, he faced her with a cold smile. "I know that you have lived with the barbarians for a long time, but where I come from, it is a matter of grave offense for a guest to cause undue difficulty to her host. I hope you will remember that."

Miriam's resistance faded and she followed him outside. He saw her eyes quickly take in the camp and the surrounding terrain even as he guided her toward the gates of Arsuf and the prison cell that would be waiting for her inside the citadel. He knew that she was trying to absorb everything at once in the hopes of devising some way out of her predicament.

The Lionheart suppressed a smile. He wondered how many times and through how many clever machinations she would try to escape in the months to come. Or how many misguided rescue efforts her love-struck Saladin would mount. Well, he would have to prepare for all of them. Of course, Richard had no intention of harming the girl, but the Sultan did not need to know that. In any event, any concern Saladin might have for Miriam's welfare would soon be eclipsed by the new crisis that Richard was about to cause among the Saracens. The surprise that would lead to the downfall not only of Jerusalem, but also of the entire Muslim empire.

50

Maimonides sat at the council of war in his usual seat to the left of Qadi al-Fadil. The vizier had been uncharacteristically polite to him over the past few days, but his forced civility only increased the rabbi's anger. Maimonides wanted to lay all the blame on the courtier's shoulders for the terrible series of events that had befallen his beloved niece. If the sniveling rat had not betrayed her to the Sultan, she would likely still be safe in Jerusalem. But in moments of lucidity when his rage and despair died down just enough for him to think honestly, the rabbi understood that the old man was just another unwitting pawn in a ruthless game played by the late Sultana.

In truth, he knew who was ultimately responsible. Miriam had ignored his impassioned advice and chosen to follow her young heart, to predictable calamity. But even she was not truly at fault. That responsibility lay solely at the feet of one man. The man who now sat at the head of the carved table looking tired and defeated.

It was the Sultan whom Maimonides blamed above all else. Miriam was just a child, unfamiliar with the dangerous path that his alleged friend had placed her on. The rabbi's stomach turned at the thought that a man whom he once esteemed above all others had pursued such a reckless course with a girl young enough to be his daughter.

Maimonides had sought to leave the court and return to Egypt with Miriam. He had no desire to remain in service to the throne, with all of its worldly glory and prestige. All he wanted was to spend the final days of his life reclining in his quiet garden in Cairo, reading the latest books on medicine and finishing his magnum opus on the Jewish faith, *The Guide for the Perplexed*. And he wanted to help his lovely niece put her terrible ordeal behind her, to work with his wife, Rebecca, and the local matchmaker to find her a suitable partner who would heal the scars of her youthful heart.

But Saladin had refused his request to leave, citing his desperate need for clear advice as the tide of the war against the Franks steadily worsened. Maimonides no longer cared about either the Crusaders or the Muslims, locked in their eternal battle for Jerusalem, a Jewish city that belonged to neither of these interlopers. Let these two upstart heresies that had severed ties with their mother faith waste all their energies destroying each other. Perhaps when they had ground each other into the dust, the Children of Israel could reclaim what was rightfully theirs.

But he had kept his bitter thoughts to himself and bowed to the Sultan's command. Saladin's behavior had grown increasingly erratic since the series of Frankish victories threatened to unravel his life's work, and his brutal and uncharacteristic decision to execute the Sultana had sent a chill down the spine of all the courtiers. Not that Maimonides had any sympathy for the coldhearted queen, but the incident had made clear to all that Saladin had reached a terrible breaking point and anyone who offended him was in dire jeopardy. For the sake of his wife and his niece, who had both suffered far too much since he foolishly invited them here, he had held his tongue and remained gainfully employed at the Sultan's side. At least Miriam would be safe, far away from this madhouse.

And then his world had been shattered a second time. When he received word of her capture, his heart sank into the depths of Gehenna. Rebecca, who had wept for days when Miriam had been imprisoned as a result of the Sultana's schemes, had fainted at the news. She now refused to leave her bed, and Maimonides watched her waste away in despair, refusing most food and surviving on a few crumbs and water. Rebecca had lost her will to live, and he had a terrible feeling every morning that he would awake next to her cold, unmoving body. He could not imagine his life without these two women. They were the pillars that had held up his body and spirit for so many years. A world without Miriam and Rebecca was not worth living in. The rabbi knew that suicide was forbidden by the Law, but he no longer cared for the dry, heartless rules of a God who would send so much agony into the world, and then force His befuddled slaves to stay and suffer like prisoners.

✦ ✦ ✦

EVEN AS MAIMONIDES TEETERED on the edge of sanity, the Sultan had taken the news of Miriam's captivity with stoic acceptance. If the girl had been someone else's flesh and blood, perhaps the rabbi could have been more charitable. Word had spread through the realm of the fall of Arsuf. The Franks held the coast, and more ships from Europe were likely on their way. In the eyes of others, the fate of one woman could not be weighed on the scales of war. But in the rabbi's heart, there was no other point left to this losing conflict except to save that one precious life. And the fact that Saladin did not appear to share this perspective only increased the rabbi's estrangement from his master.

Maimonides stared into space, uncaring, as the bombastic al-Adil argued matters of military strategy yet again with his brother.

"The Franks will probably attack from the north with the help of their supporters at Tyre," al-Adil droned on. "From their vantage point at Arsuf, they are poised like a dagger at the very heart of the sultanate. Jerusalem *will* be their next target. We have no choice but to double the number of our soldiers outside the city. Conscript every village boy above the age of ten in Palestine if we have to."

Saladin steepled his fingers in front of him, as he always did when he was thinking.

"What you say is logical, but this Lionheart is wily," the Sultan said, to everyone's rapt attention except Maimonides'. "I think he is planning something very different."

Al-Adil hesitated and then cast a glance at the sullen rabbi.

"The strategy I describe fits with the documents stolen by that Jewess."

An uncomfortable silence fell over the council room.

Maimonides felt hot rage building inside at the cavalier mention of his niece by this uncouth Kurd. He was about to say something unwise when, to his surprise, the Sultan spoke.

"Her name is Miriam, brother. Never address her except in tones of utmost respect if you wish to live."

Saladin's tone was acid and his face had turned cold. At that instant, Maimonides saw the break in the Sultan's carefully cultivated façade. Saladin met his eyes, and yes, there was real anguish there at the memory of the tragically heroic girl who had turned his life upside down. The rabbi's wounds were still too deep for forgiveness, but for one brief instant he saw a glimmer of his old friend again.

"I apologize, my brother," said al-Adil, and for the first time in anyone's memory, he actually sounded contrite. "The lady Miriam did a brave deed in stealing their plans, an act of courage that will undoubtedly be sung by both Muslims and Jews for many generations." He paused and bowed his head to Maimonides, and then continued his harangue about military strategy. "So far, their actions have followed the documents to the letter. We should honor her memory by using the information she gleaned wisely."

Maimonides felt a flash of resentment at al-Adil's implication that Miriam was lost beyond hope of rescue, but he realized that the man was only stating what everyone already believed in their hearts. Including Maimonides himself.

Saladin glanced a final time at his rabbinical adviser, then swiftly returned to the debate at hand.

"That is what bothers me," he said. "Even if the Lionheart did not plant false information, he should know by now that we have these documents. A wise man would have altered course. Yet he appears to be walking straight on a course of which he should know that we are fully aware."

Al-Adil grunted.

"He is a Frank. They think with their asses."

There was ripple of nervous laughter as the courtiers released the tension that had built up over the past few moments.

Saladin considered for a long moment, then lowered his steepled hands to his sides, as he always did when he had made a final decision.

"I will increase the guard around Jerusalem by fifty percent, but I want enough soldiers in the field in case Richard tries to surprise us somewhere else."

Al-Adil saw that further argument would not be tolerated. He bowed his head in acquiescence.

"As you command."

Saladin stood up, followed by everyone else in the room. Maimonides made no effort to rise with the respectful haste of his colleagues, but rise he did.

"Go about your routines with cheer in your hearts, my friends," Saladin said unexpectedly. "We are far from defeated. In fact, I believe that Allah has a few surprises in store for our overconfident adversaries."

The courtiers and generals nodded and took their cues to leave.

"Stay, Rabbi."

Maimonides was surprised to hear the Sultan's voice addressing him. Saladin had not spoken more than a handful of words to him since word arrived of Miriam's capture. Al-Adil and Qadi al-Fadil glanced at the old doctor as he stopped in his departure and turned.

When they were completely alone, Saladin moved to stand beside his estranged adviser. He put a firm hand on the old man's shoulder, and Maimonides flinched despite himself at the intimate contact that now felt so alien and inappropriate.

"I have not forgotten her, my friend," Saladin said in a soft voice that trembled with emotion. "A messenger will be dispatched to Richard to negotiate her release." The Sultan paused. "I know that all the pain that your family has endured—that Miriam has endured—is my fault, and by Allah I will bear the responsibility on my shoulders until the Day of Judgment."

Maimonides forced himself to look into his master's eyes. In that instant the veil was lifted and the rabbi saw sorrow, regret, and shame swirling in those dark pools. And the terrible anguish in his own heart began to ease. The knowledge that this powerful and proud man could admit the truth of his own failings was a first step toward healing their shattered bond. Maimonides doubted their relationship would ever again be as it once was, but that was without a doubt for the best. Perhaps, when Miriam was safe in her bed again, they could begin anew, not as potentate and subject, but as two mortal men who saw in each other the best and worst of themselves.

And at that instant, watching the Sultan take responsibility for the terrible fate of an innocent girl, the rabbi knew what he had to do.

"Let me go."

Saladin did not appear surprised at the request, but he looked closely at the rabbi's lined face before answering.

"I worry for your health."

Of course, the idea was preposterous. Sending an aging man whose hands suffered from tremors and whose heart might stop at any moment as a diplomatic envoy on such a critical matter—it was utter madness. Yet Maimonides knew without a shadow of a doubt that he was the only one who could shoulder this burden.

"My health will only worsen if any harm comes to Miriam," Maimonides said. It was the simple truth.

Saladin nodded at long last.

"Go then, and may the God of Moses be with you."

With that, the Sultan turned his back on his elderly adviser. The man who had once been the most powerful ruler in the civilized world slowly left the room, his shoulders slumped under the terrible weight of the world. A weight that grew heavier by the day, until it would at last force him, and the sultanate, to its knees.

51

Miriam was getting used to spending her life inside prisons. At least this cell was better furnished than the one she had languished in for a week while Saladin had gone about his lethal purge of the harem. Richard had locked her in one of the plush state bedrooms in the governor's castle at Arsuf. The bed was covered in soft blankets made of deer hide. The stone walls were decorated with delicate tapestries left over from the citadel's century-long turn as a Frankish military outpost. While she felt no emotional connection to the silken images of the Madonna holding the infant Christ, examining the delicate artwork at least provided her with something to do while she languished in the company of the enemy.

At least she had a window in this cell. The Crusaders had not bothered to install any bars on the arched frame, assuming that the fifty-foot drop would discourage any escape attempts. Of course, none of them knew that Miriam was willing to choose the ultimate escape if the conditions of her captivity worsened or she suffered any abuse at the hands of the barbarians. She still regretted the failure of her first suicide attempt when the caravan fell into the clutches of these beasts.

Miriam stared out the window as the sun disappeared beneath the horizon, drowning the sea in a pastel wash. Far beneath her she could see the legions of the Crusader army finishing their monotonous drills and training sessions. The men put away their javelins and maces and turned toward the direction of a flat brick building that she assumed was the mess hall from the disgusting odors that seemed to float upward every evening at about this time. Perhaps the Sultan had nothing to worry about. Even if the Crusaders were able to launch their inland attack from Arsuf and cut through the layers of defensive barriers that Saladin had erected around Jerusalem, they would eventually fall victim to the poisonous gruel that seemed to serve as the soldiers' only source of nourishment.

Even as she wrinkled her nose at the thought, the door to her room opened and two soldiers entered with her usual repast, a steaming bowl of the disgusting soup. She mused to herself that while the accommodations in the Sultan's prison were rather grim in comparison with her current cell, the food was markedly better. Perhaps there was some hidden meaning in the fact—the Sultan's simplicity disguised a heart of gold, while the Franks efforts to appear civilized would never alter the fact that the Europeans were unsophisticated ruffians.

These guards whom Richard had assigned to watch over her were Italians, one from Rome and the other from some city-state called Venice. She had gathered this from surreptitiously listening to their conversations over the past several nights. They were apparently unaware that she understood the basics of Italian, a fact that Miriam had kept well hidden from her captors. She had always had a fascination with languages and prided herself on her ability to read and speak several of the barbarian tongues. Her uncle, whose knowledge was limited to the primary Crusader language, French, had never understood her desire to study the infidels' speech. But then he had never had the terrifying experience of running from a horde of angry Franks that was murdering and pillaging a harmless merchant caravan, screaming curses at an escaping teenage girl with words that made no sense but which were repeated hundreds of times in her nightmares. She had hoped that by mastering their tongues, she could silence their haunting, incomprehensible cries in her sleep.

While her skills in languages had not dampened the cold terror of her dreams, they had proved remarkably helpful during her imprisonment. She had gathered much from the men around her, who were unaware of her fluency in Italian and English, including the layout of the camp and the placement of guards at various points in the citadel—information that would be vital should she eventually formulate an effective plan of escape. She had also picked up on the daily complications facing the occupying army in its efforts to subdue resistance from villagers in the areas immediately surrounding the coast. While the Franks went out of their way to appear utterly confident in their mastery of the conquered territory, their own nervous words betrayed their inflated bravado and empty posturing.

Miriam turned to face the guards carrying her dinner. They were both tall and lanky. The brown-haired one had recently begun growing a beard, apparently to hide a rash that had erupted on his cheeks as a result of some undiagnosed desert ailment. The other, a blond with curly hair and ears that jutted out at an amusing angle, stepped forward with the wooden tray holding the offensive broth that served as breakfast, lunch, and dinner.

She sat down on the bed and grimaced as the guard placed the tray beside her. The soldiers moved to stand by the door, giving her only a modicum of privacy as she held her nose and sipped the vile gruel off a wooden spoon. She could feel their eyes on her as usual, undressing her in their minds. Miriam did not care, as long as their fantasies remained locked squarely inside their heads. Richard had made it clear to her that his men had been ordered not to touch her, although his commands could not control their perverted imaginations.

The blond turned to his rash-covered colleague and spoke in Italian.

"I was talking to one of the men who served in Guy's Jerusalem regiment, a survivor of Hattin. He was saying that Jewish women are animals in bed."

Miriam made every effort not to react. It was their nightly ritual of degradation, made especially sweet to the young fools' minds through their belief that she could not understand a word they said. Every evening she would endure their lascivious talk as she ate, refusing to give them any indication that she understood them. She was not going to give up her only strategic advantage in this disastrous situation out of a foolish sense of feminine dignity or pride.

The brown-haired guard ran a hand over the unwashed stubble on his cheeks, scratching at the splotchy rash. Miriam hoped it kept him up at night with itchy discomfort.

"Do you think the king has tasted her yet?"

"No, but I hear he will drop by any night to sample her wares."

Miriam struggled to keep eating, despite the icy claws that were beginning to squeeze her throat. She had suspected that Richard was attracted to her. But for a murderer and a barbarian, he had been remarkably courteous so far. She did not know what she would do if he tried to force himself upon her. Her eyes had flitted to the window and its deadly drop, when she realized the men had stopped talking and were watching her with curiosity.

Damn, she had let down her guard. Miriam was not sure what she had done to send off a telltale sign, but it was obvious that her body language had tensed at the thought of Richard trying to have his way with her. She glanced up at the men and spoke in French, a language they knew she understood.

"It is very rude to speak in a foreign tongue among those who know not the language," she said, speaking slowly and with feigned discomfort at the unusual sounds. "I have endured your disrespect for far too long. Perhaps I should discuss the matter with the king. He is a true gentlemen, unlike you swine."

It worked. The soldiers laughed at the irony of her words given the most recent turn of their conversation. Her veil of incomprehension was back in place.

"She is feisty," the bearded warrior said in Italian, and smirked. "She must have brought Saladin much pleasure."

Miriam shook her head in feigned frustration at their continued disrespect. She went back to eating the gruel with a pout of affected resignation.

The blond leaned closer to his companion, but she could still make out his words.

"Did you hear? The infidel has sent a messenger to negotiate her release. That doctor who she came with last time."

Miriam's eyes flickered, but she continued eating with her head bowed. This was utterly unexpected and it took every inch of self-control to restrain a gasp. Her uncle was here? Perhaps the nightmare was finally about to end.

"That old fart? He looks like he'll keel over any moment," the bearded guard exclaimed. "Are we actually going to hand her over without even a little fun?"

Keep eating, her mind screamed. *Don't look up. Don't acknowledge a word.*

"Don't worry, she's not going anywhere," the blond replied. "But I am sure the king will reunite her with her lover Saladin in prison when he seizes Jerusalem."

Miriam slowed her eating. She sipped at her food, hoping to prolong the meal and gather as much information as she could.

"It's too bad that the conquest of Jerusalem will be delayed for some time."

What? Richard wasn't going to attack?

"The king is wise." The curly-haired fellow shrugged. "First we take Ascalon, then Cairo. With Egypt under our control, we shall conquer not only Jerusalem but Damascus and Baghdad."

Ascalon. Oh my God.

Miriam stopped eating. She could not maintain this pretense much longer. She needed to end this before her guard dropped and the soldiers figured out how they had been manipulated by a woman. And she needed time to think, to plan.

She set the half-finished bowl aside and turned to the bearded guard.

"I cannot eat any more of this camel dung," she said in her halting French. "Now get out and take your uncouth braying with you."

The soldiers laughed again, but they complied. The two guards turned and left, locking the bedroom door behind them and leaving Miriam to rapidly consider her options.

Richard was moving on Ascalon, the gateway into the Sinai, even as Saladin concentrated all of his forces in the country's interior. Egypt was unprotected. If Richard's army held the oasis, they would be able to launch a devastating attack on Cairo that would shatter the sultanate.

Jerusalem was not the goal of this new brand of Crusaders, as it had been for their fathers. Their design was much grander. They were seeking to reverse the humiliating conquest of Christendom that had been unleashed five hundred years before when the armies of Allah, led by Khalid ibn al-Waleed and Amr ibn al-As, had smashed the Byzantine Empire into the dustbin of history. This new breed of holy warrior understood that Christians would never hold Jerusalem for more than a few years as long as the Holy Land remained surrounded by hostile Muslim nations. So they would eliminate the threat at its source. Conquest of the sacred city would be the inevitable by-product of a Crusade launched to destroy the caliphate itself.

Suddenly Miriam realized that Richard the Lionheart was not the foolish, impetuous boy she had presumed him to be. He was a military genius with the audacity to turn the world upside down. Richard was the new Saladin, except that his victories would be followed not by amnesty and reconciliation, but by blood and vengeance. The Muslims would be destroyed. And her people would be left with no allies, no protectors, in a world ruled yet again by those who saw in their faces only the dripping blood of a slain god.

All thought of her own predicament vanished at that moment, along with any lingering resentment toward the Sultan for the disastrous end to their affair. All that mattered to Miriam now was warning Saladin about the impending threat to Ascalon.

She had fancied herself a spy once, had risked her life to save her people from the Franks. The king had tricked her then, used her youthful ambition and adventuresome nature against her. But this time she would not fall prey to Richard's manipulations.

Failure was not an option, for civilization itself was on the brink.

52

Maimonides stood in what had once been the office of the military governor of Arsuf, a position that had rapidly passed from a Frankish overlord to one of Saladin's deputies and then back to the Franks yet again. All in a span of less than three years. Maimonides remembered the overwhelming sense of victory he had felt at Hattin and at the fall of Jerusalem, when it seemed that the Franks had been forever banished from these lands. And yet here they were again, stronger and more vindictive than ever. In truth, he had lulled himself into wishfully thinking that the victory at Hattin meant the end of the war. But it was no more than a temporary turning of the tide, and with clockwork regularity, evil had again risen to even the score. Perhaps that was the way it would always be. Even if Saladin managed to repel this invasion, it would be a brief respite before the dogs of war were unleashed yet again in the paradoxically named Holy Land.

If the King of England noticed the rabbi's discomfort at standing for such a long period, he did not appear to care. The golden-haired boy, dressed today in a tunic of purple silk and a flame-colored cloak, was watching him with an arrogant smile that made Maimonides wish he could forget his oath about never causing harm. Ever since Miriam had been captured by this petulant child, the rabbi had asked himself why he had been cursed with the task of saving Richard's life. With word of the terrible number of casualties at Acre and Arsuf, and daily rumors of Frankish atrocities against the coastal villagers, Maimonides felt personally responsible for the suffering of every victim of this war.

The king seemed perfectly comfortable sitting in the high leather-backed governor's chair. Beside him stood his usual retinue of scowling advisers, including the scarred devil Conrad. But there was no sign of the one Crusader whom the rabbi had come to respect. Perhaps Sir William was out on an expedition such as the raid that had captured his unlucky niece. Or perhaps he had died in one of the battles and was buried under some anonymous mound on the coast. He hoped that this was not the case. William's death would be a terrible loss for decent men on both sides of the conflict. Without a voice of reason to rein them in, the Franks would undoubtedly unleash the worst that was in their black hearts.

The gilded door opened and Maimonides' bitter thoughts were pushed out of his mind by the sight of Miriam. She was led in by two lanky, pale-faced men and he saw that she was wearing an unusual blue gown covered in white lace that must have been of some European design. At least Richard had seen fit to keep her clothed, although the rabbi shuddered at the thought of what he might have asked from Miriam in return.

His niece broke free of the restraining hands of the guards and flew into his arms. He held her tight, and for an instant he forgot all about the war and the terrible tragedy that surrounded them in all directions. She was alive, and did not appear to have been ill-treated. But Maimonides knew that some forms of abuse did not leave a visible scar.

"Have they hurt you?" His voice sounded strange to him, and he realized it was because the tears he was suppressing had found their way into his throat.

Miriam looked at her captors, and then affected a smile that Maimonides instantly recognized as false.

"The king and his men have been perfect gentlemen."

Maimonides saw Richard's sneering face, and decided that he had had enough of courtly pretense.

"Well, that's a change."

The king threw his head back and laughed heartily.

"I see you retain your caustic humor, good doctor," Richard said. "I hope you will join my medical staff in my new headquarters in Jerusalem."

Maimonides felt cold needles piercing his heart. Richard's men smiled broadly at his confident words. All except Conrad, whose face appeared to darken and grow more malevolent (if that were indeed possible) at Richard's proud boast. Perhaps the Crusader forces were not as unified as everyone believed.

"That will never happen." Maimonides wanted this audience to end as soon as possible so that he could leave this wretched castle and return his niece to safety.

"A shame," Richard said with an exaggerated shrug. "Well, as you can see, your niece is unharmed. You can relay the fact of her safety to your master. Is there anything further I can help you with?"

Maimonides felt the stirrings of shock and anger in his belly. Richard was talking as if he would not release Miriam. The rabbi had not come this far into hostile territory to be trifled with.

"The Sultan wishes to know the ransom," he said. Maimonides had been authorized to agree to a sum of up to fifteen thousand gold dinars, an extraordinary figure that far exceeded the ransom paid by any of the Frankish nobles for the release of their loved ones during Saladin's initial conquest of Jerusalem. And Saladin would pay the sum out of his own stores of wealth rather than dip into the already strained treasury. The Sultan's willingness to empty his own purse had gone a long way to rekindle the rabbi's affection for the man.

Richard leaned back in his chair.

"Very simple really," he said through shining teeth that looked distinctly menacing. "If Saladin surrenders Jerusalem, I will surrender the girl."

Maimonides turned beet red with rage at the boy's impudence. Miriam stood stoically by his side, as if she had never expected to be released in the first place.

"How can you do this? She nursed you on your deathbed!"

Richard's smile faded and was replaced by a cruel grimace.

"That is why she is a guest of honor and not buried underneath a sand dune in the Negev."

Miriam placed a soft hand on her uncle's arm. Maimonides saw the warning in her eyes and realized that if he went too far over the line of propriety with this dangerously unstable youth, there would be consequences for Miriam as well as for her aged uncle. But Maimonides, flush with frustration and defeat, could not hold back a final, ill-advised taunt.

"History will remember you as a tyrant, Richard of Aquitaine."

A cold silence fell over the governor's office. The courtiers glanced at each other in shock. No man had ever openly spoken like that to the king, especially not a Jew. Richard leaned forward and for a moment Maimonides thought he was about to order the offending doctor's execution. And then, as if to convince Maimonides of his madness, he laughed.

"That depends on who writes the history, Rabbi."

* * *

MAIMONIDES WAS HALFWAY BACK to Jerusalem before he found the note Miriam had slipped into a pocket in his cloak. On a torn piece of linen, scratched in some strange brown liquid that smelled faintly like lentils, she had scrawled a message. It was a poem addressed to Saladin. Although the words made no sense to him, Maimonides had a strange feeling in the pit of his stomach as he read her note that the course of the entire war—the course of history—was about to change.

53

Maimonides stood before the grim-faced Sultan in the hall of judgment as he finished explaining Richard's ultimatum. Saladin sighed and shook his head wearily.

"It is as I expected. I am sorry my friend," the Sultan said. "But do not despair yet. Miriam is highly resourceful. I expect that this boy king will find keeping her under lock and key rather difficult."

Maimonides coughed uncomfortably.

"I have indeed seen evidence of her resourcefulness, *sayyidi*. But I do not know to what end."

Saladin's eyebrows rose in expectation. Even al-Adil, who had shown little interest in Miriam's fate, perked up.

"What are you talking about?"

Maimonides removed the torn bit of linen and passed it along to Saladin's hands.

"She slipped this to me at some point during our meeting, I'm not sure when," the rabbi said, hoping that he was not embarrassing himself or the Sultan with a message that might turn out to be nothing more than some lovelorn poem written by a lonely and isolated girl.

The Sultan looked at the note with surprise. He read it to himself once, then raised his head and repeated the words aloud, apparently not caring how they were interpreted by the courtiers.

"Love is the only thing worth fighting for. You once told me of an oasis where you first loved a woman. Our destiny lies in the shade of its palm trees."

There was a rumble of surprise from the nobles present, although Maimonides noted that Qadi al-Fadil remained silent. He appeared deathly ill at any mention of Miriam, and the rabbi had realized that the arrogant premier actually felt shame and sorrow for his role in her downfall. The rabbi had not forgiven the vizier yet, but he was beginning to think that perhaps his heart would be open to that possibility one day. If it swayed the Deity to bring Miriam back safely, Maimonides imagined he would pardon the whole sorry, treacherous lot.

Still her unusual message, with its frank allusion to the Sultan's controversial affair, stirred more than a few nasty glances in the rabbi's direction. The grumbling suggested to Maimonides that even if he were willing to forgive Miriam's enemies in the court one day, the sentiment would probably not be mutual. He steeled his mind and returned his attention to the message.

"My niece is not prone to writing poetry, my lord. She risked terrible punishment in passing it along. What does it mean?"

Saladin looked first at al-Adil, and then at Qadi al-Fadil, before turning back to face Maimonides. For the first time in many months, the rabbi saw a bright light in the Sultan's eyes. A look of wonder and joy. Considering how precarious the situation had grown, with the Crusader invasion of Jerusalem likely to be undertaken any day, the expression on his features seemed inappropriate, verging on madness.

"I was wrong about Miriam. She is truly a great spy." Saladin rose from the golden seat of judgment and turned to al-Adil, who seemed completely perplexed by the Sultan's behavior.

"My brother, summon the council of war," Saladin said in a voice that sounded remarkably like that of an excited child who had discovered where his mother had hidden a box of sweets. "Richard is not on his way to Jerusalem."

There was tumult of shock at his words. Even Maimonides wondered whether the pressure had grown too much for him. Richard and the Crusaders were poised for a massive attack from their vantage point at Arsuf. That was obvious to even the common people who had no experience in military matters, and had resulted in the spontaneous evacuation of villages surrounding the Holy City.

"What are you talking about?" Al-Adil looked at his brother suspiciously, as if wondering whether the Franks had placed some enchantment upon Saladin. "Where is his next target, if not Jerusalem?

Saladin faced Maimonides, his eyes twinkling.

"Ascalon."

And then it all made sense.

54

Maimonides hated horses. He hated camels even more, so he agreed to travel yet again on Saladin's gray-spotted mare that had accompanied him on his failed mission to Richard. Well, his efforts at rescuing Miriam had failed, but the entire court was abuzz with news of Richard's plans to invade the Sinai. From the perspective of military strategy and espionage, the rabbi's diplomatic mission to Arsuf had been a resounding success. Unfortunately that gave him little solace when he considered the fact that his brave niece remained locked in the devil's lair. A fitting reward for her heroic service, courtesy of an ironic, teasing God.

They had left immediately after Saladin had discussed the matter with his war council. Maimonides had managed to squeeze in an hour back at home desperately trying to explain to his ailing wife that Miriam was safe, but could not yet return to them. And then the Sultan's twin brutes were banging at the door to his apartment, telling him that he would accompany the Sultan on the mission.

He understood the necessity of having a trained doctor present during an arduous trip through the desert, but there were many physicians in the city of Jerusalem. Younger, heartier, less likely to keel over in the blistering heat of the Negev. But it was not his place to question the Sultan, and despite Rebecca's wailing cries for him to remain by her side, he had been forced to participate in the Sultan's carefully planned response to Richard's stratagem.

Of course, the need for urgent action was clear. The Franks had nearly trapped them with a well-devised gambit. By positioning their forces so as to suggest an imminent attack on Jerusalem, they had forced the Muslims to focus all their resources on defending the Holy City. The entire southern border with Sinai was undefended. And Ascalon, which stood at the gate of the desert, was the main supply corridor into Egypt. Possession of the city, with its wells and date trees, was necessary to supply an army to survive the long trek into the wasteland where his people had first received the Divine Law. If Ascalon fell, Richard would be able to use it as a base into Africa. With the resources of Egypt in Frankish hands, not only Jerusalem, but also the entire caliphate, would fall.

Protecting Ascalon had suddenly become the primary focus of the Muslim army. A massive counteroffensive to Richard's attack would be required if they were to stop a disaster that would make the fall of Acre and Arsuf look like minor military blunders.

But instead of finding himself part of a huge expedition force capable of repelling the attack on Ascalon, Maimonides had been shocked to discover that the Sultan was embarking with only thirty men. Some of the finest soldiers in the army, certainly, but by themselves utterly incapable of taking on an army of thirty thousand fanatical Crusaders. The rabbi concluded that these men were simply chosen to lead a much larger force, perhaps consisting of Egyptian and Syrian conscripts would be waiting for them as they traveled south.

But after days of traversing the lonely waste of the Negev, with no sign of even a single Bedouin camp pitched in the desolate gray sand,

Maimonides was becoming alarmed at the possibility that the Sultan had indeed gone mad. That he expected this puny raiding force, consisting of two dozen horses and a handful of camels, to take on the might of the Frankish hordes. Perhaps Saladin thought that the mystical favor of Allah would be upon them, as it had been on the incredibly successful armies of the Prophet. The rabbi had, of course, read of the many astounding victories of Muhammad and his Companions, usually against impossible odds, but even the Prophet had never to his knowledge won a battle in which he was outnumbered a thousand to one.

A sentry wearing a green turban rode up from behind a towering sand dune that had obscured their vision. He galloped over to the Sultan's side and spoke words that were drowned out by the moaning Negev wind. Saladin apparently understood him and he turned to nod at Maimonides, who spurred his mare on to the Sultan's side. Maimonides grimaced at the sudden increased pace of the animal, his hips burning from the strain of riding the wretched beast nonstop for days. Saladin laughed when he perceived his discomfort.

"My friend, it appears as if the doctor is in need of medicine himself."

Maimonides was aware of the less-than-charitable grins on the faces of some of Saladin's men and he forced himself to hold his head high with dignity.

"Men of my age always appear ill, *sayyidi*. We use that to get attention."

Saladin laughed heartily, and then raised his voice for all in the raiding party to hear.

"I have just received word that the Lionheart is only two days away."

He sounded ebullient, apparently thrilled at word of the impending arrival of the juggernaut. Maimonides bit his lip and decided to find out for sure if the Sultan was truly mad as he was beginning to suspect.

"Will we be able to garner reinforcements in time?"

Saladin's smile slipped away and he became sober. Maimonides was startled to see a hint of sadness rising in his dark eyes.

"We will not need reinforcements."

Maimonides hesitated, unsure what to say. None of this made any sense. Saladin obviously saw the conflict on his face, between desire for a rational explanation for the strange course of action they were taking and fear of learning that there was none.

"The 'Guide for the Perplexed' appears perplexed himself," the Sultan said.

Maimonides took a deep breath.

"Forgive me, *sayyidi*, but we cannot hold Ascalon with this small band."

At that instant their horses cleared the top of the massive dune and Maimonides gazed down upon the emerald island that was Ascalon. It was as if God had dropped a slice of Paradise to serve as a bridge between the twin hells of the Negev and the Sinai. Sparkling rows of palm trees, rich with clusters of dates, walled the city in. White stone houses, sparkling like pure marble, stood in the midst of a carpet of manicured grass, lined with well-tended rosebushes.

Saladin caught his breath and Maimonides thought he saw the glistening of tears in his eyes as he gazed upon a city that he had often proclaimed the most beautiful gem in all the caliphate.

"You are correct, my friend. This petty band cannot protect Ascalon." He paused. "Do you remember that note Miriam sent?"

Maimonides nodded. How could he forget? But he sensed that the Sultan was no longer even speaking to him. It was as if he were addressing someone else whom the rabbi could not see.

Saladin rode over to a sturdy palm tree set by a well on the outskirts of Ascalon. The city's residents were beginning to emerge from their homes, perhaps thinking a trading party had arrived with goods for Egypt. Merchants were the lifeblood of the city and utmost courtesy would be extended to them. The curious onlookers, many of them children in bright-colored tunics or women in black Bedouin head scarves, appeared unaware that their visitor today was not just another ordinary trader selling pottery. They had probably never seen the Sultan and would not have believed that such an august man would bother to visit their tiny backwater town. Little did these poor people realize that the fate of the world ran through the verdant and well-groomed streets of the oasis.

Saladin dismounted from his horse and knelt before the palm tree, as if in prayer. No, Maimonides realized, not prayer. As if he were reliving a tender memory.

"I first made love to a woman under this tree," Saladin said, running a battle-weathered hand along its thick trunks as if he were caressing that very lover of whom he spoke. "I was fourteen. I wish I could recapture that moment, make it last forever. Alas, everything must come to an end."

A terrible premonition hit Maimonides in the stomach. He glanced around at the curious onlookers. The children were laughing at the visitor's strange behavior. Some of the women pulled their charges back inside, obviously worried about the intentions of the mad newcomer and his heavily armored party.

Maimonides felt the tightening in his stomach rise to clench his heart.

"You aren't going to save Ascalon, are you?"

Saladin rose and turned his back on the palm tree. There was something dark and terrible in his eyes now.

"Oh, I will save Ascalon, my friend. By destroying it."

Saladin grabbed an ax from the harness of his ebony steed. And without saying another word, he turned on the palm tree that bore the memories of his first night of love and hacked with cruel, unflinching brutality.

The men immediately dismounted from their steeds and began running through the oasis. Some entered the homes of the terrified residents to order them out, while others stood at the center of the township, holding high the eagle standard of the Sultan. They were not bandits, they proclaimed as outraged Bedouin men emerged brandishing scimitars, but any man who interfered in their duty would be treated as one. A group of well-placed archers stood poised to turn the threat into a reality.

Maimonides watched with utter horror as the Sultan's soldiers systematically destroyed the city of Ascalon. They tore down the trees then set them ablaze. The flames swept through the manicured grass and rosebushes and began to consume the thatched roofs of buildings. It seemed as if in a matter of minutes the entire oasis was on fire.

The rabbi's eyes filled with tears as he saw some of Saladin's troops empty bags of white powder into the wells that served as the lifeline of Ascalon. The next unsuspecting man that pulled a cup from one of the water holes would soon feel his throat burn with the lethal ash. The Prophet had forbidden Muslims from burning trees or poisoning wells, and Saladin had been strict in adhering to the Islamic code of war through many years of conflict with the Franks. But the Sultan obviously saw no other way. Ascalon had to be utterly obliterated to force Richard to abandon his plans to use it as a base from which to strike at Egypt.

Such is the madness of war. In order to save the land, they had to destroy it. Make it useless to their enemies, who needed Ascalon as a supply center for the long, unforgiving trek through Sinai. With the oasis in flames, Richard's armies would be forced to turn back. Maimonides knew that with this one terrible act of destruction, Cairo had been rescued. One city, one pristine oasis of beauty in an unforgiving and cold desert, would die, in order that a thousand cities, from the edge of the western ocean in the Maghreb to the lands of the rising sun beyond India, would live.

But as he stared at his friend, who watched the devastation in silence, he wondered whether something in Saladin himself did not in fact die that day.

With the oasis burning around him, Saladin knelt one last time before the ruined stump where he had found love and the nurturing joy of a woman's touch. And for the first time in many years of friendship, Maimonides watched tears flowing down the Sultan's cheek.

The most powerful man in the world wept for lost love and a world in which beauty must sometimes be sacrificed on the altar of power.

55

Richard stared with stunned disbelief at the pillar of smoke rising a thousand feet into the heavens above. The only clouds that floated in the cobalt-blue sky were the billowing black fumes from the still-smoldering ruins of Ascalon.

The Lionheart felt a terrible combination of righteous anger and unholy despair battling for preeminence in his heart. He withdrew his sword and flung it into the desert sand in a display of petulance. Richard's rage almost exploded when he heard the thick, rich laughter echoing behind him. He whirled on the Jewess, who rode behind him as a captive. Her hands were bound and her legs were tied to the side of the brown mare that Richard had provided her. The king realized as her arrogant laugh echoed around him that he had made a mistake in not wrapping her mouth shut as well.

"Your Sultan is mad."

It was a powerless, foolish thing to say, but these words were all that came to his mind, filled as it was with the devastating knowledge that he had been outfoxed by his adversary.

Miriam continued to smile, despite the lethal rage evident on her captor's face.

"It is a warning, Your Majesty," she said proudly. "Any man who would destroy what he loves most to thwart his enemy—such a man has no limits."

Richard had endured enough disrespect at the hand of this infidel lady. Chivalry be damned. He picked up his sword and approached. Her smile vanished, but he did not see the onset of fear. No, she looked more insulted than frightened at the implied threat. Well, perhaps she would react more appropriately if the threat was more than implied.

"If I sent him your head on a platter, he might see how far I am willing to go as well."

The ebony-haired beauty merely shrugged.

"I think you overestimate his affections for me. He has many women, and I am probably long forgotten."

And then she winked at him. Winked!

Richard felt the anger subside and in its place a feeling of astonishment took hold. Who was this remarkable woman that did not fear death? Standing there before this girl in the burning sun, the heat doubled by the flames still raging through the shattered oasis, the greatest king in all of Europe felt utterly powerless. The only other woman who had ever made him feel so helpless was his mother, Eleanor, on the rare occasions when he had earned her displeasure as a child. His mother had the ability to make even the mightiest of men feel small under the unblinking gaze of her disapproval. Eleanor and Miriam were separated by a gulf of faith and upbringing wider than the entire world, yet they somehow shared one trait—the ability to reduce proud soldiers to little more than ashamed children with just a change of inflection in their voices.

"I doubt that, Miriam," he said at last, lowering his sword for good. Miriam locked eyes with him and he had that strange feeling again. As if he had known her for a very long time, longer perhaps than he had lived on this cruel and fractured earth.

The strange, hypnotic moment was shattered by the arrival of William. The knight rode to the king's side after inspecting the devastation up close.

"Sire, the wells are poisoned," he said in his usual straightforward tone. "Several of our men, driven mad by desert thirst, dipped into them and have paid the price."

Richard's outrage was gone, sapped away by the stark reality of the flaming wall before him. He saw no point in fuming and raging at a truth that could not be undone.

"We have no choice but to turn back," he said in an exhausted voice. "The men cannot make it through Sinai without supplies."

There. It was done. A brilliantly crafted plan, developed over months of careful analysis and discussion with his advisers, had gone up with the same smoke that now blanketed Ascalon.

Richard mounted his steed and pulled the reins, ready to turn his back on the shame of defeat, when a sentry rode up from across the sand dunes. The freckle-faced Sicilian was red with excitement and urgency.

"Sire, we have spied a group of Saladin's scouts in the desert. A party of six men heading east."

A soft smile appeared on Richard's lips.

"Then the day is not completely lost," the king said. He turned to his favorite knight, from whom he had been somewhat estranged since the butchery of Acre. Perhaps a little hunting expedition would give his men a chance to release some of their anger and frustration at losing Ascalon. And a joint effort might give him a chance to rebuild some bridges with his old friend. "Ride with me, William."

The knight raised his eyebrows in surprise, but he quickly complied. "Yes, my lord."

Richard grabbed his royal banner, a purple flag emblazoned with a golden lion, from a nearby page. Waving the flag as a sign to his Templar knights to follow, the king rode off into the desert in search of his prey.

＋　＋　＋

FROM THEIR HIDDEN VANTAGE point above rocky incline, a group of Saladin's soldiers watched the decoys below. A small band of the Sultan's men had been left on the outskirts of the Ascalon, waiting patiently for the arrival of Richard's legions. They had very strict instructions—lure out some of Richard's knights from the main force and capture at least one of the Templars alive. The Sultan had suffered from a lack of reliable intelligence since the onset of the war, and no one expected the Jewess to come through again with significant information.

The ploy appeared to be working. The handful of soldiers posing as errant spies rode about the dusty plain below in open view. They had already spotted a sentry hiding in the craggy boulders to the west. He would soon sound the alert and a raiding party would be dispatched to capture the Muslim stragglers. Saladin had guessed rightly that his young adversary would seek to soften the blow of failure at Ascalon with the capture of some of the Sultan's men who had engineered his humiliating defeat.

They did not quite expect what happened next. A dust cloud rose over the western hills and the thundering hooves of a dozen horses echoed through the valley. The Crusader raiding party erupted over the boulder-strewn mounds and charged straight at the decoys.

From his hiding place above the field, an Assyrian foot soldier named Kamal ibn Abdul Aziz, who had been placed in charge of this mission by the Sultan, pulled out a small viewing lens to get a better view of the battle. The Franks were bearing down on their quarry, who feigned surprise and horror and put to flight. The decoys led the outraged Crusader knights deeper into the sand dunes.

Kamal prepared to lift his sun-blackened hand to signal the ambush, when he caught sight of something unbelievable through the lens.

The man leading the charge was dressed like all the other knights, his face shielded by the heavy Frankish helmet. But he bore in his left hand a flowing purple banner. The roaring lion shone golden in the midday sun.

Kamal had seen that banner before. He had been one of the lucky survivors of the debacle at Arsuf. The young man had witnessed a man riding down the central column as the Crusaders reversed course en masse and turned on their pursuers. He had watched with unmitigated shock as their looming victory had swiftly turned into defeat as the Franks rallied behind the man whom they saw as both a king and a god. Richard the Lionheart alone bore that standard into battle, and any who escaped Arsuf alive would never forget the terrible sight of the billowing pennant that preceded the rout and massacre of the Muslim troops.

Was it possible that the enemy king, the most hated man in all the world, was even now riding straight into their trap? Kamal did not know if his brain was addled by the unforgiving desert heat, or if he was truly about to serve as a witness to history. He turned seeking confirmation from Jahan, a gruff infantryman from western Iran, who was also watching the events unfold below.

"Do my eyes deceive me, or does the Lionheart himself take part in the fight?"

Jahan peered through his own lens at the standard, and then burst out laughing, a raspy sound that succinctly expressed the awe and incredulity that surged through Kamal's heart.

"He is brave but foolish."

"He is also worth the wealth of nations," Kamal said, his eyes gleaming at the incredible value of their catch. He turned to face the archers set in the ledge behind him. In a second he would give the signal that would change the world. But first he had to get word to the cavalry hiding behind the hills to focus all their efforts on capturing one man.

Saladin had asked them to bring back a single soldier who could provide them intelligence of value to the war. Instead, they were about to hand the Sultan his greatest enemy on a silver platter.

Kamal saw the hungry look in Jahan's eyes and smiled. They were about to become the most celebrated warriors in all the land.

—◆ ◆ ◆—

RICHARD FELT HIS HEART beat faster as it always did when he was about to slay a foe in battle. The fleeing horseman before him, wrapped in a blue robe and turban, was about to meet his Maker at the end of Richard's razor-sharp lance. He thrust his spear out toward the rounded plates of the Arab's lamellar armor, expertly aiming for the weak spot he knew existed just at the crease under his left arm. Then all hell broke loose.

A series of horns resounded through the valley and the fleeing horsemen suddenly swung their steeds around to confront their pursuers. The Crusaders outnumbered the little band of infidels by more than two to one, and their offensive would have been a suicidal gambit had it not been for the exploding ambush all around them.

Over thirty horsemen erupted from their hiding places behind a series of large rocks at the base of a massive sand dune. Richard felt all blood drain from his face as he realized that he had foolishly ridden right into a trap. He wanted to curse himself for allowing his hunger for revenge to overcome his strategic thinking, but there was no time for self-recrimination. They had to escape the Saracen forces before the grand Crusade ended here in a flood of arrows. Richard had no intention of dying in this lonely valley and being remembered in the annals of history as the idiot king who fell for what was truly the oldest trick in the book.

Richard managed to turn his horse a full 180 degrees in retreat while fending off a charging Muslim with the force of his lance. The spear embedded itself deep in his pursuer's chest and snapped in two as the king turned to flee. His men attempted to create a protective circle around him, and several of his knights took the full brunt of the rain of arrows that were clearly meant for him.

One of the arrows flew through a crack in the wall of human bodies around Richard and smashed into his left shoulder. Tearing through layers of steel and mesh, the barbed head pierced his flesh, stopping only when it met final resistance at his shattered collarbone.

Richard felt like his entire body was on fire. It was as if the gates of Hell had opened to claim him, and the sparks of damnation were even now racing through the length of the wooden shaft embedded in his shoulder and flowing through his blood like boiling acid. The king struggled to keep his eyes open, but his vision was rapidly disappearing inside a dark tunnel. Blackness surrounded him and the blinding light of the desert seemed to be falling away from him.

And then a familiar voice broke through the void and he could see again. William was at his side, riding like the wind. The knight reached over and grabbed the royal banner that still hung from Richard's hand. And then, without looking back for a moment at his injured master, William Chinon broke out of the defensive ring that was trying to get the king to safety. The knight held aloft the pennant with a hearty laugh even as the Saracen raiders descended on him from all sides.

"Saracen fools, I am Richard the Lionheart, Lord of the Angevin," William screamed. "No heathen will have the honor of my capture today."

The knight rode off into the sand dunes in the opposite direction of the king. The Muslim soldiers, anxious to capture the man they believed to be the lord of their enemies rode off after him en masse.

And then William was gone.

Richard saw a surviving Templar who rode beside him jump off his own steed in full gallop, landing on Richard's horse in a brilliantly executed maneuver that he would probably never be able to repeat but for which he would undoubtedly be honored by his comrades for the remainder of his military career. The man grabbed hold of the horse's reins and guided the injured king out of the empty wastes of the Negev toward the safety of the Crusader army camped before the burning remnants of Ascalon.

56

Al-Adil waited tensely at his brother's side. Word of the Lionheart's capture at the hands of the Sultan's ambush party had streaked through Jerusalem like a wildfire. The king was being transported under heavy guard to the palace and was apparently refusing to speak to anyone except the Sultan himself.

His brother had ordered the guard around the Holy City strengthened. With their king a captive and their plans to invade Egypt in ruins, there was no telling what the Crusader army would do. Many of the courtiers were hoping that the double blow would utterly smash the foreigners' morale and they would merely climb back into their ships and sail home. But al-Adil did not believe that for a second. The most likely outcome would be a desperate, all-out attack on Jerusalem. The fanatics would throw every man they had at the Holy City in a final decisive battle whose outcome was far from certain.

The tension of impending doom hung over the hall of judgment as Saladin's court lined up in full-dress regalia to greet the infidel king. Al-Adil knew that his brother was a stickler for protocol, especially between rulers but he personally wanted nothing more than to slit the throat of the boy king who would had wreaked so much devastation on their people. The blood of Acre and Arsuf could not go unavenged.

A gong sounded in the outer hall and a blast of trumpets echoed from every parapet in the castle. Al-Adil glanced at Saladin, who sat upright on his throne, his face displaying no emotion at the thought of finally meeting his nemesis.

The massive silver doors to the chamber were flung open and the guards immediately stood at perfect attention as the young commander of the triumphant ambush force, an Assyrian named Kamal ibn Abdul Aziz, proudly stepped forward. The lad was already being spoken of as one of the true heroes of the war, and al-Adil had little doubt that the lucky bastard would reap the rewards for this improbable victory for the rest of his life.

A terrible hush fell over the nobles as the man in shining armor followed Kamal inside. He was tall and wearing a sparkling breastplate gilded in gold. Every head strained to see what the boy king looked like, but his features were still masked behind his heavy helmet.

Kamal bowed low before the Sultan, and then raised his head with the brash confidence that comes easily to youths who have stumbled on to fame.

"*Sayyidi*, may I have the honor of presenting to you your esteemed colleague King Richard Plantagenet, Lord of the Angevin, King of England and France."

Saladin did not move. He was watching his rival like a hawk. Al-Adil saw a strange look on his brother's face. Was it amusement?

The armored man stepped forward to stand directly before the throne. He lifted his helmet and revealed his face.

It was Sir William Chinon, the knight who had served as Richard's emissary to Saladin and had pleaded for the Sultan to save his master's life.

A terrible gasp spread through the room. The nobles' heads flew from William, to the Sultan, to the boy Kamal, who was obviously perplexed at everyone's sudden shock.

And then, to al-Adil's surprise, Saladin burst out laughing. There was no irony or anger evident, just pure, unadulterated mirth at the ridiculousness of the situation. Al-Adil felt his own outrage evaporating under the Sultan's contagious belly laugh, and against every bit of willpower he could muster, he found himself joining in as well.

Al-Adil realized at that moment that in the midst of war and madness, there was sometimes nothing left to do except laugh at the utter absurdity of the human condition. He laughed at the confused Kamal, who still thought he had reeled in the mother of all fish in the ocean. Sir William stood stoic, his head held up proudly. Finally, even the knight could not hold back a smile.

"It is an honor to meet you again, Sultan," William said, and a hush fell over the crowd. He had spoken in Arabic, strangely accented but passable. Clearly he had made some progress over the past few months in learning the tongue of the men whom he had traveled across the world to kill.

Saladin snapped a finger at one his guards.

"Prepare the finest stateroom in the palace for Sir William," he said. "Once you are refreshed, perhaps you would join me for dinner."

And then he turned to face the boy who had gone from hero to imbecile in the span of a moment. Kamal looked terrified as he waited to hear the fate of the fool who had turned all of Jerusalem upside down by capturing the wrong man.

"I hereby proclaim that Kamal ibn Abdul Aziz shall receive a reward of one thousand gold dinars for his successful capture of William Chinon, one of the greatest warriors to adorn our adversaries' forces. And he shall be promoted to the rank of my personal bodyguard."

There was a murmur of surprise from among the nobles. Al-Adil grunted. If it had been left to him, he would have flogged the boy before the entire army for falling for a stupid ruse. Apparently Kamal expected that something along those lines would indeed be his fate, and appeared utterly taken aback by the Sultan's generosity. The boy fell prostrate on his knees.

"Your mercy knows no bounds, *sayyidi*."

Saladin smiled broadly.

"It is only fit payment," the Sultan said. "You have provided a truly valuable service, for which I will be eternally grateful. Today, you made me laugh, and in a world burdened with sorrow and death, joy is a most precious commodity."

57

Miriam gingerly stitched Richard's shoulder with a needle and silk thread. The hard part was over. Removing an arrow so deeply embedded in the king's shoulder, while his suspicious men watched over her for any sign of lethal intent, had been the first challenge. When she finally managed to wrest the razor-sharp edge from between his shoulder blades, she had been faced with the problem of stemming the sudden rush of blood. For an instant Miriam thought she had ruptured an artery and that the Lionheart would soon be dispatched to the grave. No matter how much she would have enjoyed sending this murderous dog straight to Hell, she knew that her own death would soon follow, and she did not wish to give Richard's men the satisfaction of executing her.

Using a pouch of special herbs that she had carried for her journey to Cairo, she had been able to stem the bleeding at long last and hopefully had halted the spread of infection. Now all that was left to do was sew him back up.

Throughout this torturous process, she had been surprised to see Richard cling to consciousness. Most men would have happily succumbed to the blackness as a means of escaping what must have been excruciating pain. But the Lionheart appeared determined to prove either to her or to himself that he was stronger than all other men.

So she kept talking to him, realizing that the sound of her voice would at least distract him partially from the agonies of surgery she was forcing him to endure. She was able to gather enough information from his mumbled ramblings to determine what had happened. Saladin's men had ambushed the party and Sir William had allowed himself to fall into a trap that had been laid for the king himself.

"Your men must love you greatly if they would allow themselves to be captured in your stead," she said as she continued threading the long gash in his left shoulder.

Richard appeared better now that the healing plants were doing their job. He motioned for his soldiers to leave him. The men hesitated, but a quick look at their master's forceful eyes and they exited. Miriam realized that she was alone in his private tent for the first time. Most women would have been uncomfortable at the sudden intimacy, but she had been waiting for such an opportunity for a while. Her position had been terribly precarious over the past several weeks. And now, with the destruction of Ascalon, there was no telling what Richard would do, especially if he ever deduced her role in the failure of his grand scheme. She knew there was only one way to ingratiate herself with the king and win herself more precious time to live.

It was strange how all roads seemed to return to Ascalon for her. It was here almost a dozen years ago that her parents' caravan had stopped briefly on the long journey from Cairo to Damascus. And it was in Ascalon that a Frankish raiding party had descended from the cover of the sand dunes to wreak havoc. Her mother and father had perished there, and for many years she had believed that her own spirit had died with them. And now Ascalon was destroyed and she was seeking to win over the affections of the king of their murderers in order to live. Ah, the God of irony at work yet again.

Richard shifted as she went about her careful business with the needle. He was staring off into space, clearly thinking of his friend and the terrible tortures he must be suffering at Saladin's hands by now. Of course, Miriam knew that William was probably being treated as a guest of honor according to the Sultan's code of chivalry, but such gallant behavior would be incomprehensible to this barbarian. And Miriam found that Richard's distress gave her the advantage over his heart that she needed to effect her plan.

"William is a man of honor," he said at last, his voice streaked by evident sorrow. "I often disagree with him, but in my heart I know that he is the better half of my soul."

Miriam could see that Richard was no longer hiding behind his normal bluster and bravado. Obviously the loss of his friend combined with the humiliating failure of his primary military objective was weighing on his heart, causing him to let down his carefully erected guard. Miriam hoped she could play his feelings to her advantage.

"You never cease to amaze me."

Richard looked at her with surprise.

"Why do you say that?"

"I have heard that you are ruthless and cruel, and I have seen that side of you," Miriam said, choosing her words carefully. "Yet I sense that it is only a façade."

Richard faced her with an odd look, as if she had unwittingly stumbled across one of his great secrets.

"You speak boldly for a prisoner."

Miriam laughed, making sure to add a slight feminine lilt to the sound.

"I thought I was an honored guest."

Richard smiled for the first time since he had been brought in from the field.

"Touché."

Even as Miriam carefully sewed up his wound with her right hand, she let the long fingers of her left hand gently massage the muscles of his shoulder.

"Richard of Aquitaine, why did you come here to turn our world upside down?"

The Lionheart turned his eyes away from her, his smile vanishing.

"It is my duty, as King of England."

Miriam decided to try a risky gambit.

"Your father—Henry was his name?—he is said to have counseled against this Crusade."

She felt Richard stiffen. His eyes turned cold and his shoulder jerked slightly as her needle brushed up against raw flesh.

"Forgive me," she said. "The wound is still fresh." She would leave it to Richard to interpret the injury of which she spoke.

The king reached over with his hand and brushed the soft skin of her left arm. She forced herself not to cringe. This was, after all, what she was hoping would happen.

"Tell me, Miriam. Where would you be today had I not arrived on your shores?"

"Perhaps I would be in the harem in Jerusalem, hatching schemes against whatever new girl the Sultan took a fancy to."

"You deserve more than that."

Miriam finished the last stitch and put the needle and thread down on a small beechwood stand by the military cot that served as his bed.

"What more could a woman want than to be queen? Surely, every man seeks to become the king."

Richard sighed and stood up. He flexed his injured shoulder and winced.

"The throne is a prison," he said. "Everything a ruler does is scrutinized by his enemies for a sign of weakness. Every sleep is troubled with the knowledge that an assassin may lie awaiting in the shadows of the room."

Miriam allowed herself a brief, pleasurable mental image of just such an assassin sneaking up on Richard in his sleep. Then she drove it out of her mind and continued to pretend that she was interested in his innermost thoughts.

"What would you have done, if you were not burdened with the crown?"

Richard turned to face her, his eyes suddenly bright with intensity.

"I have asked myself that a great deal since I arrived in Palestine. Perhaps I would have been an artist."

Of all the things she had expected him to say, that was not one of them.

"You . . . draw?"

An impish smile appeared on the young king's face and he strode over to his cot. Underneath the silken duvet that covered his bed, he removed a scrolled piece of parchment and handed it to her. Miriam took the sheet and intentionally sat down upon the bed. She unfurled the paper and stared in shock.

It was a drawing, hand-stenciled in blue ink, of what she presumed was the Virgin Mary holding the Christ child at her bosom. It was actually quite well done, but what shocked Miriam the most was the sad face of the Virgin.

It was hers.

"It's remarkable," Miriam said, trying not to be distracted by the chill that was coursing down her spine.

"No one will ever see it, except for you," Richard said, sounding like a child delighted to be able to share a special secret at last. "The nobles do not want a painter for a king."

No, apparently they wanted a ruthless murderer who did not even spare women and children in battle.

"I shall keep your secret," she said, feigning shy pleasure at being granted such a privilege.

Richard smiled at her, and she saw a hint of his usual arrogance.

"Like you kept my war plans?"

Miriam stiffened. Did he know that she was responsible for the fall of Ascalon? If so, this game she had been playing was about to end very badly.

But Richard burst out laughing and she could hear no cruelty in the sound.

"Fear not. I admired your courage when you raided my general's tent during your first visit."

Good. He was still thinking of the embarrassing incident when she had fallen into his trap. He appeared blissfully, unaware that her abilities as a spy had improved quite dramatically since then.

Richard shrugged. He sat down beside her on the bed. Miriam felt her heartbeat quicken. *Stay focused*, she commanded herself.

Richard took the drawing back, rolled the sheet closed, and returned it to its hiding place beneath the bed.

"In any event, your Sultan saw through my deception." He paused and became somber. "He is apparently a master tactician. I would have thought my conquest of Ascalon would be the last strategic move he would have anticipated. Clearly I must factor his genius into my future plans."

Miriam touched his hand.

"I have heard that the greatness of a king is measured by his ability to learn from his mistakes, Your Majesty."

Richard took her hand in his and squeezed. She forced herself to smile bashfully. His grip was tentative, as if he was not used to touching a woman.

"Call me Richard. I have not heard my own name spoken since I left England."

Miriam looked down, feigning sudden shyness.

"Richard, then."

Richard leaned forward, his face dangerously close to hers. She saw that his cheeks were flushed, and his eyes betrayed something that looked almost like fear, as if he were a child stepping into water for his first swimming lesson.

"This war has left me tired, Miriam," he said softly. "And alone. William was my only friend, and I may never see him again."

He brushed a strand of her hair and she was unable to stop herself from cringing. Thankfully, Richard misinterpreted the source of her discomfort.

"You love him, don't you?"

Miriam had to answer that carefully. She was walking a thin line between seduction and disaster.

"Yes, but I do not think we are fated to be together."

Richard seemed satisfied with her response. It sounded truthful, made her appear loyal and sure of heart, at the same time open to other possibilities.

"Can I ask of you one thing, Miriam?"

"You may ask."

Richard stroked her cheek, mistook her blush to be one of modesty rather than the suppressed heat of rage.

"Forget him for one night."

"Richard . . ."

The golden-haired youth put a finger to her lips to halt her wavering protests. She felt it tremble against her flesh.

"We are both far away from the people we love," he said, letting his voice drop to a whisper. "Trapped in a heartless conflict. I have not known love and a tender touch for an eternity. Can we spend one night as a man and a woman, without the burden of history?"

And then Richard kissed her.

As Miriam felt his arms wrap around her waist, she forced the image of Saladin into her mind.

+ + +

WITH THE NECESSARY DEED over and done with, Miriam lay in Richard's bed staring up at the folds of the crimson tent. The Lionheart was nestled against her, asleep from a combination of the healing herbs she had given him and the lethargy that always seemed to possess men at the completion of the act of love.

She kept telling herself that she had had no choice. The only way to guarantee her survival as a prisoner was to slip inside Richard's heart and take hold. But now that they had crossed the threshold, she knew that her status as the king's lover would have other advantages. He clearly underestimated her abilities and her loyalty as a Jew to a Muslim sultan. This mistake could be used to provide her nation with a critical advantage.

She would pretend to be enamored of the lonely Richard and use her status as a concubine to learn the innermost secrets of the Franks. It was not only a way to save her life in the company of the barbarians, but a chance to help the people she loved the most stand up to these ruthless invaders.

The Muslims believed that Paradise lay under the shadow of the swords. But she knew better. Her people had been trapped under the warring shades of the Crescent and the Cross for centuries, and there was no eternal garden waiting for them, only shifting sands and raging waters. Not that it mattered. Miriam no longer believed in such mystical promises anyway. In a world filled with betrayal and death, the only Paradise that could be found was one built by one's own hands. She would no longer rely on the whims of Deity to rescue her. She would take matters into her own hands.

Miriam was aware that her warning about the attack on Ascalon had changed the direction of the war. It was a fact of which she was deeply proud, even if no one in history would know that the Crusaders had suffered a resounding defeat because of the carefully chosen words of an anonymous Jewess. And she would do whatever else she could to drive these monsters into the sea.

But lying there in the arms of a butcher, feeling his warm, sticky seed infesting her womb like poisonous pus, she had to keep from vomiting at the thought of what she was doing. As she struggled to come to terms with her choice, Miriam remembered her favorite story from the Bible. The tale of Esther, a Jewish girl who had disguised herself as a Persian princess and taken to bed a foreign king, all to save her people.

Perhaps she would be the new Esther, a heroine who endured the caresses of her enemy in order to effect God's plan for the salvation of the Chosen and their allies. Yet that hopeful thought was balanced by a sudden, terrible premonition. No matter how hard she tried, she could not shake the feeling that this path she was on would end in only one place. Death.

58

Maimonides sat beside William at the Sultan's table. Saladin had arranged to eat with the knight every evening for the past fortnight. Sometimes it was just the two of them. Other times he would invite select advisers to join them. Tonight was the third time he had invited the rabbi. None of this would have been all that unusual, except that Saladin usually dined alone. Maimonides had come to understand that the Sultan, who was always surrounded by a buzz of activity, saw the evening meal as the one time in his daily routine when he could collect and process his thoughts in silence. At least that was true before the war began consuming every moment of his daily schedule.

Initially, the doctor had thought that Saladin's regular dinners with William were just an extension of the Sultan's hospitality to their "guest," but after watching the two men conduct often lively discussions late into the night, he concluded that Saladin had found in this enemy knight something of true value—an intellectual equal whose company invigorated and delighted him.

This conclusion was apparently shared by al-Adil, who picked away at his skewered lamb kebabs with little enthusiasm. He glanced over every now and then at William with a sour face whose expression looked remarkably like maidenly jealousy as the Frank regaled the Sultan with stories about his military exploits in some barbaric region known as Walls or Wales or something.

The dinner table in the long stateroom was covered with the bounty of the land. Succulent roasted hen along with a variety of meats, ranging from spiced rabbit and lamb to fare more suited to the desert—chunks of goat meat and camel. The latter was set aside almost exclusively for al-Adil, who had never developed an appreciation for more sophisticated cuisine. Maimonides had been taking his own doctor's advice and refrained from eating red meat, which had of late been troubling his stomach more than usual; instead, he filled his gold-embossed plate with an aromatic stew of spinach, beans, and chickpeas, along with a healthy slice of bread dipped in olive oil. He noticed that Saladin seemed perfectly happy with his usual small bowl of lentil soup. Despite all of his medical admonishments to the contrary, Saladin insisted on eating as frugally as his men guarding the frontier against the encroaching Franks. Until they could come home and feast on fowl and fatted steak, he would deny himself any such luxuries as well.

Saladin was asking William about the universities in England and how they compared with institutions such as Al-Azhar in Cairo. The knight, with obvious discomfort, admitted that organized schooling in his homeland was still in its infancy. But the Frank seemed very interested in learning more about the education system in the Muslim world. He appeared particularly intrigued by the Islamic system of funding universities through private endowments. It was a long-standing tradition that wealthy Muslims would bequeath arable land and shares in business concerns to these endowments, providing the income needed to allow the schools to exist independently of the whims of state financing. Al-Azhar had managed to grow and thrive over the past several centuries, despite the tumultuous changes of government and state ideology in Egypt during that time. The university had been the finest center of Islamic learning when Egypt had been the domain of the Shiite imams, and it remained so even though Saladin had supplanted the Fatimid caliphs with Sunni rule.

Saladin suggested that what England needed to emerge from its economic and educational backwardness was a similarly endowed university that would stand apart from the government and train the youth of the kingdom. Perhaps if the Europeans came to value learning over warfare, as their forefathers the Greeks once did, they could reinvigorate their stagnant civilization. William appeared to be deeply moved by Saladin's vision, and he seemed ready to press for more details about Al-Azhar, when the embossed wooden doors to the dining room opened. A balding page nervously approached the Sultan. The room went instantly quiet. The Sultan did not like being disturbed at dinner unless it was for an emergency.

"What is it?"

The page glanced at William for a second, then proceeded.

"*Sayyidi,* an ambassador from the Franks has arrived."

The Sultan raised his eyebrows in surprise. He turned to face William.

"Were you expecting this?"

William shook his head.

"It is my king's rule not to ransom captured soldiers," he said, his voice tinged with a mixture of regret and bitterness. "My men understand that if they are caught, they will be left to the fate their carelessness has justly brought upon them."

"It is a cruel and wasteful policy," Saladin said. Maimonides knew that no matter how hard he tried, the Sultan could never truly understand the callous and primitive Franks.

William shrugged and smiled almost apologetically.

"Perhaps. But then there is a good reason why your men have been unsuccessful in bringing back alive any of my soldiers for interrogation."

Al-Adil slammed his goblet of fatty goat milk down on the table.

"We have you."

"I thought I was a guest, not a captive."

"Like my niece?" Maimonides spoke before he could stop himself. William did not meet his eyes, and the rabbi felt suddenly ashamed. This man was a decent soldier and not responsible for his brutal king's behavior.

Saladin stood up and gave both al-Adil and Maimonides a reproachful glance.

"Let us leave these matters before we cross the bounds of propriety," he said in a cold voice. Then he turned his attention to the dark-haired knight. "Perhaps you would like to meet your countryman and see what news he brings us from the noble King Richard."

✦ ✦ ✦

WHEN THE DINNER PARTY had hastily reconvened inside the Sultan's judgment chamber, and a few notables such as Qadi al-Fadil had been summoned from their homes to take their places at the surprise diplomatic meeting, the Frankish ambassador was let in. And the rabbi's mouth fell open in disbelief.

Conrad of Montferrat, dressed in a dark cloak and hooded robe, stood before them. His chest was puffed up with affected pride, and while his face was stoic and unreadable, his eyes burned with a hint of shame and humiliation.

Al-Adil's hand flew to his sword, but one fiery look from the Sultan caused him to stand back. While Saladin was obviously not going to tolerate the murder of an emissary in his hall of judgment, he nonetheless appeared utterly bewildered by the nobleman's appearance. Conrad was an even more hated figure than Richard, for he was the last remnant of the old Frankish kingdom that had managed to hold off the Sultan's victorious troops for almost two years. While Richard might be a foreign adventurer motivated by misinformation and propaganda, Conrad was a true Crusader at heart. His hatred for the Muslims was ironclad and had been forged through years of fighting alongside fanatics such as Reginald of Kerak. He had been Saladin's nemesis long before Richard had arrived.

This made no sense to Maimonides. Surely Conrad knew that he was in Saladin's eyes an even greater enemy than the petulant boy king. Indeed, the Sultan had placed a staggering bounty on Conrad's head, enough to fund a small principality. Why would this man who claimed to be the true heir to Jerusalem risk immediate execution by walking in to his adversary's lair?

Maimonides was not alone in his consternation. Sir William stepped forward, his face flushed with outrage at the sight of the nobleman with the graying curls and scarred cheek. The rabbi remembered the enmity that he had seen between the men during his visit to Richard's camp.

"This is a trick," William said in a voice quivering with hatred. "My king would not send this dog to speak for him."

Conrad met William's eyes with a cold glance, and then he returned his gaze to the Sultan.

"You are right, William," he said, his voice booming imperiously in the marble-and-ivory hall. "I speak only for myself . . ." He paused, and then added the words that would change the course of the war.

". . . and my troops."

For an instant Maimonides thought that William would follow through with what al-Adil had started. Even though the knight no longer bore a weapon, he looked ready to tear out Conrad's throat with his bare hands.

Saladin blinked several times, as if trying to process what he had just heard. He continued to stare at Conrad's face, as he often did when attempting to gauge a man's veracity. When he spoke, it was with calculated slowness, emphasizing every word as if to make sure that nothing he said was misunderstood in the slightest.

"Am I to understand that there has been a break between you and Richard?"

Conrad smiled, but there was no warmth in the expression.

"There will be, if we can come to an understanding."

＋ ＋ ＋

THE SOUND OF THE muezzin echoed across the city from the Dome of the Rock as first light broke through the black of night. Maimonides had been up late participating in heated discussions with Saladin and his closest advisers. While Conrad retired to a pleasant bedroom in the palace, guarded by men who had been instructed to kill him at the first sign of trouble, the rabbi and a dozen courtiers and military commanders had debated the merits of an alliance with the treacherous Conrad. Despite al-Adil's vociferous protests, the Sultan had permitted Sir William to participate in the discussion. The knight knew Conrad better than any of them, and hated him apparently as much as they did, and they needed to hear every perspective before embarking on a partnership with a man who had been their most intransigent enemy for years.

Maimonides struggled to stay sharp, but exhaustion was setting in. Both his body and soul were weary of the never-ending twists to this conflict. But he really should not have been surprised. The God of irony had struck yet again. The break against the Frankish assault they had been praying for had come in the form of a ruthless politician willing to betray his own people.

While some of Saladin's men, and even Sir William, argued that Conrad's offer was likely a ploy meant to trap the Sultan in some nefarious plan cooked up by the wily Lionheart, the rabbi was not convinced that this was another of Richard's schemes. Maimonides had deduced from his own assessment of Conrad's character and bloated sense of self-importance that he was probably serious about an alliance against his fellow Christians. Conrad had apparently concluded that Richard had no intention of installing him on the throne of Jerusalem once the war was concluded. His years of struggle against the Muslims, his stubborn resistance to the overwhelming might of Saladin's forces despite his lack of men and resources—all of his valor had been forgotten by the power-hungry newcomers. In the nobleman's mind, Richard could not have advanced so far along the coast of Palestine without the bitter sacrifice of Conrad and his men. And despite all his services to the Crusader cause, he had been betrayed at the moment of impending victory.

So the Marquis of Montferrat appeared to think his only course of action to correct this injustice was to betray the betrayers in turn. Conrad had offered to join his forces with Saladin against Richard, in exchange for dominion over the coastal cities. If he could not be King of Jerusalem, then being Lord of Acre would do.

Of course, Maimonides had his doubts about trusting a self-serving worm like Conrad, and in this he was supported by Sir William. But the Sultan clearly felt they had little choice. The Franks would inevitably welcome more troops from over the sea and wave upon wave of invading forces would eventually wear down their defenses. Unless the allies could divide and destroy Richard's forces now, the fall of Jerusalem was certain.

And so, as the first streak of crimson cut through the dawn sky, Saladin held up his hand to signal that he had made his decision. The Sultan had concluded that a pact with one devil would be necessary to destroy another.

Maimonides glanced at William, who stoically accepted Saladin's pronouncement with a bow of his head. The rabbi's heart went out to the enemy soldier. For every other man in the room, the pact with Conrad was a necessary evil that could lead to a final, glorious victory against the hated forces of the Lionheart. But for William alone, it was the beginning of a terrible tragedy, a civil war in which Christians joined with heathens to kill other Christians.

Perhaps the young man had never known the ironic nature of God, but the rabbi realized that this was indeed a masterstroke of the divine humorist. Only a few weeks before, the Christian forces appeared invincible. A storm had been rising on the beaches of the coast that appeared poised to sweep inland and tear asunder the very foundations of civilizations. And yet, in an unexpected flash, the tempest was about to turn its destructive rage against itself.

The Crusaders would fall, not in the cold light of the Crescent, but under the terrible, crushing weight of their own Cross.

59

For Richard, the surprise arrival of his sister, Joanna, on a ship from England was nothing less than a divine blessing. Ever since his failure at Ascalon, he had been weighed down by a terrible feeling that his hopes and dreams were unraveling right before his eyes. His men had retreated to Arsuf and were growing restive. More and more voices were clamoring for a direct assault upon Saladin in Jerusalem. But Richard knew that such a move would play straight into Saladin's hands. Of course, his men were tired and anxious after countless months holed up in a foreign land. Their dreams of conquering the pyramids had been shattered, and now the hotheads in the barracks saw only two options—launch an all-or-nothing strike against the Holy City or retire with shame to their boats for a bitter journey home. The longer Richard dallied about on the coast of Palestine trying to find a third choice, one that would actually provide a real chance of defeating Saladin without risking utter annihilation of his own army, the more his men grumbled about his indecisiveness. It was at times like this that Richard missed William the most. He had a calming effect on the men, many of whom saw in him the very noble qualities of chivalry and honor that their comrades among the Franks had long since sacrificed on the altar of expediency.

But the arrival of a ship bearing the fluttering golden lion of his family's crest had heartened Richard. Perhaps the nobles of England had received word of the challenges facing their countrymen in this Crusade and more reinforcements were on their way. Such an act would have, of course, been uncharacteristically magnanimous on the part of his brother, John, who was serving as the Lionheart's vicegerent in London. So Richard had been disappointed but not surprised to see that the *dromon* sailed alone.

Yet his gloom had given way to joy when he saw Joanna seated on the small rowboat that detached from the warship and docked on the sands of Arsuf. He had ignored all protocol and swept his golden-tressed sister into his arms, planting a dozen kisses on her cheeks, which quickly turned red with embarrassment.

She was as beautiful as ever, dressed in an unusually low-cut gown of purple-and-violet lace that showed the line of her cleavage—probably the latest fashion back home. But her face looked unusually wan and sad. He had wondered what troubles she had endured under John's bitter hand, and their mother's cruel tongue, since Richard embarked on this foolhardy adventure. John had resented Joanna's support for his elder brother's claim to the throne, while Eleanor had never forgiven the girl for her closeness to her estranged husband, Henry. Joanna had therefore been trapped between two of the most powerful figures in the realm, and Richard knew that her only comfort would have come from knowing that her mother and her brother hated each other more than they despised her.

After a brief tour of the citadel at Arsuf, Richard took Joanna to his private chambers and spent the better part of the afternoon recounting the long and bitter story of his experiences in Palestine. He did not even hold back from her news of his affair with the captive Miriam. Ever since they were children, they could speak to each other easily and openly about the most intimate details of their lives. Miriam had increasingly become a fire in his breast. He had told himself that he was simply seeking solace and company in the midst of a lonely war, but his feelings for the Jewess were blossoming into something much deeper. Something that terrified Richard.

Joanna had listened to Richard's tale with rapt interest, although she was obviously unhappy with the news that the first girl to capture his attention was so far beneath his station. And a Jew, no less. She began to list for him all the reasons why he needed to end the affair before word got back to the nobles. It would delight John no end to spread stories of how Richard had betrayed the sacred cause by consorting with a Christ-killer.

As fate would have it, their argument was interrupted by a knock on the cypress-paneled door to his chamber. When Richard summoned the visitor, he was startled to see that it was Miriam. But then, of course, he had forgotten in all the excitement of Joanna's arrival that he had promised to dine with her that evening.

The moment Miriam and Joanna laid eyes on each other, a terrible stillness fell upon the room.

"Miriam, let me introduce you to my sister, Joanna. She just arrived from England."

Miriam bowed in her usual clumsy fashion, her face unsmiling. Joanna looked at her below arched eyebrows, then turned to face Richard.

"So this is the Jew who fills your bed, my brother?"

Miriam's eyes flashed at Joanna's breach of etiquette. Richard realized that he needed to keep these two apart before a miniature war erupted inside the beleaguered Crusader camp.

"Forgive my sister," he said with an uncomfortable smile. "Her tongue is renowned."

Miriam shrugged as if it were beneath her to take offense at anything Joanna had to say.

"That's all right," she said, in the contemptuous tone that both infuriated and excited Richard when it was used on him. "If a woman cannot claim renown from her beauty, then her tongue must suffice."

This was going very badly. As King of England, he commanded the absolute obedience of thousands of men. He knew how to motivate warriors to go out and sacrifice their lives on his behalf with nothing but an illusory promise that they would attain the "hereafter." But the Lord of Christendom apparently had no way to keep the two women he loved from clawing each other's eyes out.

But, to his surprise, Joanna laughed at Miriam's insult, not with prideful disdain, but with genuine mirth.

"She has spirit," Joanna said. "Remember what I said, brother. If you cannot tame such a woman, she will tame you, and the throne with it."

And then, to Richard's complete confusion, Joanna and Miriam shared a look of sudden understanding. Perhaps even the stirrings of mutual respect. Women made absolutely no sense to him whatsoever.

"Enough of such chatter," he said, flustered that he felt out of place in his own castle. "What news do you bring of England?"

Joanna suddenly became somber.

"I will not speak it in front of this Jew."

He thought Miriam would take insult, but the girl did not flinch. Perhaps she sensed in his sister's tense tone that there were indeed some matters that were rightfully kept between siblings. Miriam excused herself without another word, closing the door behind her.

Richard saw the sadness in Joanna's face again and realized that it was not just fatigue from a long journey, or grief at the melodrama of their family life back home.

"What's wrong?" Richard sat down on his velvet cushioned bed, and Joanna joined him.

"What we feared is happening," she said, her shoulders falling under the weight of her words. "John is gathering the nobles under his wing. They grumble that this Crusade is destroying our nation."

This was not a surprise to Richard. It was natural for his brother to seek to discredit him during his long absence. He had expected as much, and had put in place his own allies in the court to quash the murmurs should the hint of real sedition become apparent.

"So John has grown a spine at last," he said with a dismissive wave of his hand. "It was to be expected."

Joanna looked at him, perplexed by his nonchalance.

"You do not seem frightened by this threat to your throne."

"Why should I be?" Richard asked in a tone that was slightly sharper than he would have liked. He found himself growing mildly irritated at his sister. Joanna had never been so easily cowed by the ever-present court intrigue during their father's reign. Did she have less confidence in his ability to thwart whispers in the corridors before they erupted into rebellion in the streets?

"John will wait a few more months," Joanna said softly. "If you fail to seize Jerusalem, he *will* depose you."

Richard felt a flash of anger in his breast. She seemed so certain that he would lose in this chess game against John. He could not understand why his sister appeared to have resigned herself to such an outcome. Unless perhaps some of his stalwart allies had gone over to John's side . . .

"That is truly rich," Richard said as a terrible thought entered his mind. He had embarked on this Crusade, not for Christ or for the honor of Rome, but to undercut his brother's efforts to steal the scepter. But perhaps Richard had thoroughly miscalculated. And now John was able to use against him the fact that the war, in which he had once held the initiative, had now descended into a frustrated stalemate. If Joanna was right, the Crusade would not bolster Richard's kingship. Rather it would send his head to the executioner's block at the command of the newly crowned King John.

His father's last words still haunted him. Perhaps John was the future of England after all. Throughout his life, Richard had confidently believed that he was the one who rode the wave of destiny in his family. It would be the greatest irony of all to discover that he had been nothing more than a mere stepping-stone for the destiny of John Lackland.

Richard suddenly burst out laughing at the madness of the whole situation. He turned to face his concerned sister with a weary smile.

"Miriam says her God is a master of irony," Richard said. "If John only knew our father's last words, he would not wait another day to seize the throne."

Joanna stood up and placed a comforting hand on her brother's arm.

"I have kept my silence these many months out of loyalty to you. But soon my life will be in danger as well."

If she was looking for words of comfort and reassurance, he wasn't sure he had any.

A loud banging on the door brought their troubled conversation to an end. Joanna's hand flew to her throat and Richard whirled as the wooden door flew open. Several of Richard's generals stood stone-faced in the shadowed corridor outside his private chambers.

So had it come to this? Was rebellion finally upon him, not in the distant halls of London and Tours, but here in the trenches of Palestine? He realized that his hand was already on his sword hilt, his heart thundering in his chest.

"What is the meaning of this?"

One of Richard's commanders, a Templar from Brittany named Reynier, stepped inside and bowed stiffly, followed by a half-dozen other men. Richard saw they were all unarmed, but the king remained tense. Something was terribly wrong here.

"We have received terrible news, my lord," Reynier said. "That snake

Conrad has broken the alliance and made peace with the infidels. Even now his soldiers are embarking toward Acre, which they plan to hold in Conrad's name alone."

Richard felt like he had been struck with a mace to his gut. The war was no longer at a stalemate. The outcome was not in dispute anymore.

The Crusaders had lost.

— — —

RICHARD HAD EXPECTED HIS hastily convened strategy session with his commanders to be raucous, filled with outrage at Conrad's betrayal and calls for vengeance against the traitors. Instead, his men absorbed the news in utter silence. They were all looking at him with blank, defeated expressions that he had never before seen on the confident faces of the Templar and Hospitaller leaders. Only Joanna's face registered any emotion, and it was the dreaded gaze of pity.

"Conrad's betrayal has placed us in a difficult position," Richard said, stating the obvious in a desperate effort to generate some discussion from the silent generals. "We cannot defeat the Saracens with only half of our men. What counsel do you offer?"

Apparently none. Not a single man spoke up in the brightly lit marble hall at the center of the Arsuf citadel where they had all been summoned. Richard felt his rage building.

"Are you men or frightened children?"

Joanna, who sat beside him on a red-velvet lined chair, leaned forward and spoke, her voice sounding like a mother desperately trying to help her grieving child accept the death of a family pet.

"They give no counsel as there is none to give, brother. The Crusade has failed."

Hearing the words stated so bluntly, before all of his leading soldiers, filled Richard with a terrible despair. But he could not—would not—accept defeat so easily.

"I can summon more troops over the sea." Even as he spoke, he felt ridiculous.

"In the climate I described, the nobles will not accede to your summons," Joanna said in a soft voice.

Richard banged his fist on the ornate table that once belonged to Saladin's governor in Arsuf. Its unusual black wood finish, polished to mirror brightness, splintered under the force of his fury.

"So you are all ready to go back to your homes without your honor? You sicken me."

Joanna laid a hand on Richard's arm to calm him. He wanted to wrench it free, but her gentle touch had a soothing influence on his blood, as it always did. There was a moment of absolute quiet, and then, to everyone's surprise, Joanna stood up.

"There may be one way," she said unexpectedly. He looked at his sister and saw her forehead crease as her rapid mind went to work. The king turned his gaze with contempt on the defeated, tired faces of his soldiers.

"It is a dark day when my brave knights are mute and a woman must guide the king."

A golden smile blossomed on Joanna's face. It was the first time he had seen any light in her eyes since she had disembarked from her boat that morning.

"Let us do what Conrad has done," she said with sudden confidence, as if her suggestion were self-evident. Of all the things he had expected anyone to say about the solution to their quandary, those words had not crossed his mind.

"What do you mean?"

Joanna faced the generals, who were beginning to sit up and take interest. Her enthusiasm was cutting through their despair, even if they did not understand what she was talking about.

"Conrad has bartered away his troops in exchange for the coastal cities. But from what you have told me, your forces are better equipped and still pose a threat to the infidels."

He saw where this was going. And it was either insanity or utter genius. Perhaps it was both.

"You cannot be suggesting . . ."

"A truce. We will offer Saladin an end to hostility in exchange for maintaining the status quo."

It actually made perfect, twisted sense.

"So we, instead of Conrad, would retain the coast. And when the climate improves in Europe, we will bring reinforcements to crush the Saracens."

Joanna beamed, just as she did when they played riddles as children. She was always inordinately delighted when she uncovered a truth that had been carefully veiled from the mind of her brother.

"Exactly."

The men were stirring now, looks of renewed hope on their faces. As much as the idea of making a truce with Saladin was offensive to their warrior minds, the thought of fighting a united force of infidels and their wayward Christian brothers was even less appealing. If Conrad solidified his alliance with the Muslims, none of them would escape this wretched, unholy land alive. But if they wrested the banner of truce from his traitorous hands, they could bide their time and seek vengeance against the unbelievers at the opportune moment.

Richard stood up and embraced his brilliant sister, who had single-handedly rekindled their spirits and showed them a way out of the deadly pit that loomed in their path.

"Our father would have been proud of you."

Joanna's face darkened at the mention of Henry, a stalwart opponent of the Crusade to the end.

"Perhaps," she said, without conviction.

Richard turned to Reynier, who rose to meet the king's gaze.

"Send a herald to Saladin with the offer," Richard said. "I wish I could see the look on that bastard Conrad's face when he gets word."

60

Conrad of Montferrat had turned the distinct shade of purple that Maimonides normally associated with drowning victims. Conrad's reaction was not really out of the ordinary, considering the utterly astonishment on the faces of all the Sultan's courtiers upon hearing the herald's words. Walter Algernon had come offering a truce between Richard and Saladin in place of the one drawn up by Conrad. Conrad's stunned face had gone from red to violet when he heard Richard's condition that the Marquis of Montferrat be immediately extradited to face execution for treason against the throne of England.

The only one who did not appear at all startled or perturbed was Saladin himself. The Sultan leaned back in his throne, his hands caressing the golden lions that served as armrests. Maimonides saw the beginning of an amused smile on the Sultan's lips.

"It is an intriguing offer," he said after a dramatic pause.

Conrad went from purple to green. Maimonides really hoped that the man would get a grip on himself. If he fainted from lack of blood flow to the brain, the unenviable task of saving the wretch's life would fall on the rabbi. It was a duty he really would rather not be required to perform in this instance.

"We have an agreement!" Conrad shouted. He strode toward the Sultan in outrage, but the twin guards immediately blocked his way. They looked as if they were waiting for him to take one more step so that they could appear justified in beheading the sniveling rat on the spot.

Saladin looked at Conrad with narrowed eyes.

"We have a negotiation, my lord. That is all."

Staring at the drawn scimitars that hovered precariously before his neck, Conrad stepped back. With obvious difficulty, the betrayed betrayer took a deep breath to calm himself. When he spoke again, his voice sounded almost reasonable, although a murderous mask still covered his features. The scar under his left eye seemed to be glowing red like a hot coal.

"Richard seeks to trick you," Conrad said. "He is simply biding time to bring more troops over the sea."

Saladin could no longer restrain his smile at the nobleman's discomfiture.

"Well, of course he is," he said, as if Richard's ulterior motives would have been obvious to a toddler. Saladin turned his attention back on the herald. "My dear, Sir Walter, the only way that I could agree to such a truce under the circumstances is if I had some security."

This was unexpected. A murmur grew among the nobles, and for once Saladin let them whisper without calling for silence.

"Security, illustrious Sultan?" the herald said, playing over the word again in Arabic as if he might have misunderstood its meaning.

"Yes. Our friend Conrad rightly reminds us of the threat posed by future invasions. I wish to end this constant state of war between our civilizations. The only way this is possible is if we unify our interests."

Algernon's face betrayed confusion.

"I do not understand." He was not the only one. All eyes were on Saladin as the court anxiously watched the Sultan lead their nation through very uncertain waters.

"Word has come that the king's sister, Joanna, is visiting our shores."

Sir Walter blanched. Even Maimonides had not heard this, but obviously the Sultan's methods of gathering intelligence about the Franks had vastly improved since his tragic triumph at Ascalon.

When the herald spoke again, he was clearly hesitant, unsure how much to reveal, how much to conceal.

"Yes, Princess Joanna graced the king with a brief visit, but she has long since—"

"She is still there, at his camp in Arsuf." Saladin's cold tone suggested that he would not tolerate any deceit from the herald.

"What does the king's sister have to do with our offer of truce?"

It was a question that Maimonides, and everyone else in the chamber, was asking themselves as well.

Saladin's eyes gleamed.

"Tell your king that I propose a truce of my own. A truce of marriage." His words caused an immediate shocked stir. Maimonides stared at his friend in disbelief. How could the Sultan be thinking of yet another woman while Miriam languished in Richard's captivity?

The rabbi saw that the Sultan was looking at him when he spoke the next words.

"I speak not for myself, Sir Walter. I am more than content with the beautiful women whom Allah has sent to grace my harem. But if the princess Joanna will agree to marry my brother, al-Adil, our people will have a unified ruling family. Palestine will then be home to both the believers and the Franks, under one government."

There was a tumult of shock that ran through the nobles. Maimonides saw that al-Adil appeared the most stunned of all. The red-haired giant's mouth opened as if to speak, but no words came out. The Sultan had just proposed a marriage of his own brother to the infidel's sister. It was utterly insane. But as Maimonides thought about it for a second, he realized that, even more than it was insane, the stratagem was utterly brilliant.

The herald seemed as taken aback as everyone else, but he managed to squeak a nervous reply.

"I cannot vouchsafe my king's response to your, er, most generous proposal."

Saladin glanced over at Conrad, who obviously could not care less whether Saladin's brother married all the ladies of the court in London. All that mattered to the ruthless politician was the terrible truth that his dangerous gambit had just backfired on him. Conrad had followed the path of Judas, only to find himself trapped in the snares of his own betrayal.

"Just send him the message," the Sultan said to Algernon. "I prefer the subtle intrigues of politics to the cruelty of war."

61

ichard shook his head in disbelief at Algernon's words.

"Saladin is indeed mad."

The herald bowed his head in embarrassed agreement. Richard's courtiers joined in a round of exaggerated laughter. What could the infidel be thinking, sending back such an outrageous proposal?

"Do not dismiss the offer so easily, brother." Joanna's voice rang out in the marble chamber, and all laughter instantly vanished.

The king turned to face his sister, shock etched on his suntanned visage.

"You would consider this?"

Joanna stood up and faced the row of nobles, who were staring at her as if she had spoken treason. She jutted her chin out in a look of defiance.

"If it would end this vicious war, then yes."

There was an explosion of outcries from the knights and noblemen. The idea of giving a woman of the royal family in marriage to a heathen was incomprehensible, a violation of both divine and human canon.

Richard put a hand on his sister's arm, partly as a reminder to the courtiers that she shared his blood and was under his protection. He had to dissuade her from this madness before she fell victim to the slinking whispers of the nobles.

"But you would let an infidel into your bed? Betray your Christian virtue to the lust of a heathen?"

Joanna turned to face him with a triumphant smile.

"That has not stopped you."

Her words cut into him like a dagger. And he could see that the outraged eyes of his men now fell with discomfort to the floor. Everyone knew of his affair with Miriam, but none had risked speaking of it in public.

Richard looked at his sister's face and saw the same unwavering determination she had displayed when she had refused Henry's command to forget her lover Edmund of Glastonbury. When Joanna made up her mind, no one in Heaven or on earth could dissuade her.

"I swear that I shall never understand women."

Joanna laughed merrily, her eyes twinkling at the scandalized courtiers. As her eyes passed over them, each of the men looked away, unable to withstand the blue fire that shone through them.

"That is as it should be. Our power derives from our mystery."

62

Conrad had found William at last. The young knight had been assiduously avoiding him since his arrival in Jerusalem. Even though they were both housed in the same heavily guarded corner of Saladin's palace, William had apparently gone out of his way to make sure their paths did not cross. In the loyal puppy's eyes, Conrad had betrayed his master, Richard, an unforgivable crime. But the Marquis of Montferrat knew that William was still young and hot-blooded. He had never borne a responsibility greater than making sure some half-educated soldiers managed to come back alive from a battlefield. When William had carried the burdens of a nation on his shoulders, perhaps he would understand the difficult choices that face a king every day. Just as the decision to seek Saladin's aid had come after much deliberation and careful thought, so Conrad had been forced to spend a great deal of time weighing his options after Saladin's apparent rejection of their truce. And now, with his mind firmly set on the course he had to travel, he needed to speak with William. Perhaps his unthinking loyalty to the boy king could finally come in handy.

Conrad caught up with William on a balcony. The knight was staring out at the yellow crescent moon that hung over the mighty towers of Jerusalem. He appeared deep in thought and did not react until the nobleman stood directly behind him.

"What do you want?" William's tone suggested that he really did not care what Conrad's answer was.

"Just to speak to a fellow believer," Conrad said, staring out at the sparkling Dome of the Rock that he used to visit regularly while it was a church. Was that just four years ago? It felt like a lifetime. "I tire of the company of these infidels."

"That does not prevent you from betraying your king to them," William snorted.

Conrad shrugged, prepared for the younger man's derision.

"He betrayed me."

William whirled and grabbed Conrad by his tunic. He rammed the nobleman against the limestone wall and Conrad had a moment of sheer terror when he thought the outraged knight would fling him off the balcony to meet his death on the rocks far below.

"If you were not protected by the Sultan, I would run you through right here," William hissed. And then, as if he had made his point quite clear, he let the nobleman go and turned his back on him.

Conrad managed to calm his wildly beating heart and called out after the knight.

"I was surprised that you did not cry out in shock at the Sultan's indecent proposal."

William turned to face him again. He had managed to restore the mask of stoic patience that he normally wore, although his eyes still burned with loathing.

"It is a good idea," William said. "We must live together in this land. It is better to be unified than to be at each other's throats."

So, Saladin's propaganda had found a sympathetic ear among the Franks. Conrad wondered how his enemy Richard would have felt knowing that his favorite knight now parroted the infidel's line like a loyal member of Saladin's court. Still, he needed to get through to William if his plan was to have any chance of success after all that had happened.

"Can you set aside your hatred of me for a moment and speak as a brother Christian?" Conrad tried to put a penitent lilt in his voice and was unsure if he had been successful.

William crossed his arms but did not move to leave.

"My feelings are my own affair," the knight said. "But speak as you will."

Conrad took a deep breath.

"I have reconsidered my plan and realize that I made a bad decision. We cannot make peace with these infidels."

William's face darkened. He stepped forward until his face was only inches away from Conrad's.

"What are you saying?"

Conrad forced himself to remain focused under the knight's savage glare.

"I will approach Richard and offer to renounce Saladin and restore the alliance."

William burst out laughing.

"You are truly a swine. You break your oath to kings the moment the wind changes."

Conrad did not care what the boy thought of him. All that mattered was that he set aside his personal hatred for the good of the Christian cause. Without William's backing, it would probably be impossible to effect a reconciliation between the rival Crusader kings.

"You have Richard's ear. Will you support me?"

William leaned dangerously close to Conrad, and spit in his face. Without another word, the knight turned on his heels and stormed down the corridor to his bedroom.

As Conrad wiped the spit off his face, he felt his fingers brush the awful scar on his cheek. He reached into his pocket and pulled out the jade charm that served as his constant reminder of the events of the terrible day in the desert.

The Marquis of Montferrat was trapped. He could not go back to Richard without William's help. And he could not go forward and face the unified forces of the Lionheart and Saladin. After years of intrigue in the name of power, he had finally woven a web so intricate that he himself could not escape it.

Feeling the first terrible pinpricks of despair striking his heart, Conrad stared down at the jade necklace that had belonged to some anonymous woman he had ravaged and killed in the desert outside Ascalon. And then, feeling his rage boil over, he flung the charm across the hall. It clattered against the marble floor and vanished into the shadows.

The nobleman turned and stormed back toward his own heavily guarded bedchamber. He had to finish packing. Saladin had been gracious enough to give him the night to gather his things. Tomorrow, an honor guard would escort him into Christian territory. Perhaps when he was back among his men, he could find a way out of this mess.

The defeated nobleman left the corridor and did not look back. He did not see a figure emerge from a hidden vantage point in the shadows.

Maimonides bent down and lifted the jade necklace in his wrinkled hands. He stared at the Hebrew letters etched into the charm, and then raised his eyes. Tears of grief and fury rolled down the rabbi's cheeks as he stared in the direction of the treacherous nobleman who had been revealed in that instant for the monster he truly was.

63

Maimonides finished explaining what he had overheard to Saladin. The rabbi had kept his voice carefully calm and detached. He did everything he could to hide the terrible turmoil raging in his heart at the discovery of his dead sister's necklace in Conrad's possession.

There was no doubt in his mind that it belonged to Rachel. The charm had been unique, carved from real jade. He had purchased it from a rare Chinese trading caravan that had arrived to much fanfare in Cairo a few weeks before his sister's wedding. He had personally inscribed the sacred letters of God's name, *YHWH,* on the charm with the same pen he had used to finish his transcript of the Torah scroll at the end of his studies. Rachel had been wearing the necklace on that terrible day when Reginald's men attacked her traveling party. When news of her death came back to Cairo, the rabbi had sworn a terrible oath that transcended even that which he had once made to Hippocrates. Maimonides promised that he would one day find out who had taken Rachel from him, and he would exact a vengeance that would rival that of Joshua against the Canaanites. And now, over a dozen years later, the God of irony had sent her murderer into his very midst, but protected under the mantle of diplomacy. Well, that shield would vanish quickly enough now that the Sultan knew of Conrad's most recent betrayal.

The Sultan listened to Maimonides with a grave face. The rabbi saw traces of red around his eyes and he knew it was not from sleeplessness or the normal fatigues of kingship. Word had recently arrived of a great tragedy in the family of Ayyub. The Sultan's beloved nephew Taqi al-Din, who had vanished from the court in self-imposed exile after the fall of Acre, had been struck down by fever in a camp on the outskirts of Armenia. The news had hit the Sultan and his brother, al-Adil, like a thunderbolt, and the palace at Jerusalem was covered in a blanket of mourning. That Taqi al-Din had agreed to return to the court, his penance complete, and help his uncle through the worsening crisis of the war only added to the loss. The Sultan was in a dark place emotionally, and it was, in all likelihood, the wrong time to bring up Conrad's betrayal, but Maimonides found that his own inner demons would not be silenced.

After the rabbi finished speaking, Saladin nodded and shrugged. He turned back to a sheaf of documents he had been examining when Maimonides had barged in with the news of the nobleman's plans to reestablish the Christian alliance.

"You were right about that lizard," he said, but with little apparent interest.

Maimonides was confused by the Sultan's nonchalance, but continued to press the matter.

"We can make this work to our advantage."

Saladin kept reading, but he waved his hand for the rabbi to continue.

"What do you suggest?"

Maimonides was thankful that he had done a little investigation before presenting the matter to the Sultan. Being prepared usually paid off.

"Conrad has already sent Richard word of his proposal," he said, leaning close to the Sultan. "My spies say the two are set to meet in a few days' time."

Saladin put the pages down and faced the old doctor. He seemed unconcerned by this sudden twist of fortune. But perhaps he was simply used to such changes by now. The course of the entire war seemed to change on a daily, even hourly, basis.

"You think we should negotiate with Conrad prior to this meeting?" the Sultan asked politely, his tone suggesting that he already believed such an action would be fruitless when dealing with a perennial backstabber like the Marquis of Montferrat.

Maimonides held his breath. He had never said the words that were now on his tongue. And he prayed to God that they would never cross his lips again.

"No, *sayyidi*. We should kill him."

Saladin's eyes went wide and the blood seemed to drain from his face.

"What?!"

Maimonides found the words now flowing from him in an intense rush, as if a dam of emotion had burst in his soul.

"Let us slay this two-faced rat and make it appear as if Richard did so as an act of revenge for his betrayal. The Franks will turn against each other over this crime and we will drive them all out of Palestine."

Saladin looked at his adviser in utter disbelief.

"And they say you are a man of God." His tone was gentle, almost as if he was trying to remind Maimonides of who he truly was.

"My people believe that God chose us to make the world a better place," the rabbi said slowly, trying to keep the hate he felt toward Conrad out of his voice. "Letting these barbarians rise again cannot be His will for mankind."

Saladin's face hardened. His eyes turned cold. It was a look that Maimonides had seen before on the Sultan's face, when he was suppressing anger. But he had never seen that look directed at himself.

"While your suggestion is appreciated, I cannot go along with it."

The rabbi knew he was walking on the edge of a cliff, but he could not let the matter drop. In his mind burned a memory of the terrible dead look on Miriam's face when she returned as the sole survivor of the ill-fated caravan.

"Why, my lord?"

"It is dishonorable to treat kings in such a fashion." Saladin sounded exasperated at having to explain himself to his adviser.

"Conrad is not a king; he is merely a pretender." Maimonides found that the fire of vengeance that burned in his heart was taking away any sense of restraint or diplomatic wisdom in dealing with his master.

"But the Lionheart is my equal," Saladin said, his voice rising. "I will not falsely accuse him of murder."

"*Sayyidi* . . ."

The Sultan slammed his fist down on the polished table where he had set aside the documents he was reading.

"I have made my will known!" And then, seeing Maimonides cringe under his wrath, Saladin calmed himself. "Now please leave me, old friend. I must prepare for this reunified Frankish threat."

Maimonides bowed and walked out of Saladin's study, past the Egyptian guards, who stared at him with surprise. While they did not like the rabbi, they had never heard the Sultan shout at the old man before. Maimonides ignored them. He knew what they thought of him and he did not care. He had a task he must perform. The rabbi knew that the Sultan would not help him do what had to be done. But there was someone who could.

64

Maimonides was led blindfolded into what he presumed was a cave set deep in the hills outside Jerusalem. He wondered whether the black-veiled man who had appeared as if by magic at his bedside that night was planning to kill him and leave his body deep inside the bowels of the earth as a fitting punishment for the temerity of his request. Thankfully, Rebecca slept through his yelp of surprise when he awoke to see those terrible yellow eyes staring at him from above the dark mask. The man wordlessly threw the frightened rabbi his travel cloak and gestured for him to follow him outside, where an ebony horse that looked like it should have been pulling the chariot of Hades stood. How the masked man had gotten inside the apartment, much less known which cloak the rabbi wore on journeys, remained an absolute mystery. Maimonides guessed that he would behold many more mysteries that night.

The veiled man, who had not spoken a single word during their entire trek, now put his hands on the rabbi's shoulders and pressed down. Maimonides was forced to his knees and he felt his heart leap into his throat. And then, without further ceremony, his silent guide undid the wrappings around his eyes. Maimonides blinked, but it made little difference. Even with the blindfold off, he could barely see anything, except that he was inside some vast, deep vault beneath the earth. He had lived in Jerusalem for almost four years now and he had never had any notion that such immense caverns existed in the surrounding countryside.

The only source of light in the massive chamber came from a small oil lamp set on the ground before him. A single flame flickered softly, casting strange shadows all around. It was unseasonably cold down here, and icy stalactites hung directly above him, like the teeth of a giant dragon waiting to clamp down on their prey.

Just outside the circle of light cast by the tiny lamp, Maimonides could see the outline of a figure dressed all in black and seated crossed-legged on the hard stone floor. He could make out that the man wore a dark turban, but the contours of his face were otherwise masked by the shadows.

It did not matter. Maimonides knew instinctively who this was, although he was shocked that the man had been able to arrive in Jerusalem so quickly. It had only been a day since he had sent out a carefully worded summons through one of Saladin's spies who owed the rabbi his life. A chill went down his spine. Perhaps this man had been in Jerusalem all along, rather than hiding out in the mountains of Syria to the east, as was generally believed by the few who dared even speak his name aloud.

So this was where his quest for vengeance had brought him. In the presence of a man whose crimes made the atrocities of the Crusaders look like generous acts of mercy. If his loved ones knew how far he had fallen into the Devil's grasp just by sitting in the same room as this man, they would have disowned him. So be it. He had sworn an oath. Conrad of Montferrat had to die, but there was only one man capable of penetrating the Crusader defenses and executing the monstrous nobleman. And that man now sat before him in an icy cave that Maimonides guessed probably led straight down into Hell.

He was called Rashid al-Din Sinan, but his name was rarely spoken aloud even by those who dismissed his very existence as a tale spread by elderly matrons to frighten little children. He was known instead as the Old Man of the Mountain, a respectful title that masked his terrible power. For Sinan was the leader of the most feared warriors in all of human history.

The Assassins.

"I apologize that we could not meet under more auspicious conditions, Rabbi."

When Sinan spoke, it was with a hiss that sounded just like a serpent. Maimonides felt for the first time a terrible fear constricting his throat. He had no desire to see Sinan's face after hearing that inhuman voice.

"I thank you for agreeing to meet me," the rabbi said, forcing himself to keep his mind on the matter at hand. The sooner he could get this over with, the sooner he could get out of this hellish place. Or so he hoped. "I know my request is most unusual."

Sinan leaned forward, but to the rabbi's relief, his face remained buried in darkness.

"My associates have told me of your plan," he said in that same terrifying voice. "Bold. Treacherous. You surprise me, Rabbi. I would not expect a doctor, much less a man of God, to devise such a plot."

Hearing moral judgment coming from the lips of the most evil man on earth increased Maimonides' self-loathing. But he had no choice. He doubted he would be allowed to leave the cave alive if he suddenly chose to change his mind. Perhaps he would not leave here alive in any event.

"Even Lucifer was an angel once," the rabbi said softly.

Sinan laughed, a bone-chilling sound like steel cutting through armor.

"Your plan has merit, but why not hire my men to slay Richard rather than this weak snake Conrad?"

Maimonides did not want to reveal his personal reasons to this criminal. Somehow the thought of Sinan knowing about Rachel filled him with dread. His own soul was bound to this man now, perhaps for eternity. He did not wish Rachel's spirit to owe any debt to him from beyond.

"My intent is to sow division among the Franks," he said carefully. "Richard's death would be blamed on Saladin and would only fuel the fire of their Crusade."

"You are indeed wise," Sinan hissed. "You realize that your sultan would kill you if he knew you had summoned me."

"Yes." Maimonides bowed his head. Sinan seemed bent on shaming him in return for carrying out this evil deed. If that was the price of vengeance, he would gladly pay it. But he sensed that the cost of his arrangement with this devil would be far greater than he could yet imagine.

"Do you know why he hates me?"

Maimonides did not, nor did he care to. He just wanted to make the arrangements and leave. But he kept the thought to himself.

"I have many theories. Perhaps you can enlighten me."

Sinan breathed heavily. It was a hungry, panting sound that was more unnerving than even his laugh.

"I am the only one to ever hold the life of the great Saladin in his hands. I will not bore you with the details of our feud. Suffice it to say, one night he awoke with a dagger at his throat. He could not believe that my men could penetrate the inner sanctuary of the palace and enter his very bedroom. The great Sultan was so frightened that he wet his bed."

After having witnessed the ease with which the masked intruder had come upon him that night, Maimonides had no doubt that Sinan was telling the truth.

"Yet you spared him."

Maimonides suddenly knew that Sinan was smiling in the darkness, although he had no idea why, since his face remained as invisible as ever.

"Yes. He serves my purpose. My minion was sent to show Saladin that he, like every man on this earth, lives only according to my good pleasure."

Perhaps it was out of a desire to remind himself who he truly was, the man he had always been before the need for revenge had consumed him, but the rabbi could not let this madman persist in his delusions of worldwide grandeur. It was an affront to the Almighty and to everything Maimonides believed in.

"Only God has that power." Even as he said it, he regretted the words. What was the point of challenging this vicious killer's bloated sense of self, except to invite his own death?

But Sinan laughed again with no hint that he had taken offense.

"I agree."

And then Maimonides understood. The rumors were indeed true. The Old Man of the Mountain had created the ultimate cult of warriors, men who would lay down their lives on his behalf because they believed he was Divine. It was said that he kidnapped young men and brought them to his secret mountain lair that had been designed as the most breathtaking garden on earth. The boys were told that they had died and were in Paradise. Surrounded by lush springs and abundant fruit, provided with the company of the most beautiful women in the world dressed as the voluptuous *houris,* and fed daily a near-poisonous dose of hashish, the boys were told that that they were Sinan's angelic warriors. Brainwashed and utterly obedient, the young men would do anything he asked. They had no fear of death, since they believed they were already dead and therefore immortal. Sinan had convinced his men that he was God. And hearing him now, the rabbi suddenly realized that this demon truly believed it as well.

Not knowing what else to do in the presence of such madness, such unadulterated evil, he persisted in his mission.

"Will you do as I have asked?"

"Yes. But I will need the help of your niece. I hear she sleeps in Richard's bed."

The rabbi's mouth dropped. Sinan knew about Miriam. And had apparently heard the vicious, impossible rumors of her trysts with the villainous king.

"I do not know how to get word to her," he said when he could speak again. He had no desire to involve Miriam in this insanity, but he had a terrible feeling that it was already too late.

"My men will take care of that," Sinan said dismissively.

"I fear placing her on this path," Maimonides said bluntly.

Sinan leaned back.

"I understand that she endures Richard's caresses as she fancies herself a spy for your Sultan's interests. Let her prove her loyalties."

All of this was new to the rabbi. But there was a terrible ring of truth to Sinan's words. Miriam had demonstrated on more than one occasion her willingness to engage in espionage in this war. If she had joined Richard in bed, it would only be for that reason. And Maimonides had a strange feeling that the matter was out of his hands. Sinan's curiosity had been piqued and he would not stop until he had concluded the affair the way he wished. Miriam would be pulled into participating in this terrible deed with or without the rabbi's approval.

"I know Miriam," he said at last. For some inexplicable reason, he found himself unable to lie in front of this brutal killer. "If you can get word to her, she will help you."

Sinan cackled with delight. Maimonides had a strange feeling Satan must have laughed in exactly the same way when he witnessed Adam and Eve partaking of the forbidden fruit.

"I will need your sister's necklace."

Maimonides suddenly wanted to run out screaming into the night. He realized at that instant that Sinan truly was a monster from another world. Whether it was through the whispered help of the djinn, *ifreet,* or some other desert demons, or some forbidden magic passed down through the disciples of Solomon, the Old Man of the Mountain clearly had access to knowledge that no mortal soul could possess.

Yet he found himself complying. As if in a trance, Maimonides reached into his pocket and withdrew the charm. The green jade twinkled in the lonely lamplight. Not wishing to come even an inch closer to Sinan, he gently tossed over the necklace. Sinan caught it effortlessly and the rabbi felt his heart sink to think that this creature now held the holy letters of the Tetragrammaton in his hands.

"Excellent. Then all that is left to be discussed is my fee."

Maimonides prepared himself. He sensed that whatever it was Sinan wanted, the price would prove to be too great, on many levels.

"I am a poor man, but I will find some way to—"

Sinan raised a hand in the shadows to stop him.

"I do not need your wealth."

Maimonides held his breath.

"Then what?"

Sinan stood up, but did not approach the circle of light.

"I hear that you are nearly done with a treatise on the Jewish faith. The so-called *Guide for the Perplexed*."

Nothing surprised Maimonides anymore.

"Yes. What of it?"

"In return for Conrad's death, I require that you provide me with a copy of this treatise with all of your original notes. That is all."

Whatever the rabbi had imagined in his darkest thoughts, he had not been prepared for this.

"Why?"

When Sinan spoke, his voice sounded strangely distant.

"Questions of the Divine interest me more than any mundane treasures. You may find this hard to believe, Rabbi, but I too am on a holy mission. I administer death, and in death, we truly experience the Divine."

The lamp flickered as he spoke, although Maimonides felt no wind, nor would he have expected a breeze so far beneath the earth. The rabbi glanced at the flame for an instant. When he raised his eyes again to the spot where Sinan stood, he felt all the color drain from his face.

The Old Man of the Mountain was gone.

65

Miriam had fallen asleep after another disgusting night of coupling with the King of England. Richard seemed completely infatuated with her, and she had honed her acting skills to their finest over the past several weeks to keep him under the delusion that she shared his feelings. Every night, while he slept with his head against her breast, it took every ounce of willpower she possessed not to tear out his throat with her bare fingers. Perhaps she would indeed go through with it one day, but only after she had fabricated a foolproof escape plan from the prison that was Arsuf.

"Miri . . ."

Miriam opened her eyes and found that she was no longer alone with the king. A woman stood at the foot of the bed dressed in a flowing blue robe, her face covered by a white veil. The strange woman reached out a hand and pointed to her, and Miriam felt a terrible chill.

"Miri . . ." the woman said again, her voice echoing oddly, as if she were crying out from a great distance. Miriam had not heard that endearment in over a dozen years and she felt tears welling in her eyes. Only her mother Rachel had ever called her Miri.

Pulled by a force she did not understand, Miriam found herself getting out of the bed where the sleeping Richard still lay. She followed the veiled woman through the door, and saw to her surprise that the king's guards who were normally stationed outside his bedroom were on the ground, fast asleep.

The veiled woman led her down the hall. Everywhere soldiers lay sleeping, some snoring loudly. Miriam would have thought someone had somehow drugged everyone in the citadel with a sleeping draft, but of course that was impossible.

The veiled woman took her through a wing of the castle that she had never been allowed to enter. Down a longer series of steps, she led Miriam to a bronze door, before which lay two armored guards. Miriam gasped when she saw that they were not asleep like the others. Instead, their throats had been slit and a pool of blood had formed before the door. The veiled woman stepped over the corpses without even looking down. She opened the door, which swung inward with a groaning creek, and beckoned for Miriam to follow her. Miriam gingerly stepped over the bodies, raising the hem of her linen sleeping gown so as not to soak it with blood.

Inside, she saw a man who was awake, but kneeling on the floor, bound by black ropes around his waist and arms and gagged with a velvet cloth. One look at his scarred face and she knew who he was. Conrad of Montferrat, the treacherous noble who had betrayed Richard and then betrayed Saladin.

Miriam had seen Conrad on only a handful of occasions, but every time she looked at his scarred face, she had felt a strange queasiness in her stomach, and the sensation returned now. It was as if she had seen him before, many years ago, but of course that was impossible. Wasn't it?

"You know who he is, Miri." The woman spoke for the first time since they had left Richard's bedroom. And the voice sounded remarkably like her mother's.

"No, I . . ."

And then she did. Staring at the terrible red scar on his left cheek, she remembered. The man who had raped and killed her mother before her very eyes. How he had chased her and pinned her to the desert sands. Even as his terrible member had torn her hymen, mixing her mother's blood with her own, she had managed to reach his waist and pull a dagger from its scabbard. And then she had slashed upward, hoping to slit his throat but managing only to tear a line through his cheek.

A line through his cheek. Just like the one on Conrad's face.

The man had fallen off her, screaming curses in a language she did not understand. She had run, blood coursing down her thighs. Miriam could no longer even remember how she had escaped her pursuers as she fled from the ravaged caravan. Up one sand dune. Down another. Running for her life, she had finally seen the outcropping rocks under which there had been a small hole. An entrance to a cave that was just barely large enough for her to crawl through. And there she had hid. He had coming looking for her, had nearly found her hiding place. But she had been rescued by a sandstorm that had forced him to return to his fellow soldiers. When she finally emerged, she had followed a campfire that had led her back to the site of the caravan. A tribe of wandering Bedouin who had come upon the carnage had already buried her parents and the other victims. She had walked like the living dead toward them, her legs caked over with sand and dried blood. She had hoped they would put her out of her misery, take her life too so that she could be with Rachel again. But a kindly Bedouin with a scraggly beard had put her on his camel, given her a flask of water, and then taken her on the long journey back to Cairo.

And now she was here. Facing the man who had taken everything away from her. He had haunted her dreams for over a decade, but she had never known his name. Until now.

Conrad of Montferrat.

The veiled woman approached her, holding a knife in her hands. Miriam recognized the jeweled hilt and the etched lion on the blade. It was the king's personal dagger.

"You know what you have to do."

And Miriam did. She took the blade and turned to face the terrified Conrad. He was trembling wildly, tears pouring down his cheeks. Miriam knew that he wept not for her mother or the hundreds, the thousands, of others he had killed. He wept only for himself, for the end to his life of butchery before he could fulfill his mission of destruction through the world.

She felt no pity for him as she approached with the knife, nor any hesitation.

Miriam placed the blade against his neck, saw the first line of blood trickle down from contact with the razor-sharp edge. She felt something warm at her feet and realized that she was standing in a pool of Conrad's urine. The great warrior, the man who claimed to be the true King of Jerusalem, had wet his pants at the thought of death.

She slit his throat.

Blood gushed like a geyser from the wound. She was hit with a splash of the burning liquid and her white nightgown was suddenly covered in scarlet. Conrad fell to the ground, his face splashing in the pool of his own piss.

Miriam turned to see the ghostly woman holding out her hand. Miriam saw that she held something green and sparkling in her fingers. It was her mother's favorite jade necklace.

"I'm proud of you, Miri," the woman said. Miriam dropped the blade on the ground and took the charm in her hands. How she had loved her mother's necklace.

Her delight faded when she looked up. The mysterious woman was no longer standing in front of her. Instead a veiled man in midnight-black robes and a turban stood before her. His eyes glowed yellow like a cat's and he was laughing, a terrible, scratching noise that sounded like sheets of metal being torn asunder.

Miriam screamed . . .

. . . and awoke. She was back in Richard's bed. The king was lying on his stomach, sound asleep as the first light of dawn seeped in through the arched windows of their bedroom.

Trying to calm the terrible beating of her heart, she stepped out of bed to get a glass of water. And then she froze. She was no longer in her white nightgown. Instead she was wearing a blue robe and her skin felt wet, as if she had just bathed and wiped her body with a towel.

And then she realized that she was wearing something around her neck. With trembling hands, Miriam lifted the necklace and gazed upon the green jade and the octagonal charm with the name of God inscribed in Hebrew.

She wanted to scream from that moment on until eternity. But no sound came from her throat. She felt herself losing her balance and she managed to fall back against the bed as the darkness took her.

The last thing she saw as her mind slipped into the black of unconsciousness was the glowing yellow fire of a serpent's eyes burning into her mind.

66

Miriam sat with dread inside Richard's study. She assiduously avoided looking at his pale-faced sister, Joanna, but she could feel the woman's eyes boring into her from across the marble-tiled room. Word of Conrad's murder had spread through the citadel like a flood and tensions were running high. Richard had spent the better part of the morning with Conrad's lieutenants, who had joined him on this ill-fated mission to reestablish the Crusader alliance. Most of Conrad's soldiers were holed up inside Acre, but word had probably already reached them by carrier pigeon of their leader's assassination while under Richard's protection. She knew it was only a matter of time before shock and outrage boiled over into mutiny.

Miriam could still not believe what had happened, or her own apparent role in the assassination. But the strange charm, which looked exactly like her mother's necklace, remained tied around her neck. It was impossible, but then again, there it was. She reached up and touched the beads, almost hoping they had returned to the world of the imagination, the same strange realm where she had seen herself murder Conrad of Montferrat in cold blood.

Miriam had always prided herself on the clarity of her thinking. She put little stock in so-called feminine intuition as the basis for perceiving the underlying realities of the world. Aristotelian logic, the art of deduction and analysis, had been her tools for examining life's mysteries. But such an approach failed her utterly now. What she had seen in that dream state, what she had done . . . none of it could be explained by rational means. And yet it had happened, all of it. The possibility that her stubbornly held view of an ordered world, one without magic or mysticism, was false was in some ways far more troubling to her than the fact that she could kill a man with such ease.

Of course, if Conrad had indeed been the man who had savagely attacked her mother on that fateful day in the Sinai, she would hold herself blameless of any crime. But she doubted that the Franks would be so merciful if indeed they ever learned the truth.

She thrust her thoughts aside as the door flew open and Richard stormed in, followed by his adviser Reynier. She had never seen the king look so angry, even at the unexpected destruction of Ascalon. Miriam felt a chill go down her spine as she realized that he looked just the way Saladin did when he walked in on her in bed with Zaheer.

"Sire, we must prepare," Reynier pleaded. "Conrad's generals will rally their troops against us. They claim that you ordered their master's death."

Richard turned on the aide, who took a step back in fear.

"Preposterous!"

Reynier hesitated, and then spoke without looking at his king's mad eyes.

"My lord, a dagger bearing the royal insignia was found by his side."

Miriam felt her heart stop for a beat. When she looked up, she saw Richard's unnerving gaze upon her.

"This is Saladin's work," he hissed. "He claims to be a man of honor, but he conspires to commit this murder to divide us."

"He is not like that . . ." she said out of instinctive loyalty before she could stop herself. It was, of course, a terrible mistake.

"Silence!"

Suddenly Richard was upon her. His hands grabbed at her throat with animal ferocity. She desperately tried to move, to breathe, but his fingers closed around her neck like a torturer's vise.

"It was you, wasn't it?" the king bellowed. "You lulled me into a daze with your kisses, all the while you were plotting against me . . ."

Miriam wanted to scream, but no sound emerged from her lips. Tiny blue lights flashed in front of her eyes as her brain signaled its desperate thirst for oxygen.

". . . you stole a royal dagger and gave it to Saladin's men. Admit the truth!"

"She can hardly admit to anything if she is dead, brother." Joanna's voice cut like a knife through the air. Richard relaxed his grip and Miriam fell to her knees. Her lungs sucked in air in desperate gulps.

"In God's name . . ." was all she managed to say before Richard kicked her in the stomach, his leather boot smashing hard against her gut. She felt herself losing consciousness and struggled with all her will-power to stay lucid, despite the terrible pains racking her body.

"Do not blaspheme!" Richard's voice thundered in the small room. "Your people betrayed God and delivered Him to His death. And you have the audacity . . ."

He raised his foot to kick Miriam again, and she knew that she would not remain conscious after the second blow. Suddenly Joanna stepped forward and put a restraining hand on his arm.

"My brother, calm yourself."

But instead of assuaging his fury, her words only seemed to intensify Richard's madness.

"Tell me, Joanna. Were you a party to this plot too?"

Even in the midst of excruciating agony, Miriam was aware that Richard had fallen over the edge of rage into something far worse.

"Have you gone mad?" Joanna shrieked, voicing Miriam's thoughts.

Richard grabbed Joanna forcefully by the shoulders. The princess threw a desperate glance at the stunned Templar Reynier. The young knight clearly had no idea what to do, so he turned his face away from the scene.

"I wondered why you were so eager to share your bed with the infidel," Richard seethed, his eyes filled with blue flame. "Perhaps you have been in his embrace all this time."

Joanna slapped him. But instead of snapping him out his insanity, the blow pushed him deeper into darkness. He struck her back, sending his beloved sister crashing to the floor.

Miriam watched through eyes blurred with tears as Richard stood above his trembling sister. Her right cheek was swollen and a thin line of blood was issuing from her lips. At another time, Miriam would have taken dark pleasure at watching the proud bitch humiliated by the cruel man whom she so adoringly called brother. But now, as currents of fire ran through her own body from Richard's brutality, she could feel only empathy for the terrified girl.

The king pulled Joanna up with one forceful tug of his arm.

"Richard, please . . ."

"I trusted you with our father's last words," Richard hissed. "Did you reveal them to John? Is that why he is bold enough to challenge me?"

Joanna was crying too profusely to answer. Richard tossed her aside and turned his attention to the petrified Reynier.

"Send a message to all the Frankish generals, including Conrad's men in Acre. They are either with me or against me. Any who rebel, I will kill them with my own hands. Once we have cleansed ourselves of traitors, we will wait no longer."

He turned to look at Miriam, who still lay sprawled on the ground, her hands covering her pain-filled stomach.

"Mark my words, Jewess," he said with a coldness that was much more frightening than the heat of his rage. "Jerusalem will be ours. I will let you live long enough to see the city burn. And then I will toss you into the flames myself."

67

Maimonides sat at the council of war in silence while the generals heatedly discussed the rapidly deteriorating military situation in Palestine. Although he was in his usual seat of honor to the left of the prime minister, Qadi al-Fadil, he felt very much out of place. Even the Sultan no longer made any effort to include him in the discussions. In fact, Saladin did not even acknowledge his presence at the table.

Ever since word of Conrad's murder had reached Jerusalem, the Sultan had avoided his old friend. They had not spoken a word in the tumultuous days that followed, and when the rabbi attempted to enter Saladin's study to speak to him about what was becoming an obvious rift between the two men, the twin Egyptian guards had blocked his way. And this time the Sultan did not hasten to his rescue.

Perhaps it should have been expected. Saladin was no fool, and he had obviously deduced that the rabbi had somehow been involved in the assassination plot that had thrown the Crusader forces into disarray. For a time it had seemed as if the old man's prediction had come true. Richard's forces had been forced to turn away from their efforts to conquer Palestine in order to quell the revolt of Conrad's men. While there had been much rejoicing in the court at the news of the Frankish infighting, the mood had grown more somber when word came of Richard's rapid victory against the rebels. The Lionheart had crushed Conrad's most violent supporters at Acre, and then proclaimed an amnesty for the rest of the Frankish backsliders. Richard was able to convince the defeated soldiers that they had been tricked by Saracen intrigue and that the true murderer had been the devious Saladin. The only way to avenge Conrad's death was to bring the leader of the infidels to justice.

Having secured unified control of the once-divided Christian forces, Richard had returned his attention to Jerusalem with renewed rage. Convinced that Saladin had ordered the assassination to besmirch the king's reputation among his own men, the Lionheart was now treating the war against the Muslims as a personal vendetta. The petulant boy appeared to have dispensed with his cautious strategy and was planning a full frontal assault on Jerusalem to avenge his soiled honor. Maimonides, in his efforts to destroy the Crusader alliance, had unwittingly strengthened it, and had exposed the Holy City to its unbridled wrath.

All in all, things had not quite gone as he had planned.

Ever since his fateful meeting with the mysterious leader of the Assassins, Maimonides had endured terrible nightmares that taunted him with the details of Conrad's murder. The dreams had been remarkably vivid, as real as if he had witnessed the events with open eyes. The Marquis of Montferrat was always kneeling on the floor while a dark figure whose face Maimonides could never see properly slit his throat. The man would then fall face-first into a pool of his own urine, the yellow soon turning sickly crimson as blood mixed with piss.

Each night he would wake up gasping for breath, his eyes flitting wildly about his bedroom, as if something terrible were hiding in the shadows of the room, waiting to take him on a dark journey that was an unspoken part of his deal with the Old Man of the Mountain.

Maimonides had told himself a thousand times that what he did was a grand sacrifice for his people, not just an act of personal vengeance on behalf of his beloved sister and her daughter. The Franks had massacred the Jews before, left not a man, woman, or child alive when they last stood inside the gates of Jerusalem. If they conquered Palestine, they would do so again. Despite his vivid dreams, he had not been present when Conrad died, and his heart felt no sorrow when the news reached him. Yet every night, just before he awoke with a cry, he would see Conrad lying in his own blood. But as the dead man lay there soaked in his own waste, he would be transformed from the angry and bitter man that Maimonides had known. And he would become again the beautiful child that he perhaps had been once, filled with hope and joy. A child lying in a pool of blood who would never play again.

Maimonides forced the image out of his mind and compelled himself to listen to al-Adil, who with his booming voice was, as usual, drowning out disagreement.

"The end is at hand, mark my words," he said as again his fist slammed hard against the black tabletop. "The Lionheart will no longer play cat-and-mouse games. He is preparing for the final battle, one for which we have no choice but to be prepared. Either we will emerge victorious, or the Franks will wash the streets of Jerusalem with our blood."

There were some startled glances passed back and forth at the table. The little speech was as close to eloquence as the lumbering brute had ever come in his life.

Maimonides saw the Sultan smile slightly for the first time that day. It was an expression he had missed seeing on Saladin's face, which had aged rapidly over the past year. His once midnight-black hair was now peppered with gray, and worry lines had wrinkled the skin around his eyes. Maimonides had grown increasingly worried about the toll the war was taking on a man who had once seemed ageless and invincible, but he had been unable to perform any medical examinations of his patient since the news of Conrad's death had driven the invisible wedge between them.

Even now, as the Sultan glanced at his different courtiers while adding his own thoughts to his brother's tirade, he conspicuously failed to meet the rabbi's eyes. Perhaps Maimonides would never regain Saladin's trust, and if that were indeed the case, then the rabbi would have lost something far more precious than his standing in the court. Maimonides knew that even if his actions ultimately saved the world, they would have been at the cost of the most rare and valuable commodity of all. A friend.

"...according to our spies in the neighboring countryside, the Frankish forces are leaving their citadels at Acre and Caesarea en masse," the Sultan said as he pointed to a large map of Palestine that had been laid out on the table before the nobles. "It appears likely from their movement that they are planning to rendezvous at a central point on the coast before they make their way toward Jerusalem."

All eyes followed Saladin's finger as he pointed to a dot representing a small village on the map, south of Arsuf and northwest of the village of Ramla. Only a day's march west from Jerusalem.

"Jaffa," Saladin said with the certainty that came from years of planning and waging wars. "Jaffa is where they will launch their attack."

There was a dread moment of silence at the table as reality set in. The war was finally coming to them.

"We must increase the defensive barriers around Jerusalem." It was Keukburi who spoke, his sad face seeming gloomier than ever.

"No." Saladin's response caught everyone by surprise. The Sultan stood up before his men, his shoulders straight, his head held high. He was not a tall man, but at the moment he towered above them like a giant.

"I will not permit any more blood to be shed inside the Holy City," the Sultan said firmly. "If we are to face Richard's army, it will be on the open plain of Jaffa, not cowering like women inside our houses."

"We have substantial stores of rations within the city, *sayyidi*," the vizier, al-Fadil, argued. "We would be more likely to survive the siege if we remain inside the walls . . ."

Saladin turned on the prime minister, his face filled with righteous indignation.

"You are not a soldier, Qadi, so I will pardon your cowardice," he said in a deadly voice that few had ever heard before. Al-Fadil hastily bowed and murmured terrified apologies.

"If any of you have studied the sorry history of Jerusalem, you would know that there is a terrible spirit that hides inside her sacred stones. A specter that hungers for death and chaos. This phantasm beckons the foolhardy to take refuge inside her so-called impenetrable walls, her allegedly inviolable gates. And then betrays them at the first sight of an invading army."

Maimonides recalled all the stories he had heard about the first Crusader assault on Jerusalem, and he knew that Saladin's words were true.

How those men and women who had thought themselves safe inside God's city must have felt when the supposedly impassable iron gates crumbled and their holy refuge became a hellish trap . . .

"My friends, if we lose this war, we shall die like our forefathers, in the open fields beneath a clear sky, not seeking a coward's refuge inside stone huts covered by the shadow of mortared walls. If we die, we will do so under the blazing sun of Jaffa, not the spires of Jerusalem."

With Saladin's intentions now clear, the generals bowed their heads and rose from the council table. There was much work to do if the bulk of the Muslim army were to march into the waiting shields of the Crusaders massing at Jaffa.

Maimonides stole a final glance at the Sultan, who continued to ignore him, as he slowly walked out of the limestone chamber. The rabbi felt a leaden weight in his breast that was due neither to age nor to infirmity. He mused bitterly to himself that the heart was truly a peculiar organ. It felt no pain in arranging the death of one man. Yet it grieved inconsolably at the loss of conversation with another.

68

Sultan Salah al-Din ibn Ayyub, known to the Franks as Saladin, the conqueror of Egypt and Syria, the liberator of Jerusalem, took off his curved wooden shoes as he stepped onto the sacred soil of the Haram al-Sharif. The immense limestone platform, spanning one and a half million square feet, had once served as the site of the Temple of Solomon, and was now host to the two most sacred mosques outside of Arabia. To his right stood the silver-domed Al-Aqsa Mosque, where the caliph Umar had first prayed upon entering Jerusalem five hundred years before. The blaspheming Crusaders had used the building as a stable for their horses during their wretched years of rule over the Holy City, filling its revered halls with filth and manure. But even the ignorant savages had found it impossible to desecrate the beautiful building that towered above him now. The majestic cupola of the *Qubbat as-Sakhra*, the Dome of the Rock, reflected and amplified the light of the crescent moon as if it were shining with its own fire.

Built by the Umayyad caliph Abd al-Malik sixty-nine years after the Prophet's fateful emigration from Mecca to Medina, at a cost of all of Egypt's tax revenue for a period of seven years, the Dome was beyond a doubt the most splendid work of architecture in all the world. The octagonal building was covered in turquoise-and-emerald tiles etched with verses from the Holy Qur'an. The exterior walls were of veiled marble and overlaid with arches that were embossed with golden geometric patterns made to resemble stars and flowers. The shining cupola of the dome soared ninety-eight feet above the platform and spread out to a diameter of almost sixty-five feet. Hidden inside the Dome was the Sakhra, the sacred limestone slab that served as the peak of Mount Moriah and the focal point for the passionate spiritual hopes not only of Muslims, but of their Jewish and Christian brothers as well.

The Dome of the Rock had become the ultimate symbol of Jerusalem for the whole world, and the Haram was usually filled with worshippers and pilgrims who had come from the four corners of the earth to pray within it sanctified precincts. But not tonight. The platform, lined with ancient olive trees, was utterly deserted, as was most of the city below. With the Crusaders marching steadily east, Jerusalem had been abandoned to its ghosts.

Saladin was alone tonight, but he was accustomed to solitude. For most of the fifty years he had walked upon the earth, he had been alone. Not in the sense that other men thought of the word. No, of course, in those terms, he had barely had a moment to himself in decades. His life was filled with the inescapable throngs of soldiers, courtiers, spies, friends, and enemies. At times it was almost impossible for petitioners even to see the face of the Sultan through the huddled masses that demanded his attention every day of the year, every moment of the day.

But Saladin knew that such interactions were only a shadow of real companionship, a frenzy of superficial communication brought about by the realities of power that guaranteed a meeting neither of minds, nor of hearts. In this respect, in the silent chambers of his soul, Saladin had been truly alone for as long as he could remember.

Here and there he had experienced a fleeting moment of connection, a flickering sensation of understanding, between his charges and himself. But Saladin had rarely opened his heart to another for any length of time, for fear that the truth would be unmasked. The truth that the great invincible Sultan was just a man, with fears and weaknesses like any other.

There had been a few within his inner circle with whom he had become close. And yet every time he came near to letting his guard down, a terrible force that delighted in his tortured solitude arose and tore them from his bosom. His beloved wife Yasmeen, who had consumed his heart when he was just a boy—Saladin had imagined once that he would, when the battles were behind him and victory secured, rest his head on her milky shoulders and confess all the fears and doubts he had been forced to hide from the world. But the battles never ended and victory remained a mirage. And the years of conquest that had kept him away from Yasmeen's side had created an impassable chasm between their hearts.

Saladin had resigned himself to being alone forever, and then fate played a terrible trick on his heart. Kismet had dangled before him a sparkling sapphire, one that he was forbidden by the laws of God and man to touch. Miriam had entered his life like an unexpected storm rising from the sea and brushing aside the protective walls of his soul with her green eyes and sparkling smile. In her arms, Saladin had felt alive again for the first time in years, and he could forget during their time together that he was meant to be the Sword of Allah upon the earth, the champion of the Muslim *ummah*, and could again become what he secretly had always wanted to be—just a man, without the burden of destiny forever crushing his spirit.

And for his sin of adultery with the Jewess, they had all paid a terrible price. Miriam was lost to slavery in the infidel camp, perhaps forever. And Yasmeen he had been forced to slay, before her murderous machinations unleashed a wave of death and scandal that would have torn his court asunder even as the enemy bore down on the gates of Jerusalem. In his desperate effort to fill the terrible void in his heart, he had managed to destroy the only two women who had ever managed to find their way inside it.

Saladin forced the thought from his head before the dam of his sorrow and regret, built over decades of war and betrayal, burst open wide. The Sultan knew that if those emotions were ever released, he would be consumed with grief beyond madness and the lives of a hundred thousand innocents in Palestine would be sacrificed on the altar of his self-pity. He had to keep his mind razor sharp, his heart as hard as Damascus steel, if he was to steer the ship of the nation through this final storm.

That was why he was here tonight, standing before the Dome of the Rock, where Heaven and earth were united for all time. To beseech his invisible God for guidance through the impenetrable mists of history that were swirling all about him. And to ask His forgiveness for bringing the Holy City yet again to the brink of calamity.

Saladin climbed the ancient stone steps that led to the Dome and passed under the four-arched Gate of Ablutions. He let his hand rest briefly on the ancient brass knocker that protruded from the western door of the sanctuary, then slowly stepped inside.

The interior of the dome was brightly lit by dozens of copper lanterns encircling the walls. Those who had done no more than glimpse the outside of the Dome were stunned to discover that its ethereal beauty was only a pale shadow of the glorious architecture that was hidden within. Each of the building's eight walls was lined with stained-glass windows that stood twice the height of a man. The floors were covered in the richest red-and-green carpets imported from as far away as Persia and Samarqand. And the roof was paved in tiles of gold and jewels to form intricate patterns of overlapping circles that seemed to swirl toward infinity.

At the center of the grand monument, directly beneath the Dome itself and encircled by a screen made of carved cedar, stood the Sakhra. The Rock of Abraham. Saladin approached the massive stone slab that was shaped like a horseshoe—straight as an arrow on one end and curved like a crescent on the other. The Sultan wondered at the sheer improbability that this craggy boulder should have played such a central role in the history of Creation. For the Jews, it served as the foundation for the Holy of Holies, the sacred enclosure where the Ark of the Covenant had stood for hundreds of years. For the Christians, it was the last vestige of Herod's Temple, where Christ had challenged the power-hungry priests and the greedy money changers. And for the Muslims it was all that and more. From here, the Prophet Muhammad had ascended to Heaven on his fabled Night Journey, a mystical voyage that had culminated in the Messenger kneeling before the Throne of God. It was said that the world revolved around the Sakhra, and that the angel Israfil would one day stand on this very limestone slab and blow the trumpet that would signal the Resurrection of mankind and the Final Judgment.

Saladin normally obeyed the protocols around which believers kept a respectful distance from the Rock itself, but tonight he shifted open the wooden screen and bent down to touch the cold gray stone as if to prove to himself that it was indeed just that—a stone like any other, but one that had been chosen by God for a grand purpose. The thought crossed his mind that he was not all that different from the Rock. A man like any other, but destined to forever stand apart from his kinsmen on the shoulders of history.

"I am always amazed, O Sakhra, by the annals of history." The Sultan spoke out loud, addressing the holy stone and his own heart. "You have stood here since the days of Adam. You have witnessed the Flood and the rise and fall of empires. Our father Abraham almost sacrificed his son on your cold surface. David, Solomon, Jesus. They have all stood where I am now. And our Holy Prophet, Muhammad, flew to Heaven when his feet touched your sacred stones. Yet in all that time you have never spoken to any man. What secrets you must have to share. Will you, at long last, converse with a weary soldier tonight?"

Despite his plea, the Sakhra did not choose that moment to break its eternal silence. But the Sultan continued, his eyes peering deeper into his own soul even as he stared at the shadowed crevices of the Rock.

"I am afraid, my friend," he said, a phrase he had never spoken out loud before. "I have never been more terrified than I am tonight. My entire life has been dedicated to fighting the Franks. I cannot remember ever desiring anything else. But all things, at least those not made of stone, will end. So too is my battle ending."

Saladin gazed into the cupola a hundred feet above, his eyes following the majestic circle of Qur'anic calligraphy that was etched into the gold leaf and spiraled toward the center of the grand Dome. Few could look straight into the interior of the Dome without falling to their knees in utter awe. It was like a blind man receiving the miraculous gift of sight, only to stare directly into the sun. For this was the secret of the *Qubbat as-Sakhra*—its greatest beauty lay hidden within. Just like the human spirit.

"You see, I am not afraid of dying or losing to the Franks," Saladin said to the timeless Presence that he felt permeate the chamber as he gazed up into the hypnotic spire of gold. "I have always been ready for that possibility. No, sacred Rock, I fear only one thing."

Saladin lowered his eyes and fell to his knees as he admitted aloud a truth he had never truly faced before.

"When this battle ends, in victory or defeat, my reason for being will end too," he said, fighting the terrible chill that was running along his spine as he brought his most feared inner demon to the surface.

"Everything beyond this final battle is shrouded in shadow," Saladin said, tears spilling down his cheek uncontrollably. His voice cracked in a terrible sob that seemed to have been trapped inside his breast for a lifetime.

"And of that darkness, O Sakhra, I am most afraid."

Saladin, the most powerful man on earth, stayed on his knees, seeking solace from the Divine Force he knew was there with him tonight. A quiet blanketed the shrine, a silence that was deeper and more profound than any moment of prayer or introspection that he had ever experienced. He felt his eyes weighed down with a sleep that had escaped him for two nights.

In that all-encompassing silence, as the veil of slumber descended upon him, the vault of memories was laid open at last. He saw his life flash before him, even as it was said to happen to men at the moment of their deaths. And then the vision grew and consumed him . . .

→ → →

SALADIN WAS RUNNING THROUGH the mud-caked streets of Tikrīt like a carefree child while his beautiful mother called out to him lovingly. It was time for dinner and she had made his favorite lamb stew. Life was so simple here, no war, no hate, just the exuberant play of children who knew the meaning of neither death nor suffering, nor the terrible weight of destiny . . .

He was riding a horse as a teenager, awkwardly clutching a spear in his right hand, while his formidable father, Ayyub, scolded him for his poor form. How could Saladin ever expect to be a soldier if he could not even hold a lance upright? The youth bowed his head in shame. All he wanted was for his father to accept and love him for the boy he was. But he knew that he could never earn that love, until he was free of all flaws and weakness. And so he set his goal at that moment to be the greatest warrior of all time. To be perfect . . .

He was standing over the bloodied corpse of the first man he ever killed in battle, desperately fighting the terrible impulse to vomit as he stared down at his sword thrust deep into the chest of his victim. The dead boy was a dark-haired Syrian rebel, not much older than himself, who was looking up at him, shock and surprise forever frozen on his features. He felt his father clasp his hand on his shoulder, his eyes shining with pride at his son's first kill. Saladin had waited all his life to see that look on Ayyub's face. But instead of joy at his success, he felt only the stirrings of terrible despair as he gazed into the grime-soaked face of the youth who had perished at his hand . . .

And then he was standing over the bodies of the many thousands he had sent to their deaths, the remains of his soldiers and his enemies piled all around him in a sea of devastation. Their lifeless eyes stared up at him accusingly: "Behold the cost of your legacy, Great Sultan. Your name shall be remembered for eternity, but who shall remember our sacrifice?" Saladin wanted to scream but no sound emerged from his throat. He had crossed the valley of his life, and he knew that it ended here, washed in the blood of those who had given their lives so that he could fulfill his terrible destiny . . .

And then darkness set in over the grisly tableau and he was alone at the end of the journey.

Except that he was not alone, and this was not the end.

A woman stood before him now, her body glittering with a halo of silver light. It was Miriam, resplendent in her flowing blue gown and chiffon scarf, her hair sparkling like black silk. Her eyes burned with emerald fire.

"We are all slaves of history, Miriam," he heard himself say. "It is a river that no man can harness. We cannot swim against its power. Indeed, we drown in its torrent."

And then she laughed and he felt all the frost that had gathered over his heart over the decades melt in an instant.

"And when you are drowning, my love, know that I will be there to rescue you. Always." Miriam held her arms out to him, her face filled with divine forgiveness, summoning him to her eternal embrace . . .

╼ ╼ ╼

THE DREAM, IF IT was that, ended and the Sultan's eyes flew open. He was still kneeling before the Sakhra, but the terrible weight on his soul was gone.

Salah al-Din ibn Ayyub rose to his feet in wonder at the vision he had experienced, even as the first light of dawn filtered in through the sparkling stained-glass windows of the Dome of the Rock. He reverently kissed the gray stone before turning his back on the Sakhra and stepping out of the ancient sanctuary. He did not know if he would ever enter its precincts again, but it no longer mattered.

The Sakhra had broken its eternal silence tonight and Saladin had received his answer. There was still one thing left to fight for.

69 The Plain of Jaffa—AD 1192

S ir William Chinon sat upon the gray steed that had served him loyally from its home in the Welsh countryside across the world to the Holy Land. He rode beside Saladin as the Muslim leader surveyed the sea of battle tents arrayed across the plain of Jaffa. Although no emotion was visible on the Sultan's features, William did not doubt that he was impressed. Richard had managed to take the greatest defeat of the Crusade—the death of Conrad and the resulting civil war among the Franks—and transform it through the sheer force of his will. The divided Christians were now unified under a single commander and were focused on the task that had bedeviled them for years—the final defeat of Saladin. The snowy-white pavilions, adorned with crimson pennants, shone defiantly under the hot Palestine sun, beckoning the Muslims to fight as they had never fought before.

By the time the bulk of the Sultan's army of thirty thousand had arrived, a major skirmish between the forces had already taken place. Saladin's advance troops had managed a daring raid on Jaffa even as Richard's fleet was sailing straight toward the beach. The citadel had briefly fallen into the hands of the Muslims, but the occupiers were pushed out after only two days by the wave of Crusader forces disembarking from the sea. William had smiled when he heard the reports that Richard had personally retaken Jaffa, leading the attack with only a few hundred men. The retreating Saracens had been filled with wide-eyed tales of the bravery of the English king, who had marched into battle against the defenders of the citadel with little more than a sword and a battle-ax. William had not been surprised, and he found it encouraging to know, that his king had not changed much since he had seen him last, despite the vicissitudes of war.

Staring out across the plain at his countrymen, William felt a sudden pang of sadness. He had spent almost a full year in the gracious company of the Sultan and had never been treated like a prisoner. The Muslims had shown him the utmost courtesy and he had grown to respect and admire their culture, traditions, and yes, even their religion. But he was still a foreigner. His home lay across the sands in the camp of his Christian brothers. He did not know if he would live to see the next day, but if he were to die in battle, he wished it to be in the company of his own people. William no longer knew or cared which side served God and the cause of right. All he knew was that he belonged with his nation.

He turned his head to see Saladin watching him closely. William had come to believe that the Sultan possessed an almost mystic power that allowed him to read the hearts of men, and when Saladin spoke, that belief was again confirmed.

"Return to your master," Saladin said with a gentle smile. "He needs you this day."

William blinked. He had assumed that he had been brought along with the army from Jerusalem to serve as an interpreter or a bargaining chip—the usual roles played by prisoners of war in such circumstances, but he realized now that it had been Saladin's plan to let him go all along.

"You are the most gracious of men, Sultan," he said in his now flawless Arabic. "But know that if I go, and we meet on the battlefield, I will not hesitate to slay you."

Saladin nodded, unperturbed by the knight's warning.

"No quarter shall be given on my end as well," he said with the same polite frankness. The Sultan stared at the buzz of activity a thousand feet away in the Crusader camp, but to William's eyes he seemed to be looking much farther away, beyond the limits of time and space. "Perhaps we will meet again in the hereafter, Sir William. I would like to think men of honor may dine together in Paradise, regardless of which side they fought for in this world."

William extended his hand to the Sultan.

"It would be my honor to dine with you at the table of the Lord."

Saladin grasped his hand firmly. William took a moment to look into his enemy's eyes—his friend's eyes—and then rode down toward the row of sparkling tents that was his home.

— — —

WILLIAM TOOK A SEAT at Richard's table and enjoyed a glass of wine as the beaming king clapped his hand on his shoulder in joyous welcome. The knight was struck by how different his monarch looked. His face

was still young, his features bronzed by the Palestine sun, his hair sparkling like red gold, but his eyes had aged terribly. The fire of enthusiasm
that had once burned in them had been replaced by a cold bitterness, an
edge sharper than any blade in the Crusader arsenal.

"What can you tell us of their forces?"

William let the cold draft soothe his throat, which had been parched
by the long trek from Jerusalem under the unforgiving sun. It was the
first drop of alcohol that he had tasted since his capture by the Muslims,
who abhorred fermented drinks as the work of the Devil.

"Evenly matched to ours. They have more archers, but we have an
advantage in horses."

Richard nodded.

"Then the Battle of Jaffa must be in close quarters to press our
advantage."

William finished the wine and rose to face his master.

"I have always thought it more honorable to face your enemy in
hand-to-hand combat than in a siege from the distance."

Richard's face fell and he suddenly looked remarkably like the late
King Henry, tired and worn down by the world he commanded.

"I have learned a great deal about honor in this strange land. The
Saracens speak much of it, yet the way they put it into practice is peculiar. Particularly when it comes to the honor of kings."

William put a gentle hand on Richard's arm. He knew that the
drama and the intrigues of the war had taken a terrible toll on his friend's
heart.

"Saladin did not betray Conrad to Sinan," William said suddenly.
For some reason, he felt the need to restore the reputation of his former
captor. He hesitated, and then added what he had come to learn from
the whispers of the court. "It was the Jewish doctor."

Richard stared at him with wide-eyed surprise, and then burst out
laughing.

"This is all madness. All of it."

William had never heard such weary exasperation in Richard's voice.
"My lord?"

Richard turned to face him, a hint of sadness on his handsome features.

"William, I finally understand what my father said so many years
ago. We should never have embarked on this Crusade. It was insanity."

William was shocked at the admission, but he saw a cloud lift from Richard's face even as he spoke.

"I always agreed with him, sire," the knight responded truthfully.

Richard walked to the opening of his command tent and stared out beyond the rows of his own forces to the shining blur on the horizon that was the camp of the enemy army.

"Part of the madness is that I have lived in this land for many months, yet I do not even know who these men are," Richard said softly. He turned his eyes on William again. "You have spent time with the Muslims. Are they good people?"

William hesitated, and then decided that his king really did wish to hear his honest thoughts on the matter.

"Yes, sire. They are good people."

The king nodded, but pressed the point.

"Are they like us?"

William gazed out at the Saracen forces and then said aloud a truth which he believed neither side was ready to accept, and perhaps never would be.

"They *are* us."

A thoughtful expression crossed Richard's features, and then he clasped a firm hand on his knight's shoulder and led him outside into the merciless sunlight.

"Come, let us finish this. The judgment of history awaits."

70

Al-Adil stared out across the field as the armies prepared for the final battle. He squinted through his brother's viewing lens as he took in the defensive line gathered at the edge of the Frankish camp. Actually there appeared to be two lines. The front row consisted of infantry, footmen who were leaning with spears fixed in the sand and pointing up diagonally. Al-Adil realized that they were positioned in such a way that any Muslim horsemen who charged would risk having his stallion impaled by the lethal lances. Slightly behind these soldiers stood a row of crossbowmen, each archer placed between two of the kneeling defenders. All in all, about two thousand men were lined up to serve as the primary human shields against the Muslim onslaught, about a fifth of whom were armed with the lethal crossbows that were the bane of the Muslim forces.

Al-Adil had to grudgingly admit that the strategy was smartly conceived, but relied on absolute discipline among the Crusader infantry who would bear the brunt of the Muslim attack. Any break in their resolve and there would be an opening that his men could exploit. As the giant Kurd took in his pale-faced enemies through a sweep of the lens, he froze. A familiar soldier in sparkling armor was riding up and down the line, but this was no ordinary general. The golden-haired youth carried in his hand the lion standard of the king, and beside him rode William Chinon, the knight whom his brother, succumbing to sentimentality, had unwisely freed on the eve of the battle.

So this was it. The Lionheart himself would lead the attack.

Al-Adil quickly passed the lens to his brother, who sat beside him on the raised command post. Although al-Adil had met the arrogant king during several diplomatic missions over the past year, the Sultan had never before seen his adversary in person.

"The Lion's ass graces us with his presence."

Saladin raised an eyebrow and stared through the lens at the place where his brother was pointing.

"He is younger than I expected," the Sultan said with genuine surprise. Al-Adil remembered that he himself had reacted the same way when he had first met the barbarian leader. The boy had struck him as pompous and rash, two qualities that seemed to be much in evidence today as Richard put his own life on the line with his troops.

"He is also a fool if he intends to lead the charge," al-Adil said, rubbing his hands with delight at the thought of the Angevin leader falling under a hail of his men's arrows.

"Bravery and foolhardiness are all shades of the same color, brother," Saladin said with a shrug. And then his brother's face darkened. "What word of Miriam?"

Al-Adil grimaced. He had been placed in the unhappy position of supervising negotiations for the release of the Jewess, but his heralds had come back empty-handed.

"She is being held in the king's pavilion. He refuses to bargain for her freedom."

Saladin nodded. The Sultan leaned closer and spoke in a voice that was almost a whisper.

"If I am slain today, I will expect you to rescue her."

Something in Saladin's voice cast a pall over al-Adil's heart. His brother always acted before every battle as if victory was assured, even when the odds were heavily against him. But now Saladin not only seemed prepared for death; he sounded as if he welcomed the idea. Al-Adil turned to protest, and then saw a strange light in his brother's eyes that chilled him and choked the words back into his throat.

"I do not love the Jewess, but I love you, my brother," al-Adil said at long last. "You have my word. She will live to a ripe old age, pampered in the gardens of Egypt."

Saladin nodded, satisfied.

"*Insha'Allah.* If God wills."

The Sultan stood and faced the waiting legions that had gathered around the command post. Normally at such times, the Sultan gave a well-prepared, rousing speech calculated to fill his men with the courage of battle. But today he simply stood before his men, without fire or pride, but with a steady, earnest courage. He looked at the faces of his commanders, then into the eyes of the common soldiers who adored him, revered him more as a myth than a man, and finally he spoke words that al-Adil knew came directly from the heart.

"O warriors of Allah, hear me! For five years we have faced the Franks in a ruthless war to seize control of this sacred land. In all that time I have watched countless men, just like you, walk without fear to their deaths. How many of your brothers have you buried in that time? Men with wives and children. How many mothers have wept, knowing that the fruit of their loins, the beautiful babes that they once suckled at their bosoms, lie rotting in an anonymous sand pit, their names forgotten to history? You all know who I am, yet I must fear to say that I do not know most of you, and for that I am deeply ashamed. Not just of myself. I look with loathing at every throne on this earth, where a man may sit in ease and send others to their deaths, without ever knowing their lives. But such is the way of the world, my friends. Kings command, and soldiers die. And so, because I have led you here, many of you will die today as well.

"But I say this to you now, my brothers. Do not die for me. I am not worthy of such a sacrifice. But your wives, your children, your mothers—

it is for them that you stand here today. When you face the thundering charge of the infidels, when you see the flash of their swords descending toward your necks, the tips of their spears aimed at your hearts, remember that you stand and fight—and die—to protect those whom you love from such a fate. In the end, no cause, no idea, no strip of earth, sacred or profane, is worth the shedding of a single drop of blood. But there is one thing—indeed, the only thing—in all the heavens and the earth that is worth dying for. And that is love. If you fall today fighting for the sake of love, then my brothers you will reach a Paradise that is beyond any described by the poets or the theologians. It is a garden that transcends the eternal fountains and palaces and lovely maidens of the Hereafter. For love itself is Divine, and to die for love is to embrace immortality."

Al-Adil felt tears welling in his eyes and saw that many of the soldiers, men who had stoically withstood the terrible injuries of war and hate, were weeping openly. He looked up in wonder at his brother, whose very person seemed to radiate a glow that outshone the fierceness of the Jaffa sun. Like Moses descending from the mountain carrying the tablets of the Lord, Saladin's face emanated such intense light that it was impossible to look upon him directly.

At that moment he realized that he had never truly known his brother. Saladin had been born into the family of Ayyub, but he was not of them. He was more than a mere scion of the simple clan of Kurdish mercenaries from which he had sprung. He was a holy spark descending from the firmament, and for some inexplicable reason, he had chosen to set his feet among the most improbable people—uncouth ruffians who had sold their allegiance to the highest bidder for a thousand generations. Al-Adil felt suddenly truly humbled by the knowledge that he shared his blood with this man, in whose striking features and noble character it was said that a last hint of the Prophet could be found on earth. He did not know why someone as coarse and mean as himself was fated to be Saladin's brother. But he did know, in that instant, that he loved this man more than his own life and the world combined.

Saladin turned to face the enemy camp a thousand feet away. He raised his fist in a final call to defiance against the forces of hate and barbarism that stood gathered on the doorstep of civilization. And then he let out the battle cry that would send thirty thousand men hurtling toward death in the name of love.

"Allahu Akbar!"

＊ ＊ ＊

THE CLASH WAS UNLIKE anything either side had seen before. Wave after wave of Muslim horsemen raced toward the defensive lines of Richard's forces, which held their ground under the steady barrage. Horses fell to spear and crossbow, hurling Muslim knights to the hard ground; those who survived the fall picked themselves up and charged the infantry directly. Scimitar met broadsword in an explosion of steel. Richard's crossbowmen fired volley after volley, but every soldier who fell to a bolt was quickly replaced by two others madly rushing toward certain death and the promise of Paradise.

It had become almost impossible to see the battlefield under the thick cloud of dust and smoke, but Saladin continued to peer through his viewing lens for any sign of a breakthrough. The infidels were valiant, he had to give them that. Their defensive lines held, despite the tidal wave of turbaned soldiers that flung itself against the human wall that stood between them and the Crusader camp. He could smell the terrible stench of piss and blood wafting across the field on the hot summer wind, the twin manifestations of the fear and rage that fueled men in war.

And then, as the cloud of battle cleared for an instant, Saladin saw the golden-haired boy who had been identified to him as his archenemy charge on his horse straight into the onrushing Muslim forces. Behind him was a contingent of fifty or sixty heavily armored knights, their massive shields held out before them as they followed their king's suicidal attack.

Richard seemed to have absolutely no fear as he struck out at attacker upon attacker, his sword cleaving the heads and arms of anyone who dared stand in his way. The dramatic thrust of the Templars into the center of Saladin's advancing army was quickly spreading confusion and terror in the hearts of his men. Many of the Sultan's soldiers began to flee at the approach of the Frankish stallions, even though they vastly outnumbered the knights on all sides.

"He is a great warrior," Saladin admitted at last to al-Adil, who sat beside him on the raised command post and was following the battle through his own lens.

"His death at our hands will be sung for many generations," his brother grunted confidently.

Saladin sighed.

"No, my brother. There is no music in war."

Saladin stood up and mounted his ebony steed, al-Qudsiyyah. He knew he needed to enter the fray on the field in order to reinvigorate his men, give them a rallying point to inspire their courage. Al-Adil immediately followed him and jumped onto his own stallion without a single word, although Saladin could see the glee in his eyes at the thought of joining the battle. The two sons of Ayyub rode out across the field, followed by forty of Saladin's greatest knights who would not let their leader charge into battle alone.

As he rode into the haze of death, Saladin kept his eyes out for the Lionheart, but he was impossible to see in the confusion and chaos all around him. And then the Sultan saw a Crusader knight rushing toward him and he held out his scimitar, prepared for the challenge.

It was Sir William.

Saladin hesitated, but saw that the knight did not slow in his advance, and he knew he would have no choice. *Maktub*. It was written.

"No quarter, Sultan!" William shouted above the din of the madness swirling all around them. Saladin raised his shield just in time and absorbed the bone-cracking blow of William's lance. In one swift move, he spun around and struck the lance with his scimitar. The Damascus steel tore through the wooden spear like a knife through butter.

"No quarter, Sir William," Saladin said softly as the knight dropped his shattered lance and withdrew his broadsword.

The two rode directly at each other. Their swords clashed and sparks flew. Saladin was no longer young, but he had trained daily with his scimitar since he had first learned of the new Frankish invasion. He knew that his age and experience helped him on the throne, but that the only thing that mattered on the battlefield was brute power.

William appeared surprised at the ruthless force of Saladin's attack, but even as he countered and parried, Saladin could see him grin under his helmet, as if they were two schoolboys and this was nothing more than a game. He smiled softly in return, even though he knew that there would be no joy at the outcome of this battle.

Blow after blow, the friends who were enemies circled and lashed out. Saladin forgot the battle raging around him and focused his mind on his opponent. They were alone in the desert. Dancing. He felt himself go to the still, small place of peace that always shrouded his heart just as he was about to deal death to a foe.

And then Saladin lunged and severed William's hand at the wrist.

The knight appeared more startled than in pain as he looked down at the blood spurting from the stump of his sword arm. He looked up and faced the Sultan, their eyes meeting for what felt like an eternity.

And then, without breaking his gaze into William's soul, Saladin plunged his scimitar through the knight's heavy breastplate, felt it tear the wire mesh beneath, rip through skin and bone, and pierce the other man's heart.

And then, incredibly, William smiled with a warmth that bordered on love.

"Until we dine in Paradise, then . . ." he said, even as his eyes began to close.

Saladin felt his own vision blur.

"Until then, my friend."

Sir William Chinon slumped forward on his mount.

Saladin reached forward and took the horse's reins in his hand. As the battle raged all around him, he led William's stallion that carried the body of his adversary back toward the Muslim camp.

He heard al-Adil ride up behind him. When his brother saw William's corpse, he removed his helmet and saluted the fallen knight.

Saladin dismounted and did not look at his men. He did not wish them to see the tears that were streaming down his face. In all his years of warfare, he had never allowed himself to weep for a slain comrade while a battle still raged. But today he allowed himself to weep for an enemy. An infidel and a heathen. And the truest man of God Saladin had ever met.

"Send him back to Richard with an honor guard," Saladin called out to his soldiers without raising his head.

71

Richard stared in disbelief at the body of his lifelong friend William. Wrapped in a sheet of white silk, the corpse had been carried to the war-ravaged Crusader camp under a herald's flag. Saladin had sent an honor guard of seven knights to escort the remains, but after seeing the look of horror and animal rage on the king's face, the men had quickly turned on their heels and ridden to their own zone of safety.

Richard knelt before William and saw his tears drop on to the bloodstained and torn breastplate of his fallen comrade. He choked back a sob as his eyes fell upon the jagged stump where the knight's right hand had once been.

"Forgive me for bringing you here," he said softly. It was his fault. William had counseled against this mad adventure, and yet Richard listened only to his pride. And now the one man in the world whom Richard loved like a brother was gone.

Richard let out a terrible scream of hate. Hatred for Saladin and his murderous hordes. Hatred for the nobles whose machinations had compelled him to resort to this bitter and intractable conflict. And finally, and most fiercely, hatred for himself. It should not have been William who died this day. It should have been him.

And then, with a sudden burst of white fire in his heart, Richard stood up and stamped over to his horse. Before any of his commanders could react, the king jumped on his stallion and rode like lightning straight into the midst of the churning battleground. He tore his jeweled broadsword free of its scabbard and then lashed out at anything that moved. He did not care whether he killed Saladin's men or his own. He would deal death to the world as easily and unthinkingly as it had dealt death to William.

"Murderers! Feel the wrath of the Lionheart!" He heard his own voice but it sounded like it was coming from a great distance. Men fell before him to his right and left, their heads severed, their eyes slashed out, as his blade flew in a whirlwind of bitter rage.

He was vaguely aware that he had single-handedly penetrated the Muslims' defensive perimeter and was deep into the enemy's side of the plain. There stood before him a legion of a thousand men on horseback, their spears pointing at his heart. He was alone on the enemy's terrain, without a single ally near enough to aid him, and he did not care.

Richard rode up and down the stunned lines of turbaned soldiers, who stared at each other, wondering whether this was some elaborate ruse. Why would the king of the Christians ride out and challenge the entire Muslim army alone, unless he sought to trap them in some fashion? Some of the horsemen stared down at the ground before them, their eyes scanning to see if hidden trenches filled with thousands of Franks were about to burst open at their feet.

Richard waved his sword before him, challenging the entire Muslim cavalry to take him on.

"Are you all cowards?" he bellowed. "Behold, the king of your enemies is in your midst. Fight me!"

One knight rode forward tentatively, his scimitar raised. Richard rode at him, pouring all of his rage on the one man who'd had the temerity to confront his madness. The knight had barely raised his weapon to strike when Richard sent his sword tearing through the lamellar plates that protected his stomach. His blade went in with such force that he could feel the man's spine snapping at the force of his weapon.

As the turbaned knight fell to the ground, another rose to take his place. And then another. Richard felt like he was swimming in a strange dream. A dozen men seemed to be coming at him, and yet he felt no fear. He channeled all the hate and rage that had weighed on his soul over the past year through his sword arm, and the enemy fell one by one, like paper dolls.

And then he heard the high-pitched keen of an arrow flying across the plain, and he raised his head with a smile, welcoming the sought-after release of death.

But the bolt fell low, striking his valiant horse in the side. The animal reared in agony and flung Richard from his saddle. The Lionheart crashed into the blood-soaked earth as the steed fell over and lay still.

Dripping with black mud and the blood of the soldiers he had slaughtered with such ruthless ease, Richard stood up and held his sword aloft in continued challenge. Yet the line of archers did not move. They sat there on their steeds watching the raving monarch with awe and dread. Here was obviously a man with a wish to die, yet he was far deadlier to those who sought to grant him his wish than they were to him.

"Damn you all! Dogs! Swine! Are there no men among you?"

A terrible silence hung over the plain. And then Richard saw a strange sight. The cavalry parted and made way for a turbaned giant riding a gray charger. He was holding the reins of a magnificent black Arabian stallion, which he led toward the king.

Richard recognized the man. It was the red-bearded brute known as al-Adil, the brother of the Muslim Sultan. The Kurdish warrior stopped directly in front of the dismounted king and nodded a curt greeting.

"A gift from my brother the Sultan, to Richard, King of the Angevin," al-Adil said. "This is al-Qudsiyyah, the Sultan's personal stallion. A man of your courage deserves to fight on a steed of equal valor."

Hearing al-Adil address him by name broke the strange spell of madness that had taken possession of Richard's mind. He felt dizzy, as if he had just awakened after another bout of the dreaded camp fever that had nearly killed him a year before. He managed to keep his unsteady legs from shaking as he stepped forward and grasped the offered reins with a gracious bow.

"My brother also sends his regret for the death of Sir William. He was a good man," al-Adil said. "You should know that your noble knight did not fall by the hand of any man less than the Sultan himself."

Richard felt his heart grow cold at the giant's words.

"Tell your brother that even as I have lost someone I loved, so will he," the king said in a loud, controlled voice. "Out of respect for his chivalrous actions this day, I shall spare the traitorous Jewess for one more night. But on the morrow, the Sultan will receive her head in a gold box."

Then, without another word, the Lionheart climbed atop Saladin's horse and rode back through the vortex of battle toward the Crusader camp.

72

Night had fallen and the warring forces had retreated to their respective corners of the Jaffa plain. There was no point in continuing the conflict as they could barely see each other in the pitch-black that had descended upon them with the setting of the sun. The new moon was a slim crescent hidden behind the billowing clouds of smoke that covered the devastated battlefield. The only men moving on the cracked and bloodied earth were dark-robed workers belonging to both sides. These were conscripts from neighboring villages that had fallen under either Crusader or Muslim control over the past few months who worked under a flag of mercy to remove the thousands of rotting corpses from the battlefield before pestilence set in and soldiers on both sides died of the plague.

As the grisly process of clearing the field and preparing for another day of slaughter continued, one of the workers broke from the others and slid carefully toward the Crusader camp. Moving with remarkable speed and stealth, the figure eluded detection by the roving patrols of Crusader guards as he crept toward his goal: the crimson command pavilion of King Richard. The act of espionage he was attempting was sheer madness, but the man who was attempting it was not a normal spy.

Saladin had slipped out in the middle of the night from his own camp without telling anyone, including his brother, al-Adil. If he were captured now, the Muslim forces would be thrown into absolute disarray and the war would likely end in their rapid defeat. The Sultan knew that he was risking not only his life, but also his entire kingdom by this uncharacteristically reckless act. And he did not care.

Saladin stealthily approached a hillock overlooking the battlefield. Towering a hundred feet above him was the scarlet military tent that was his destination. There were no sentries on the southern face of the hill, as the Crusaders had deemed passage along the sheer, vertical cliff wall to be beyond the capacity of anything that lacked the natural gifts of a spider. While the Sultan did not claim to possess such abilities, he did have his own means for scaling the heights. From within his slave's robes, he removed two specially crafted daggers, forged with the sharpest Damascus steel in the Muslim armory. Saladin plunged the blades as deep as their hilts into the dark rock of the wall. And then he began his careful ascent, clawing his way a foot at a time toward the summit.

The Sultan lost all track of time as he scaled the wall of earth. As the safety of solid ground vanished far beneath him, he forced himself to look straight up and ahead. Saladin knew that his vaunted courage would likely vanish in a moment if he dared even to glance down at the deadly rocks that were far below him.

After what could have been hours or even days, so little was he aware of the passage of time, he scaled the side of the cliff and fell to his knees on a patch of cold gray mud. His heart was still racing and he found it difficult to refocus his mind on the task ahead. Saladin took a series of deep breaths and recited the ninety-nine names of Allah softly as he sought to regain the calm and confidence necessary to fulfill his mission. Raising his head at last, he saw the ruby cloth of the master pavilion only a dozen feet away from the yawning edge of the cliff. Glancing around rapidly, he was gratified to see that there were no guards posted here. The Crusaders had assumed, like most rational men, that natural topography would serve as the greatest defense for the command pavilion. But Saladin had long since left the world of rational men.

The tent was a sprawling complex a hundred feet high and twice that in diameter. He guessed that it contained chambers where Richard's most important generals were housed, conference rooms where matters of state and war were debated, and storage facilities for the booty of war. But he was not interested in any of that. He was looking for only one room in the tent, a compartment that held the most important treasure in all the world.

Carefully reaching inside his black robes, Saladin removed a small but deadly sharp knife. He tore a hole in the side of the pavilion just large enough for him to slip inside, then whirled in all directions, prepared to kill anyone who had witnessed his arrival. But he was alone.

Saladin cautiously wandered through the darkened pavilion, ducking into a curtained section when he heard the sound of approaching voices. Two Crusader soldiers walked by, probably on their way to some late-night strategy session with their commanders, but they did not see him hiding in the shadows. Saladin allowed himself a small smile as he wondered what they would have done had they known that the king of their enemies stood less than ten feet away. Probably pissed in their pants before they tried to raise the alarm, although they would have been dead before a sound could have formed in their throats.

He continued along a cloth corridor, his eyes darting around for any sign of danger, and then he froze. A sleepy-looking soldier stood guard around the corner, his portly body standing in front of a small chamber that Saladin immediately knew was his destination. Stepping up carefully behind the bored man with the curly brown beard, Saladin pulled from his robe a razor-thin piece of wire. And then he had his arms around the man's neck, the garrote cutting his breath off with vicious efficiency. The corpulent guard died without ever knowing that he had the honor of being cut down by none other than the great Sultan.

Pulling the corpse inside the chamber, Saladin turned to gaze at last upon the treasure for which he had risked everything.

Miriam had heard the muted sounds of struggle and had leaped from the cot on which she had been sleeping. She was dressed in a pale blue gown, her hair flowing wildly down her shoulders. At the sight of the dead guard and the dark-robed stranger, she sprang up, her fingers held out like claws before her.

"If you touch me, I will scream."

Saladin smiled, his face still hidden beneath the cowl of his slave robe.

"Yes," he said softly. "I recall how you used to respond to my touch. I was always rather flattered."

All the color rushed from Miriam's face as she recognized his voice. Saladin stepped forward and lowered his hood.

"Sayyidi . . . ?" Her face froze in an expression of disbelief.

And then she was in his arms. He felt his heart race wildly as her soft lips pressed against his. But she did not stop at his mouth. She kissed his cheeks and forehead in a frenzy bordering on hysteria, as if trying to convince herself that he was not a dream or a phantom.

"But this is madness," she gasped.

"You are right," Saladin said, taking her hand in his. How he had longed to touch her again! "This whole war is madness. But if it is insanity that will be my death, I would rather it be one that was rooted in my heart."

He kissed her again, felt the wonderful warmth of her bosom against his.

"But why did you come for me yourself? You have many trained spies."

Saladin caressed her cheek.

"Last night I stood at the Dome of the Rock and wept that I could see no light beyond this day. There was nothing to fill me except this wretched war. But then I dreamed of you and I knew that there was one thing still worth fighting for. Dying for."

Tears welled in her perfect emerald eyes and he felt his heart leap into his throat. And then the look of love on her face changed, to one of terror so deep that he felt a chill rush up his spine even before he heard the cold voice behind him.

"How touching."

Saladin turned to see Richard the Lionheart standing at the entrance to the cell, a gleaming broadsword in his hand.

ichard stared at the two-faced wench and her improbable savior, an aging Saracen with more gray in his beard than black. Ever since he had met Miriam, she had been full of surprises. Well, this would be the last surprise she would spring on him. He had long since told himself that his feelings for the Jewess had been no more than a disease of the heart, and one from which he had been permanently cured. But seeing her now, huddled intimately with the spy who had infiltrated the command pavilion, Richard found himself feeling the stirrings of jealousy.

"You have shared the bed of kings and yet you frolic with a commoner?" he asked with contempt before he could stop himself.

"Say nothing." Miriam had leaned forward to whisper to her rescuer in Arabic, but Richard caught the words. And he had lived in this land long enough to learn the basics of the infidel language.

"This spy will not have much to say after I tear out his tongue," Richard snarled. He stepped forward, raising his sword.

"So it comes to this at last." It was the spy who spoke now, and he did so in remarkably fluent French. Richard froze, realization of the impossible beginning to dawn. The man broke free of Miriam's embrace and opened his robe, letting the dark cloak fall to his feet. Underneath, he was dressed in sparkling lamellar armor, and on his steel breastplate was engraved the image of an eagle. "Peace be upon you, Richard of Aquitaine. I regret that kings must meet under such circumstances."

Richard stared at the man with the flowing hair and thick beard, his gaze peering into the eyes of his archenemy at last. It was the first time he had ever laid eyes on Saladin—

No. It was actually the second. A memory flashed unbidden into his mind, pulled from a jumble of mad images that had plagued him during the camp fever . . .

. . . The figure raised his bloody head, and Richard saw his blood-soaked, bearded face. A sudden cold terror gripped his heart. This was not his Lord, Je-

sus of Nazareth. Although he had never met the man in person, one look in his dark, ancient eyes revealed the truth.

The figure on the Cross was Saladin . . .

. . . And, impossibly, there he stood, in the flesh.

"Can it truly be?" Richard asked with sincere wonder. "So, you are the great Salah al-Din ibn Ayyub. This war never ceases to amaze me."

Saladin smiled and nodded courteously.

"It appears Allah has given you a unique opportunity. If you slay me now, Jerusalem will be yours without a fight."

Richard was well aware of this, and it made the situation only more unbelievable. He should have moved forward and decapitated his hated enemy with one blow, but he found himself frozen to the spot.

"Why did you come here?"

Saladin's face turned grave. His eyes met Richard's for a long moment before he answered.

"Why did you ride to certain death among my men?"

Richard stood like a statue before the Sultan. He knew the answer to that question, of course, but even as he willed himself to speak, he could feel the cold talons of pain and regret tearing into his heart.

"For William," the king said, fighting hard to keep the tremor from his voice.

Saladin nodded. There was a sudden look of deep compassion on the Saracen's face that reminded Richard again of his vision of Christ.

"You loved him," the Sultan said. There was something in his voice that suggested that Saladin understood, perhaps even shared, Richard's feelings for the fallen knight—the soldier whom the Sultan had murdered with his own hands earlier that day.

Staring at Saladin as he stood protectively beside Miriam, the woman they had both loved, Richard also suddenly understood. When he spoke again, it was as if a spirit from outside himself had taken possession of his tongue.

"Yes. I have learned that love is the only thing worth dying for."

Saladin glanced at Miriam, whose eyes were brimming with tears.

"Then you have my answer as well."

Richard stepped forward, as if pulled by a force greater than his own will. The unstoppable summons of fate.

"I have often wondered what kind of man you were," the Lionheart said, knowing full well what he had to do. "But I never really understood until today."

Saladin unsheathed his scimitar, his eyes never leaving the face of his steadily approaching adversary.

"Shall we end this here, then?" the Sultan asked simply, as if he were offering Richard a choice of drinks over dinner.

Richard grinned. This was all utterly mad, and yet standing here before his life's greatest enemy, he felt more peaceful and calm than he had ever experienced before.

"A war between civilizations to be decided by a duel?"

Saladin shrugged and raised his curved blade, assuming a ready stance. The men began to circle each other, their hips lowered in anticipation of a sudden move on the part of the opponent.

"What is any war ultimately but a conflict between two men?"

He was, of course, right.

"You are a wise ruler, Sultan. Now let us see if you are a warrior as well."

Without another word, Richard lunged at the Sultan, who met the slash of his broadsword with an elegant parry of the scimitar. Miriam screamed as the two utterly insane kings traded blows in a dance of destiny. As his sword clashed hard against Saladin's blade, Richard felt a rising wave of exhilaration in his soul. It felt as if his entire life had been nothing more than a rehearsal for this grand moment.

The sound of Miriam's cry and the lethal clanging of blades drew the attention of every guard in the pavilion. When the men arrived, they stood stunned at the sight of their leader locked in an epic struggle with the bearded Saladin. One quick glance from Richard's cold blue eyes signaled to his soldiers to stay back. This battle was between the king and the Sultan.

Saladin was an elegant fighter, with considerable skill and dexterity, but Richard still maintained the physical advantage of youth and the psychological advantage of fighting in his own territory. He pushed the Sultan back again and again, until he was trapped against the cloth walls of the pavilion.

Saladin raised his scimitar to strike, and Richard feinted to the left. Before the Sultan could lower his blade to block the attack, Richard's sword had smashed against the circular plates of his lamellar armor and cut into his side. The Sultan fell to his knees in pain.

"NO!" Miriam tried to jump on Richard from behind but one of his men grabbed her and pinned her arms to her sides. She continued to kick and scream like a crazed demon as Richard held his blade to Saladin's neck.

And then, at the very moment of the greatest victory of his life, the terrible vision intruded into his mind's eye again, so real that he felt as if he had been transported into the dream by some devilish magic . . .

. . . He could see Saladin, bloodied and covered in scars, hanging from the Cross as a Roman centurion, a solider bearing Richard's face, stabbed the tortured man with a spear to the side.

And then he heard the voice of his father echoing through the plain of Golgotha.

"You cannot fight for him, my son. He has already won."

Richard raised his head and stared at Saladin, who gazed down at him from the Cross, his gaze filled not with hate or recrimination but with gentle compassion. The veiled woman kneeling before the Cross, the lady he knew to be the Virgin Mary, was looking at him as well. Her scarf fell and he saw that she bore the tear-streaked face of Miriam . . .

Richard was frozen, unable to move. As his eyes glanced involuntarily at Miriam, Saladin took advantage of his mental confusion and pounced. With incredible speed for a man of his age, the Sultan threw himself against the king and knocked Richard's broadsword across the room. As his men watched in helpless horror, the tables turned. Richard the Lionheart now stood before Saladin with a scimitar at his throat.

Richard gazed into the Sultan's midnight-black eyes without any fear. He was ready at long last for the end.

"Kill me and be done with it."

He saw Saladin glance at Miriam, who was still being restrained by the guard but had stopped struggling. And then, as if he had never given it a second thought, the Sultan lowered his blade and threw it across the room. It landed atop Richard's sword with a clang.

"It is not fitting for kings to tear each other apart like rabid dogs," he said, like a teacher passing on a final lesson to a student. Saladin reached out his hand toward Miriam. The guard looked at the king in utter confusion, but Richard nodded. The man let her go and she ran into Saladin's arms.

The Sultan turned his attention back to the Lionheart.

"Neither of us can win this war," he said with finality. "We both know this to be true. Let us end it without further bloodshed." He paused, his face becoming grave. "The world should not lose any more Williams."

At the mention of his dead friend, the vision played out one last time before Richard's eyes . . .

. . . One of the disciples who bowed before Christ turned to face him, his face strangely peaceful, filled with forgiveness.

It was the face of William . . .

. . . And the king understood at long last.

"So be it," Richard said with a bow. Even as the three simple words of acquiescence, ratifying the truce, fell from his lips, he felt a weight lift off his shoulders. A burden that had always weighed down his soul, and yet he had never even been aware of its presence. The crushing weight of history had vanished and Richard Plantagenet could at that moment be a human being again.

Saladin nodded and moved to leave the arena where this final drama of the war had unfolded. Richard's men stepped forward to stop him, but the king raised his hand. The confused soldiers backed away as the Sultan and his beloved Miriam walked toward freedom.

Saladin turned to smile at his enemy one last time, and Richard heard himself uttering words he could never have imagined himself saying to a Saracen.

"In another life, we could have been brothers."

The Sultan's eyes twinkled. He took Miriam's hand in his and kissed it softly, gazing into her sea-green eyes for a long moment. And then Saladin turned to face Richard the Lionheart, his greatest enemy, his smile seeming to radiate the light of a thousand suns.

"Perhaps in this life, we already are."

Epilogue

Jaffa—September 2, 1192

aimonides gazed across the plain of Jaffa at a sight he could never have imagined. The two armies were still camped at either end of the field, but there were no more arrows being fired across the expanse. Instead thousands of soldiers from both sides stood at attention in front of a massive cedar platform that had been hastily erected during the final days of the negotiations.

Their swords had been sheathed. They cast no shadow today.

The ceremony had been carefully planned by representatives of the warring parties to grant equal dignity and honor to the opposing leaders. The sun shone directly above them, but the torturous heat of August had faded into the lulling warmth of September. A gentle breeze was wafting in from the coast, where Richard's fleet was preparing to lift anchor and begin the long journey back to Europe.

Richard and Saladin stood together a few feet away from him. Both were dressed in full military regalia. The Lionheart wore a sparkling suit of dress armor that likely had never seen a day in combat. The Sultan, for his part, stubbornly refused to part with the dented and time-worn lamellar vest that had saved his life through the years, but in deference to the ceremonious occasion, he had donned a sparkling green turban and a gray cloak emblazoned with his eagle insignia. Saladin was saying something to Richard in a low voice, which made the king laugh heartily. Anyone who did not know the bitter history between the two men would have thought that they were the closest of allies, the elder ruler serving as a wise father figure to the golden-haired youth who had been entrusted with the guidance of a nation.

The Sultan glanced at Maimonides, and to the rabbi's delight, his old friend smiled warmly. The rift between them had not yet fully healed, but he was confident that with the ending of the war, they would be able to resume their former intimacy. That the same was true about the Sultan's relationship with his beloved niece, he could not say for certain.

The old man's eyes fell on Miriam, who stood beside Saladin resplendent in a sparkling gown of blue silk, her hair covered in a shimmering scarf that looked as if real diamonds had been sewn into the fabric. He felt a sad tug in his heart. The rabbi knew not what life held in store for her, nor did he think she herself knew. She had refused to speak of Saladin to her uncle when they had been tearfully reunited after her release. All she would say was that she was heading back to Cairo with the Sultan's blessing. The subject of Saladin's plans to join her, as he had once promised to do in the rabbi's presence, neither had mentioned, nor did the rabbi press the matter. But as he caught the gentle glances that passed between the Sultan and Miriam, he knew, and accepted, that the bond between their hearts would remain, even if they could not be together under the laws of God or man.

Behind the Sultan stood a pale, yellow-haired creature that the rabbi had been told was Richard's sister, Joanna. The princess was whispering to al-Adil, the man whom she had nearly married in an effort to end the vicious conflict. Rumors were spreading among the people that al-Adil had been so flattered by the beautiful girl's willingness to enter his bed for the sake of peace that he had begun to woo her in secret. Maimonides did not usually give much credence to gossip when it came to dalliances among various nobles, but seeing the pretty girl giggle and blush at something the uncultured al-Adil whispered in his poor French made him wonder all the same.

The ceremony was about to begin and all attention turned to the black-garbed Patriarch of Jerusalem, who stepped up to an oak table at the center of the platform, behind which Saladin and Richard stood. In front of each of the kings was a copy of a lengthy document, prepared in Arabic and French, which listed the terms of the peace treaty. Heraclius handed both men quill pens as he read aloud the agreement of truce for the benefit of the thousands who had come to witness the ceremony. The priest's voice boomed across the field, echoing with such power that Maimonides wondered whether God had not adjusted the winds in order to spread tidings of the triumphant proclamation of peace through the world.

As the Patriarch spoke, Maimonides gazed in wonder at the nobles gathered on the dais. Born in different corners of the world, they had been thrown together in this strange land that seemed to bring out the best and worst in the human spirit. Destiny had caused the paths of their lives to cross. And yet they had chosen to free themselves from the shackles of fate. They had seized the pen of fortune in their own hands and written a new course for themselves and their nations. These men and women had left behind the beaten paths of war and enmity, and were now walking together through an uncharted realm toward an uncertain destination. They did not know what awaited them as they marched toward the horizon of time, but they all knew that they could no longer look back to a past filled only with sorrow and savagery.

And so it was that the two men of war met that day on the plain of Jaffa as men of peace. The truce was a victory for neither side, and, yet, a victory for both. The Muslims and the Jews would retain Jerusalem. The Christians would hold sway over the coastal cities. It was an imperfect arrangement, but what more could be expected? They were, in truth, all imperfect men. It was a lesson in compromise and forgiveness that the rabbi hoped his children and their children would remember. But he feared in his heart that the God of irony had some more twists and turns in store for the Holy Land that he could not as yet envision.

Then again, perhaps he was wrong. Perhaps the days of war in Jerusalem were finally over. Perhaps the city of Jews, Christians, and Muslims would at last fulfill its destiny as the Abode of Peace.

Salah al-Din ibn Ayyub and Richard the Lionheart signed the treaty, bringing the Crusade to an end. As thunderous applause echoed throughout the plain, the cries of jubilation soaring up toward heaven, the warriors of God reached out across the divide of civilizations and shook hands.

Author's Note

$\mathcal{W}$hile based on historical events, this book is a work of fiction. Readers who wish to learn more about Saladin and Richard the Lionheart should consult the many reference books written about these pivotal figures in history. One of the oldest books still in print about the Third Crusade is *Saladin and the Fall of Jerusalem* by Stanley Lane Poole. Originally published in 1898, this classic text was reprinted in 2002 by Greenhill Books and remains one of the most important and scholarly books about this period. More recent books that examine the remarkable personalities involved in this conflict are *Lionhearts: Richard I, Saladin and the Era of the Third Crusade* by Geoffrey Regan and *Warriors of God* by James Reston Jr. *Saladin: The Politics of the Holy War* by Malcolm Cameron Lyons and D.E.P. Jackson is a wonderfully detailed book that brings to life this great Muslim hero and the world that he lived in and ruled over. To get an eyewitness view of life during Saladin's reign, readers are referred to *The Book of Contemplation: Islam and the Crusades* by Usama ibn Munqidh. The book is a twelfth-century autobiographical account by an aristocrat in Saladin's court and is published by Penguin Classics.

For those who wish to learn more about the general history of the Crusades, *A History of the Crusades, Volumes 1–3,* by Steven Runciman is a magisterial work that has been popular since the 1950s. A more recent and well-received work of scholarship is *God's War: A New History of the Crusades* by Christopher Tyerman. *The First Crusade: A New History* by Thomas Asbridge focuses on the origins of the clash between Christianity and Islam whose impact is still felt on the world scene today.

Many readers who are accustomed to viewing the history of the Crusades from a Western perspective may find several books that relate these events from the point of view of the other side to be enlightening. *The Crusades Through Arab Eyes* by Amin Malouf and *Arab Historians of the Crusades* by Francesco Gabrielli provide an eye-opening look at how these epochal conflicts are perceived by Muslims.

For those interested in the figure of Maimonides, the great rabbi who served as Saladin's personal adviser, many books are available. *Maimonides: The Life and World of One of Civilization's Greatest Minds* by Joel L. Kraemer does an excellent job of capturing the personality and impact of this great Jewish thinker. *Maimonides* by Abraham Joshua Heschel gives readers a sense of why the rabbi remains central to Jewish identity today. And for those who wish to read the works of the Rambam himself, *The Guide for the Perplexed* by Moses Maimonides is available in a variety of translations from the original Arabic.

For readers fascinated by Jerusalem, Karen Armstrong's wonderful book *Jerusalem: One City, Three Faiths* explores the magical power that this city has held over humanity throughout the ages. Another great book that explains the history and meaning of this sacred city is *Jerusalem: City of Longing* by Simon Goldhill.

Students of history will recognize that I have taken some liberties with facts in order to write this book. Several characters are purely fictional. Miriam, Sir William Chinon, and the Sultana Yasmeen are products of my imagination, although I have endeavored to make them feel real to the world in which they are projected. Miriam symbolizes the tough spirit of survival evinced by the Jewish community throughout history, and her relationship with Saladin is meant to explore the intimacy that once existed between Muslims and Jews before the recent political conflicts in the Middle East. The character of Sir William is based partially on Lord William Marshal, one of the most important knights during Richard's reign, and is an attempt to dramatize how a sincere Christian would have viewed the horrific events of the Crusades that sullied the reputation of the Church for centuries. As for Sultana Yasmeen, little is known of Saladin's wives, allowing me room to create a vivid character who reveals the tremendous power women of the harem actually wielded in Muslim royal courts.

For those who know little of the history behind these events, some moments in my story may appear so improbable as to have been purely fictional, and yet they are historically accurate. Saladin's chivalry was renowned by both Christians and Muslims, and gestures such as his decision to send a doctor to save Richard's life, and his gift of a horse to Richard in the heat of battle, are recorded by historians. Saladin's character was quite remarkable, and he remains a personal hero of mine. His honor and generosity toward his enemies represent a nobility of soul that is rarely seen in politicians and leaders today, and I hope I have captured the essence of his spirit.

My portrayal of Richard the Lionheart, on the other hand, may be troubling to some readers who are accustomed to seeing him through the lens of myth. Richard remains a fixture in Western popular culture today because of his association with the legendary exploits of Robin Hood. And yet the Richard of history is a far darker figure than the one portrayed in these heroic fantasies. He was deeply anti-Semitic, and barred Jews from attending his coronation. When Jewish leaders made the mistake of arriving at his court with gifts of honor for the new king, he had them stripped and flogged. Richard's brutality during the Crusades, particularly his execution of nearly three thousand innocent hostages at Acre, weighs on any historian's efforts to paint a positive picture of the man.

And his ruthlessness ultimately led to his downfall. After Richard left Palestine and returned to Europe, he was arrested and imprisoned in Austria by disgruntled nobles until his mother, Eleanor of Aquitaine, finally secured his release in 1194. He returned to his native France, where he continued to battle against his many enemies. In March 1199, Richard suppressed a revolt led by the Viscount of Limoges, devastating the land surrounding the viscount's castle with fire. His attack on this poorly defended building proved to be his final act of hubris. Richard was struck down by a young archer he had taunted, and the arrow wound led to his death on April 6, 1199. Richard the Lionheart was by all accounts a brave warrior, but he was also proud, cruel, and often unwise, and I am hopeful that my characterization of the king will be seen in that light. In many ways, I have attempted to portray Richard as being more complex and conflicted in his conscience than history credits him as being, simply because I find one-dimensional villains to be uninteresting.

By contrast, Saladin is revered throughout the Muslim world as a shining exemplar of morality and justice, and so I understand that some Muslims will take offense at my decision to portray him as having faults and weaknesses, especially in the love story I have crafted. But I do not apologize for my use of poetic license. As a practicing Muslim, I believe that only God is perfect, and it is extremely dangerous (and un-Islamic) to place human beings on a pedestal of infallibility. Saladin's legacy of honor speaks for itself, and yet he remained a man, and he would not have wanted to be turned into a plastic saint. My decision to show him as a complex and flawed human being, I hope, will only bring attention to the majesty of his soul and his remarkable achievements. Saladin was one of the few men in history who single-handedly changed the world. His death on March 4, 1193, a few months after Richard's fleet had departed, was greeted with tremendous grief throughout the Middle East. During preparations for his funeral, it was discovered that the Sultan had given nearly all his wealth to charity, and there was not enough money left to pay for his burial. Saladin was ultimately laid to rest in the garden of the Umayyad Mosque of Damascus, where his tomb remains to this day.

My hope in writing this book was to bring to life not only these remarkable personalities and events, but to encourage modern leaders to reflect on the lessons the Crusades hold for us today. In a world still torn by religious fanaticism, holy wars, and terror in the name of God, perhaps we can find within ourselves the ability to transcend the past. Perhaps we can see beyond labels such as Jew, Christian, and Muslim to look into the hearts of our adversaries. And if we are wise, perhaps we can see that ultimately we are all nothing more than mirrors. Those we love—and those we hate—are just reflections of ourselves.

To my readers, I wish you peace.

Acknowledgments

his novel has a long and special history. Although it is my second book to be published, after *Mother of the Believers*, it was written first. The manuscript was originally a screenplay that was written shortly after the horrific terrorist attacks of September 11, 2001. I had wanted to look at the issue of holy wars and religious fanaticism through the lens of history, and the Third Crusade was rife with lessons for people today. The original script attracted much interest in Hollywood, but visionary director Ridley Scott beat me to the screen with his wonderful film *Kingdom of Heaven*. Once it became clear that my movie script would be eclipsed by Mr. Scott's cinematic juggernaut, I turned the screenplay into a novel. The manuscript was completed in August 2003. I spent the next four years attempting to find a publisher, and was often disheartened by the constant stream of polite rejection letters.

And then in May 2007, I was introduced to Rebecca Oliver, a literary agent with Endeavor (now WME Entertainment). I had recently come to the agency as a screenwriting client, and my television agent, Scott Seidel, promised to pass along my manuscript to his colleague Rebecca. Scott was true to his word and convinced a reluctant Rebecca to look at a first-time novelist's epic manuscript on the Crusades.

By then, I had received so many rejections that I had little faith that Rebecca would respond positively. But miraculously, she did. And the rest is history.

My agent, Rebecca Oliver, single-handedly turned me from an unknown writer into a published author with an international following. And for that, I am beyond grateful. Rebecca was the first person to believe in me, and her commitment changed my life forever.

There are many others, of course, to whom I owe deep thanks. Scott Seidel for sending my novel to Rebecca and convincing her to read it.

Suzanne O'Neill, who originally purchased the manuscript for Simon & Schuster and secured a two-book deal that led to the publication of *Mother of the Believers* along with this novel. Peter Borland for his wise guidance as an editor and friend. Rosemary Ahearn for her detailed editorial advice on my manuscripts. Nick Simonds for his tireless support and enthusiasm. Erica and Anthony Samadani for their invaluable help reviewing the final manuscript. And Judith Curr and her incredible staff at Atria Books, who championed my books despite the difficult political climate in the world today.

And special thanks to my family. My sisters, Nausheen and Shaheen, who are talented writers and inspired me to keep plugging away at my novel. And to my parents, who encouraged me to follow my heart, even if the path was unclear and terrifying at times.

And, finally, I want to thank you. An author without a reader is just a lonely dreamer. It is for you I have written this book. Thank you for making my dream a reality.

SHADOW OF THE SWORDS

KAMRAN PASHA

A Readers Club Guide

In this sweeping historical novel, Kamran Pasha brings to life the Third Crusade and the epic battle between Richard the Lionheart, King of England, and the Muslim Sultan, Saladin. Just when Saladin has finally taken Jerusalem for the Muslims and believes a time of peace is setting in, King Richard is departing from England to regain the Holy City for Christianity. Another bloody war is launched in the name of God, as these two men fight for the honor and glory of their faiths and the love of one beautiful Jewess. In this deeply moving and thought-provoking novel, Pasha re-creates some of the most earth-shattering moments in history that still impact us today.

DISCUSSION QUESTIONS

1. Many examples of leadership are presented throughout the book: Saladin, King Guy, King Henry, Richard, Conrad. Discuss the leadership style of each of these characters. Is it better to be feared than loved? What makes each of these rulers successful or not?

2. Sir William muses that love is "the antidote to power" (p. 107). He believes that if more of his people were capable of reading the Bible and interpreting Christ's teachings for themselves, they would not be so eager to pursue a holy war. Reread this passage and discuss whether or not you agree with William. Could his thoughts also imply that knowledge is an antidote to power?

3. Miriam often serves to expose the weaknesses and human nature of the male protagonists. What do her relationships with Saladin and Richard show us about each of these men?

4. While the Muslims and Christians fight for Jerusalem, Maimonides reminds us that the Holy City had once belonged to the Jews; that "His people had once ruled this land where he now stood, from the emerald sea to the sparkling waters of the Jordan, and beyond" (p. 202). Does Saladin have any more right to the Holy City than Richard does?

5. Many references are made throughout the book to God's love of irony. How does irony play a role in the book and in the basic notion of the Crusades?

6. "Such was the nature of all men—they would move Heaven and earth to protect their loved ones, but would rarely raise a finger to

save a stranger, even if they were bound by all the laws of God and men" (p. 269). How is this notion supported in the book? Do you believe this is true of human nature?

7. The Sultana is a jealous, conniving, and manipulative character. Do you think her death was justified? Why do you think her maid was put to death as well?

8. Discuss Maimonides' act of revenge. Was it out of character? Can you sympathize with him? Do you think he regrets his decision when everything is said and done?

9. William is both a loyal friend to Richard and an admirer of Saladin. Why do you think he remains so loyal to Richard when it is clear that he has disagreed with this war all along? How is it possible for William and Saladin to be both friends and enemies at the same time?

10. What symbolism do you interpret from Richard's dream in which Saladin's face appears on the crucified body of Christ, Miriam is the Virgin Mary, and Richard himself drives a spear into the body on the cross?

11. It might be said that war was both more savage and more civilized during the Crusades than it is today. In what ways is this demonstrated in the novel? Do you agree with this statement?

12. Reread Saladin's speech on pages 359–360. How does this put the *jihad* in perspective? In what ways does it move you?

ENHANCE YOUR BOOK CLUB

1. What would it really have been like for a woman during the time of the Crusades? Find out at www.crusades-encyclopedia.com/womenandthecrusades.html.

2. Islam, Judaism, and Christianity are the three main forms of the Abrahamic religions. To learn more about the similarities and differences among these three faiths, visit www.spiritus-temporis.com/abrahamic-religion/.

A CONVERSATION WITH KAMRAN PASHA

Have you always been interested in the Crusades? What inspired you to write a book about this particular moment in history? How did you decide where to begin your story and where to end it?

I have always been interested in the subjects of religion and history, and the Crusades represent one of the most important periods historically in the relationship between Christianity and Islam. Indeed, the conflict between these two civilizations that began when Pope Urban called the First Crusade in 1095 C.E. arguably continues to this day, with extremists in both cultures seeking to continue the deadly feud between these religions that was ignited almost a thousand years ago. The horrific events of September 11, 2001, served as the specific catalyst for me to write this story. The terror attacks on that day had a deep impact on my soul as a Muslim and as an American. Like my fellow Americans, I felt as if a dagger had been struck in my heart when I watched the World Trade Center come crashing down in a cloud of fire and death. But as a Muslim, I had the added burden of knowing that evil men who claimed to be following my faith had done these acts. As September 11 soon gave way to America's wars in Afghanistan and Iraq, it became clear that we were entering a new period in this age-old conflict between the West and the Muslim world. And I wanted to write a story that examined the ancient roots of animosity between these two cultures.

I specifically chose to write about the Third Crusade for a variety of reasons. First, it truly was an epic tale in which the protagonists were some of the most important people in world history. Both Richard the Lionheart and Saladin remain archetypal heroes of their respective civilizations, and this moment where both men clashed on the battlefield is truly a remarkable convergence of history. But, more important, the Third Crusade represents in my view the closest analogy to the events of today, with one crucial difference—the "heroes" and the "villains" are reversed. The Crusaders were the terrorists of their time, slaughtering innocents, including women and children, without remorse, and Saladin was considered by both sides to be a man of great honor and civility. This was a time when Islam was the dominant world civilization, advanced in every area of science, art, and culture, while the Christian West had slipped into illiteracy, feudalism, and barbarity. The destructive social problems in Europe led to violence and the use of terror by Christians to regain their lost dominance. In my view, this is exactly parallel to what is happening in parts of the Muslim world today, a thousand years later. Al-Qaeda and its sympathizers seek to reverse the flow of history in which the West has become dominant and the Muslim world feels militarily and culturally besieged by outsiders. Like the Crusaders, the Muslim extremists are resorting to barbarism and brutality to fight a war they feel they cannot win any other way. But as a practicing Muslim myself, I know that Al-Qaeda and its supporters violate the fundamental precepts of Islam and I oppose them with all my being. In some ways, the character I personally feel most connection to in this novel is that of the Christian knight William, who sees some of his fellow believers acting in ways that violate his faith and must make a moral stand against extremists among his own people. That is why I wrote this novel, and I hope it will open many eyes among people of all faiths.

Which of your main characters are completely fictitious? How do you manage to seamlessly blend fact and fiction?

There are several important characters that are the product of my imagination. Miriam is fictitious, as is Sir William Chinon, although the latter is based loosely on William Marshal, an important knight who lived during Richard's time. These characters were created in order to voice important perspectives in the narrative. Miriam is the heroine of the story and she serves to give a woman's point of view of the war as well as a Jewish perspective on both Christian and Muslim actions. She is the necessary observer who is distinct from all the principals in terms of gender as well as faith, and in many ways Miriam serves as the reader's guide into this unfamiliar world. Sir William is an important character because he represents what I believe is the true face of Christianity, a religion like Islam that at its best is about love, humility, and service.

Saladin amply reflected those values from the Muslim side, but regrettably Richard in my view is not a noble exemplar of the Christian faith, and so I created a character to fulfill that role. In writing this novel as a Muslim, it was very important for me to avoid the impression that the actions of the Crusaders represent the teachings of Christ. They do not. William exists to remind the readers that the Crusades were a perversion of the Christian faith, just as modern terrorism is a perversion of Islam. William represents the core values of Christianity, and it was important that his character stand for truth and justice even when faced with wrongdoing by men in his own community. With regard to blending fact and fiction, I made sure that the major events described in the book—the battles, the political intrigues—were accurate to history, and then I allowed my fictional characters to behave as their personalities naturally would under the circumstances. Whether I have done so successfully must, of course, be judged by the reader.

By writing this book in the third person, you give readers the privilege of direct access to many characters' thoughts. Why did you decide to write it this way? Did you ever consider focusing on one perspective?
In my first novel, *Mother of the Believers*, I wrote from one perspective, Aisha, the wife of Prophet Muhammad. But here I chose a third-person narrative. The primary reason for the shift in storytelling is that I wanted to be fair and true to the varying points of view about faith, politics, and warfare presented in the book. In *Mother of the Believers*, it was very important for me to show one perspective that has rarely been explored in Western literature—that of a devout Muslim woman. That book's purpose was to present how Muslims in general, and Muslim women in particular, see their faith and understand their history. But in *Shadow of the Swords*, we have an epic moment in history where three major religions are caught in a vortex of conflict. Each side—Jew, Christian, and Muslim—has a perspective of the events that unfold, and I was excited to examine these different points of view authentically. The third-person narrative device was the most appropriate way to show each character's thoughts and highlight how people of different backgrounds can interpret the same event in completely different ways.

Was there a lot of research involved in creating this story? How did you go about it?

I researched the story for several years. In my author's note, I discuss some of the scholarly works and resources I turned to in crafting this tale. The Crusades have been heavily documented by historians, but rarely has the Muslim perspective been examined in Western literature. Being raised in a Muslim family, I had access to a perspective that is often ignored or misunderstood by other writers. I am hoping that my novel will inspire readers to learn more about this historical period and to examine it from new and important points of view.

What was the most interesting thing you learned while conducting your research?

What fascinated me in my historical research was the extent to which Jews and Muslims were not only allied during the time of the Crusades, but how intimate the relationship between the two communities really was. In our current moment in history, there is a great deal of tension between the two faiths over Middle Eastern politics, and yet during most of the past thousand years, Jews and Muslims were considered natural compatriots. The two religions, Judaism and Islam, are remarkably similar in theology and ritual, as they both emerge from a common Semitic cultural heritage. Christianity, by comparison, is a very distinct tradition that owes much of its intellectual and theological heritage to Greco-Roman civilization. Christians and Jews often have difficulty understanding each other's theologies and concepts of God and salvation, because they are actually speaking very different languages even though they share a common scripture, the Bible. Judaism and Islam have different scriptures, but their understanding of God and approach to worship are deeply parallel. I have suggested throughout this novel that "God loves irony," and perhaps that statement is proven true in the dynamic triangle of these three faiths. Jews and Muslims have the most in common and were historically friendly, and now they are often at each other's throats. Judaism and Christianity have much greater theological differences and were historically antagonistic, and yet today we talk of a common Judeo-Christian heritage in America. That is true irony. I hope that in this novel, particularly in how I draw the relationships among Saladin, Maimonides, and Miriam, I am able to awaken a memory in both the Muslim and the Jewish communities of a time not long past when they saw each other as family and not as enemies.

How did the love story aspect of the book evolve?

I understood when I crafted this novel that the fictional love story among Saladin and Miriam was a potentially explosive device that could offend some readers, both Jews and Muslims. And yet for the reasons I discuss above, it was very important for me to bring these two characters together in an intimate way, so that the true commonalities and differences between their communities could be examined. Saladin has been portrayed as such a saintly figure in the Islamic tradition that I realized that depicting a covert affair with a Jewish woman was liable to upset many people. And yet I do not believe in placing human beings on idolatrous pedestals. I hope that the love story I have crafted will help readers to embrace Saladin as a real human being with a heart and soul. And I hope that romantic aspects of this story will only serve to highlight the noble aspects of Saladin's character in not just grandiose mythic terms, but in very relatable and believable human experiences, too. Saladin was our brother, and I hope we can learn from him and emulate his nobility in our daily lives. Turning him into a plastic saint incapable of feeling the emotions that we all share does a disservice, in my view, to his incredible life example.

As a Muslim, did you find it hard not to take sides and let your personal beliefs influence your portrayal of certain characters?

I do not believe there is such a thing as objectivity when writing about matters of faith. Everyone has an opinion on religion, and that perspective serves as a paradigm in how one views the actions of men like Richard and Saladin. I am a believing Muslim and for me the Crusades represent an act of unholy terror and aggression. And yet I am honest enough to know that the Crusaders saw themselves as heroes fighting the forces of evil. What I hope I accomplished here is to present each character's perspective as he or she would have authentically seen things, and let readers judge for themselves where the truth lies.

Is there anything in particular that you would hope your readers will take with them after reading this book?

I hope that my readers will walk away with an understanding of the importance of seeing things from someone else's point of view, especially if that perspective appears hostile or opposed to our own. The only way we human beings can transcend the cycle of fear and hate that feeds war is to learn empathy. And the first step in that journey is to recognize the humanity of our adversaries and the authenticity of their viewpoints. It does not mean we have to change or abandon our own beliefs, but in order to live in this world in peace, we must give others the right to have different views from our own. It is a lesson that I sought to have the characters in my novel learn, and I hope that it is a lesson that we can all incorporate in our lives.

In what ways did the experience of writing *Shadow of the Swords* differ from that of writing your first book, *Mother of the Believers*?
Shadow of the Swords was actually written before *Mother of the Believers*, even though the latter was published first. In many ways, this novel was far more challenging for me as I had to incorporate multiple viewpoints about the Crusades, many of which conflicted with my own personal perspectives on the conflict. *Mother of the Believers* gave readers an intimate view of what Islam means to me as a believer. But *Shadow of the Swords* will, I hope, give my fans a deeper sense of my values as a human being independent of my particular religious or cultural heritage. It is a book that perhaps reveals the universal aspects of my own soul, and I hope that it will encourage my readers to look within their hearts to find what truly matters to them about being human in a world full of diversity and conflict.

What do you think your next project will be?
I have a few projects I am developing. They are all works of historical fiction, but my readers may be surprised at the new genres I plan to explore. One project that I intend to complete in the near future is a novel on the birth of Christianity, told from the point of view of Jesus Christ's family and friends. I have been heavily researching the world in which Jesus lived, and I hope that it will provide real insight into how his life and teachings impacted the people of his time. And I think many people, both Christians and Muslims, will be surprised by some of my conclusions as to what Jesus was really about and how the religion founded in his name evolved in its early years. A second project that I am very excited about is actually a vampire epic set in the world of Victorian England! Many of my readers may be startled that I would choose to go from writing about matters of religion and history to the horror genre, but I think that they will be intrigued by

how I meld the spiritual questions I love into a rollicking, fun vampire story. A friend who has read an early outline of the novel jokingly commented that I am becoming Anne Rice in reverse—a "serious" writer focusing on faith who evolves into a purveyor of vampire stories! Since I have the greatest respect for Ms. Rice's talent and career, I took that as a compliment.